"Tom Doyle has taken every Syfy channel and *Coast to Coast* radio show concept and incorporated them into a very entertaining novel. At first, I was startled to encounter so many themes, then I was drawn to admire the skills he used to weave them together, and then I just sat back and enjoyed the show. I also learned the truth about how Stonewall Jackson was killed. Great fun."

— Jerry Pournelle,
New York Times bestselling author

"Tom Doyle's *American Craftsmen* is a fast-moving and intriguing novel that incorporates features of combat fantasy, special operations, alternative history, black ops, and even a touch of romance into a seamless action tapestry offering a far richer read than most action adventures without sacrificing either action or speed."

—L. E. Modesitt, Jr.

"Other authors have blended soldiering and sorcery, but few have brought Doyle's well-crafted prose style, carefully paced plotting, and depth of characterization to the trope. The gradual revelation of the intricate 'secret history' behind the spell-wielding soldiers and the long-simmering family feuds intertwined with that history add intrigue and depth to the slam-bang action of the opening chapters."

—*Library Journal*

"Tom Doyle blends an intricately reenvisioned history of America with literary references, some bold, some sly, in this genre-bending thriller. It's a feat of craftsmanship to be celebrated." —Jacqueline Carey

5/28/16

AMERICAN CRAFTSMEN

TOM DOYLE

Tom Doyle

TOR®
fantasy

A TOM DOHERTY ASSOCIATES BOOK • NEW YORK

AMERICAN CRAFTSMEN

Copyright © 2014 by Tom Doyle

All rights reserved.

A Tor Book
Published by Tom Doherty Associates, LLC
175 Fifth Avenue
New York, NY 10010

www.tor-forge.com

Tor® is a registered trademark of Tom Doherty Associates, LLC.

ISBN 978-0-7653-7692-3

Tor books may be purchased for educational, business, or promotional use. For information on bulk purchases, please contact the Macmillan Corporate and Premium Sales Department at 1-800-221-7945, extension 5442, or write to specialmarkets@macmillan.com.

First Edition: May 2014
First Mass Market Edition: July 2015

Printed in the United States of America

0 9 8 7 6 5 4 3 2 1

For Dad, a book with ancestors

ACKNOWLEDGMENTS

I'm very grateful for the hard work, specific help, and general support of the following people:

Claire Eddy, whose excellent craft and contagious enthusiasm made every stage of the editorial process a joy.

Also at Tor, Bess Cozby, Anna Chang, and Irene Gallo.

My agent, Robert Thixton, whose perseverance was epic.

The current and former members of the Writers Group from Hell, especially Stephanie Dray, whose early comments were crucial for the direction of the story, and my other initial readers and advocates—David J. Williams, Jeri Smith-Ready, Mindy Klasky, Gerry Doyle, and Doug Texter.

My friends and family, particularly my brother and fellow writer, Bill Doyle; my partner, Beth Delaney; and my mom (who indulged her young son with a membership in the Military Book Club).

The Washington Science Fiction Association, including William Lawhorn (aka #3) and Lee Strong.

Science Fiction and Fantasy Writers of America and the late Ann Crispin, for the many ways they assisted my entry into the professional community.

John Francis Wester, for discussing his time in the navy

with me, and Boobie Dutch, whose advice on military matters was invaluable (and any mistakes are my own).

Atoussa Rahimi, for her help with some of the Farsi terms.

The Pentagon Tours program, though they refused to take me to H-ring.

The real-world military families, old and new, who are an inspiration for much more than this book.

PART I

THE VETERANS OF
A THOUSAND PSYCHIC WARS

*And he was bent on making us feel as he did, and of
course his magic accomplished his desire.*
—MARK TWAIN

*your magic errandboy's
just made a bad guess again*
—ALLEN GINSBERG

CHAPTER

ONE

As I hustled out from the hangar into the Persian Gulf twilight, my muscles tightened, and power flowed into my hands. Soon I would do what I did best. Soon I would kill a sorcerer.

The U.S. Army base tarmac gave off a blistering heat mirage as I scrambled across it. A helicopter's blades rotated at ready; their wash blasted hot as I boarded. The door slammed behind me, and the copter, christened *Valkyrie,* took off.

The five men of my team saluted, then went back to checking their equipment. They showed no impatience at having waited on the pad for orders; they were used to the bullshit. I sat toward the front for quick off-headphone interaction with the pilot when we hit the spooky stuff.

For a silent aircraft, the *Valkyrie* made plenty of noise inside. Next to me, Cpl. "Vulture" Volant yelled my nom de guerre. "Casper. Is that like the friendly ghost, sir?"

"Not that friendly, Corporal."

"A killing ghost, sir?" But, seeing that I was unamused, Vulture again inspected his sniper rifle, and I was grateful that I didn't have to order him to shut the fuck up. It was my fault for choosing a shitty cryptonym, and not just because of the ghost reference. "Casper" gave a clue to my job. Casper, or Caspar, had been one of the Three Wise Men. A magus, or what Americans with knowledge called a craftsman. Why hide my identity only to give it away through the back door?

My father had written me a warning that "We Mortons are too practical about the craft, and too crafty about the practical." Yeah, my real name was Morton, Captain Dale Morton. Other craftsmen tended to have strong opinions about my family. I didn't blame them.

My men didn't know about my family or magic, but they aimed uncomfortable glances at me. I didn't blame them either. These five had trained together, a seamless whole, but not with me. I was too important a secret to expose to others for too much time. Our unit designation, MAC-66, appeared in no records. The Pentagon didn't formally acknowledge Delta Force and SEAL Team Six but allowed their existence to be known. Craft ops were different; knowledge of their existence could be fatal.

Two of my five were boot camps, green as Uncle Sam's toilet paper. Vulture and Lt. Shaheen were more experienced. Shaheen knew Arabic and regional detail and doubled as team medic, so he was Doc. And there was the old man, my NCO, Master Sergeant "Zee" Zanol.

All good men, but I couldn't get too close. They were smart enough not to question the bullshit, but they would know the word from this land to describe me: *assassin*.

Hours before, I had stood in a prefab conference room shoved in a corner of the base hangar. The room served as an office for people who weren't officially there. Colonel Hutchinson had explained my mission. She was my favorite officer, my favorite craftsperson, and my favorite living human being, all packed tight into a tall fortysomething mix of Kate Hepburn and triathlete.

"H-ring is calling it a snatch and grab, but you'll assume your usual prejudice against the target," she said in her easy rural New England way, as if she weren't sentencing some stranger to death. "Intel says he's a Farsi speaker, a Persian." *Persian*—better than any existing nation's name to describe ancient loyalties. Hutchinson pointed to a printout map. "He's been farseen here, about fifty klicks southwest of the bridge."

"A long ways from home, ma'am," I said.

"He's not such a wise man for a magus," said Hutchinson. "We expect a go before sundown."

"Isn't Sword up next?" Code name Sword was the third craftsperson on base, though for security I was kept sequestered from him. I wanted this mission, but I had a gut suspicion of irregular assignments.

"This mission has been called by Sphinx herself," said Hutchinson, "and Sphinx doesn't want Sword. She said something to the effect that if we didn't send you on this mission, we could pack up Western civilization and shove it up our asses."

"*Me,* ma'am?" As far as I knew, neither the Peepshow at Langley nor their top oracle Sphinx ever selected the individual for an assignment.

"Don't let it go to your head, Morton. This bozo isn't important. Must be a butterfly-effect scenario."

"So I crush the butterfly," I said.

"Right," agreed Hutchinson.

I respected Hutchinson more than my rarely seen parents, and whatever Hutch said, I would execute, with my usual and extreme prejudice. But it was more than personal loyalty. I shared the sense of duty of my ancestors: Philip "Foggy" Morton who delayed the British with bad weather at Brooklyn Heights to save George Washington's army, Richard "Dick" Morton, who calmed the storms over the English Channel for the D-day invasion, and Joshua Morton, who gave the last full measure for the Union he loved. Like them, I would serve my country to the utmost.

I checked my watch. We'd be within forty klicks by now. We were coming in low and below radar, but I wasn't worried about the conventional firepower of the locals. The target would strike soon. I kept my anticipation of the supernatural blow to myself.

The first sign of attack came as a gut-lurching, sideways drop, followed by another. The chopper shook as if an oversized child was pelting it with boulders. Yes, a probable SPACTAD—spooky action at a distance.

I clambered forward and crouched behind the pilot, Lt. Nguyen. She had "Born to Kill" on her helmet. "What's that turbulence?" I asked.

"Sir, we need to turn back," said Nguyen.

"Just because of some wind?"

"Look at this," said Nguyen. On the radar, a wall of disturbance moved toward us. Sandstorm.

"Fly above it?"

"I've never seen anything go so high," said Nguyen.

"Keep flying," I said. "We'll be fine."

"But, sir . . ."

"That's an order."

"Yes, sir." Fortunately, Nguyen had been thoroughly warned to follow my every order, no matter how apparently suicidal. But she didn't sound happy, no ma'am.

I made a controlled tumble back into my seat, and held some laminated maps in front of my face. But my mind followed the storm. I felt the enemy craftwork behind it, craftwork that had been wreaking havoc on air and land traffic in this sector for months. I could try to fight the whole spell, but I wasn't on my own ground, so that would drain me, and that was probably what the target wanted.

So I'd shield the copter. It would look strange, but what could the pilot say? I touched my hand to the wall of the aircraft, and rubbed and patted it like a horse. I felt the pulse of the life of the air beyond. "*Calm air, calm* air," I murmured, and the air around the speeding copter flowed calmly by.

My headset crackled. "Sir," said Nguyen, "the sand is blowing, but we seem to be in a clear pocket."

"Roger that. Carry on, Lieutenant."

Compulsively, I checked my weapons and gear again— way beyond the necessary. I carried a Heckler & Koch MP5 submachine gun with its clean first shot and a Sig Sauer P226 9mm pistol, because I didn't want to adapt my father's .45 with the electronic safeguards. My team's equipment appeared standard for a Special Ops unit, but it had hidden features for craft-enhanced ops. The surest weapon in a craftsman's hands is his opponent's mind. Each weapon had a "Stonewall" chip that would prevent firing at a team member (including oneself) under any circumstances. I smiled at the chip's name. As my ancestor Joshua Morton had illustrated to General Jackson at the end of an otherwise bad day at Chancellorsville, getting the enemy to shoot their own took very little craft.

After the mission, the team would be kept under 24/7 surveillance and quarantine for a month, in case any craft time bombs had been dropped into their psyches. I grimaced in sympathy, but their minds wouldn't be great concerns if I eliminated the target quickly.

The men had technical explanations for these safeguards. Too much Syfy Channel had accustomed them to all kinds of nonsense—that they might be subject to chemical hallucinogens, microwave mind control, or perfect holographic projections. Like Dad had written, any sufficiently advanced magic is indistinguishable from technology.

For a long mission, another man might carry amphetamines or other stimulants. I carried only one pill: a black cyanide capsule. And in case I hesitated, there was an exception to the Stonewall chip. One man in the unit would have the order and the means to kill me rather than allow my capture. I bet it was Sergeant Zee.

I felt the gs as the copter veered right. "Sir," said Nguyen on headset, "we're about two klicks from the target location, approaching from due south."

I didn't look up from my equipment. "Keep flying north, full speed."

"But the target is . . ."

"He'll run," I said. I moved forward again for a face-to-face.

"But we're coming in quiet," said Nguyen.

"He knows that we're coming." The pilot looked at me, horrified at this hint of a security breach.

I viewed the ground through the copter's night-vision

screen. Sure enough, far ahead on the lone road leading out of the village, a jeep raced toward the north. In night vision, the jeep glowed bright green with heat, but in my vision, the target burned red with craft. Perhaps if the target had tried to flee quietly without throwing sand in our faces, he would have made it, but that wasn't magi style. "That's our man. Try not to lose him."

"Yes, sir."

If the target was talented enough, he would shake us with some sorcerer stealth unless I could guess where he was heading. That's why I was here, and not some Predator drone—this chase required craft and intuition.

Where will he run to? My objectives liked old ground. Any other place, I could just pick out the nearest ruin, but here in the Near East ancient sites with occult potential dotted the landscape. Wait, there on the map, straight down the road, a familiar name. Drones had seen some recent small-unit activity in the area, but that wasn't what concerned me. I stepped back to show the map to Doc. "Isn't there an archeological site here?"

"Yes, sir, an Assyrian settlement near the town. Looters have been digging pits during the recent unpleasantness."

"Pilot, head to MC 9146 4211."

"Roger, wilco—wait a minute. He's off the scope, sir."

"Understood. Circle the point where you last saw him for ten minutes. Then, head to MC 9146 4211 on a curved vector, veering thirty degrees west of true until midpoint." I didn't want the target to see us pursuing in a straight line behind him, and I didn't want to beat the target to the site.

I called up maps and photos of the dig on my handheld.

Yes, an old tunnel excavation into a nasty temple to Assur-Marduk—the target would like that. And something more organized than looting had been going on in the last two years, with the maze of tunnels opened up to the surface, then covered from view with a series of tarpaulins.

I turned to Sergeant Zee and pointed at my map. "Let's run through the mission. We'll insert a few kilometers downwind of the town, here." It was a small town with a long Arabic name, and before that a Greek name, and before that something in Assyrian. And something else before all that. Every place they sent me was like that. Small towns with large history lessons.

"Don't make me pronounce it right, sir," said Zee. "I just forget them all afterwards."

"Doesn't matter," I said. "Our objective won't go to the modern town. The drones have spotted activity just to the west in the excavated mound."

"What kind of activity, sir?"

"Hostile activity." Zee didn't need to know about the other aberrant sandstorms and equipment failures. Like me and many of my ancestors, my target was a weatherman. "Vulture will clear the entrance to the dig. Then, you'll all cover the town and any approaching bad guys." Any *conventional* bad guys.

"You're going into the tell alone, sir?"

"That's correct." Odd that Zee knew the word *tell*.

"An ancient city? Hmm." He narrowed his eyes at me. "I've seen some strange missions, sir. A crypt in the bottom of a mine in Bosnia, a temple older than the Mayans in Central America. I don't like that kind of strangeness, but it doesn't frighten me."

"I hear you, Sergeant." The man was saying that he understood something about craft ops—that I could rely on him not to panic in the face of magic and to keep his mouth shut afterwards. That I could talk to him. That I didn't have to go into those ruins alone. But craft was different from most military secrets. Besides, I preferred to hit the target myself. A mundane soldier was just somebody I'd have to protect.

"We'll talk afterwards," I continued. "So we understand each other, no one else is to enter the ruins under any circumstances. You understand my orders, Sergeant?"

"Yes, sir."

Having completed my checklist, I prepared my most important weapon—my craft. I focused on my breathing to find my center. I hit the mute button on my senses. The chopper engines, the camouflage colors, the smells of fuel, equipment, and sweat—all perceived through foam insulation. Very internal, intimate time, turn the lights down low, baby. Some of this quiet bubble was common to most elite soldiers before a mission, but some of it was the peculiar meditation needed for my power.

Ritual and formula were just two possible focal points for magic. The essence of craft was to hold two exact images in one's mind at once—the thing as it was and the thing as it would be. Then, still holding the images, the craftsman placed the word of action between them. To do all this instantaneously required talent, practice, and energy.

But with my power running high, one of my natural gifts showed itself without effort. The team's auras flickered around me; the small letters of their sins, scarlet a's of petty fornications and k's of military duty, tried to distract me. I ignored them. In my bubble, I waited. I was alone; nothing else existed. I felt the craft energies flow up and down my spine. More than enough juice for one sorcerer. I was ready.

Nguyen signaled: two minutes. I resurfaced. I mumbled a prayer to an absent God that, this time, my team would just face flesh and bullets, leaving the more powerful horrors to me.

"Get ready." The copter slowed to a hover. "Move out!"

The metal door flew open with a slide-slam and we were down the ropes and fanning out through clouds of dust in a scattered deployment. Better for this sort of op that, until it was done, the aircraft not touch the ground, or stick around too long. The pilot swooped away like a bat copter from hell. My night-vision goggles gave the world a greenish hue. Unlike most Special Operations Forces, this unit had no video equipment. No recording of a craft op would ever be made; no amount of operation review could justify the inevitable leak that would endanger all practitioners.

"Let's move." We started jogging toward the tell. I loved the desert at night. Human beings seemed like a blot on its purity. Cumin, nutmeg, cardamom, lamb, exhaust. Sure enough, the inevitable smell of Middle Eastern cuisine mixed with diesel wafted over from the town, making me hungry and queasy at the same time. I hoped the civilians would, unlike their smells, stay at home. Home, and safe from me and my team.

We found cover behind the piles of moved earth. An all-weather tarpaulin, the first of many over the dig, made a tentlike roof to the mound entrance; its loose corners wagged or flapped in the wind. Someone had organized the digging and the tarps, creating a flimsy yet safer ceiling for their ancient home.

Two bad guys stood guard at the entrance, talking, one in a burnoose, the other in a deracinated uniform. Doc listened with a parabolic mike (a craft op standard) and sent me their text. "Heard chopper. Concerned." Not concerned enough by half. They were lighting cigarettes, which glowed like flares in my night vision. But the guards didn't glow with craft. Vulture lined them up in his silencer's sight. Conventional means for conventional people. Always better to take life with a bullet, as the law of karmic return was more lenient and indirect with nonmagical action.

Two bullets snapped. Unavoidable sounds, but they didn't matter. Any target worth his craft would be tipped off at this point.

I let go of the breath I had held. "Thanks, Vulture." Then I turned to Doc. "Keep the site sequestered. Talk any civilians out of coming near. We want zero casualties for us and them. I'm going in. Sixty minutes. Mark." No craft duel had ever lasted longer than an hour, if the craftspeople meant business. Simply not enough energy in one person to go longer at full throttle. A battle with multiple practitioners relieving each other in shifts could go on longer, but that didn't happen very often. If I wasn't back in an hour, I was dead, or a danger to my own team, or something worse.

Outside the hangar, Colonel Hutchinson shook her head at her other favorite killer, code name Sword. In contrast to Morton's dark features, Native American cheekbones, and expressive mien, Major Sword's blond hair and nor'easter gray eyes framed a long angular face of iron. That face had just gotten harder. Poor boy was understandably pissed.

Sword pointed at the red horizon, eyes on Hutchinson. "Was that my mission that just took off, Colonel?"

"No," said Hutchinson, "that was Casper's mission that just took off, Major."

The major's real name was Michael Endicott. If he had known Casper's real name, he would have been more pissed. The major's ancestors were the Endicotts of Salem. Sure, he could serve under her, a Hutchinson, descended from that notorious heretic woman—hell, the boy actually seemed to like and respect her. But she doubted he could extend that tolerance to Captain Morton. The pagan Mortons with their "craft" were anathema to the Puritan Endicotts and their "gifts of the Spirit." A shame, because she was fond of both Dale and Michael, and would have loved to see them fight together against enemies foreign and domestic. But ever since 1628, when John Endicott and his men had attacked Thomas Morton's colonial settlement, the two Families had feuded, and had even tried to exclude each other from the secret covenant that George Washington had made with all the craft Families in return for their service during the Revolution. Then the Left-Hand Mortons had scared the shit out of everyone, and the Endicotts had never let the later generations of Mortons forget it.

"Casper went under your orders, Colonel?"

Hutchinson knew where this was going. "My orders came from higher up, Major."

Endicott looked about to shrapnel. "Permission to speak freely, ma'am?"

"What the hell is it, Michael?"

"Hutch, don't these sudden changes in assignment bother you?"

"They sure seem to bother you," said Hutchinson. "But you never appreciate assignment by farsight."

"This is different." Endicott lowered his voice. "If the Peepshow and our PRECOG can't agree, it means something powerful is blocking one of their farsights. The general says it could be a sign that *they* are back."

Hutch snorted. Michael's father, General Oliver C. Endicott, had never liked Sphinx or her Peepshow, kissed Pentagon farsight ass, and was close-to-discharge insane about the imminent return of the Left-Hand Mortons.

"OK, Michael. Never mind that those evil kin-fuckers have all been exterminated. Let's hold that branch of ancient history over the heads of the modern Mortons like a cudgel, make them keep toeing the line, never let them above the active rank of captain, because God knows they haven't saved our asses enough to trust them again."

Endicott's face cracked into a small grimace. "It's not like that, Hutch. Just don't be surprised if something goes wrong."

Hutchinson's tough heart skipped a beat. Dread, then anger, used up her remaining patience with all things Endicott. "That had better not be an oracle, Major."

"No, ma'am."

"Good. Then get packing, soldier. You're due in Prague tomorrow."

"Prague?" Poor boy sounded positively wounded by the new assignment; Hutchinson tried not to chuckle.

"Yes, Prague. I'll brief you in the conference room in one hour." She hesitated, trying to separate the threads of command instinct from an almost maternal concern, until she found they agreed. "But I'm keeping you here tonight." Because she refused to be surprised if something went wrong.

At the entrance to the dig, my feet came to an unordered halt. A ward, very formal and fancy pants. If I broke the ward's craft circuit, it would trip an alarm back to its maker. I said *"break."* That would certainly get the target's attention, even if his mundane guards hadn't.

I stepped under the tarp and scrambled into the maze of passages. Glowing LEDs that hung irregularly along the broken walls gave me a twilight view without the night-vision device. The lights were on, so someone was home.

Why the hell did my duty always seem to take me to confined spaces, sometimes far, far underground? At least the dirt was no longer overhead. My family had reason to fear live burial.

The tell was not large in conventional space. But ruins that had been around this long had aeons of unconventional space to move through. Over the crumbling mix of stone and mud brick, ghosts of buildings shimmered with gold, lapis, and tapestries in my peripheral vision. I ignored most of the lavish details, focusing on those bits of translucent décor that might guide me through the maze to a former temple, palace, or crypt.

Then, out of the ether, two horrendous Assyrian genii blocked my way. Blood dripped from their eyes, gore from their teeth. My heart hammered for fight or flight.

After a second, my pulse continued to race with self-disgust. Obvious fakes. Nonhuman spirits, if they existed, must be rare. I stepped forward, then froze—what could these images be distracting me from? Ah, there, behind the one on the right, a trigger that would probably cave in this portion of the dig. But no trap that I could sense beyond that. If this was designed to make me waste energy, I wouldn't bite. *OK, we'll be trapped for a while together— some nice intimate time to exchange craft secrets.*

I ran through. The walls collapsed behind me. But the cave-in was a shit job, and I would still be able to squeeze through or climb out, if it didn't get any worse.

Little enemy probes of my power prickled my nerves, but like gunfire, they also guided me to their point of origin. A voice in my head: *"Allahu akbar . . . ?"* Then, "Greetings friend, in the name of Allah, the compassionate and merciful." Shit, the fucker could think in panglossic, and with an annoying British accent. I preferred not to have much time for talk.

"Pretty pagan surroundings for 'Allah,' friend."

"Necessary for my little trap."

"You'd better spring it soon. I'm just about there." I cocked the hammers of three spells in my mind: a parry, an external thrust, and an internal one. I would have to improvise the specifics.

"We practitioners should not kill each other," said the sorcerer. "We should stay in our own land, our own power."

"Right," I said. The tarp rippled in the night breeze. I came to an L in the maze, turned right, and found myself at the lintel. I used a small mirror to peer into the room beyond.

Through the doorway was a long hall that had once been a temple. The sorcerer sat in a beat-up lawn chair where the altar to Assur-Marduk should have been. His head was framed by a back wall bas-relief of the god's bull horns, symbols of the long gone Taurean Age. Amidst priceless objects, the sorcerer wore a Red Sox jersey and shorts. His teeth were mostly gone, his eyes stared up at the sky and seemed half-blind. Unarmed? Probably preferred craft-on-craft action.

I raised the MP5, prepared to turn and shoot.

A cold hand of craft squeezed at my lungs. *"Break hand,"* I said, using my first spell.

Another hand of force reached for me and made my gun feel too heavy to aim. With the MP5 dangling from my right arm, I spun around the corner and drew a circle around the sorcerer with my left forefinger. *"Move air."*

The laws of thermodynamics are funny things. They don't forbid most of the air from moving away from one's head; they just say that it's more likely the universe will expire before that happens randomly. A weatherman can put a spin on the forces and probabilities of nature. I was good at tweaking the improbabilities and making them happen.

The sorcerer gasped, but he could still think up mischief. I pointed my left hand straight between my target's eyes. *"Short sharp shock."* The sorcerer jerked rigid. A lot of these backwoods magi had trouble thinking of their minds as mechanisms. They wasted time on hallucinations and ignored the raw synapses.

I moved closer to the sorcerer. That hadn't been too bad. Now to kill him.

I could not take him prisoner. Confining such a man, much less putting him on trial, was prohibitively difficult. My orders might violate the law, but the law didn't know

about the craft, which was a damned good thing, given
what the law used to do to craftspeople.

I held my MP5 inches from the old man's head.

The sorcerer ceased convulsing and sat bolt upright,
eyes fixed on me. I sought a protection to employ. The
sorcerer cackled at me like a dirty old farmer at Internet
porn.

I didn't shoot. No further malevolent energies sought
me; I could afford to grant a few seconds. "If you've got
any prayers to say, say them now."

The sorcerer closed his eyes and spread his arms wide,
palms out. "You are here to take me out. Fine, I am old
and ready. But I am going to take you out too. Not kill,
just stop."

Threats were not the prayers I had in mind. I leveled my
gun and shot the sorcerer between the eyes.

The report echoed down the ancient hallways; in a red
burst of craft, the sorcerer's spirit left. Mission accomplished, I considered my exit.

No exit. The cool night air rustled the tarp, carrying the
sound of automatic weapons fire and a crushing sense of
dread. My gun shook in my hand as I waved it in the dead
sorcerer's face. "What have you done?"

A voice like a recorded message played in my mind.
*Feel that, ferangi? We know your family, your country.
Your Left-Hand ancestors were an abomination before
God. You can violate our land, parade your filth in front
of us, even take our lives, but you will not take our magic.
You will not take our souls. Feel it, ferangi.*

I felt it. Successive explosions of fear, then pain, then a
gaping, aching nothing.

A bearded man, hands outstretched, stands as a human shield in front of his house and a veiled woman; then hands and body are ripped with agony, and both man and woman fall into the dusty doorway.

A mangy dog bares its teeth, then whines in final, crippled terror.

A little girl wearing only a "Hello Kitty" T-shirt runs and screams down the street, then her heart bursts as two rounds pierce her chest, and my own heart screams.

I felt the curse. Driven by the power of the sorcerer's self-sacrifice, my team saw enemies everywhere, and killed every man, woman, and child they saw. The sorcerer's own death spared him the karmic consequences of his heinous magic. Each murder instead became a cancerous part of my own mind.

In the dungeon of my skull, a voice like my own laughed at the curse, and the murders. The voice of the Left Hand, trying to get out.

Part of a wall tumbled stones at my feet. The dig started to slowly cave in—a dead man's craft switch. Nothing that I couldn't have outrun, if I cared to. I didn't care. I was dying inside, over and over again.

A rip like a Little Bird's guns. At the other end of the room, the point of a KA-BAR slashed open the tarp. A soldier peered through the newly created gap. "Captain. Where are you?" It was Master Sergeant Zanol.

"Sergeant, I ordered—"

Zee jumped down to the floor. He dashed toward me and pushed me out of the way of another cascading stone. "I don't give a fuck, sir." Zee pointed his rifle at me. "They're . . . I . . . you've got to help them."

After that, my memory was a jumbled slide show. Zee

gave me a lift up and out of the excavation, then scrambled up after as I ran across the tell for the town. I hurtled down the mound's side and screamed into the *snap-snap* of bullets, *"Cease fire! Cease fire! Goddamnit, cease fire!"*

Far too fucking late. Night vision showed me the cooling bodies of women and children everywhere. My team was staggering around, covered in the sacrificial blood, starting to realize what they had done. I couldn't let that realization sink in. *"Valkyrie,* immediate pickup. That's ASAP. Over."

Like someone half-asleep, Doc protested on the com. "Captain, I think there's some wounded civvies here. Should I treat?"

"Negative, repeat negative. Withdraw."

"You heard him," yelled Zee, voice nearly breaking with rage and despair. "Move out!"

We jogged to the pickup point. We climbed back in our ground-hovering copter and started home.

I grabbed the chopper's transmitter. Duty still compelled me; I mouthed the necessary words to base. "Ike, this is MAC-66. We need immediate steam vac, MC 9146 4211."

"MAC-66, this is Ike. We'll need to clear that with Mamie."

"Negative, Ike," I said. "I'm calling this, priority Alfa, Last Best Hope."

"Roger that, 66. Wilco. Over and out." It would be easier to explain a mistake from the air than what we had done. I would be destroying a town and ten thousand years of history to do it. I didn't care.

I clamped my jaw shut until it ached. Each death

exploded in my head. If I opened my mouth without something to say, I'd start screaming and never ever stop again.

I had to maintain appearances, if only for my men. But they wouldn't leave me alone. "Captain, what happened back there?" asked Doc.

"Nothing. Understand? Nothing happened," I said. "You fired at some bad guys. We withdrew. That's your report. You'll speak of this to no one else."

But it would have taken more craft than I had left to convince my sergeant. Zee's face was in his hands. He was sobbing.

We landed back at the base. Dawn was coming up over the dead land like an interrogator's lamp on my soul.

As we left the copter, Colonel Hutchinson was already on the tarmac and moving right into my face. "Captain, what the hell is going on? Where do you get off calling in an air strike? We aren't even supposed to be there!"

I gestured over my shoulder, like a drunk at a bar passing the bill. "Colonel, my team . . ."

"Oh, of course." One of Hutch's supernatural talents was to calm and reassure in a crisis. "*Good work, men.* Get your gear stowed. I'll debrief you myself at 0800."

But my team didn't look calm or reassured as they left me. Some looked back at me with silent questions and confusion. Sergeant Zee's red eyes never left the tarmac as he crossed it.

The colonel spoke in a low voice. "Now, Morton, what the fuck happened out there?"

I held at attention, silent and steady, until the last member of my team was out of sight in the hangar. Then, my legs buckled, and I crumbled to the ground, retching, trying to be sick, but nothing was coming up.

Hutchinson put her arm on my shoulder. *"Dale, I'm sorry."* But her craft couldn't reach me. "Dale? Captain Morton!"

The dungeon voice in my mind said, *Kill her. Kill them all.*

I struggled back to my feet. *We know your family. Cease fire!* "I'm stopped," I said, my mouth like a computer reading a speech. "Done."

"Good. Now, what happened?"

"No, ma'am, I'm done with this. All this. The military. Life. Done."

Hutchinson smiled, shook her head. "Some R & R . . ."

"Done done done."

"We'll talk about it later."

"No, right this fucking minute." Cold fire flew out from my hands. "I resign. Discharge me now."

Hutchinson said, "Sword." As if they were expecting this, two men ran across the tarmac and tackled me. The craft fizzled in my hands. With nothing more to say, I screamed into the face of one of the men. I hated that face, but had forgotten why.

Hutchinson nodded, a sedative went in. I roared, but didn't care enough to fight it. Being knocked out just made it official. I was done.

All the way back to the U.S., every time I woke up, I screamed until they knocked me out again.

CHAPTER

TWO

Major Michael Endicott gave the high castle a glance and thought of trivial injustice. Prague, beautiful bullshit Prague. Prague's old-world occult irritated him. Every assignment turned noir here. Like foreign movies, Prague missions tended to end badly and absurdly.

Endicott played the gaping tourist and waited for his call. To his right and above loomed Prague Castle, locus of alchemy and occult practices until the Thirty Years' War. The old European aristocracies had attempted to monopolize spiritual power in their realms, but the New World's openness to new Families had helped to put an end to that. To Endicott's left, a picturesque rabbit warren of streets and alleyways led back down to the town, every shadow potentially filled with Central European nasties who sought his demise. Further up the road stood the old monastery, site of tonight's rendezvous.

Lovely Slavic women passed to and fro, irritating in their own way. A wife or girlfriend back home was overdue, but a Christian relationship took time, and in his position he couldn't have any other kind. He had his doubts that God cared much about his sex life, but his superiors and family did.

In response to these insubordinate thoughts, his satphone finally rang—General Dad calling. Other branches of the military could afford to move family members to separate chains of command, but not spiritual ops. Endicott answered.

"Sir?"

"Sword, the target has moved up your rendezvous. You'll proceed directly to the site. Operate under Moscow Rules." This precaution meant nothing; in spiritual ops, almost anywhere overseas was hostile territory.

Endicott's irritation got the best of him. "Sir, why am I here?"

To Endicott's relief, his father seemed to view this question as legitimate. "Pentagon PRECOG wanted you in the desert, but that freakshow Sphinx vetoed it, and that Hutchinson woman concurred on the ground, so we've given you Casper's milk run. Try not to screw it up."

"Yes, sir." Dad didn't think much of Hutch and Langley's Sphinx, but it was PRECOG's Chimera that always gave Endicott a queasy feeling. An H-ring joke had it that the motto of Pentagon farsight was "We know, but we don't care."

The general's voice lowered into a confidential, wily tone. "Remember to ask about the Left Hand and the Mortons."

Lord, would he never cease on that? "Roger, sir. Wilco. Sword out."

Left-Hand: the craft relativistic euphemism for "evil." Endicott hated the word almost as much as the fact. In spiritual ops, evil was Evil.

Endicott strode up the cobbled road. He carried a long and narrow box that enlarged at one end, as if he were a professional pool player with a bridge cue slung over his shoulder. Perhaps he shouldn't have bothered hiding his thirty-inch sword; in this town, carrying an archaic weapon with a decorated hilt wasn't so unusual. Endicott's weapon was the source of his code name. He bore the blade of the first American of his ancestral line.

Endicott was proud of his family, whatever its excesses, and Old John of Salem was the most excessive Endicott. John had used this sword in May 1628 to hack down Thomas Morton's maypole and drive away his drunken followers. John had brandished this sword during the trial of Ann Hutchinson, ancestor of the colonel. In America's first declaration of independence, John's sword had sliced the red cross of Saint George the Dragon Slayer from every flag he could find.

Major Endicott could laugh at a man who had wanted veils for women. But Old John had been right about the things that mattered: faith, discipline, and freedom.

Old John took a distant second place in Endicott's heart to his later ancestor, Abram. At the siege of the House of Morton, Abram had carried this sword. With it, he had defeated Roderick, leader of the Left-Hand Mortons, the man who had taken the name and guise of the Red Death. Abram had slain the greatest evil in the history of the Fighting Families. Just thinking of Abram gave Endicott an electric feeling of pride.

From generation to generation, the Endicotts had handed down this sword as the symbol of their Fighting Family's commitment to military service. Other talents in other Families might forget their duty to country and either forego their spiritual gifts or use them only rarely and in secret from government practitioners, but Endicott could not imagine living without either his spiritual duty or practice.

He reached the entrance to the baroque monastery, now a tourist haven. A long line of stocky Germans chattered in soft gutturals at the entrance. Germans still had a way of annoying everyone in American spiritual ops. Dear God, was this Sphinx's sense of humor? Send the Puritan to a Catholic monastery to meet an atheist with a bunch of Germans nearby. Endicott was tolerant, but he didn't appreciate being laughed at.

Endicott's target was Karel Macha, an aging Cold War leftover. Macha had double-dealt too many times, and any number of nationalities would still love to kill him. The Czech wanted to eyeball his contact before coming over.

Endicott didn't ready any specific spells. He would rely on his strongest spiritual gift: the power of command. His Family had centuries of practice at telling others what to do. Unlike some other Families, his didn't believe that God played dice with the universe. When Endicott prayed, he felt like a vessel for divine certainties, not skewed probabilities.

"In the name of Jesus, let me through." Endicott gave commands in simple panglossic, another useful gift of the Spirit. Repeating this simple prayer, he was admitted to the limited tour area, then the caretakers-only area of the monastery library.

In the old library, Endicott's nose itched. Despite preservation and cleaning efforts, the air was saturated with the dust of decaying books. Many rows of volumes were rebound in bland communist gray, contrasting with the rich dark woods of the shelving. A brief search and he found his goal: a not-terribly-secret passage led downstairs.

On the steep stairway, fancy stone gave way to brick and natural rock. The farther belowground Endicott went the more the very air pulsed with hostility. He remembered what Abram Endicott had written about the House of Morton under the Left-Hand Roderick and Madeline, how he could feel its malice against him. This place was like that, a vessel for the chthonic power of those who dwelt here.

When Endicott reached the last stair, he found a source for the anger. An old man glared at Endicott, his head bald and choked with veins, his glasses almost bulletproof thick.

The man's splotched face moved quickly from malice to surprise, and then added a dash of confused fear. Just traces of expression, but enough for Endicott to read.

"You are Casper?" asked the old man. What the hell? Who had given this guy code names?

"I'm your contact," said Endicott.

The man nodded, smiling with his remaining cigarette-stained teeth. "Not Casper. OK. I am Macha." He pointed to a dusty seat snagged from the antiques upstairs. "Please. We talk, then we go to USA."

"Not quite." Endicott placed his hands on the chair, but remained standing. "You're old enough to know how this game goes. You tell me things that are worth my government's time and resources, and you get a nice life in Florida or wherever you like. You tell me shit, you get shit. Understood?"

Macha nodded and didn't smile.

"Good," said Endicott. "Now you sit, and we'll talk."

Macha told his bio, and he didn't mess up any of the details that Endicott already knew. He spilled about American spiritual ops that had gone bad, and gave the preliminaries on the real reasons they had gone bad. Though these were old files, it was interesting news, and might be worth the cost of making this man's remaining years comfortable.

Endicott took pages of notes as Macha went on, describing Russian ops, East German ops, Czech ops, Russian ops again. Yes, the old man was talking enough, perhaps too much. He seemed to have forgotten his part in the negotiation—to hold something back until he was on U.S. soil.

Endicott wiped the sweat off his forehead. Macha's yammering was giving him a headache. Maybe that explained the feeling that the room's hostility had grown. How could the old man stand it here?

Endicott didn't have to take it anymore. "Enough!"

Macha smiled and stood up. "We are done? We go?"

Endicott wanted to say, *Yes, let's get the hell out of here,* but realized he had one more question that, no matter how absurd, he was ordered to ask.

"Just one more thing. What do you know about the Left-Hand Mortons?"

"Left-Hand?" sputtered Macha. "Nothing. Absolute nothing."

But Endicott was no longer listening. He stared at the door behind the old man. It glowed with the black light of very bad craft.

"What's in the back?" asked Endicott, trying to keep his tone even.

"Not your business."

"Yes, my business." He pushed by Macha.

"I'm working for you," said Macha. "USA! USA!"

The door was shut but not locked. In spiritual warfare, this was a bad sign—it meant that mundane protections were superfluous. *But how bad could it be, Lord?*

The back room was long and narrow, with two rows of benches running from end to end. The stench of chemicals familiar and strange made Endicott's eyes water. On the benches nearest the door, body parts, mostly heads, some in jars, some not. Some desiccation, but no rot. No blood, not a drop. *OK, pretty bad.* But Endicott had seen death before. If Macha was a serial killer, it wouldn't be the first time that Uncle Sam had sheltered a sociopath.

Farther down the benches, the news got worse. Conventional formaldehyde gave way to alchemical vats, bubbling above gas jet flames and humming with craft. In the vats, attempts at homunculi. Not good, but their failure was comforting.

But what did these alchemical experiments have to do with the dead heads and limbs all around him? *Lord, help me understand.*

A sound like butterfly wings. The eyelids of the nearest head fluttered open. A groan came from mouths without vocal cords. Arms bent at their elbows, reaching for him.

In a flash, Endicott had his revelation. No, not dead, nor truly alive, these potential golems of flesh and bone. Macha was trying to assemble a deathless body with no soul, a prospective vehicle for another's spirit. The Left Hand had always striven to defy death, but even Endicott's father hadn't dreamed that anyone could go so far.

"Abomination!"

With a few reflexive moves, Endicott's sword was out

of its box and in his hands. He forgot his mission, forgot himself, forgot everything except perhaps God. With main force and little method, he started destroying all things within reach.

Gnarled hands tried to restrain him; Endicott had forgotten Macha. The old man bellowed with surprising strength. "I do not care who fuck are you!"

Endicott wanted to toss Macha aside and get on with the Lord's work, but he noticed that the man was no longer alone. Two young goons with semiautomatic pistols stood at the doorway.

Macha chuckled and coughed. "You leave now, maybe I let you live."

Meanwhile, the undead limbs and heads were crawling and rolling toward Endicott, as if to smother him in their sheer mass. He was outgunned, outmanned. As for spirit, Macha didn't have much personal juice, but the chamber's black-light force seemed to flow through him. Endicott couldn't take him in a straight-up duel of power.

But Endicott would not leave this room without ensuring its destruction. Even if Macha were telling the truth, Endicott couldn't live knowing its evil continued.

Only one weapon left, the distinct spiritual strength in which the Endicotts exceeded all others. The power of command.

He prayed at Macha's goons. *"In the name of Jesus, I compel you. Shoot each other."*

Each goon turned toward the other, hands shaking, shooting, but shots flying wide. The old man's voice rose to a shrill cry. *"Stop it. Shoot him. Shoot the American!"* The force of the place aided him; the goons stopped shooting at each other.

Now another commanding prayer, one which Endicott had no assurance of being answered. He prayed at the heads, hands, and feet. *"In Christ's name, attack these men."*

With unnatural speed, these soulless things somehow obeyed, crawling and rolling toward his three enemies, wrapping around their feet, biting at their ankles. But the goons' hands had ceased to shake; soon, their wills would be their own.

Endicott had one more prayer, a completely silent one outside his usual expertise. *Extinguish flame.* The fires under the alchemical vats snuffed out. He prayed his enemies wouldn't notice.

Endicott faced his enemies, sword out. One of the goons was slowly aiming toward Endicott; the other was still struggling. Both blocked his exit. The writhing arms and legs on the ground seemed less lively and affectionate.

The gas under the vats continued to hiss. Time to go.

Waving his sword, Endicott charged the goon with the better aim. If he got a shot off, show over. *"Fall! Fall and . . ."* Macha started to say something nasty; Endicott slashed at him with his sword as he plowed shoulder first into the goon. Macha dodged the blow; Endicott spun off the goon and tumbled onto the hard floor of the sitting room.

The old man screamed, *"Die, die, die!"*

Endicott suddenly felt slower, weaker. But such poorly planned craft could not stop him. In a second, he was up, and running for the stairs.

Endicott reached the stairway and raced up with grasping arm and pumping legs, sword gripped down at his side. The room tugged at him, wanting him to stay. *"After him!"* cried Macha.

The tramp of goons' feet on stone echoed behind him. No more time. *"In the name of God, flame on!"*

The explosion rumbled through the stone. The concentrated gas acted as catalyst for other chemicals in the room, which added their destructive force in rumbling crescendo. A furnace of flame roiled up, impelled by alchemy and the dark spirit of the place, reaching for Endicott with the dying screams of his enemies. His clothes were on fire. He was on fire.

Oh God, out, out, out! He burst out of the passageway and rolled on the antique carpet, then lay there, exhausted. *For these gifts I give thee thanks, Lord.*

He prayed for healing, but that wasn't his strong suit. His painful burns weren't that severe. *Just get me through the day, Lord.* Caretakers and security men were running past. One stopped and shouted at him in Czech. Endicott grabbed his arm. *"Take me to the American Embassy. Now."*

Endicott sat huddled in a safe room deep within the U.S. Embassy, still in charred and singed clothes, wrapped in a blanket. Feeling bad and absurd, feeling blistered and burned. The infirmary could wait; first, he had his duty. He cleared his thoughts and phoned the general.

"Sir, target was terminated. Termination was unavoidable. There's significant mess for cleanup. Intel is . . . Intel is very significant, sir."

Silence for a ten count. "Sir?"

"Never mind all that now, Sword. You can report to me in person. You're needed back home, ASAP."

"Sir?"

"Something is wrong with, um, Casper. We want you to monitor him."

Casper. The captain he had helped restrain. Endicott's sword hand itched at the name, and he didn't know why. "I saw him at the airbase, sir."

"Right. I expect your report on Prague tomorrow." The general cleared his throat. "You should know that Casper is a Morton."

"Understood, sir." His father must have detected the pause in Endicott's response and known the emotion it contained. But his response was certain. If his father of all people could give this order, Endicott could damn well obey it.

Containing his strong feelings completed Endicott's exhaustion. Duty done for the moment, he let himself be cared for and wheeled onto a plane for Washington. Tomorrow he would just report the facts, but he knew what the general would say. The old Czech had been working with some serious Left-Hand craft, craft at a level that he did not fully comprehend and control, or Endicott would have been toast. Only one Family had ever achieved that dark height. The general would say that the Left-Hand Mortons were back. They were trying to make new bodies for their old corrupted souls.

And coincidentally, something was wrong with Captain Morton. Only, in spiritual ops, there were no coincidences.

All this was profoundly disturbing, like a move to DEFCON 2 on a sunny day. But what really stuck in Endicott's craw (along with the monastery's splinters) seemed trivial in comparison: why had PRECOG originally assigned the Prague job to a Morton? And why had Sphinx switched this job to an Endicott?

If all had gone well, a Morton would have been fine in Prague, perhaps even too cozy with the monastery's Left-Hand abominations. But if all had gone as badly as it had? God had granted the Endicotts the strongest power of command, and it had taken all of Endicott's compulsive power to get out of the monastery alive. If Casper had not played nice with those Left-Hand elements and had gotten into the same fight, he would have died down there.

The steady vibration of the plane was a lullaby. Endicott could not answer the riddle yet, not without knowing more, certainly not before sleep took him. But, within the limits of duty, he would answer it. And whatever the answer, someone would have to face divine wrath and Endicott power. *So help me, God.*

THREE

I was in the desert again, fighting the sorcerer. *"Break hand . . . move air . . . short sharp shock."* Then, I was running, trying to stop my men: *"Cease fire! Cease fire! Goddamnit, cease fire!"*

Kill them all.

I stopped yelling and blinked my eyes fully awake. Sunlight streamed into the rural bedroom. I felt cold and wet in a pool of my own night-terror sweat. I rolled off the firm mattress of the oak bed onto the thick shag floor and went to the bedroom door. I knocked. "I'm awake," I said.

"No shit?" came the answer.

"Thanks for the sympathy." But I actually appreciated the attendant's nonchalance. I showered and dressed in my flannel shirt and new jeans with on-duty precision. That was more than I could say for the dining room staff— shirts untucked, shoes scuffed and muddied, symptoms of low discipline and morale. The staff was tired of this shit detail. I had been here too long.

I cut my pancakes with an antique silver knife on fine porcelain. They apparently weren't worried that I'd use the knife on self or others. As usual, they served me too much breakfast, and, as usual, I ate too little—just enough to avoid the threat of forced feeding. I told myself I didn't want to put on weight and lose my fighting edge.

But that's the idea, to stop fighting, said the voice of the curse.

Never, kill them all, answered the dungeon voice that enjoyed the memory of bloodshed. I recognized too well the sound of that voice. I had heard it whisper from the subbasement of my home, the House of Morton. I had fought that Left-Hand voice my whole life. Had the curse weakened me enough to lose?

Caught between the argument of my mental aliens, I could barely think. A thump behind me. Two of the attendants were helping someone downstairs with their elaborately tattooed arms. The pale, thin young man wore a thin black tie—an LDS craftsman, no doubt. The Mormon was still breathing; I hadn't yet killed in my sleep. But my unconscious night-terror assault had hit a target again.

Maybe they thought the massacre was my fault. Maybe they were worried that I'd gone the Left-Hand path of my ancestors, Roderick and Madeline and the rest. Maybe they feared the voice in my head. If this damage kept up, they might have to consider putting me down like a broken horse or a rabid dog.

If I went for the door or a window, they'd have trouble stopping me. But then the Gideons would find me. Those hard-assed special ops trackers probably patrolled the grounds, sniffing the air like bloodhounds, keeping outsiders out and me in. Was the one called Sakakawea here? She had hunted magi on every continent, including Antarctica.

And if I got past the Gideons, where would I go? The

other Families, Abram Endicott at their head, had taken the House before. I could seek the Sanctuary and invoke the compact, but that wouldn't stop their pursuit. Hell, first, I would have to get past the Sanctuary's guardian, the Appalachian, and she was no fool; compact or no, she wouldn't let me in.

That killed my already small appetite. I drifted to the study to read from the dusty Harvard Classics that filled several shelves, and to ignore the WWI poetry that some joker had stuck in there. *It must be visiting hours.* In an army dress blue uniform, my father blocked the doorway. "Hi, Dad."

"Hi, Dale. You're looking thin."

"Not very hungry," I said. "You look . . . unchanged."

"One of the few advantages of my condition."

"Being dead as coffin shit?"

"Doesn't mean I won't kick your ass if you start talking smart."

"Sorry."

"No, I'm sorry, son. I'm here to help."

"Help?" That was new from this ghost. "OK. Can you move over? I'd rather not step through you." I could touch ghosts, but they triggered an unpleasant sensation, like a combination of cold and wet. I carefully stepped into the study. "You want to help me, Dad? Tell me where I am."

"I don't know." My father sighed, a hollow sound with no air in it. "You know the rules." I knew: my father was like a recording that couldn't really tell me anything new, only how things had been. He could help more with Morton family matters, but not much. A sad, rude, and true way to think of my father.

"Sorry, forgot," I said. "Haven't seen you for a while. Why did you wait until I was crazy to show up?"

"I've been around you a lot," said Dad. "Why did you wait until now to see me?"

"I have your letters," I said. "And Grandpa. They're usually enough."

"At home?" Dad asked.

"Yeah."

A silence. My father couldn't come home. For reasons he wouldn't discuss, Dad had chosen burial at Arlington instead of the family mausoleum. Grandpa wouldn't let his ghost past the door.

My keepers could listen to my side of the conversation, so I couldn't ask him my real question: what did he know about Sphinx, the woman who had sent me on my last mission, and probably set me up?

Instead, I asked, "Did the other Mortons end up like this?"

"Left-Hand? No son of mine is going down Roderick's road."

"They say you did," I said. "Before the end."

"*They?* Don't speak ill of the dead, son. It makes us uppity."

"Sorry," I said.

"Before the end, I was here. But I didn't know where I was then, so I can't help you now."

"You went nuts?"

"They seemed to think so." Dad shimmered like a heat mirage. "Look, between the happy memories and the craft security, I'm a little tired. We'll talk later. In the meantime, think about how to lie low—"

"Like you, Dad?"

"—and would you say hi to your mother for me?"

"She's remarried, Dad, I don't think—"

"What?" My father shook his head in confusion. "Oh, right. Never mind." And he was gone.

Not for the first time, I wondered about my mother.

In one of the upstairs rooms, Endicott reported in to Hutchinson. She looked as beat up as he felt from their constant containment of Morton's outbursts. Yes, practitioners were valuable, and ones with Morton's power were rarer still, but they had given Morton more energy for his recovery than any other spiritual soldier had ever received. Time to ease Hutch toward the inevitable conclusion.

"Ma'am," said Endicott, "he still isn't under control. The general is concerned."

"We're all concerned, Major," said Hutchinson. Her voice held steady with command, but her eyes were slits of fatigue.

"Five weeks," said Endicott, "and we still don't know if he can recover, or if he's been permanently compromised."

Hutchinson's sharp jaw tensed, relaxed, tensed again. "Time to see what he'll do under pressure. We're bringing a new shrink into the craft secret. Let's give him to Morton."

They took me in the middle of the night, out of the first dreamless sleep I'd had in months. They must have used drugs or craft so I wouldn't unconsciously hurt my awakeners. They took me upstairs to what looked like a dentist office, if one's dentist had the equipment for waterboarding and electroshock. Interrogation? They must think I'd gone Left-Hand. But that didn't make sense: if they thought I had gone that rotten, they should kill me thoroughly now. And if they were serious about torture before murder, surely they'd use craft.

The goons sat me firmly down in the chair and strapped me in, then left the room. A man in a doctor's white jacket and oversized mustache turned on an old tape recorder. "I want to hear about the mission, Dale."

"You already know about the mission."

"I need the truth."

Those in the know about craft were a small community. I hadn't seen this doctor before. "Are you cleared to hear about what I do?"

"That's not for you to decide. The sooner you cooperate, the sooner you can leave here."

I studied the doctor, and found him wanting. His sins were trivial, and he had no craft. "I'm not going to tell you anything."

"Then I'm authorized to use harsh techniques."

"You're going to torture me?" I laughed. I spoke toward the recording equipment and those listening outside. "You get all that? He's trying to push me around. If you don't want him to know, you'd better stop this right now." Then I turned to the doctor, all humor gone. "OK. Joke's on you, pal."

"Tell me about the mission, Dale," said the doctor.

"No, let's start at the beginning. My ancestor, Thomas Morton, was the first great American craftsman."

"What did he make?" asked the doctor.

"I'm getting to that. He arrived in Massachusetts in 1624, and found that, in this new land, he had strange new powers. He could alter the weather. He could see the sins of men, and could influence their will. He could fight and kill with preternatural efficiency."

"Who, um, told you these stories?"

"My father," I said.

"Your father? My records say that—"

"Thomas Morton," I continued, "tried to form a new society of native and European. He took several Indian wives, and they taught each other much magic, or what we call craft. But the Puritans stopped him, shipped him back to England—twice."

"I see," said the doctor. "So, Puritans versus your polygamous ancestor. Do you feel the Puritans are against you, Dale?"

"Oh they are, they are. But, for the sake of the nation, we've come to a modus vivendi." I too much enjoyed skewing my story to this prick's psychological worldview, but I'd get around to the punch line soon. "So, Morton passed his abilities to his part-native descendants."

"And you're one of these magical descendants?"

"That's right," I said. "I'm a craftsman."

"Dale, if you have these abilities—"

"*If,* doctor? Are you calling me a liar?" More psycho role play. So obvious.

"What, you say some backwards Latin mumbo jumbo . . ."

"*Shut up,*" I said. Compulsion wasn't my usual strength, but this mundane doctor was easy.

The doctor's mouth flapped, but nothing came out. He reached for his throat, covered his lips, a dumb show of muteness.

"No, not Latin," I said. "Despite the papist tendencies of my Cavalier ancestor, we Mortons have never seen the charm of Latin. Magic is sensitive work, and it's best to mean exactly what you say. That means Webster's English. Which you seem to be lacking. *Speak*."

"Hypnosis." The first word exploded from the doctor's mouth. "I'm a suggestible subject. But that's not magic."

"Maybe not." Good. Now for the scarlet-letter treatment. "Neither were your experiments on students, you fuck. Your late-night sexual exploration seminars with undergrads, did they get college credit for those? And that one patient—you let her snuff herself. Very convenient. All good practice for the harsh techniques."

The doctor stood up, enraged and in my face. "Bullshit. You're insane. You've got no powers." He pulled a hypodermic off a tray, and seemed to calm. "Let's get serious. You'll tell me about the mission now."

Now it was my turn for anger. *"Sit."* The doctor sat down hard on the floor, the hypo clacked at his side. "Drugs and craft don't mix. You're almost right about my powers. I've been crippled. My last target was a sorcerer. He allowed me to kill him, then gave his postmortem craft unusual power through the blood sacrifice that he caused my own men to perform. He's cursed me, and it's tearing me apart. And that's what put me here, in this improvised rubber house for a shell-shocked craftsman. Not just psychological guilt, but blood craft. Do you understand now, you fucking joke?"

The doctor looked at me in amazement. "Um, um . . ."

The chair rattled beneath me. I felt like lightning in a bottle. *Murder him,* insisted the dungeon voice, *for starters.* The curse retorted, *Then kill yourself, for starters.*

My superiors were testing me, and failure meant death. I found my center, and played to the unseen gallery again.

"I was on that mission for a reason. Farsight should have seen this setup. Somebody wants me out of the game."

Now, to end on a light, good ol' Dale Morton note. "I think we're done for the day, don't you? Please help me undo these straps. Outstanding." I rubbed my wrists. I had tensed against the restraints more than I'd realized. I stood up. "They're gonna explain everything later, I expect, but you might as well hear it from me. Even if I hadn't stopped you, they were never ever gonna allow you to administer serious psychoactives or pain. You know why that is, doctor?"

The doctor shook his head. I said, "Please speak for the microphone, doctor."

"No."

"Because my family scares the shit out of them." I laughed. "I don't blame 'em. We once produced pure evil, and they're terrified we'll do it again. But we're useful. So they'll never really hurt me, unless they mean to kill me." I turned to go, but my disgust at this American's willingness to torture harmonized with the darkness inside me, and I needed to give voice to both.

"Doctor," I said.

"Yes?"

"Don't let me see your fucking face again. Ever."

S atisfied?" asked Hutch, shutting off the tape.

"He sounds more than a little paranoid," said Endicott.

Hutch raised her brows ironically, but Endicott refused to take the bait. "He still wants to quit," he said.

"Horseshit," said Hutch. "He'll change his mind."

Endicott nodded, but thought, *And when he leaves, he'll be the general's problem, and you won't be able to protect him anymore.*

T he next day, I went back to the old schedule. Night terrors, breakfast, my father in the study. Today, Dad smiled sadly. "Looks like you've got a visitor coming. I'll get out of the way."

A familiar man stood at attention in the study's doorway. Sergeant Zee. "Hello, sir. I hope you don't mind my stopping by."

I must have gaped. "Sir?" repeated Zee.

I pulled myself together. "No, Sergeant, I don't mind at all." I managed a smile. "Please, at ease. Have a seat. I'm not exactly on duty here."

"Thank you, sir." Zee sat on the edge of an overstuffed chair, somehow preserving his military posture. I sat on the small sofa.

"So, they let you out of quarantine," I said.

"Yes, sir," said Zee. "It was a difficult month."

"Yeah, I understand. You've probably noticed my accommodations." I patted the sofa. "The padding is nicer, but it's a cell all the same. And not much company."

"Yes, sir," said Zee. "That's part of why I wanted to see you."

"I appreciate that, Zee. I'm glad to see you. But how did you know?"

"Well, sir, as I tried to tell you, I'd served on a few missions like yours," said Zee. "They gave me the order to kill you, rather than let you be captured."

"Yes, I guessed that. Still, to get permission to come here . . ."

Zee said, "I didn't need permission, sir."

I felt a cold hand reaching for my heart. "How's that?" A stupid question.

"I'm dead, sir," said Zee. "I'm sorry, I thought your father would have mentioned it."

"No," I croaked. "Must have slipped his mind." Shit. I easily missed the ghostly about ghosts. I had once spent a whole evening with a friend at a bar before finding out the next day that he had been dead for weeks. "Your death," I said. "Something to do with our mission?"

"Yes. I remembered it all, over and over again."

"You killed yourself," I said.

"Seemed to make sense at the time. I left a note. 'I'm sorry.' That was it. I left behind my wife and kids." Zee's image flickered as his calm lapsed. "Seemed to make sense at the time."

"What's happened to the others?"

"They're more or less OK. They don't remember much. They've been discharged or placed on light duty. They don't quite understand why, but their survival instincts told them not to fight it too hard. So why are you fighting it, sir?"

"I tried to resign," I said. "They won't let me go."

The ghost considered. "Then think about this, sir. Was it worth it? Your target was protecting a little shit town that no one cared about—not us or them. He just wanted us to stay away. You show up, and it makes him crazy, makes him sacrifice them all, just to stop you."

"I think about it all the time."

"Well, think about this too. I have my last orders. I'm not going to let you feel any better until you've stopped, sir."

"You'd serve a terrorist sorcerer?"

"Oh no, sir. I've been watching you, and listening. It's you who's going over to the enemy." Zee grinned, face full of rage and malice. "This is for me."

I felt it all over again, the man, the woman, the dog, the child, the deaths of a whole town. The scream came to my throat, but I wouldn't let it out.

Instead, I walked through Zee and went to the doctor on duty. In the measured tones of desperate need, I said, "I need to speak with Colonel Hutchinson."

I sn't it time you got over what happened?" asked Hutchinson.

The steady pulse of death, death, death, still beat in the veins of my skull. "This isn't about the mission, ma'am. It's about me needing to resign. This treatment you've arranged isn't working."

"What about the night terrors?" asked Hutchinson. "You've . . . been causing some difficulties in your sleep. We can't have that on the outside."

"I know, ma'am. I have reason to believe my sleep problems will cease to hurt others once I've left the military. And if they don't, the Family House should contain them."

Hutchinson shook her head. "This is something the target did to you, isn't it? Why don't you fight it?"

"If it were just a curse, a craft time bomb, I would, ma'am," I said. "But it's beyond that now. When the massacre happened, something in me . . . wasn't upset."

For the first time in my presence, Hutch's eyes betrayed surprise. "The Left-Hand Mortons are dead and gone," she whispered.

"And they're going to stay that way," I said.

Hutchinson said, "No craft soldier has ever quit in time of war."

"War? Feh."

"But what about the Right side of your family? The Morton legacy."

"What legacy? How are you going to get your baby Mortons if I'm too bugged out to take a girl on a date?"

Hutchinson sighed. "Do we really need more Mortons?" She stopped my objection with a wave. "Our superiors agree that we do. And that's the one reason we're agreeing to this." She opened her briefcase. "We have a special discharge for craft soldiers."

I read the discharge papers.

Section 2. Conditions. 1.1 After the Discharge Date, any action violating natural laws will constitute an act of treason against the United States.

"This says I can't do craft. Ever."

Hutchinson nodded. "Same rule for any craftsperson not in government service, only more so. No parlor tricks at a kid's birthday, no nice weather to watch the baseball game. Nada."

"And I can't even talk to another craftsperson?"

"Call it paranoid," said Hutchinson, "but wherever two or more witches or wizards are gathered without his say-so, Uncle Sam's balls go cold."

"If I don't sign?" I asked.

"You can't leave," said Hutchinson.

"If I . . ."

"Don't make me answer that question," said Hutchinson. "You know how this administration feels about craft work. National security only. We won't risk the general public knowing this. Everything else is Ex-22." Exodus 22:18: "Thou shalt not suffer a witch to live."

I signed. The colonel nodded. "Good. That was for them. Now I want your personal word on it."

"My word?"

"I want you to swear by the craft."

"What if I can't control it?"

"You come back here until you can. Look, don't get all Sunday-school questions about this. Take the prohibition seriously, and we'll all be fine. Push things, and we'll push back."

The deal was bullshit—a Morton could no more completely stop practicing craft than completely stop breathing. But I could swear to keep it to a low background, ambient kind of thing. That oath would have real power. My honor was more than an abstraction, it was tied into my being and my practice of the craft. But what about my family's duty?

I had no choice. "I swear to you by the craft and my ancestors not to willfully practice magic anymore."

That night, as I lay down to a tentative sleep, Sergeant Zee came to me. "Thank you."

"Fuck off," I said. I had found my own solution to the competing voices: a separate war.

I thought of what I couldn't tell Hutchinson, but what I had tried to tell them all in the interrogation. *I was on that mission for a reason.* In magic, there were few accidents. Someone, probably Sphinx, had set me up. There was a mole in the craft, and oath or no, I would kill the traitorous sorcerer. It was what I did best.

PART II

SCHEREZADE AND THE OTHER HOUSE OF SEVEN GABLES

You cannot depend on your eyes when your imagination is out of focus.
—MARK TWAIN

(I am large, I contain multitudes.)
—WALT WHITMAN

"For craft's sake, is that really necessary?" I asked, nodding at the blindfold.

"You aren't the first mage to be treated here," said Hutchinson, "and unfortunately, you won't be the last, so this location will remain classified." She tied the blindfold over my face. "Good luck. I'll see you soon."

After a car, a plane, and another car, I felt the steady deceleration of a confused driver. "It isn't here," said a voice from the front seat.

"Stop," said the escort at my right. "This is close enough."

The car stopped. A front door opened, then the door next to me opened. Someone tugged me outside and took off my blindfold. My large, black-suited escort asked, "This close enough?"

In the middle of the road, I blinked at an ancient mansion obscured by craft. "Bull's-eye."

"Shit," said the suit. My bag was tossed to the pavement. Doors slammed, and the better-than-regulation sedan squealed off. I stood alone in front of the House of Morton.

I hesitated. I felt eight years old, after a bad day at school. *But I've got no place else to go.* I picked up my bag and strode toward the House.

The House had the wild asymmetries that could only accrue over centuries. Stables partially converted into a garage extended in an L to the right side. A terraced garden faced the street, rising to a walled courtyard with a Chinese balcony thrust forward above it from the third floor. Trumpet flowers bloomed everywhere. The overall look was that of a Victorian medieval folly, a gothic fortress against the inevitable peasants with torches.

The core of the old House had seven gables. For the Mortons, this was not an accidental feature. The House had been designed as an occult mirror to the Endicott mansion in Salem, in deep sympathy with the Mortons' enemies for times when it became necessary to powerfully remind the old foes of their errors.

I stepped up through the garden into the courtyard. A wave of hot hate rolled out from the House; the heavy wooden door swung open. A stern-faced old man stepped forward, raised a shotgun and pointed it at me. "Freeze, you yellow bastard."

I froze. "This isn't going to solve anything."

A voice came from behind me. "He wasn't talking to you, sir." I looked back. Sergeant Zee grinned like a feral dog.

"We had a deal," I said.

"Fuck you and your deal, sir," said Zee, approaching me. "I like it here."

The old man waved his gun to the right. "Boy, step aside so I don't have to shoot through you."

Zee spat. "Whatchya going to do, old man, kill me?"

"Not kill," said the old man. *"Erase."*

I hit the ground as the old man pulled the trigger. Zee roared as ectoplasmic bullets ripped through him. Then he dissolved into a glowing mist, driven away for now.

"You going to spend all day kissing the dirt, boy?"

I pushed myself to my feet. Smoke drifted up from the barrels of the gun. The old man yelled at the empty air. "Goddamnit, I don't care if the Bavarian Illuminati and Poe's bird are giving you juice, you better be hitting the highway to heaven." Then the man looked me right in the eye, and a jagged smile broke the stony face. He threw his arms wide. "Welcome home, boy!"

I ran up to him, arms wide. "Grandpa." We came close, but did not touch. Grandpa's ghost would feel uncomfortably cold; he had been dead a long time. Still, damned good to see him again.

Remembering Grandpa's words as I approached the House, I bit hard on my emotion. "I thought . . ."

Grandpa shook his head. "What your father did was different. At least according to me." He nodded toward my bag. "Get your things. Your room's ready."

As I stepped across the threshold, the House embraced me with the warm smells of fresh baked bread and cinnamon. "I missed you too, House."

The wood floors creaked in minor complaint. "Nonsense," I said. "You don't look a day over three hundred. Still as beautiful as—" A *gong* interrupted me, marking the hour.

"Do I have to tell you again?" said Grandpa. "That clock belongs in the subbasement." He set the gun down and it vanished. "With the other Left-Hand Morton nastiness."

The great clock in the hallway ignored Grandpa and continued to tick through its second century with preternatural accuracy, low like a heartbeat, with each swing of its shiny, steel pendulum. The spade-shaped weight glinted sharply in an otherwise dull-toned antique.

"Later, Grandpa," I said. The House was whispering, wanting me to see every thing, each in its place, older, but unchanged.

To one side of the main hall, the parlor held neoclassical busts of Revolutionary Mortons, whose dead white eyes seemed to follow any guests, despite their lack of pupils. In this otherwise finely furnished room, the sickly yellow wallpaper stood out, interrupted by only two small bookshelves, two uncatalogued Copley paintings, and some Pelagic pottery and Revere silver. Even if the guest avoided looking at the wallpaper, in the corner of one's eye it seemed to breathe like a tired old woman.

We moved on to the library and study side of the House. On the library table sat the book I had made from my father's letters, instructing the young me in the craft "in case I should perish before I can teach it myself." Such letters were a Morton tradition, validated over and over by early death, including Dad's.

On this side of the House, shelves of rare books almost completely covered the walls: original editions, manuscripts, and notes of Hawthorne, Poe, Lovecraft, and other friends of the Mortons.

"Let's say hi to the Founders." I bound up the stairs toward the third-floor hallway, Grandpa trailing.

"Goddamnit," said Grandpa. "We're not ancient Chinese or Louisiana creoles. Why do we pay so much attention to our ancestors?"

I stopped, raised an eyebrow at Grandpa, then trotted on. There was someone I needed to see.

Portraits of the Mortons going back four hundred years lined the hall. Sounds like insect scurryings voiced disapproval. They always disapproved. But two portraits—each with the same frame, each with the same blackened canvas—were silent. The obliterated images of Roderick and Madeline Morton hung as a paired reminder of their horror. Not what I needed to think about now.

I was focused on another Morton. "Joshua."

"Joshua," said Grandpa. "The best of the Mortons."

"Not very honorable, what he did," I said. Joshua Morton, the assassin at Chancellorsville, used his craft-propelled voice to tell the Confederates to "pour it into them, boys." But instead of Union troops, they shot their own General Jackson.

"Not brave," said Grandpa, "but necessary. Brave was that summer, in Pennsylvania."

"That was just plain crazy," I said. Joshua had stood alone against the combined craft weight of the South, against his own brother Jeb, and against the stars in their courses on the Union left flank.

"Crazy," said Grandpa, "and necessary. My dad said whenever Joshua shook the hand of a former slave, he would flinch at the freedman's memory of every stroke of the lash. So that day at Gettysburg, Joshua didn't flinch."

I stared for a moment, letting the chills fade. This was why I had served, why I would always serve. I might be out of the army, might have sworn an oath not to practice, might never receive much respect from the other Families, but that all made little difference to a Morton. I had a duty to perform, a very *necessary* duty. I had a traitor to kill.

The person who had given me my last assignment must have known the probable outcome. *Sphinx.* I knew her legend, but I needed mortal details. I could only get those from the dead.

"Grandpa?"

"Yep, boy." My grandfather manifested in a blink; one second nothing, the next as solid-looking as life. The glass of bourbon in his hand gave a whole new meaning to "spirits." "Ready to tell me about the trouble you're in?"

It was best to be calm talking with an ancestor. If they saw you angry (or scared), they might get too sympathetically agitated to be of any help. So I asked, as casually as I could, "Grandpa, did you know Sphinx?"

At Sphinx's name, Grandfather came unstuck from the floor and didn't float back down to Earth immediately. "If it's the same code name, yep, I knew her."

"Who is she?"

Grandpa sat down in his old chair like he used to when he told me long stories of Morton wars. "We found her at Woodstock."

"No shit?"

"No shit," said Grandpa. "And watch your language. She was prophesying the end of the war in Vietnam."

"Hell," I said, "I could have told you that."

"She spoke like a goddamned teletype, giving cold specifics of body counts and operational code names, then painting sweeping vistas of helicopters taking off from the American embassy roof."

I whistled. "Still, would have been difficult to find her in all that noise."

"Hell yes," said Grandpa. "We might have lost her in the sixties sea of anarchic craft, but our intel had been checking all purported prophets against the facts."

"How did you know her?"

"I helped bring her in. She was non-Christian, one of ours."

Grandpa took a sip of his bourbon. In life, a sip after a bet in poker had been Grandpa's nervous tell. I said, "That all?"

Grandpa stared down at his bourbon. "What do you mean?"

"Nothing," I lied.

"I was about twice her age," said Grandpa, still defensive.

"Right. Sorry." Had the old goat slept with Sphinx? That might bias his story, but it wasn't what I needed to know. "So she joins the Peepshow to foresee the bad news professionally. She ever call in a bad mission?"

"No, never," said Grandpa.

Until me. "That you knew of," I said.

"No," repeated Grandpa. "They *gave* her the bad ones. They thought she was insubordinate. She would use ancient names for locations rather than military coordinates because they sounded cooler, so they gave her punishment detail. They had her looking years down the road. Anyone else observing that far ahead would mostly generate meaningless noise. But she was too good. She would see the shit long before anyone was ready to understand it."

"Oh come on," I said, deliberately provocative. "Nostradamus quatrains aren't intel."

"How about these verses?" said Grandpa. *"Evacuate the embassy in Tehran. Close all the airports in September."*

"Oh."

"Her most famous warnings marked America's spectacular failures," said Grandpa. "No wonder that, despite her record, she was as ignored as Cassandra. But they must take her very seriously by now. She must be a director or a DD."

"Maybe she didn't want to be understood," I said. That was enough tiptoeing around. "If she lied . . ."

"She never lied," said Grandpa.

"If she's lied," I repeated, "if she's warned the Peepshow against me, that would explain what happened in the desert." Grandpa stared at his boots, lost in dead thoughts, so I got in the old man's face. "This is Morton business, Grandpa. This is family survival. Can she see inside this House?"

Grandpa sighed. "If anyone could, Sphinx could. But no. The Left Hand pulled all kinds of wicked shit in this place, and no one saw. They can't see everything."

"What's her real name, Grandpa?" With that simple question, I crossed a line. It wasn't like the fairy tales, where names meant magic vulnerability. Disclosing your real name meant vulnerability in the flesh, in your ordinary home, with your ordinary spouse and kids. Grandpa had brought her in, so he must know her name.

"It won't do you any good," said Grandpa. "Last I knew, she lived alone at Langley. She's Dare Smith of the Virginia Smiths."

Shit, that was an old lineage, going all the way back to Captain John Smith. Grandpa was right: if she kept within Langley, she wasn't vulnerable in the mundane world. But no one stayed in a secure site forever. I would still track her.

Grandpa's image rippled with restlessness. "Now, I'm tired. And I think you're tracking the wrong cat. Sphinx was many things, but never evil."

He vanished. It couldn't be easy to hear that your grandson planned to kill an old friend. Though the target was still uncertain, that was the direction I was traveling. If the top farsight had gone bad, then America's existence might be at stake. But even if I decided that Sphinx was a mole, how could I kill someone who could see me coming?

I packed my camping gear, flung myself into my souped-up '57 T-Bird, and peeled out of the stable-garage. I would drive to northern Virginia to stake out the area around Langley. I wouldn't fly to D.C. They would watch for me, particularly at those airports.

"You shouldn't be out."

I nearly veered off the road at the sudden voice. My father sat solemnly in the T-Bird's passenger seat. "Shit, Dad, are you trying to push me to the other side early?"

"God, I still love this car," said Dad. "Go home, Dale. Too much bullshit in the air. This is where it all goes wrong." Then Dad was gone.

"Dammit, Dad." Ghosts couldn't do precog, so I wasn't stopping.

I was close to the freeway ramp when I saw the first surveillance vehicle: a black sedan carrying three agents in stylishly cut black suits. They pulled up close to make sure I knew they were following. Their windows weren't tinted; they wanted me to know who they were. One man had curly blond hair and the other had no hair at all, while the woman appeared Celtic fair and red-haired. I hadn't seen them myself before, but knew them by reputation and code name: blond Bumppo, bald Carson, and Sakakawea. The Gideons, the trained trackers who hunted down rogue craftsmen, were on me.

The T-Bird wasn't the best car to shake a tail, but I might manage. With a growl from the old motor, I veered away from the ramp and went back into the tight blocks of College Hill. I was pretty certain my tailers weren't Providence natives. Sure enough, a couple of sudden turns later and I had lost them. I got on the highway.

Two women in a convertible bopped along to the radio, nice lookers in summer colors that might have gotten a smile from me on another day. Something very wrong about that, about attracting my interest without scrutiny. Despite my oath, I did some craft that nobody else would detect: I checked the women's sins. Big capital red letters flashed moralities more suited to counterintelligence professionals than party girls. A leapfrog surveillance, with at least two cars devoted to me. Not good.

I got off the freeway at the next exit. Now I was on my way to the reservoir in fucking Pawtuxet, which they insisted on calling Cranston. Not my territory, and craft stealth wasn't my strength. Frustration burned.

You should just kill them.

And that seemed like a grand idea. I had a pistol in the glove compartment. The two women weren't craft. I could take them before the Gideons arrived. I could . . .

Cease fire! Shit. I spun the wheel violently, and the car squealed painfully to a stop in the parking lot of a strip mall. The tail drove into the lot and past me as if nothing were amiss, parking a few rows down.

I held my throbbing head in my hands. Between the sorcerer's curse and the Left-Handish voice, my skull was about to explode. I wouldn't get to Virginia tonight. I'd find another way, with more appropriate transport, or maybe the surveillance would loosen up. Time to develop an alibi for this excursion. An out-of-place heavy metal club occupied one section of the mall. *I'm just out for a drink.*

I pulled into a parking space and shut off my car. A drumbeat of craft malice pulsed around me, red like blood. A sudden squeal of rubber. The tailing convertible pulled out of its space and out of the lot, nearly creaming a pedestrian. Something was wrong. Before I knew why, I grabbed the gun from the glove compartment.

My brain caught up: the agents must have been ordered away from me ASAP, meaning someone didn't want them to witness what happened next. I tucked the gun into its holster built into my leather jacket. Again driven by instinct, I sprung from the T-Bird.

I spun around, searching for the next strike. Down the road, the Gideons' sedan came barreling toward the mall. The pedestrian had moved on, and no other person stood close enough to see details. Good. If my own government was trying to kill me, then any witnesses would be at serious risk.

That was why I wasn't going to drive home. If they had decided on my death, then termination in a speeding car would just lead to more collateral damage to innocents and my spirit.

Behind the mall was a wooded park area, which might even the odds a little. As good a place as any for a showdown. I ran for it, past the storefronts toward the edge of the mall building, where I would turn and enter the woods.

The Gideons' sedan screamed to a stop, and two of them were already out the doors and in pursuit, fast as feral cats.

I reached the end of the building. A woman stepped out from the corner restaurant. I stepped to dodge her. I was going to yell a warning—*Get inside, bad people are behind me!*—then draw my gun.

But then, drawing breath to speak, the smell hit me, savory and dreadful. Cumin, nutmeg, cardamom, lamb, exhaust. The scents of a "Mediterranean" restaurant blended with the low stink of auto fumes.

I stumbled to a stop, my way blocked. Zee was standing in front of me. "You've been a bad boy, sir."

I fell to my knees. All went blank, except for foreign gutturals from somewhere close. From my own mouth.

Then the woman from the restaurant was speaking low, angry and close, using the same Farsi-sounding syllables, and I could see again. The woman had bent down so that her perfect almond eyes and short gamine hair were only inches from my face. Her eyes seemed wide with surprise and outrage. Her right hand had gone straight into her purse, forearm tensed, probably packing a knife.

My limbs were lead, but I could move my neck. I looked over my shoulder, expecting a bullet or some unsubtle craft to blow my head clean off. But Sakakawea and Carson stood still, fifty feet away, weapons concealed. Tall and lean, Sakakawea held a hand out to her side, restraining her colleague, speaking low into her headset. Maybe they didn't yet have authorization to act with witnesses. But they would get it soon.

"You need to get inside," I said to the woman from the restaurant. I struggled to get up off my knees. No good.

She repeated the Farsi syllables with emphasis, as if I

were a particularly thick child. I shook my head. "I don't understand."

She stared, incredulous. Beautiful too. More than a few of my kind had perished at the hands of terrible beauty. She asked, "Are you threatening me?"

"What was I saying?"

"The dogs will lick your blood."

"Oh. Sorry. Wasn't talking to you. Can we discuss this inside?"

"To whom were you speaking?" she asked, with unusual grammatical precision.

Someone higher up must have found the Gideons' leash, because they went walking away at a fast clip, and the paralyzing red drumbeat of craft malice seemed to be withdrawing with them. I stood up and brushed the bits of asphalt from my knees. "A flashback. I think this restaurant caused it."

"Then you are threatening me," she said, but she relaxed the arm in her purse. "This place belongs to my family."

"Oh. Really sorry." I breathed through my mouth to avoid the restaurant's exotic odors. The Gideons' sedan was pulling out of the lot. "I should go." I walked toward the T-Bird.

The woman trailed me. "You're a soldier. You were in Iran?"

"No. Long story."

"Where, then?" she asked. "Iraq? Why Farsi? Who were those people running after you?"

Then both the Left Hand and the curse exploded in my head, for once in total agreement, screaming at me. *Kill her now.* "I need to go." I stumbled and fell again into blackness.

S ir, we had him. Why did you stop me?" Leaving
Bumppo and Carson behind in the sedan, the woman
they called Sakakawea was speaking on her headset with
her commander. On the opposite side of Prospect Street
from Brown's Carrie Tower, she paced back and forth on
the sidewalk like a freshly caged predator, neon green eyes
still hunting for prey.

Sakakawea had seen power radiating from where Morton had knelt, driving back Chimera's force. But she had
felt no limitation on taking a clean shot—or two, if one
counted the mundane witness. H-ring would have rubber-
stamped it as killing a rogue with collateral damage.

"Chimera said this wasn't the time for us to act," replied
her commander. He masked his emotions, but she could
hear his frustration.

"A half hour before, Chimera said this was the damned
time. What's the holdup?" Chimera had been predicting
for months that the last of her kin might kill her and her
commander, and destroy Chimera as well. The good news
was that the old Endicott would slay the younger, which
wouldn't be a problem no matter how interpreted.

"You know his deceptions better than anyone."

"Yes, love," she said, dropping their formality. Thank the dark gods that, unlike her commander, she did not have to see Chimera on a daily basis anymore. Her commander had taken the body of Chimera's technician in the Pentagon's secret H-ring. She would have killed Chimera long ago if that hadn't been exactly what he had wanted.

Her commander ignored her endearment. "Morton will report this up to Hutchinson. She's the only one he trusts. We need to remove her."

"When?" asked Sakakawea, not hiding her eagerness.

"Soon. Chimera suggests immediately bringing our force to bear on the House, followed by a coordinated attack."

Sakakawea demurred. "He's a Morton. He'll have a foreboding of his death."

"Good. He'll just appear more insane."

"Are we strong enough?" she asked, but only for her commander's benefit.

"Yes," he said.

As she ended the call, Sakakawea found herself standing near the simple stone and plaque of the H. P. Lovecraft memorial. She chuckled to herself, and loped back to the car.

A warm hand touched my forehead. I opened my eyes, and saw the perfect face of the Persian American woman peering back at me. Did I mention she was beautiful? For the first time since my last mission, the voices in my mind were completely quiet, though I was extremely focused.

She stepped away from me. In her other hand, she held a dripping gray cloth, which must have been meant for my brow. I felt the weight of my gun in my jacket. Good, she hadn't taken it.

I assessed my position. I was seated in the detritus-filled part of a restaurant kitchen that no customer should witness. In the kitchen proper, a Persian-looking man with a wrinkled face and dark hair chopped vegetables with a large knife and almost preternatural speed. His sins were many and familiar. A woman of similar age (his wife?) discreetly tossed some seeds into a gas flame. Their little popping noises distracted the younger woman; she said, "No need for that, *Madar*."

I assumed the seeds were protection against the evil eye. I couldn't fault *Madar*'s perspicacity, but nobody besides me in this room radiated craft, so any problems should be mundane.

The young woman tossed the cloth into a sink and stood off to the side. She seemed a little embarrassed and concerned, but with nothing to occupy her hands, she folded her arms. In the club next door, a double-bass drum pounded a sound check.

"Thank you," I said.

"Why were you saying those things in Persian?" said the woman.

The old man tutted. "Manners, Scherie."

"OK," said the woman, eyes a little wider at the incongruity. "My name is Scherezade Rezvani. This is my mother." Mrs. Rezvani turned away. "And my father."

I stood up, wobbly. "I'm Dale Morton. I'm sorry to have troubled you."

"No, please, wait," said Scherie, stepping forward, open

palm out. "Something very bad happened to you, and it happened in Persian."

"What did I say?"

"Nothing important," said Scherie. "But the way you spoke reminded me . . ." Her dark eyes drooped. "Some people I know were hurt under the Shah or under the current regime. So I think evil things were done to you, and not so long ago."

Mr. Rezvani glanced at the fire door like these words were chasing him, so I peeked at his sins. Yes, he had done some of those evil things to others, but his sins had the fuzzy quality of old crimes in another country.

Mrs. Rezvani shook her fists. "Those thugs in Tehran cannot last. America should bomb them."

"Madar," Scherie clucked. "He doesn't want to hear us weep over lost Persia."

"My daughter wants to go back and change things," said Mr. Rezvani, ignoring Scherie's admonition. "She's modest, but I teach her this and that." He picked up a large carving knife and made it twirl and dance. Then he tossed it toward Scherie, who snagged the handle in midair. Scherie averted her skillful yet embarrassed eyes.

I shook my head. "What happened to me . . . wasn't anything important."

"I understand," said Mr. Rezvani. "I still meet with men, they know other men who work for a certain Company."

A man who met men who knew men—too many degrees of separation for me to wrap my brain around. But this family wasn't a security risk to me, and I didn't need to entangle them in my problems.

"Thank you," I said. "I should be going."

"Come back soon," said Mr. Rezvani. "We'll show you

real Persian cooking." I had forgotten about the food smells; they didn't seem to be bothering me now.

Scherie insisted on driving me back to the House. As little as I liked that idea, I agreed, because I wasn't sure that I wouldn't black out again. "Nice car," she said. She drove the T-Bird, while I called for a taxi to meet us.

As we approached the House, I remembered that she might have trouble seeing it. When it wasn't hostile, the House liked to be inconspicuous. "It's kind of hidden behind the other houses."

"What, it's behind the big old creepy mansion?"

She could see the House clearly, which meant that the House wanted her to see it. Strange. She pulled up to the main gate. "I love old houses. Can I see?"

Again I hesitated, not because of the folklore injunction against inviting a stranger across the threshold. She couldn't damage me, but the House might damage her. But the taxi wasn't here yet, and the House seemed to like her, so I chanced it.

Once inside, most guests instinctively kept away from the dark walls and strange objects, but Scherie touched everything. "This wood is warm, like someone's arm in the sun."

Now this was going too far. The House was flirting with her. Under my breath, I mumbled *"Stop it."*

Then, of course, Grandpa appeared, hair slicked back and dressed like James Bond at Monaco. "And who is this exotic gem?" A craftless stranger like Scherie wouldn't see or hear him, but he was annoying me.

My phone interrupted us: the cab calling, lost only a

house away. "Just wait there, she'll be out shortly," I said. Then to Scherie, "You've been a lot kinder than I deserve."

Renewed concern and embarrassed interest filled those large dark eyes. She handed me a card—a charming, old-fashioned gesture. "Give me a call if you want to talk."

"I'm afraid you heard what kind of talker I am."

"Call anyway," she said. "We can go shoot stuff somewhere."

"After what I said and did?"

"You seem . . . like someone I've known for years. That's usually a good sign." Her smile was a little crazy, and a lot beautiful.

Then she left, and the weight of the day came crashing down on me. I wouldn't be dating Scherie. The Pentagon was a hair trigger away from shooting me, and my death was a certainty if I found and killed Sphinx. Any friends would be at risk. And sleeping with someone? Despite the assurances I had given Hutch, I had no idea what the voices in my head were going to do tonight. Though quiet now, they had screamed for Scherie's blood when I had first seen her.

No, no dates. I had damage-control problems with my former employers. Even if the Gideons and the other agents reported the truth, it wouldn't look good. I called Hutchinson. "We need to meet."

"What the hell were you trying to pull?"

"Need to talk in person." The House was more secure than any phone line. "Can you be here tomorrow?"

"To Providence? I should have you hauled back in."

"You were going to come up here to check on me. Move it up."

"Dale, what's wrong?"

"Not over the phone, Hutch."

Once I was off the phone, I could hear all the voices. The House moaned in the wind for Scherie like a three-hundred-year-old teenager. The voices in my head returned, vengeful at their banishment, unhappy how my focus on Scherie had freed me from them, if only for a little while.

The House kept my nighttime craft attacks contained, but the nightmare of the desert returned, and sleep felt like combat. Worse though was a soothing whisper from the subbasement, promising me an end to all my troubles, if I just set the Left-Hand spirits free.

In the cab back from Dale's house, Scherie tapped her clenched fists against her thighs. She was angry at herself for so many reasons. She had practically thrown herself at a man who was return-to-sender damaged. Worse, he had given her the brush-off. Maybe it was an old-money thing—crazy and snobby at the same time.

It had felt so right with him though, standing together in that ancient mansion. The only thing that troubled her was that it looked like a haunted house in the movies. Scherie enjoyed science fiction and fantasy, but hated ghosts. She had seen too many of them as a child.

No one else in her family had seemed to notice them. They had thought the ghosts were her imaginary friends, but they were at least wrong about the friends part. Some of her childhood ghosts were uncles and aunts that she hadn't seen before. They spoke mostly in Farsi, too fast and complicated, not like her parents had taught her. She told them to slow down, but that just made them upset.

The other ghosts were worse. Years later she mentioned

the ghosts' names to her father. He got angry, but not with her. He had done bad things for Iran's ministry of intelligence. After the revolution, the Shah's secret police changed their name, but not their personnel or methods. The names belonged to those tortured and killed by one side or another in the revolution and aftermath—executed relatives and her father's many victims.

They had surrounded tiny Scherie, touched her, and she had felt the pain of their last moments. They had shrieked inside her and tried to crowd her out of her own mind, her family only slightly less brutal than Daddy's work product.

They had made her wish she could flee her body. One former friend of her father's was particularly good at this—a true ghoul. A nightmare, but the crazy-people house would have been even worse. So she had endured. She had known by her tormentors' examples that killing herself would be no solution.

Finally, as innocently as she could, Scherie had asked her mother a question: "How can I make ghosts go away?"

Her mother had smiled. "All you have to do is tell the ghosts to go away, and they will."

Scherie had taken her mother at her word, and more. She said, "Get the fuck out of my house and out of my life!"

And the ghosts had left, and had never come back. She had been very young, so eventually they had seemed like a long, bad dream. Now, that dream could only create a minor unease in a beautiful old house.

Despite her anger at herself for pursuing Dale, by the time she arrived at the mall, she was already hoping that he would call, and not just for a possible romance. She guessed that he had worked covertly in the Middle East, and might be an avenue for her to help her family's homeland. Her father had given her plenty of military talk and some combat basics, but a veteran covert soldier like Dale might have higher-level skills and contacts to share. If he didn't call, she might have to pursue him still harder. If she saw any ghosts, she would just tell them to go away.

The next day, while I was planning some means of getting to Sphinx, I felt a small uneasiness flow across the House's ambient vibe, like the play of a summer breeze on my grandmother's aeolian harp. It wasn't the curse or the voice; more like the sense of a stare across a room, or across a continent. It was a foreboding of an attack that might lead to my death. *No shit, Nostradamus.*

When Hutchinson entered the House, she cut right past our usual soldiers' bull session. "Why were you trying to shake our tail on the highway?"

"What did the Gideons tell you?"

"Shouldn't I be asking the questions?"

"OK, here's what they probably reported. They tailed me from here with the assistance of two mundane agents. I got on the highway, but then it appeared that I spotted the mundanes, and exited to a nearby mall. When the Gideons arrived, I was threatening the mundanes, but then I collapsed for reasons unknown, and all agents were able to escape unharmed."

"And that's not what happened?"

"They were setting me up for early retirement."

"You're paranoid. Where were you going?"

OK, I needed at least one ally, and that meant Hutch or

no one. "I've been thinking more about who called my last mission."

"That kind of thinking is outside your pay grade, Morton. Which is *discharged*."

"We've got a vermin in the Families."

"A craft mole?" said Hutchinson. "High-heeled nonsense. And even if true, it's not the person you're thinking."

"I was set up, and now they're trying to finish the job."

"That sorcerer was a damned good farseer," said Hutchinson. "It happens."

"Not like this. Hutch, I'd swear those three Gideons are in the mole's pocket. If somebody wants me out of commission, it can't be good for craft and country."

Hutchinson closed her eyes and spoke quietly through clenched teeth. "If I say there's a mole, they'll say it's you."

"I'm willing to take that risk," I said.

"I'm not," she said. She pulled out a long case. "I've got something for you."

I opened the case with dread. It was the Purple Heart. "But I'm not wounded."

"Not where anyone can see."

"By that criterion," I said, "a lot of other soldiers should have gotten this."

"Yeah, I know," said Hutchinson, "Keep it for them."

"Yeah. OK," I said. "You can keep it when I'm gone."

"When you're gone? What the hell is eating you?"

"Nothing," I said. I couldn't say that I would likely perish when I took out the mole, so I told her the other reason. "I had a minor foreboding this morning."

"Not from doing craft?"

"No, not intentionally."

Hutchinson closed her eyes and shook her head.

"Morton forebodings. Battlefield diaries with the last entry reading 'Today I died.' Wills with the date of decease. Taking a suicidal mission because the command post was going to be blown up anyway. And dreaming those damned Lincoln dreams."

"What the fuck, Hutch? I'm a little edgy and you've got me on the Lincoln train, first class?"

"Easy." She reached out a hand to just touch my arm. "Any time frame on this foreboding?"

"It feels like there's still some time."

"Then we'll do this through channels," said Hutchinson. "I'll check out Sphinx and these Gideons. I'll get the spooky spooks at the Peepshow on it. They'll see if anyone's painting your crafty ass."

"You're going to tell Sphinx?" I asked.

"I've got my own contacts there," she said.

"You said it yourself," I said. "They might hunt me instead."

Hutchinson fixed her maternal stare on me. "These aren't the days of Roderick and Madeline. You're my responsibility, and I'm not going to let anything happen to you."

She stood up. "I'll have intel start today. We'll stop this thing before you see me next. And you'll see me sooner than scheduled. My word on it."

"And if Sphinx is behind this?"

"Then I'll get you close enough to her to do what you do."

Hutchinson offered her hand; I gripped it. The hand was cold. I asked, "Are you feeling OK?"

"Never better."

"While you're checking on me," I said, "keep an eye out for yourself."

"Another foreboding? Don't worry. The Hutchinson tradition might be less colorful than your family's, but once we've entered the service we follow the book, and we survive. So we'll do this my family's way. Watch yourself, and stay away from the craft. I'll handle any bad guys, mundane or SPACTAD."

But when Hutchinson left, I looked at my hand, and felt the inadequacy of a handshake.

That night, instead of the desert, I was standing at the prow of an enormous ship, all glowing white in the twilight, as if carved from ivory. The ship was gliding impossibly fast over an inert ocean. I could have spread my arms out and played Titanic, but no icebergs relieved the gray view. I would have welcomed a crash, even a sinking, anything to stop the fast-approaching, dark, indefinite shore, because there, the scarlet horror of the Red Death waited.

That wasn't the greatest horror. At my side, in a diaphanous shroud billowing in the silent wind, stood Scherie. Our brief contact had tied her to my destruction.

I woke up, roaring "No!"

The Lincoln dream, and the Red Death, both Family omens of doom. Scherie and I didn't have much time. The boat dream had only given Abe one day's notice. Lincoln had been crafty alright, but a Morton was craftier. We might have a month, but no more, and a lot less if I had the second dream. The Red Death's connection to Roderick and the Left Hand only confirmed the illness of the omen.

When I got out of bed, I avoided mirrors and the inevitable double image of life and death that Lincoln had seen. The Mortons have never made great knights errant. Damsels in distress were too often traps for the unwary. But I felt a greater need to protect Scherie, an innocent, than to save myself. I couldn't see where this need had come from. My guilt about my last mission seemed a thing apart from this other emotion. As the morning went on, the urge to protect Scherie didn't fade.

Was this simple attraction? I refused to believe in love or even intense like at first sight, and goddamnit I couldn't afford it now. Instead, I told myself that a craftsman might feel a compulsion to save an ordinary man or woman who years later might do something extraordinary (even though I couldn't recall a specific instance and no one in my family had ever done such a thing). Following this crystal-clear logic, it didn't matter whether or not I was attracted to Scherie; I had to guard her. If I was going to do that while I tried to kill the mole, I would have to get close to her.

Under any other circumstances, this line of thought would have made my day.

I needed no similar logical contortions to believe that both Scherie and I were in imminent danger. Unlike a Greek tragic oracle, a Morton foreboding wasn't a trick that pushed the hero toward his fate. My foreboding was a real warning of what would happen without an exceptionally strong and clever response, so ignoring it wasn't a wise option.

So before I called Scherie, I needed another plan against Sphinx. Although I appreciated Hutch's support, it would still come down to me versus the mole. I required a backup attack.

Grandpa appeared in the combat fatigues of the sixties. "I still say Sphinx isn't your enemy. But if you want to sort this out, there's a simple stratagem, honored in antiquity. When you're totally screwed, throw a party. And make sure everyone comes."

I laughed bitterly. "You want me to poison everyone? Or should I cudgel them all in a collapsed tent?" Grandpa had told many nasty bedtime stories about such parties, and besides being unacceptably bloody, the idea didn't seem very practical. With the curse, I wasn't sure I could kill anybody, much less a crowd.

"Boy, don't be willfully stupid. You get them all here, you'll find out pretty quickly who the rat is, assuming there is one. You'll have to be improvisational, and surgically focused. It's a Morton tradition: to make oneself fatal in death."

Put this way, it made sense. "Thanks, Grandpa."

I stood at the antique secretary desk and drafted an invitation: "You're cordially invited to a belated celebration of Dale Morton's retirement from the military. He'll be leaving immediately after the party to tour America and the world. Please come to wish him bon voyage." The pretense of a farewell would hide an ambush, or maybe a last stand.

I e-mailed this immediately to old West Point classmates and friends from mundane assignments. Ah! A twinge of the curse pain, or just conventional guilt? I would try to get them out before things turned tragic, but my enemy might kill a few of them while hunting for me.

The guests I really wanted, Sphinx and her allies,

wouldn't receive this invite from me. But they'd find out about it, and realize that the party was their last best opportunity to complete the death magic that I felt on the horizon. They'd be dying to attend.

Thinking this gave me back my combat calm. Death was like an old scary friend: nothing to lose sleep over.

A slow knock at the door boomed through the House. *Who the hell could that be?* Someone who didn't know or care about the gothic doorbell. Surely my enemies weren't ready to strike here, on Morton ground. I readied a blast of wind for the House to unleash against anyone on the threshold. With no warning, I swung open the door. *"Blow . . ."*

Me away. On the warded stones stood Scherie, smiling, nervous. "Would you believe that I was just in the neighborhood?"

Major Endicott met with Colonel Hutchinson in her office, part of the secret H-ring deep below the heart of the Pentagon. This sick occult-shaped building drained Endicott's health like a tropical jungle mission. Despite that, the Pentagon's spiritual security exceeded anything on the planet. A plane could take down a towering skyscraper, yet leave the modest Pentagon relatively intact. Engineers explained, and the spirit kept its secrets.

Hutch's small desk photos of smiling nieces and nephews contrasted with the grimness of their conversation. Against reason and expectation, Hutch still supervised Dale's case, but under his father's orders Endicott commanded the surveillance of the House of Morton. For the first time, Endicott and Hutch were consistently at odds.

Endicott expected he had been called in for a general

protest against the surveillance, so he was surprised by Hutch's actual question: "Why are those Gideons on babysitting duty?"

"I suggest you take that up with General Endicott, ma'am." The general headed countercraft ops, or C-CRT, but Endicott was passing the buck.

"Michael, if I go to your father, nobody is going to be happy."

"I picked those three because they're the best." He didn't mention that Chimera had approved them, because one didn't mention Chimera more than necessary.

Hutch tapped a thin set of folders on her desk. "Do you know anything about them beyond their files?"

"No." Gideons weren't good company.

"Aren't Gideon hunter-trackers a bit overqualified for simple surveillance?"

"So far, Morton has tried to lose our tails and would have killed the mundane surveillance if the Gideons hadn't arrived in time."

"You're confident in that report," said Hutch, sounding skeptical.

"Yes, ma'am. You've heard that he made contact with an Iranian family?"

"Politically, they're typical exiles. The father has worked for the CIA, and she was born here."

"You don't see a touch of Stockholm Syndrome?" asked Endicott. "Or that Morton may have been completely turned?"

"We examined him carefully for any suborning of his will."

"This might be about character, not craft," said Endicott.

"I know his damned character," said Hutchinson. She paused, her eyes almost pinning Endicott to the far wall. "Look, Michael, you were right. That switch of operations in the desert was part of something going wrong. But whatever it is, I trust Dale. His line of Mortons has always been part of the solution."

"Hutch, whatever's going on, it would be a serious mistake not to keep the best possible eyes on Morton."

Hutch nodded distractedly. "Yes. And even better eyes on those watching. Dismissed, Major."

Back in his own office, Endicott sat in the shadow of a portrait of Abram Endicott, with his grizzled beard and iron face. On display below Abram lay Endicott's sword with its decorated handle.

He phoned the general, and reported his conversation.

"I want you to go to Morton yourself," said the general. "Play the dumb fundie. I want you to push every pagan and other button he has. Those Mortons have little self-control. He'll let something drop."

"Sir, doesn't that risk driving him toward our enemies?"

"Don't doubt it—he's already there."

Colonel Hutchinson thumbed through the limited files one more time. Craft practitioners usually bore the burden of extensive history, but these Gideons seemed positively mundane in their lack of background. She particularly mistrusted the neat and succinct file of their commanding officer, Captain Sakakawea. No normally accumulated career record should look like the well-edited work of one hand.

Once again, a Morton might be on to something big.

No use hesitating—time to call over to Langley, to the man they called Eddy. Hutchinson had received many of Sphinx's oracles through Eddy, and through other not-too-subtle hints suspected that Eddy was Sphinx's minder at the Agency.

She picked up the phone, but no dial tone. Damn, the phones were out again? Especially here in H-ring, some of the tech seemed decades out-of-date. She might have to get hold of a technician from the Office of Technical Management (OTM). Craftsmen needed their toilets and computers (and phones) to work, and H-ring's OTM saw to their needs. Its importance had grown with the use of IT in the Center. Hutchinson mused that, like their mundane counterparts, she and the older craft generation treated high tech like magic.

A knock interrupted Hutch's impatient button pushing as she sought a working line. "Yes?"

An explosion of craft light, then darkness.

A male technician, not the usual IT youngster but around Hutchinson's age, counted to ten to calm his emotions. Then he entered the colonel's office. He smiled at her slumped form. "Ma'am, I'm here to fix you."

CHAPTER

SIX

I looked out the door in the direction that Scherie was wagging her thumb. "Aren't you going to invite your friends from work in for coffee?"

On the street was a black sedan, this time with tinted windows. In the right light, the silhouettes of two men and one woman in sunglasses made shadow play for the neighbors. The Gideons. Another time, I'd have mocked their obviousness too, but here the cliché was the message: *Don't forget that you're being watched.*

"Don't worry about them," I said.

"I'm not."

But she was worried about something. *Must be me.* The House was putting on a show again; it smelled like incense and patchouli. Was she here for a date? Should I try to seduce her to keep her near me, so I could protect her? The thought was extremely attractive, but I was a solider, not James Bond. My motives were too mixed, and my own prospects too desperate, to go that route without much more thought.

"So, what brings you here?" I asked.

"Well, um, stop me if I get too stupid, but I think you can help me."

"I'd be happy to."

"I want to learn how to fight."

"Oh." My brain raced for something to say to hide my disappointment. Training her to fight would be a good way to keep an eye on her, and might help protect her, but she could get martial arts instruction anywhere. So, a question. "Who do you want to fight?"

"You heard my parents."

"You want to help the opposition in Iran? You don't think small, do you? Why do you think I could help with that?"

"Your family shows up as regular military online, but when my father talked about covert work, you didn't deny it. And you've worked in the region."

"Isn't the Iranian resistance nonviolent?"

"Mostly. I want to help with the other part."

I was in no position to help anyone pursue such efforts, particularly a mundane stranger. But if I went through the motions, that would certainly keep her close.

Then, Grandpa stumbled into the room. "Aren't you going to introduce me?"

"Not now," I mumbled.

"What's that?" said Scherie.

"I think I may be able to help with that."

"That's . . . that's great!"

"Do you have some time?"

"Now?"

"I need to take you someplace," I said. "Your father mentioned knives, but do you own a gun?"

"No. I've fired one, but not my own."

We drove the T-Bird to the southern waterfront. The black sedan didn't follow this time, but I assumed we were watched. I told Scherie enough truths about my covert activities in the Middle East to keep her interested. "But those folks in the sedan are watching me to make sure I stay retired. So we'll have to figure out some way around them. Stay away from them."

As I pulled up a gravel drive, Roman Roszkewycz slouched outside the old office entrance to a condemned mill. He was balding with a ratty khaki beard that should have been a goatee. An expatriate Slav with a knack for the illegal and a fondness for Westerns, and the latest in a long line of fixers for my family, he took care of any mundane complications. I liked the rogue, and I sometimes envied his seeming freedom from all the duties I had to family and country.

Roman eyed Scherie with unmasked lechery. "*Dobrý den,* pardner. Who is charming friend?"

"Please set up the targets for me and charming friend," I said. "And we'll need to borrow your guns."

"I set up little bunny and squirrel for friend to shoot?" asked Roman, miming bunny ears.

"Something with your shape will do," said Scherie.

"Charmed," said Roman, still grinning. He gave a little bow and went inside.

After I observed Scherie on a target run and made some minor corrections to her stance and technique, I gave a demonstration. Letting my craft idle in neutral, I fired. The feel of each weapon's kick reassured me—simple physics, action and reaction, no magic necessary to concentrate shots in a target's head and heart. This felt like

West Point again, when I had trained without craft, saving my power to defend myself against anything truly heinous from the upperclassmen. Craftless training was a point of pride with us Mortons, and an essential discipline that might decide life and death for self and others.

But I had some necessary craft to perform as well. While Scherie took the next run, I invoked my enemy. *See me now, Sphinx. See what I'm doing. Come to me, or I'll be coming for you.* To freshen the scent, I discreetly dropped a small bit of handkerchief stained with my own blood to the dusty floor. Perhaps this would bait her into the open.

Scherie lowered her gun. "Your turn again."

I fired through my clip. *Cease.* A barely audible echo of the curse mixed with the gun blasts. I clenched my teeth, and lowered my gun.

Scherie took off her headset and put her hand on my shoulder. "You alright?"

"Just a cramp," I said. "I'm fine." And I was. Something about Scherie's touch blocked the pain. But I detected no craft. Did my focus on her allow me to avert the curse? What was happening here?

Another hand, cold, on my shoulder. "She's got to go, son," my father said.

I knew Dad had commitment issues, but this was getting ridiculous. "How did your gun feel?" I asked Scherie.

"Excellent," she said. "Very comfortable."

"Roman," I called, "I want to get a gift for my charming friend."

I sent Scherie home with a load of Morton family texts on tactics. As the sun set, my doorbell rang a John Phillip Sousa riff in a minor key—Grandpa's humor with gothic patriotism.

Like responding to reveille, I trotted downstairs to the great oak door. I readied a wind against a possible intruder, but the House whispered that it was already prepared. So no, not Scherie or Hutch. Instead, a man, slightly smaller and younger than me, with perfect skin without blemish or scar. Most officers were clean-cut, but this man was clean to the bone. For the occasion, he smiled too much, and his sidearm bulged too much.

The man offered his hand. He stank of craft, and a handshake was not good craft etiquette, when mere touch was a weapon. He was familiar. From the desert?

The man said, "I'm Major Sword."

The whole House whispered anathemas into my ears. The House knew this one's blood, and I could nearly smell it myself.

"Endicott?" I was gobsmacked. "You're an Endicott."

Unlike me, Endicott hadn't learned to mask his feelings well. Right now he looked furious. "Morton, you're in violation of your contract. I'm placing you under arrest."

"Oh come on, Endicott! Would you need to exert any craft, or pray, or whatever you do, to tell that I'm a Morton in this House?"

Endicott looked around at the ancient furnishings, and I detected the slightest of shudders as Endicott felt the House's hate. "Point taken."

"Then here's another point. We don't work well with Endicotts."

"You'd prefer a Mather?" asked Endicott.

"I'd prefer a family who doesn't want me hanged," I said. An Endicott had busted up Thomas Morton's attempt at a craft union between native and European; the same Endicott had helped drive Anne Hutchinson out of Massachusetts. Later Endicotts had a talent for cheap propaganda theatrics, like the time they helped both Jefferson and Adams live until the fiftieth Fourth of July.

"That was a long time ago," said Endicott. "Our superiors don't think much of grudges."

"I'm not just talking about the past," I said. Endicotts continued, albeit nonviolently, to keep Mortons out of positions of authority.

"But we have our orders."

"No. I have a contract. And I'll keep my word." I pointed at Endicott's oversized firearm. "Planning on shooting someone today?"

"I might ask you the same thing," said Endicott. "You've been spending some time at the range."

I ignored this. "So, where's Hutchinson?"

"You mean Colonel Hutchinson?"

"I'm not in the military anymore, Mr. Endicott."

"I'm well aware of that," said Endicott. "I was upstairs during your treatment. I prayed for you."

"Oh," I said, momentarily abashed. "Thank you."

"Just doing my duty, as I am now."

"You're not going to tell me where Hutch is," I said.

"That's classified," said Endicott.

"Classified?" I couldn't believe Endicott could say the word without laughing. "Two things that Hutch is good at, and one isn't keeping out of my face. Or yours, I'll bet."

"Classified," said Endicott.

I tried another tack. "Has anyone been doing craft nearby?"

"The army has a right . . ."

"Not you," I said. "Someone else."

"Mr. Morton, I remind you again of your contract—".

"Damn it, how many ways do I have to say it? I'm not concerned because I've been practicing or whatever *you'd* call it. I've got eyes and instincts."

"Until you can tell me something more specific, I can't be of much assistance." Endicott took out a checklist, a goddamned checklist. "In the past month, have you experienced any night terrors? Has anyone in the household been harmed by nonconventional means? Have you left the state for any reason?"

"No." Hell, they knew that. "But I may need to leave town. To see my mom. She's—"

"Feeling fine, last time we checked," said Endicott.

"The ghosts say she misses me," I said. The ghosts had said no such thing, other than my father's confused message. My mother had shown only minimal interest in me since my childhood and Dad's death. One day, I would try to find out why, but now I needed my mother as a blind, not a mystery. "I know, she could come here, but . . ."

"I'll see about it." The toad was stalling.

I said, "My discharge doesn't place any limits on my movements."

"That's up to my superiors," said Endicott.

"Lying is a sin," I said.

Endicott took out a pamphlet and patted it on the table.

"What's this?" I asked.

"A little reading material," said Endicott. "Strictly as a citizen."

All True Miracles Come from Jesus. "Well, that explains a lot," I said. "Thank him for me. But I prefer the cheesy gospel of Cecil B. DeMille and his sword and sandal pals."

For a moment, I could have sworn that Endicott's lip twitched up into a smile, but it quickly tightened into something dyspeptic.

"I thought you'd appreciate this," said Endicott, "after what that be-jerseyed fakir did to you. You should know better than anyone that Islam is an evil religion."

"I'm not sure how Muslim he was," I said.

"His power wasn't from God," said Endicott. "We could have protected you. We still could. You could come back. You could be doing God's work."

"I worked for the Constitution," I said, "and no one else. For a Morton, America is our religion."

"And how has that worked out for you, for your family?" asked Endicott. "And not just you, but all the other craftsmen? We think we can do better. A Christian power for a Christian nation."

"Not really my concern anymore whose power," I said.

"I think it is," said Endicott. "We could protect you and your loved ones."

"I thought there wasn't anything to protect me from."

"I didn't say that. I also didn't say anything about the security risk that Scherezade Rezvani represents."

In God's name, go ahead, take your best shot. The alien thought intruded into my brain. A compulsion spell. I knew Endicott was trying to make me react, but when he had mentioned Scherie with menace, he had hit the right button. I couldn't help my fingers twitching for the bastard's sudden death.

Give him to us. Another alien thought, but this one came

from downstairs. Endicott had no idea the danger he was in.

Save the fool. That thought was my own. I somehow found the will to speak instead of act. "Isn't it time you were going, citizen?"

"One more bit of advice," said Endicott. "The days of privilege and immunity for the Fighting Families are over. The days of criminals and unreliables on the streets practicing black arts are over. Christian soldiers and leaders whose power comes from Jesus are the future. Men like Thomas Jackson."

I just about choked. This toad knew what a Morton did to Stonewall. "Here's something for you to think about. We Mortons have been serving and dying for this land for four centuries. We try not to think about religion too much. 'Cause it pisses us off. So you'd better go. Now."

"We're not finished," said Endicott.

"But the House is," I said. "It's slow, but powerful. It doesn't like you." *And the things in the subbasement like you even less.*

Endicott picked up his briefcase. "Please have your house better prepared for our next meeting."

After Endicott left, I leaned against the door, breathing heavy, sweating with the effort to control my anger. Shit, just what I needed: another enemy, and the Left-Hand spirits straining at their chains.

Grandpa called from the hallway. "Dale, are you OK?"

"Yes," I croaked. "I need a moment here. Alone." *Otherwise I might hurt myself, the House, and you—not necessarily in that order.*

Slowly, my body and mind cooled, and I could no longer hear the insistent whispers of the Left Hand. I had no quarrel with evangelical craftsmen as a group. Craft soldiers practiced all kinds of traditions and religions. The Mortons were rare in our complete disdain for theism.

But why was Endicott deliberately trying to piss me off? Was he part of the mole threat, or was he still fighting the old feud? Either way, he was a fool. No Morton had ever given in to the Puritans—not then, and not now.

That night I had another dream. Scherie and I were laid out in his-and-her coffins at the local funeral home. But then, like the devil's cameraman, the dream panned back to show another coffin, and another. Many coffins. The corpse faces were fuzzy, as if the identities weren't resolved yet, but the features were a mix of all the Families I knew of. The rictal-smiling Red Death stood among the coffins, with a tall ghastly thin woman with pale gossamer hair in his grasp.

I woke up. That was the second Lincoln dream. I knew the pale woman from descriptions and her association with the Red Death of Roderick Morton: his twin sister Madeline. That they were together in my dream could only have one meaning: our time had nearly run out. Time for Scherie and me to go. Again, the threat to Scherie seemed more important than any threat to me, but by now this feeling seemed natural, and I reflected on it even less than before.

I ignored Grandpa calling after me as I bounded downstairs for the phone. I called Hutchinson's office, but Endicott, somehow on duty at the early hour, took the call. I said, "I need to leave town."

"I'm sorry," said Endicott. "Your request is denied."

"Denied? Get me Hutchinson."

"No," said Endicott.

"Why are you hiding her?" I asked.

"Hiding?"

"Look, it's not just about me," I said. "My family, all the Families, are at risk. You get me Hutchinson, or I'll use any means necessary to contact her."

"That would have serious consequences . . ."

I hung up. New trouble brewed, and rain poured. A summer thunderstorm blasted outside. Nature had a way of sympathizing with a Morton. A knock at the door seemed to shake the whole House. Grandpa moaned with the wind.

Like Macbeth's porter or Poe's scholar, I went to the knock, picking up my father's Colt .45 on the way. I would be lucky to have some hot witches or a smart bird at my chamber door, and not my doom. If I needed a blast of craft, I'd draw the lightning down.

At the door, I felt the knob. Death was near, but not mine, not yet.

I opened the door. Lightning crashed, illuminating Hutchinson's face. I exhaled, nerves jangling. "Jesus, Hutch, what took you so long? Come in."

Hutch trailed silvery water, her hand was wet and stone cold. She was not well. "I understand you've been trying to unearth me," she said.

"I've had the Lincoln dreams, and Endicott has been harassing me. Where have you been?" I asked.

"I was working your case," said Hutch. "Then I got . . . distracted. I need to tell you what I've found."

"You've found something," I said. "Then I'm not crazy."

"Crazy or not," she said, "someone is trying to kill you."

"Why me?" I asked.

"Dale, it's not just you."

"I know," I said. "I saw it. They're going for the Families. Our families. But who are these assassins?"

"I don't know," she said. "And I don't know why. It could be to undermine the craft defense, it could be a revenge thing. It could be . . . something else. Dale, you know how my Family and I value loyalty. So it hurts like hell to say this, but . . ."

"But I can't trust my own government," I said.

"No. No, you can't," she said. "Even if they're not actively against you. At best, the brass fears disclosure of the craft militant, and they'd rather sacrifice you and a lot of craftsmen than risk it."

"And at worst?" I asked.

"At worst," she said, "something's rotten on the inside."

"You should come with me," I said. "We should leave."

"No," said Hutch.

"Then why are you telling me all this?" I asked. But my heart could guess why. "How do you know this?"

"Because I'm dead," she said.

"Oh shit," I said. "I'm sorry, Hutch." I took a breath. "Who did it?"

"I don't know. Dale, I can't find my body! I've got nowhere to go. I don't even know how I got here."

Can't find her body? Only serious power could hide a body from its spirit. "Hutch, was it Sphinx?"

"Whoever they are, don't let them kill you. I release you from your oath to me. Use the craft. Get them." Hutchinson started to fade.

"Hutch, don't go!" But she was gone.

Don't let them kill you. I spoke to the empty air: "How the hell am I going to do that?"

PART III

THE FALL OF THE
HOUSE OF MORTON

But evil things, in robes of sorrow,
Assailed the monarch's high estate;
(Ah, let us mourn, for never morrow
Shall dawn upon him, desolate!)
And, round about his home, the glory
That blushed and bloomed
Is but a dim-remembered story
Of the old time entombed.
—EDGAR ALLAN POE

He perceived this man fighting a last struggle, the
struggle of one whose legs are grasped by demons.
It was a ghastly battle.
—STEPHEN CRANE

I see in him outrageous strength, with an
inscrutable malice sinewing it.
—HERMAN MELVILLE

In H-ring, Michael Endicott was worried. The general would be here soon. Endicott looked up again at his portrait of Abram, envying his ancestor's certainty. Just yesterday, as ordered, he had picked a fight with a decorated and unstable veteran of America's secret wars. Not very Christian or honorable, but dutiful.

But that dubious action wasn't what worried Endicott. He still didn't know where the AWOL Colonel Hutchinson had gone. He had first noted her absence midmorning when he had wanted to confront her about Morton's firing range visit and his predawn phone call (which he had ordered routed to his personal line). Hutch wasn't answering her cell or home lines. Spiritual ops didn't take unannounced sick days.

Though only hours old, Hutch's sudden disappearance felt connected to the troubles in the House of Morton. Endicott had ordered the three Gideons to break off from Morton surveillance and find her. The Gideons were the best at tracking craft prey, but Endicott didn't enjoy thinking that way of Hutch.

With a regulation knock, the general entered. He had let

his full head of hair go silver. In an age of plastic people, Endicott's father had the face of a gray wolf sculpted in granite. The general preferred to keep his own office free from intrusion, friend or foe, so he sacrificed protocol to meet Endicott here.

"I completed my mission, sir," said Endicott. "I pissed Morton off. Baited him, pushed every pagan button. Threw in some obvious spirit compulsion. He didn't bite. He didn't even really threaten me, just gave me some crap about the house."

"That house is threat enough," said the general.

"I've heard the legends," said Endicott. "Like distilled Poe and Hawthorne."

"You've spoken with him since," noted the general.

"He asked to leave town. I said no. He wanted to speak with Colonel Hutchinson. He made another vague threat."

"What's his real reason for leaving?" asked the general.

"From what I heard at the nuthouse, he may think some-one is pursuing him," said Endicott. "He may suspect that Sphinx is a mole. His fear may be baseless, but nonethe-less sincere. His family has a history of paranoia, followed by violence, so we can expect trouble."

"And you?" asked the general.

"Sir?"

"Scared?"

"Sir, if a Morton is really frightened, that makes me ner-vous. But Sphinx?" Endicott shook his head.

"The Mortons are subtle," said the general. "They've even made you doubt your mission."

Endicott decided he needed to argue once more with his

father's obsession to be effective. "Sir, why are we pushing Morton like this?"

"He's with the Left-Hand Mortons," said the general, with a new flat certainty in his voice.

"That branch died out in the 1800s, sir."

"'Died out' is a gentle and inaccurate way of putting it," said the general. "The Families under Abram exterminated any of the Left Hand they could find. But not before the Left Hand had killed more than a few Family members, and more than a few Endicotts. And not before some of the evil escaped."

"Sir, that was a long time ago," said Endicott.

"Time doesn't matter to the Left-Hand Mortons. They have an ambiguous relationship with death," said the general. "They think long-term. Very long-term."

The general's use of the present tense chilled Endicott.

But then the general repeated his skewed version of craft history. "Left-Hand elements were active during the Civil War. We have evidence from our Latter-day friends that survivors of the Morton Left Hand, including a common-law couple, moved west, where they could be as violently perverse as their natures desired. With the First World War, they had room to hide in our ranks again. And Captain Morton's own father demonstrated a strong reversion to type."

Endicott had always doubted much of this, particularly regarding Morton's father, but before Endicott could raise old questions, the general asked, "Where is Colonel Hutchinson?"

"I have the Gideons looking," said Endicott. "When Morton asked for her, he said we were hiding her."

The general smiled. "I suspect he knows more than we do. Either he's recruited her, and she's gone underground, or she said no, and he disposed of her."

Despite his anxiety for Hutch, Endicott kept his gaze steady. "Sir, couldn't the colonel and the captain both be victims of the Left Hand? Maybe they need our help."

"No," said the general, again with his new certitude. "Chimera has seen this. This is the year, and the Mortons are the threat."

"But Sphinx . . ."

"Is part of the problem," said the general. "Morton is right about that much. Fortunately, Chimera doesn't have her biases. Anything else, Major?"

"No, sir." Endicott had ventured as much of his doubt as appropriate.

The general tapped Endicott's desk twice in thought. As if in response, there was another knock at Endicott's door. "Enter," said the general, as if he were in his own office.

One of the white-coated, quasi mundanes from OTM came in and handed the general a message. OTM technicians always seemed to be buzzing about the general and his office. They were an unremarkable bunch amidst the colorful craft-types, and Endicott only noted this tech because of the intrusion into his space. The tech would have been considered old for his job in the private sector, but maturity was an advantage where absolute discretion was important.

While the general read the message, the technician looked past Endicott at Abram's portrait. Endicott couldn't read the tech's emotion, but he didn't seem appropriately respectful.

"Please have Chimera tighten control," said the general

to the tech, who thankfully stopped staring at the portrait and departed. The general folded the note and looked at Endicott. "The Left Hand are skilled at hiding whenever the other Families come after them. Morton may even try to flee overseas. We can't let him out of our sight. My orders remain the same: he's not to leave Rhode Island. Use any necessary force."

I drove to see Roman, who was once again slouched outside the office entrance. "*Dobrý den,* pardner. I've been expecting you."

"Why's that?" I asked.

"You get a gun for a beautiful woman. I think, you'll both have to leave town soon."

"You're a wise man," I said. "I need two departure packages for Mexico." My retirement vacation party was next weekend. In my original plan, I would have obtained a similar package to support my threat of postparty flight in order to draw out my enemies. Now, I needed to provide for a very real getaway for Scherie and, if our major opponents didn't show, myself.

"No problemo, pardner," said Roman. "For you, ten percent discount."

"*Spasiba,*" I said. "But I'll need a car too."

The smile fled Roman's face. "What is wrong with the Thunderbird?"

"Nothing," I said, "other than everyone knows it's my car. And I need something a little more recent and resilient."

"Hmmm. This I do not like. Come inside. I show you horses."

At his desk, Roman displayed computer thumbnails of a stable of laundered cars. "You want something American, yes?"

"Yes," I said.

"This Corvette?"

"No, this Chevy Malibu."

Roman sighed. "Very boring."

I said, "I want the car fueled and parked along the side street near the family mausoleum by next weekend. Leave the keys in a case above the driver's side front tire. I'll be sending you some weapons, but any other special forces equipment you can obtain will be appreciated. And I'll need plenty of ammo."

"You're planning a long trip?" asked Roman.

"Very long." That could be too true.

"I'll have the car moved in stages." Roman stared out the dirty window. "You know, friend, someone maybe is watching. Watching now."

"Everybody is watching. As long as they don't know the exact details, I'll be fine."

"No one knows details. I handle myself, very quiet. But maybe I take a vacation too, yes?"

"You're a very wise man," I said. "Just a few days might be good for your health. Go someplace nice. I'll pay. In advance."

Roman nodded. "I see. Then we say good-bye." We embraced like Slavs. *"Vaya con Dios."*

"That's not Russian."

"No, it's cowboy," said Roman. "And it's what I mean."

———

When I returned to the House, I went to the kitchen. Despite some new appliances, it still had the antique dumbwaiters and cramped sense of space of my grandfather's day. I poured myself a finger of bourbon. "To absent friends." I raised my glass. "How about it, Hutch? You want vengeance, I'm going to need some help."

Nothing. Not that I would expect Hutch around the House after she had warned me, as she wasn't a Morton. I would have to be more forceful. "Colonel Hutchinson, I'm calling you." I reached out my hand as if through a curtain . . .

"Shit!" I drew my hand back. Burning, but not heat. Cold. "Hutch?" But no reply. I'd touched the void, the spirit equivalent of hard vacuum. "Oh shit, Hutch, have they gotten you there too?"

Warming my throbbing hand under my armpit, I took my bourbon down into the basement. Could anyone help me? I knew the other family names from Morton lore, but not where they lived now. The code names I had worked with gave no clue to the family identity. They were as goofy as my "Casper" and equally impersonal, once you knew craft was involved. Oz and his witchy friends were popular, as were wizards from Tolkien, Rowling, Bakshi, and King. Stupid—did mafiosi take their nicknames from *The Godfather*? Second thought, maybe they did.

As for the Morton craft bloodline, I might be the last living representative of that legendary lineage. But even if Dad couldn't come and Grandpa wouldn't help, I had the other Morton dead. I had the House.

With the House's help, my party could work as a distraction. All the craft noise of the House and my many guests would make it difficult for Gideons and others to track our exit, if I used the right route.

I stood on an iron plate attached to a long rod that passed through each floor, up to my grandfather's room, down through the subbasement and below, to ground itself deep into this earth. Here, I could tap into the power of the Morton House and ancestors. I pressed my hand up against an oak beam, and felt the thrum that was nearly, but not quite, in sync with my own pulse. It was the layered telltale of my family's magic, the time-spanning vibration that was a heart, a steamboat, a train, a car, a plane, a rocket.

"Help me, House," I said.

We can help. The voices iced me. They were not the warm collective voice of the orthodox Morton dead that was the House. They were the dungeon voices of those who had attempted to freeze time, whose attempt to snatch immortality had led only to living death. The most powerful ancestors in this House were not my friends. To help me, the Left Hand would require payment. Payment in blood.

We can help, they cooed again. *Come to the subbasement. And bring your friend.*

The next day, when Scherie arrived for another training session, I was ready. I had tucked a sheathed knife in my belt and readied a bit of persuasion craft. Right-Hand Mortons weren't good at compulsion, but we could give people a sense that life's wind was blowing a certain direction.

"If you're serious about training," I said, *"we need to go to Mexico.* There's a camp that will give you special ops training. The price is right, and I trust the operators."

"I can't afford that right now."

"That won't be a problem."

I showed her the training camp's papers. Yes, it really existed, and I had prepaid for Scherie's boot session in case I didn't make it. Still, crossing the border to a secret place full of armed men might intimidate even her a little. "You can check this out with your father. The thing is, we'll need to split up and get away without this surveillance following us. What we're doing is extralegal."

"They're not watching me."

"Don't count on that. Since I met you, they've increased their surveillance. So consider this an entrance examination."

She nodded at this appeal to her competitive streak, so I continued. "We'll leave during the party. It'll be the best time; I can set up all sorts of distractions. Unless I decide it's safe to go together, you'll leave first, and I'll follow. Work out your own route, but don't tell it to me. We'll meet in Guadalajara at the Café Madoka a week after the party. If I'm not there, go on to the camp without me—it means I've been, um, unavoidably detained." More likely I was unavoidably dead. But I thought, *Believe.*

"Why are they so interested in you? Is it about one of your missions?" asked Scherie. "The one that made you scream in Farsi?"

"Some people I used to work with have gone bad. Best just to avoid them. Here are the other things you'll need." I handed her a fake passport, some pesos, and a Luxembourg bank account number (which, if I didn't make it, would give her enough money for an ordinary life), all mundanely arranged for me by Roman.

"You were just a captain," said Scherie, "but you're able to arrange this kind of travel?"

"My family has a history of being prepared to move." True since the time Thomas Morton had fled to Maine, but not an answer, so I accompanied my words with a silent, craft-laden mantra for her not to question, just to *accept and get ready*.

She nodded slowly, all acceptance again. Then, one hand clenching into a fist, she frowned. Her brow furrowed, and she turned her face as if looking at the wall for a memory, like she had forgotten something at the supermarket.

"Scherie?"

"I know this may sound crazy." She turned to face me, to look me directly in the eye. "But all these plots and secrets, they're just the tip of the iceberg, aren't they?" She waved the passport and pesos at my face. "Here I am, about to do something absolutely crazy because you say it'll be OK. So what I want to know is, are you and your family something special? Do you have some kind of mental power?"

"Like magic?" I smiled. I would do what every Morton did to protect himself and those he cared about. I kept my breathing regular, my face relaxed, my pulse normal—the biofeedback of the lie. "There's nothing magic about me. Must be you."

I delivered the line perfectly, without any tell that a mundane would recognize.

"Sorry," she said. "I'm just new at all this." Yet, even as Scherie apologized, I sensed that she was less scared for me, and a little scared of me. Lies, like magic, always cost something. "So how do I get out during the party?"

I said, "I have a story to tell you."

You wondered about my family. My first American ancestor was Thomas Morton. He came to Massachusetts right after the Pilgrims. He and the Puritans didn't get along. He fled to Maine. He had children. One of them, Jonathan, came to Providence to build this place."

I could have easily gone on with a full family history, craft and all. But what she knew might still matter. So I told her the craft-free version—a difficult lie, because the Mortons lived in craft. The secret and true history of the rise and fall of the Left Hand went like this:

The eldest of Jonathan's sons left the House of Morton to commence the orthodox family line's tradition of military service. The Morton estate in Providence came into the hands of the second eldest son and his descendants, and fell on strange times. This Left-Hand branch of the Mortons inbred for craft with their cousins, but craft didn't work like Mendel's peas, so their descendants were no more magical than their free-range relations. Instead, they became a sad bunch of neurasthenic recessives and outright psychotics.

Not inbreeding, but the incestuous combination of energies for a bloody purpose made the Left Hand powerful. They fought mortality, and lost horribly. They searched for transdimensional monsters, but only made monsters of themselves. They conducted experiments that fed on flesh and blood. Travelers disappeared; the neighbors grew suspicious, then hostile.

The Left-Hand Mortons reified their justified paranoia in the very bones of the House. They built sturdy new walls to deflect sudden attacks by angry citizens. In Reformation style, they built "priest" holes that a craftsman could hide in for days. They also built the underground rooms of the subbasement to hide and contain their more extreme experiments.

Finally, as the Civil War drew within farsight, the orthodox Mortons determined to put their House and cousins in order. The family patriarch, Ezekiel, paid a call on the twins Roderick and Madeline, last leaders of the Left Hand. Ezekiel would make no moral arguments; rather, he would urge them to return to the hidden productive life of craft service to Family and country, lest the government break its covenant and hunt all the Mortons down.

Neither Ezekiel the man nor his spirit was ever heard from again.

That began the war against the Left Hand. Ezekiel's grandson, the young Joshua, took the family mantle and called upon the other Families to aid him in putting down his twisted cousins. The Left Hand executed a preemptive strike of terror against their likely enemies, killing and disabling many. The Families united in wrath. Some hunted the Left-Hand rogues across the country. Most laid a quiet siege to the House, camping in revival-style tents on the grounds.

Fortunately, it was a siege *of* the House and not *against* it. The House revolted from the Left Hand's control and let in the orthodox Mortons and the other Families. They found Roderick lying in a deep craft-enhanced trance far beneath the House in the subbasement. His half-alive body oozed with strange decay, and he could not be roused from his sepulchral bed. With no gentler feeling than disgust, Joshua and his ally Abram Endicott hacked Roderick to pieces.

They searched for Madeline, Roderick's partner in love and madness. In the family crypt, they found her. Her lost fingernails and battered hands indicated that she had struggled to escape her coffin. In some inexplicable "experiment," Roderick had buried his sister alive.

Concerned that the Left Hand might have some further design, Joshua commanded the House to contain their spirits.

Secret exits had been a Left-Hand obsession, though now even their ghosts couldn't leave the House. One avenue of escape went underground, and could be reached only through the evil subbasement where the House kept the Left-Hand ghosts. The other old Morton dead had faded, going wherever spirits go when they tire of playing their unchanging themes, leaving behind the thrumming remnants of their energy in the House. But in the subbasement, more than the energy of the Left-Hand Mortons survived. Their will survived. As in life, their revenants had incestuously combined into something powerful, and fearful, and hungry.

It's time to show you the way out," I said. "It's the sub-basement." I took her by the hand in a gentle but unbreakable grip. There was no other way. To secure their help, I would have to present Scherie to the Left Hand. *Guess who's coming to dinner.*

CHAPTER

EIGHT

As we walked to the cellar, Scherie tried to make conversation about my edited version of the Morton story. "So, the crazy, inbred Mortons built the subbasement?"

"Right, so you might see things that are a bit strange down there."

"If you're trying to scare me off from this," said Scherie, "it won't work."

"Just stay with me and you'll be fine." As I spoke, I didn't dare look at her. I no longer trusted my ability to deceive her.

In the cellar, I picked up a flashlight. I brought Scherie to a door, hidden as much by the accumulation of dust in its cracks as by design.

"Don't send me down here for a bottle of wine!" Scherie laughed nervously. I smiled, weakly. As I feared, she was picking up on the vibe too quickly.

With more effort than I expected, I opened the door. We passed through the archway behind it and descended carefully down wrought iron steps that shook under our weight. Down, down, down we went, past three landings.

At the bottom, I scanned my light across a long, high-vaulted hallway, a dark subterranean demi-cathedral to a science gone awry. I led the way. On each side of the passage was a line of matching doors.

"Why is this one bricked up?" Scherie pointed to an obvious break in the symmetry of rooms, the undeniable appearance of a frame around the bricks where a door would have been.

"You're the one who mentioned the wine," I said.

She might find some of the other props familiar as well. A mummified black cat that still twitched with a desire for vengeance, the skeleton of a demented great ape that had hunted human prey, a heart in a box that had beaten far longer than its owner had lived. The modern Mortons had let such nasty things remain rather than attempt to remove them. "As booby-trapped as Eva Braun's brassiere," Grandpa had warned. Susurrant dry voices like spectral carnival touts urged me to *come and see, come and see*.

A hand on my arm. "Do you hear something?" asked Scherie.

"What? No, just the draft. This way." This wasn't a tour.

"When I was a little girl, I . . ." But Scherie left the thought hanging like an icicle. I took her down another flight of stairs, these of cracked stone, to the smooth marble floor at the center of the subbasement. The room was a mini-Pantheon, lit by a pale glow from an oculus in the domed ceiling, a Roman temple-cum-catacomb. Shrines to the chthonic deities of the Left Hand lined the walls at regular intervals, their strange radial asymmetries echoing the architecture. Unlike any other Mortons, the Left Hand were semitheists. They hoped for examples of immortality, and worshipped dark mirrors of their own souls.

Scherie slowed, looked. "Did they pray to these things?"

"Pay no attention to them," I said. They liked the attention.

"But this feels so damned wrong . . ."

"Not another word," I hissed, gripping her by the wrist.

Moving to our left, we reached a heavy curtain of dark velvet a quarter of the way around the center. Scherie froze. "I don't want to go in there."

"But I need to show you," I said. Ungently, I pulled her in through the curtain into the room where Roderick had met his end.

"Hey!" Scherie cried, but did not try to flee. Silence. The room was an ossuary. Columns of long bone obscenely fused into ornate marble pillars, bejeweled skulls formed a decorative frieze encircling the space. I gave the baroque terrors little notice; my attention went to the left (always to the left). There, in raw primitive contrast, stood a grotesque altar of carved stone stolen from some pre-Mayan ruin.

You could sacrifice her to us, whispered the Left-Hand spirits dwelling in the altar. They were still hungry for the blood and flesh they had sought in life. *We could use this body.*

It didn't work last time, I thought.

The blood magic will defer your death. The horror was that the evil things spoke the truth. An Alcestis-style replacement strategy would work for a time. The Left-Hand Mortons would have made such a sacrifice, and had made it, over and over again.

Do it. The alien idea had gnawed into me since the night before. *Why not? You've let civilians die before, for the sake of the mission or to protect the craft. You could make it quick, and painless. You could . . .*

Do it.

I drew the knife from my belt, and raised it above my head. Scherie gasped. Lightning quick, I brought the knife down.

I cut my own hand. A few drops of blood fell to the ground. Some instinct at my core told me the words. *My blood, not hers.*

"You cut yourself!" said Scherie, with no sense of her own peril.

Hers! said the Left Hand.

Mine, I thought. *And our enemy's blood yet to come. I and the House bind you. Scherie gets out of here. And you pursue our enemy to her end.*

For what? said the Left Hand.

"For letting you go," I said, conceding merely the inevitable.

Now! said the Left Hand.

"Later," I said.

I could only measure the strength of the voices' compulsion as their spell let go its grip. Shit, they had powerful bad magic down here. But I had fought their temptations since childhood. As many screw-ups as I'd made, I'd never done anything deliberately evil. I believed in karmic return. I had never hurt someone I cared about for personal gain. And I cared more for Scherie than I wanted to think about.

I silently tugged at Scherie to leave the room. "Letting me go later?" she said, misunderstanding. "What kind of ritual was that?"

"Just something for luck," I said.

I would keep Scherie safe, and allow her to escape, whatever the cost to myself and the Families. With that decision, the voices of the altar faded to the indistinct rustle of vermin.

We climbed another stone stairway, and entered a dark space. I scanned my flashlight across the chamber. Cold slabs and silent effigies—we were in the family mausoleum. "Could you make this any creepier?" whispered Scherie. I didn't answer.

Here lay the Right-Hand Mortons who, unlike my father, followed the family tradition of home burial. Grandpa's bones lay within the wall to my right. Except for Grandpa, these ancestors were past conversation; either their energies were well-absorbed into the structure of the House, or they were simply uninterested.

I pointed to the low-lintel exit. "That's your way out." Scherie moved toward it. "Not now," I said.

"Will it open?" asked Scherie.

"It'll open; I guarantee it," I said. "We've gone under and beyond their likely circle of surveillance. You'll need a change of clothes, though, just in case."

"How about a caterer's uniform? My family's restaurant has some."

"Yes, perfect."

"Will you go this way too?" she asked.

"Probably. I'm not sure yet." I didn't want to risk her waiting for me here if I wasn't coming. "I may have to improvise." Or fight and die. "Let's get back."

Without thinking, I reached out a hand to guide her, though she already knew the way. My grip, unlike before, was unrushed and gentle, and I could appreciate how comfortable it was to touch her. Captain Dale Morton, supernaturally trained killer, had become a little boy holding hands with his crush.

Stupid. Every second from now on, I had to be searching for threats. Even thinking of romance could get us both killed.

We moved quickly back the way we'd come. I kept up a mantra against the subbasement voices. *Soon. Soon.* My deal with these demons was worth it. They were the perfect guardians against anyone following our escape path. From now on, others could worry about their containment.

At the door, Scherie stared at me, and though fear in itself isn't a letter *F* in Morton craftsight, I could still see the new fears in her eyes. Fear for herself, sure, but also a more intense fear of me, and another anxiety that I couldn't read.

Without warning, she grabbed me in a quick hug, fierce enough to drive my breath out. "Be careful, Morton," she said. Then she was out the door and gone.

Did she somehow, after all she'd seen, actually care about me?

Soon. The Left-Hand voices bided their time.

Calling the H-ring a "ring" was a euphemism. CRFT-CEN's corridors formed the star of an off-center pentacle below the Pentagon's central courtyard. Only the inner corridors of the star formed another pentagon. Weathermen and odd alchemical brass-colored tubing and drains made the water want to be elsewhere, despite the contrary disposition of the surrounding land. Unlike the concrete of the walls above, the Center was made of stone from every state, all supercharged with the nation's craft.

The triangular extensions from each face terminated in five round offices, the five prestige spaces. Each triangle was color-coded with one of the Tantric primaries, three of which were the patriotic red, white, and blue. Except with unusual specific abilities, craft did not divide by service, regardless of the nominal uniform of the practitioner. Craft was too rare an asset with too general a use. The five points were the five major areas of expertise:

- military farsight or PRECOG (black),
- weathermen and nature control or WENA-CON (blue),
- enhanced combat or ENCOM (green),
- countercraft ops or C-CRT (red),
- black ops: special craft operations forces or SCOF (the ironic white of Melville's whale).

All very clear, efficient, military.

Below the fearful symmetry of H-ring's inner pentagon lay Chimera, like a spider trapped in a hypergeometric web. Those who knew of Chimera sometimes called his room the "ninth circle." An airlock door, always guarded, allowed access to this master oracle's domain.

The general occupied the point office for C-CRT, and Endicott's was a convenient few doors down. C-CRT's distinction from black ops was the former's disdain for Left-Hand tactics. Endicott admired his father for preserving this distinction at any cost.

When the general came over again to his office for a report, Endicott had something to tell him. "He's definitely leaving town," said Endicott. "He's not even trying to hide it. He's throwing a damned party, then he's going to leave town."

Unlike someone who had been told he was right, the general frowned. "Language, Major. You're certain?"

"He's set up an escape," said Endicott. "Car, papers, everything."

"I suppose we have to take it seriously then. What do you plan to do about it?"

"Arrest him," said Endicott. "For starters."

"There's nothing in his discharge about parties," said the general.

"Yes, but . . ."

The general's lips tightened into a regulation smile. "That's a joke, Major. But he may be collaborating with others we don't know yet. They will approach him. We can learn much. Let him have his party. Afterward, bag him and anyone else suspicious."

"Sir," said Endicott, "regarding suspicious, we still haven't found Colonel Hutchinson."

"Sakakawea can't find her?" asked the general.

"And she's got Carson and Bumppo with her. They're confused—maybe some form of craft camouflage."

"Our best are confused," said the general, eyes looking heavenward. "Give them whatever support they need. I want Hutchinson found before this party."

"I'll also need a team for the party," said Endicott. "Craft-friendly muscle, with one advance man to make sure Morton isn't going to spring a trap on us."

"A dangerous job for the advance man," said the general. "I'll consult Chimera on the op, and you'll get your personnel."

A knock, and the same middle-aged tech as before interrupted them with a sheet of paper. The general took it. "It seems that Chimera is already on top of the situation. Chimera suggests that Morton will try to disrupt your communications and other equipment. So I'll give you technical support as well. You." He pointed at the technician. "Be ready to ship out with the major."

"I'm ready, General," said the technician.

With our escape plan in place, I turned to the possibility of a last stand. If Sphinx or significant opposition showed up for my party, I wouldn't be leaving the House alive if I could take them down with me. If they only sent a proxy, I would have to fight, then flee. The very idea raised a twinge of pain—mere preparation for combat would cost me.

Any assassin or assassins wouldn't wait for me outside. They didn't know my escape route, but they would know that I had one. The design of the grounds of the estate and its walls made a clean long-range shot with a bullet too unlikely to rely on; the House's power made a craft shot equally difficult. They would have to come in to get me.

Sensing that I was deep in thought, Grandpa appeared in the fishing garb that went with his family-proverb-spouting mood. "This House and everything in it, and every object in this very room, is a weapon."

I appreciated the reminder. Grandfather had sometimes made the dark gothic mansion seem more like a practical joke than a twisted weapon.

"House, are you awake?" There was Morton blood in

the ground beneath my feet, Morton ashes in the mortar. I pricked my finger and offered up a few drops to the hardwood floors, to remind the House of who I was, to wake it up completely.

"House, I need to tell you what's going to happen. You'll have to be fully visible and lower your resistance to dangerous guests."

Drop? whispered the House.

"No," I said, *"just enough for them to feel a little resistance. Just enough to keep out the uninvited mundanes. And later, you'll have to let the Left Hand out."*

Mistake, whispered the House.

"Necessary," I said. The Left Hand would escape anyway, if my sacrifice became necessary.

And then? whispered the House.

I told the House what would happen if my primary adversary appeared. The small crack that ran through the House from earth to sky shifted, and the wood groaned.

The day before the party, I spent long hours whispering spells to the remote control for my TV and stereo while I packed heirlooms for storage. That evening, I sat in the deep chair, eyes closed, a wineglass threatening to drop from my dangling hand, the House's oak beams softly moaning, the warring voices whispering in my brain. After all my work, an indolent despair threatened to overwhelm me. Dying young was a Morton tradition, but dying foolishly was not. I hadn't killed since the desert, and still wasn't sure I could.

The sadness of the House was a violin lullaby, I was falling, falling . . .

"Dale? Are you awake?"

"What?" I dropped the wineglass, and Scherie caught

it. She was standing in front of me, life amidst the old dead things.

"Sorry. I brought some things for the party. I knocked and rang, but you didn't come. Then I thought I heard you call. The door was open." Gently, Scherie placed the glass on a table. "You're in no shape for this party." She smiled. "It'll be suspicious."

"Nothing I can do about it," I said.

She said, "I can help." She moved behind me and began to massage my shoulders. Her long delicate fingers were surprisingly strong; her touch was electric.

She unbuttoned my shirt to work her hands farther down over my tired frame. Her face bent down next to mine. "Better?"

I could try to blame the excitement before combat, or the fear that in a day I might be dead. But those would be lies. I knew it was the worst possible idea, and I did it anyway. I kissed her.

With a slow, fiery inevitability, we progressed out of our clothes and up the stairs. Having held back completely for so many days, we had no restraint now. The House sang in triumph, its heart pounding like a heavy-metal drummer.

If I used some craft, it wasn't anything that would concern my government. The most joyful magics aren't unique to craftsmen.

When we were completed, exhausted and renewed, Scherie cried, perhaps suspecting that this first time was also our last. Certain that it was, I fought to hide my heart.

In the morning, as if as eager as I was to avoid postcoital conversation, Scherie left early to say farewell to her parents before her "vacation." I checked and rechecked my weapons; I readied my mind to exceed the limits of my craft.

The slide-slam of a van door jolted me to attention. It echoed my memory of a helicopter's door and my descent into the desert. My hands shook, ready for a fight and flight miles away and months past. A craft invective nearly came to my lips. No, steady. Whether it was the curse or simple PTSD, I wouldn't give into it.

The van belonged to the caterers. I stepped out to my back driveway to greet them. The pavement felt soft in the heat.

The caterers resembled Central American guerrillas that I had once chased into a pre-Mayan tomb, now rounded out and placid, their AK-47s beaten into plows. Steady. The head caterer shook my hand, looking up into my face with concern. "Big storm tonight, sir. And awful hot before that."

I gritted my teeth, then nodded at the caterer. Despite Scherie's tender therapy, I felt unwell, and it must have shown. Unconscious oracles annoyed me; I knew which way the wind blew. "Please set up in the yard, as planned." I wouldn't leave the local weather to chance, and I didn't want a Kurosawa film fight.

Time for a security check—an unavoidable use of craft energies. My enemies might sneak in as workers to get the jump on the competition. I closed my eyes and thought, *Show their sins*. Then I studied the letters of the catering staff. I saw the usual small *t*'s and *a*'s. Nothing to worry about.

Then, a more muscular man came from behind the van, bearing a keg in his massive arms. Through the keg, his *M* flashed slow red like a coroner's siren.

I wanted to spit at their insult of sending someone with so obvious a record. Then, my hands started to shake again. For the first time since the desert, I would try to kill.

CHAPTER

NINE

I blinked the sins out of my eyes. I spoke to the head caterer loudly enough for "M" to hear. "I'm going upstairs to see about the weather."

I went inside. M followed, violating the threshold. The House exhaled in a draft of frustrated hate. *Probably has a knife,* I thought. A knife would be quiet, and it went with the cover of caterer.

M stepped with a feline's soft pads, more like a lover than a hulking assassin. I kept walking, eyes ahead, leaving my back open, betting my life that the first blow wouldn't come yet. Slowly up one flight of steps, then another to the third floor. M remained a flight behind.

At the last stair, I stopped. M's quiet steps ceased, holding back on the second-floor landing. I glanced over my shoulder. "The bathroom is straight down the hall."

I continued down the third-floor hall, then turned on my heel into Grandfather's room. M strode past as if really seeking a toilet. This must be where he wanted me, cornered and out of sight, so what was he waiting for?

I didn't waste the windfall of time. In the far corner past the shuttered window, a wooden cane gathered dust.

Every object in this very room, a weapon. I snatched up the cane, and swung it around toward the door. No one there yet. The dust shook loose, uncovering intricate carving in old-growth oak, American Indian geometries interwoven with English paganism into an Art Nouveau whole that looked fragile. But I had been thwacked with this cane more than once, and knew it wasn't soft.

Now for a defensive position. In front of the window was this floor's iron plate, where Grandfather had tapped into the ancestral power. I stood on the plate and gave silent thanks again to my native land.

A toilet flushed. Was I being paranoid? Might as well go all the way. I visualized the coming battle, preparing my mind for whatever craft might assist me.

Then I saw myself killing M, and the curse hit me. I fell back against the shutters. My body gasped for air, fighting to hyperventilate and pass out and die an easy death. *I can't do this.* My grip loosened on the cane.

M rushed in, KA-BAR blade drawn. Then he slowed and smiled at me. "Just like they said." Leisurely, he shut the door behind him. "Pathetic." M brought his knife up to bury in my exposed chest.

No. The Left-Hand voices screamed with outrage. The House thrummed with my heart. The good and evil of this place would not let me die. Four centuries of power welled up through my feet. My mind went, and training took over. In a swift arc, I brought the cane up and parried M's downward slash.

I grabbed M's arm, using his momentum to rattle him against the shutters. But M spun free. He must have wards that made him slippery to such blows. M crouched with a new respect. I side-stepped off the plate, falling short with another cane stroke.

I moved toward the center of the room, always facing M as he circled. Time crawled, but not through craft. M rotated his knife in one hand, and made strange mudric gestures with the other. Not just thug, but thuggee? Bullshit—more fake than fakir. I ignored the theatrics and followed M's movements, testing the heft of the cane.

Then, with a disciplined grace more inexorable than M's, I strode straight at my opponent, whirring the cane from hand to hand like a spinning wheel. I spun the wood clockwise into M's body with a thud, stopped, and spun it counterclockwise back, looking for a new opening. M slashed with the KA-BAR, nicking the cane, nicking my arm. But I parried again and again, while my free arms and legs delivered select punches and kicks into M's stomach and face, all aimed for the control of my opponent that my native martial arts training prized.

With cracks against steel and thumps against flesh, I worked the cane like a short staff, and tried not to think about how much I hated archaic weapons. Dueling against my grandfather with staves, I had complained, "Thomas Morton wasn't bloody Little John." Grandfather had stung me with a quick blow across the shoulders. "We Mortons use whatever means are necessary."

The Murderer's wards worked against simple mundane blows, but my blows were not simple, nor simply mundane. With the word *strike,* a touch of craft sped my movements, and guided each hit through M's aetheric parries.

M's arms moved slower and wilder. *Knife, throat, fall.* I struck the knife from M's hand and grabbed him by the

throat. With a sweeping kick, I flung M down and held him
by the windpipe against the ground.

In execrable Latin, M whispered something like a
prayer. He wore talismans around his constricted neck,
mostly European in origin—was that a reliquary of the
true cross? Why would anybody bring this foreign crap
against a Morton? Perhaps M meant to mislead about his
employer. The possibilities tired me. "Who are you?"

"I will fear no evil, oath breaker."

I glanced toward M's mind, and found it a tar pit. I could
interrogate him, but that would take all day to find out that
he really didn't know anything, not even if he worked for
Sphinx, the Feds, Endicott, or whoever else controlled the
dark force that was stalking me. My enemy wanted me to
fall into this tar pit. M had been protected, but feebly, and
had no craft strength of his own. No one had expected him
to succeed.

Who was M? Only what he had already done. "You're
a cat's-paw," I said. "Fine. Your superior wants me to ex-
pend my strength on you. But the House and I are done
with you. When you see her, tell her to leave me and
mine alone. For all I care, if she stays away, she can have
the Aquarian apocalypse. I don't give a shit."

"You're letting me go?"

I smiled a little nervous smile. God, it was hard to get
good help. "No." With a quick twist and the word *break,* I
broke M's neck.

It was an exact kill. I had avoided shedding M's blood,
and this abrupt end would send M's spirit quickly back to
his commander instead of forward to another plane. M
would moan out the misinformation that I wanted my en-

emy to stay away, and she might rush her next attack and make mistakes.

I quickly viewed M for any remaining craft aura, any sign of a booby trap set to go off after M's heart had stopped. Such a destiny seemed likely for such obvious cannon fodder, but I found nothing. I searched M's person, and found more eclectic religious medals and relics—not inconsistent with working for Sphinx, but not an orgy of evidence either. I left these with the body; I had no use for such stuff.

For now, I didn't want the body found, so I dragged it into my walk-in closet. That room had masked some of the Mortons' core treasures for generations; it could handle one lousy corpse.

Give him to us. The Left Hand was already restive. Not good.

"Later," I said.

Now.

"You'll get what I promised," I said. "And not an ounce of flesh more."

Damn your flesh! The Left Hand wailed and gnashed their spectral teeth against the woodwork; the room seemed a little dark for comfort. I opened the shutters and looked down on the courtyard. The setup was going nicely.

"I'm back!" yelled Scherie from two floors below. "What are you doing up there?"

"Just looking at the weather."

"Is it going to rain?"

"I don't think so." I remembered my slashed sleeve, and stepped back from the window. "I'm going to change now."

Instead, sudden vertigo overtook me, and I crumpled

against the wall. *No, no, no.* But then, bitter laughter welled up. The curse's impact was weak, at worst. The sorcerer had only cared about me fighting Islam. Any concern for universal life and the law of karmic return was my own.

I took off my shirt and wiped up the blood from my arm and body. Then I waved the rag in the air. *Here I am, I've been wounded. I'm the staked goat, the chum for the sharks. Come and get me.* A vulgar display of failing power, an open wound that would attract every parasitic craftsperson in New England and beyond.

At least I knew people were coming to my party.

I cleaned the cut on my arm and slapped a patch on it. That just left the oncoming storm. Everyone always complained about New England's weather; I would do something about it. I would tease the weather over the House to the kind of perfection remembered long after a disaster comes.

I stood again on the iron plate, focused my mind, and spoke four words in the plain language of the Founders: *dry and cool air.* The storm would part at my house; the day's heat would evaporate as if my large, primeval leafy oaks had soaked it up.

I stacked nature's deck with practiced ease, and the necessary energy came from the House itself.

I descended the stairs to find the other caterers. *Oath breaker.* What oath? Hutch had released me from my oath not to practice craft, and I didn't think M had been talking about my discharge agreement with the government. The only other oath I had taken was to defend the Constitution.

But the Left-Hand Mortons had once sworn an oath, in terrible words and deeds that could bind even the utterly amoral. They had sworn in the name of the Morton Family and the House of Morton to defend each other against all other Families and to never cease in their war against death. From the Left-Hand view, I was a descendant of the great oath breaker, Joshua. So M, or more likely M's masters, had wanted me to believe he had been acting in the name of the living Left Hand.

Bullshit. I refused to believe.

The caterers were setting up the pig roast; a sow spitted over an open fire. The scene brought up several unpleasant memories at once. I would eat very little; from generation to generation, PTSD hit the Morton stomach hard.

To ensure that the caterers wouldn't look for ex-M, I slammed them with preternatural suasion. *"I sent that tattooed man home. He was rude to my family. Will you need other help?"*

The head caterer shook his head. "No, he was extra, last minute."

That dealt with M. Now, my enemies—Sphinx, her spooks, or the third parties manipulating them all—would come in among the guests. They could be anyone, a stranger or an old friend. But M's attempt had assured me on one point: they would come.

Searching again for hostile activity, I saw that my courtyard walls had a night-vision glow in all directions. The neutral color probably meant that the Pentagon's people were stationed outside to stop my supposed bolt for the border. I hoped for their sakes that they kept their asses put, and that that bastard Endicott wasn't with them. I didn't think my enemy would use someone so obvious, but I might want to hurt Endicott anyway.

In a heavily wooded patch of Rock Creek Park near the District line, Sakakawea conferred with Bumppo and Carson. The two men had to look up to speak with Sakakawea, whose long thin limbs were muscle anatomy lessons.

"Is the body ready?" asked Sakakawea.

"Yes," said Bumppo.

"Any ID features?" asked Sakakawea.

"Clean," said Carson.

"Outstanding," said Sakakawea. She opened the cell phone and dialed Major Endicott. "Sir, I've found her," she said. "Dead. Looks ritual. Looks Left-Hand. Looks horrible." A pause. "Yes, I'm sure." Another pause. "Yes sir, we'll remain on alert."

She hung up, then dialed her commander.

"The advance man is dead," he said.

"The masque has started," she said.

Like a social Normandy, the invited men and women arrived in loud, backslapping, cheek-kissing waves. Chuck O'Neill, my roommate from West Point, pushed forward in a screaming tropical shirt of a southern posting. He shook to crush my hand in his enormous paw. "I really appreciate your coming."

"Wouldn't miss it for the world," said Chuck. "You leaving the military, that's huge. Now, where you hiding the poison?"

Give him to us, murmured the Left Hand.

"Right this way," I said.

I steered Chuck toward one of the very prominent outdoor bars. Other guests arrived, with the international set forming an overdressed black-and-white contrast to Chuck and the Day-Glo Americans. People had traveled far for this show. Funny how everyone knew this party mattered, even if they couldn't say why. A good thing they couldn't. Most of the guests were here as mere tactical feints, as props to convince my enemy that this was a farewell party and not a distraction or last stand. I rationalized this. Tonight's battle could be vital to the U.S. and the world, and, worst case, I asked from them nothing more than I would certainly give. I rationalized, but looked away from Chuck's broad grinning face.

As the invited guests and their booming voices accumulated, I waited for the crashers to make quieter entrances. I played the spider, feeling for the vibration along my web. Patience was difficult. Perhaps I was the insect, soon to be consumed.

The courtyard walls hummed. There, that was one. And another. And two more. Their small eccentricities—male ponytails and female chrome domes, pentagram bolos and Masonic broaches—these they covered in the beige social attire of certain Northern Virginian suburbs. Soon, nearly as many spies as invitees roamed the House and grounds. Which ones had come to kill me, which ones just wanted to watch?

Give them to us; we'll sort them out, whispered the Left Hand.

"Grandpa, any of these Sphinx?"

Grandpa appeared at my side in an old Hawaiian shirt,

a tropical drink in his hand. "Bali Hai!" he said. Not all here, but that was OK. None of these intruders looked old enough to be the woman that Grandpa had found at Wood-stock. No sign of the Gideons either. If Sphinx or any major enemy showed, I wasn't going anywhere.

One by one, the crashers failed to avoid Scherie, who guided them to the drinks. She had a knack for this work, and staying busy meant that we didn't have to discuss last night. During a break in the arrivals, Scherie said, "A lot more spies than I expected."

"Me too," I said, quite honestly. "But better that they're right here than outside."

"That old man in the loud shirt looked like a relative."

Shit, she had seen Grandpa. What the hell did that mean? Had sex opened her eyes to the Morton ghosts? That hadn't worked with other women. "Yeah, he's a distant relative." As distant from the living as he could get. Scherie's mouth dropped open, so I added, "One of the good relatives."

"Good. Heard enough about those crazy ones. Oh, there's another spy to greet."

In front of the bar table, Scherie guided another of the shadowy crashers through the drink options. The big spook was ramrodded into his Company suit; unlike most Peep-show, he might also be muscle. "We have fine bourbons and American whiskeys," said Scherie, "moonshine from the jug, and microbrews from around the country." The connection of craft and spirits went deep. "But excuse me for a moment, I'm needed in the kitchen." She retreated, as I had told her, to initiate a pattern of disappearance, so her final departure wouldn't attract notice.

The muscle spook's eyes shamelessly followed Scherie's departure. Fine. If he read her like a billboard, he would only see the information I had posted.

But now the muscle studied me, trying to see what I had on my mind. I feigned unconcern and readied a simple defense. When someone was eavesdropping, turn up the music.

Like using an UZI to trim the hedges, I aimed my modified universal remote toward the stereo, pressed "01" and pushed up the volume. Certain songs worked best; Talking Heads, Steely Dan, Soul Coughing, and Warren Zevon knew how to confuse the fictional and real demimondes. An extension of my nerves, the remote itched in my palm for its main work. Later.

I moved near the main doorway to the House, where the smoky fresh air and loud babel of the courtyard blended with the concentrated smoke and low noise of the inside. Craftsmen couldn't cure cancer, but they sure acted like they could. I was impatient for the crash of force against force. *Let's get on with this.*

As if in response, a shadow fell over the setting sun, like that moment in a poem of battle when the warrior's fate has found him. My primary adversary was circling outside my property, drawing closer, with an obsessive, mathematical precision.

The House thrummed again and again, signaling four more uninvited guests. Two glowed with the colors of the craft specialties, while the other two were just muscle. They all looked military; they all looked Endicott's type. They scattered to keep me loosely between them, formation relaxed because there was backup outside. Their commander wouldn't be far, probably in some communications van on the street.

From inside the House, the Left Hand whispered: *Give them to us.*

No, I said. Or at least, not yet.

As I mixed about the courtyard again, an overdressed crasher managed to step into my way, sparking with his nation's distinctive craft signature as he tried to recruit me. "Just a word, Mr. Morton."

"Nein," I said.

"You know I'm German?"

"We Mortons know Germans." Petty, but Dieters got on my Morton nerves.

"Just a word," insisted the German.

"He said *nyet.*" A familiar voice over my shoulder. The German turned tail.

"Roman." I continued to face forward, smile stapled on my face, teeth clenched. "What the fuck are you doing here?"

"I'm leaving too," said Roman, accent abruptly diminished. "You should come with me."

I spun around to face him. Like an updated devil from a Slavic folk story, Roman had neatly trimmed his beard into the goatee I had always imagined for it. Like the international set, he was overdressed, and smelled of better cologne.

Roman nodded toward Scherie at the bar, who nodded back at him. "Your woman, she is charming. And very devoted to you."

"Are you tired of living, Roman?"

Roman held up his hands. "I'm not your enemy."

"My friends don't show up uninvited."

"Pardon the rudeness," said Roman. "I came because I thought you were hurt."

"You smelled the blood and came running." Like a Gideon. Here on the House grounds, I could see a chameleon-like aura I had missed before. "You're a craftsman."

"A *charivnyk,* yes," said Roman.

"You hid this from me?" Only the shock at such a thorough deception restrained me from doing something fatal to both of us.

"My talent is for hiding," said Roman, "even from other practitioners."

"Then why show yourself?" I asked. "You saw I wasn't hurt."

"Worth the risk," said Roman. "It's our last chance to speak the truth."

"Worth *your* risk to fuck me up," I said. "How do I explain that my Russian gangster—"

"Ukrainian."

"Goddamn me if I care," I spat. I gave my guests a once over. "Lots of people watching us right now."

"They're hearing something else for a minute," said Roman. Still, he spoke low. "You want to leave. We can get you out of the country, but it has to be tonight."

I asked, "Who do you work for?"

"Ukraine," said Roman.

"Yes, but what do you call yourselves now?"

Roman said, "We're the Baba Yagas."

"Scary name."

"Scary world," said Roman. "You come with me?"

I shook my head. "That offer ever work on a Morton before?"

Roman sighed. "Some might be better off if it had. Please, do not be angry for trying."

"I'm not angry," I said, unclenching my fist. "You're just acting in your best interest. Fewer people get hurt when they're clear about that."

Roman looked around at the party. "Things are not so clear here. I act first as a fellow magus. Still, you stay. I understand. I too would prefer to die at home."

"Who said anything about dying?" Roman had guessed too much.

"What about the woman?" asked Roman.

"None of your goddamned business," I said.

Despite the craft protection, Roman lowered his voice. "She won't be hurt when you . . . do whatever you're going to do?"

I brushed some lint off Roman's lapel. With quiet menace, I asked, "Is there something wrong with her documents?"

"No," said Roman. "They're perfect. I swear as a magus."

"And my documents?"

"They're in the car," said Roman. "I drove it here myself. I plan on appearing too drunk to drive when I leave."

"Then we'll all be safe." Or, in my case perhaps, safely dead. "Though your new bosses won't pay as well as I have."

"Money is only everything when you've got nothing else," said Roman. "You expect a Sphinx to answer your riddles. I do not like her. She could have given Kiev an early spring; she did nothing. Still, the world is not always as we think."

I was about to respond to this unhelpful wisdom when someone else touched my arm—a bold move by the muscle spook. "May I have a word with you?"

"I'm saying good-bye to my guest," I said. I readied a few quick spells in case this spook attacked.

"Don't you think you've said enough?" said the muscle.

I was going to protest, but Roman was gone. I couldn't see him anywhere. Damn, he really was good at hiding. "I think *you've* said enough," I said to the spook.

"I agree," said the muscle. Peepshow spooks used magic to make themselves forgettable, and they disguised certain biometrical details to make ID difficult. This particular spook wore deep brown colored contacts and dyed his hair black. He wore a quasi-Masonic "eye in pyramid" lapel pin. He wasn't trying to hide *what* he was, just *who* he was.

"And what's your name, my new friend?" I asked.

Muscle had the nerve to actually think about it for a moment. He placed a hand over his chest. "Call me Eddy."

"Are you going to keep me from talking to all my guests tonight, Eddy?"

"No, not all of them," said Eddy. "Just the ones I hear continuously repeating the ingredients to Ukrainian soup."

"I thought you guys just liked to watch," I said. But the old saw didn't cut. "Why the interference?"

"You can ask my boss."

"Your boss?" I asked.

"She'll be here soon."

"Great, another uninvited guest." I reined in my anticipation of this prospective crasher's identity. Sphinx herself was almost too much to hope for. "Meantime, try the shrimp," I said. "It's fresh."

As I spoke, Roman became briefly visible as he stumbled drunkenly across the courtyard's threshold. As a final salute, he mimed cutting his own throat. I got the message: not a personal threat, but the army sign for "danger area."

Eddy rejoined his three Peepshow pals near the bar. Their disguises couldn't hide the self-importance that common foot soldiers never had. When would they strike?

Floating around Eddy's party cruisers were a couple of turned foreigners, a beautiful woman of unclear origin too twitchy to spring her honey trap, and a corn-fed Midwestern PhD turned analyst along for the ride. I ignored them all. I followed Eddy's eyes, waiting for them to betray his boss.

The House rang like a gong, Eddy's eyes flashed, Grandpa's jaw dropped.

I turned to see the most perversely flattering thing in my life. Incredibly alone, a small woman walked up the steps of the tiered garden, long braided gray hair appearing first, then a waiflike figure in a little black dress, and finally Doc Martin boots. The crasher strode through the threshold protections like they didn't exist.

She entered the courtyard. She wore glasses oversized for her fine long nose, appropriate eyewear for the most powerful oracle in the United States.

Looking nervous, one of the H-ring men subvocaled into a hidden transmitter, not caring who saw him do it. He mouthed the same code name over and over again. I didn't need to read lips or minds to know this was Eddy's boss. But Grandpa said the name anyway. "Sphinx."

Beyond all hope, my trap had worked. She had come. If I succeeded, neither of us would leave this place alive.

Sphinx is here, Major," said the technician. He tried to keep his voice neutral, though he was surprised, and surprises made him unhappy.

"I'm going in," said Endicott, opening the sliding door of the van. "Keep communications open." And he left. That at least was good news. Now, the technician could prepare his weapons in peace.

He sat down on a coffin-sized army green box at the back of the van. Poetic that, after so many years of wandering, he was back where his conquest of death had begun. But he would not go into that House himself ever again. One of his weapons was already in place, awaiting activation. If that necessary abomination failed, the other (and he tapped the box) would go in to finish the job.

Then, all threat gone, maybe he would cease to dream of the woman with dark hair and olive skin offering him pomegranate seeds. The dream's message made no sense. He had conquered death, and no god remained to reimpose mortality and justice. Oracles of death were for others.

Sphinx looked toward Grandpa as if she had heard him and smiled cold as a Sargent painting, a smile that killed Grandpa all over again. "Try the shrimp," she said, "It's fresh." She'd been farlistening. Then she veered away from me toward the food table. So much for flattery.

My death followed with her. The dark magic encircled the block and the grounds of the estate. Waiting for her to attack would gain nothing, and perhaps lose everything. Eliminating her at once would keep the House and Left-Hand spirits out of it. But I had one other person to take care of first.

"Scherie." She came away from the bar table; I put an arm around her and spoke into her ear. "Could you see about the amontillado?"

She frowned. "But it's only nine o'clock."

"Opportunity waits for no one. Go." She hesitated, then strode away with sad efficiency and no sashay. I did not say good-bye. Sometimes silence is a lie.

I readied my craft. Two corpses would be ample distraction for Scherie's escape. I'd get close to Sphinx. Close enough to confirm her crimes. Close enough to kill her. Any spooks I left standing would kill me, but taking Sphinx down and protecting my country and Scherie from her would be enough for this life.

Scherie would be downstairs before any screams. Even if she heard something, she would know to keep going.

The chill of a ghost hand on my shoulder. "Don't do it, Dale," said Grandpa. I slipped his grasp, and his cold fingers passed through me.

I pressed "06" and the fast-forward button on the remote. The time sense of Sphinx's bodyguards slowed as I moved between them with craft-enhanced speed. Sphinx spun on her heel to face me. She adjusted time's rush with the ease that flowed from its constant observation. She exactly matched my speed, two blurs in a land of statues. "Hello, Casper," she said.

The guards were reacting now, reaching for me and for their hidden weapons. Eddy crouched for some crazy leap. Sphinx held up a hand to restrain them. She smiled again, baring her terrible, brown-stained teeth. "Are you ready to die?"

A crackle of craft sparked between us, a whiff of astral ozone burned my nose. I saw a nonsin vision: a piece of my death clung to Sphinx, like a twitching piece of lint. All the evidence I needed.

"Yes," I said. I would remind them never to allow a craftsman near the president. I was close enough to synchronize Sphinx's heartbeat to mine, then stop them both. *Stop, in three . . . two . . . one . . .*

Smack! My cheek burned with the impact of Sphinx's slap. She giggled, her face smiley beautiful, the simplicity of a cherub with a bad dental plan. "Wake up, sleepy boy."

I gaped at her; I saw her sins. She showed no murders, no guilt of any kind. Her bright pink letters were the confused jumble of the only perfect human innocence.

Sphinx, the world's most powerful oracle, was insane.

She could still be part of the problem, but in no respect was she responsible for it. I couldn't kill her. *Shit, if it isn't her, who?*

I stammered as the craft energies cooled around me. "You're not . . . the person I was expecting."

"The dark man in the woods, papa?" She spoke like a little girl dressed as an old hippie, a little girl who had lived too much Hawthorne. Her eyes darted like she was in a waking dream.

In a flash, I made my default decision: save the fool. "You've got to get out of here," I said. "Something's coming for me."

Eddy stood next to us, his presence pressing me back a few inches. "Easy, Morton. Don't feed her your delusions."

I was about to argue, to plead, to beg to get this poor woman away from my craft ground zero, when another person joined our tête-à-tête. Scherie.

My heart raced. I had faced enemy fire so many times I'd lost count, but now was the first time I'd felt close to panic. "Dear, I asked you to get the amontillado."

Scherie smiled, a tense thing that fit some minor domestic dispute. "Yes, I thought you were going to make an announcement first."

I opened my mouth to say some crypto-nonsense about going before the "announcement." But the dread on Sphinx's face made me falter. Sphinx grabbed Scherie's arm in a talon of jingling Nepalese bracelets. "Get her out of here!" she croaked.

Scherie pulled the hand off. "I don't think we've met."

Then Sphinx broke into a grin and giggled. "Go. Now. And stay. Nothing else matters."

"Excuse us a moment," I said. I grabbed Scherie's arm where Sphinx had, and we walked into the House.

S he seems a little off," said Scherie, shaking off my grip. "An old friend of the family's," I said. "Why are you still here?"

"Your friend's friends were ready to kill you. Here and now." She had seen.

"They were ready to try," I said. "And that would have been a fine distraction."

"So what do I do now?"

How much time was left? My now unknown enemy was on the grounds but not yet daring the inner spirit stones. The dark magic dimmed the illumination that came to me from my land and House. My death approached like the tenth plague in *The Ten Commandments:* a slowly flowing fog and mist.

"There's still time," I said. "But you've really got to leave."

"What about the distraction?" asked Scherie.

"That's already started. I'll improvise the rest."

"You'll get yourself killed," she said.

"Ah, this is nothing." The biggest lie yet. "Now go. I'll see you soon."

"You'd better." With a shock, I heard her meaning: *love you.* No lie.

"Yeah." I felt weak in ways I couldn't afford. I nodded toward the cellar entrance. "Please. For me."

To my relief, she didn't hesitate, but pivoted and walked away. One casualty averted.

Outside, Grandpa and Chuck were both hovering around Sphinx. With his unerring sense of the worst thing to do, Chuck was trying to speak with her. "Are you a friend of Dale's?"

"Friends don't let friends die drunk."

"Would you like something to drink?" asked Chuck.

"Some herbal tea. No, fuck it." She pointed at Grandpa's tropical drink. "I'll have what he's having."

"What who's having?" asked Chuck, bewildered. I was puzzled too. Sphinx shouldn't be able to see my dead without an introduction. But then I remembered her connection to Grandpa, and wondered again about its extent.

Sphinx giggled like a very high schoolgirl. "Dirty old man. Pussy got your tongue?"

"No one here but us, ma'am," said Chuck.

"Call me Dare," she said. She started fumbling to take her dress off. "Dirty. It'll just get dirty." Grandpa and Chuck went wide-eyed. But then she looked at her watch and lost track of what she was doing. Eddy tried to keep his secret service–style poker face on, but he couldn't hide his embarrassment.

"Hey babe, let's party," said Chuck.

"I solemnly assure you," said Sphinx, "this very night, we'll party together in hell. Unless our square host kills the buzz."

There was one person in this equation that I could handle, so I handled him. "Chuck. Front and center, soldier. Right now."

Chuck walked sheepishly over to me. I whispered, "What the fuck are you doing? She's about twice your age."

"So?" said Chuck. "She's kinda sexy."

"She's very dangerous. Don't get near her again. In fact, you should go. This party is about to get ugly."

"A fight?" said Chuck. "Bring it on."

"More like a fubar," I said. "More like something that will ruin your life if you survive it."

"But I could . . ."

"Nothing you can do, Chuck, or I'd tell you. If it wasn't my house, I'd leave with you. So go."

Reluctantly, with a look back that would have made Lot's wife extra salty, Chuck made for the courtyard entrance.

The Pentagon men split their attention between me and Sphinx, babbling frenetically into their headsets. The other guests enjoyed the party's energy, thinking they were in the midst of incognito Washington elites whose names they could later Google. By the amount of airplay, the Pentagon commanding officer would enter soon. That would limit my options.

If the enemy wasn't Sphinx, where would the blow come from? She might be able to see it. I felt our residual heart sync tugging at me. Was there still time for a chat with the Delphic schizo?

With a series of pops that sounded like lightbulbs burning out in a tomb, the outer wards on the grounds were going. A low moan. One of the faded ancestors on the periphery faded out. Not much time.

As in response, Sphinx skipped over to me, face soiled with cocktail sauce and ebullient, as if she could buy the world a Coke. I took the direct approach. *"What do you know about my upcoming demise?"* I gripped her hand, hard.

Sphinx threw off my grip with a pout. "Don't need that to see which way the wind blows along the watchtower tangled up with you here comes the twister."

A cold wind did the rounds of the compass. Someone was changing the temperature. My enemy was a weatherman. But no power in the world should be able to oppose an active Morton on his own ground.

"Who's doing this?" I said.

Sphinx cackled. "You're in the ghost story. It's coming up the street, across the yard, through the door. Coming from three directions and five horizons. Is it one thing moving or several things stuck together? Is it even human?"

"Nonhuman entities are fairy tales," I said.

"Wrong genre," said Sphinx.

"We're running out of time," I said.

"Yes," said Sphinx.

Then Grandpa came between us and put his insubstantial hands to Sphinx's face. "What the hell happened to you?"

She smiled, and tears streamed down her cheeks and through his fingers. "I'm sorry, Pops, but I tried and tried, and I can't change the cold equations. The universe always balances my little causality tricks one way," and she pointed at her head, "or another. But mostly, it just doesn't care. It just doesn't fucking budge. Smoke 'em if you got 'em, Pops. We're screwed."

As if on cue, the House thrummed. Endicott marched into the party, pushing his way through the crowd, and two of his men fell in behind him. "In your mother's womb, I knew thee," said Sphinx, grinning. "But at least that asshole will share the fun. Seriously, anyone got a joint?"

Dismal Eddy sprang to sudden life and blocked Endicott's approach to Sphinx. "That's close enough."

Endicott looked at Eddy, weighed his options, then spoke in a soldier's low anger. "In Christ's name, what are you doing here? With him?" He pointed at me.

"Jesus sends his regrets," said Sphinx, munching on some shrimp from her handbag. "Christ won't be coming soon. The other fellow will be here any minute."

"This farewell fraud just became a national security

risk. Everyone needs to scatter. Except you, Morton. You'll be coming with me."

"No," I said.

"You've got no rights, you son of a . . ." Endicott faltered on the last word, avoiding the inevitable *witch*. "I'm arresting you."

"For what?"

"Say it's for Hutchinson's murder," said Endicott.

"Hutch?" How could this asshole still appall me? "That's the goddamned stupidest thing you've said."

"You're not surprised," said Endicott. "I just find out, and you don't even pretend to not know."

"You fucking idiot," I said, "you *know* that she was more than either of my parents—"

"Say what you want," said Endicott. "Maybe you're crazier than Sphinx is, and you killed those civvies yourself, and you enjoyed it. We'll figure out the charges later. But you're leaving. Now."

Sphinx's eyes went from ticking REM to frozen sociopathic. "Not while I'm here."

Endicott winced with disgust. "And how long were you planning to stay, Sphinx?"

"Another hour or so." Sphinx's eyes began to play tennis again. "I like the shrimp."

Some of the steam leaked from Endicott. "Oh, well . . ."

Meanwhile, this little scene had motivated some guests to leave, but not enough. Too many were ignoring the altercation, or taking an unhealthy interest. Time to get the bozos out of here. I pressed "10" on my remote.

The music stopped, and an official-sounding man spoke over the speakers, "Attention, a terrorist threat has been called in against this address. Please evacuate immediately. Thank you." Then the warning was given in pan-glossic craft, so that everyone would assume the second language was their own.

Some more people made for the gate. Good. Anyone who stayed would be with or against me—most likely against.

Endicott must have heard the craft touch in the message. He was beyond pissed. "What's that in your pocket? Give it to me."

"Worse and worse," said Sphinx.

"Hey Dale!" No—stupid drunk idiot Chuck had wandered back into the party. He spun around, looking up at the sky like an airborne strike was coming. "What the fuck is going on?"

"Chuck, this is an order—"

Pop! Then a series of sharp cracks, and the sound of rock sliding against rock. The seven spirit stones in the courtyard wall failed in quick succession. I cringed at the scream of Jonathan Morton's second death. Someone was turning the Morton hallowed ground into their own abominated space. My enemy was here.

"Morton, what are you doing?" Endicott must have remembered my threat about the House.

Sphinx looked at her watch. "Right on schedule. Must be a fascist. They're such clockheads." She giggled. "Clock. Head."

Stunned, I said nothing. Large chunks of my reality were blinking out. The craft forces around me became a checkerboard of uncertain absences in the ground, the walls, the House, the sky. Between the gaps, the protests of the Left Hand interspliced like helicopter blades. A juggernaut of force closed in on me, and I was going blind.

"What the hell was I thinking?" I said.

"I spy with my little eye something that begins with *D*," said Sphinx.

Endicott was chest to chest with Eddy. He shouted at me, "You treasonous motherfucker, stop this." So much for Christian sentiment.

The blind spot had moved into my immediate vision. It circled me, the people, the courtyard, became an alternating blur. They could come right up to me and kill me.

Time to retreat. "It's after me," I said. "Stay away from the House."

As if to punctuate the point, a crash. Ward gargoyles from the roof shattered to the left and right of the doorway. I stepped away from the Peepshow and Endicott standoff.

Too late. Halfway to the door, I froze. Death surrounded me, and I couldn't move my legs. I felt the bond with my enemy tightening, could sense my opponent's focus, even as my bond with the House and the Left Hand severed. Endicott was shouting from miles away. The hair stood up on the back of my neck. Somewhere close, a rifle sight sought my skull.

No, not until I inflict casualties to protect the Families and country that I love, whatever they feel about me. Not until Scherie was farther away from here. With all my will, I stepped back toward the House and into the death of my choosing.

Too slow, too slow. I felt the rifle sight move with me, felt the tension on the trigger, the joy of my hunter, the odd ecstasy of being prey. Hailing my grandfather and my ancestors, I said, "I'm coming."

CHAPTER

ELEVEN

Sphinx moved faster than my thought. She left shrimp stranded in midair and took me in a twirl with a ballerina's grace. One hand found mine, the other found the chakra of my lower spine, like she was dancing lead, like she was completing a circuit. She ripped me into her fast-forward world.

I felt a lightness that was more sex than combat. No, I wouldn't let this happen. "Get the fuck down, nut job."

"That's my boy." Sphinx smiled, the fool with the sane punch line. Like a speed freak, she enunciated an order to her Peepshow goons: *"Protect. Casper."*

A screech of psychic feedback froze me as Sphinx's command echoed shock from my brain to my enemy's to the blind force pulling a trigger. Too late. With an eldritch blast, the rifle fired.

The craft-guided shot came in like a heart-seeking missile on a spiral path of untraceable origin. The bullet made a little *pock* sound as it passed between Sphinx's ribs. The accompanying craft sizzled like black static, ensuring death. My heart, tied to hers, felt the pain. Sphinx's grip on me tightened spasmodically, then released. "Hunh.

Chimera. Go now." The heart sync broke; Sphinx's soul exploded in blinding craft, bolts of sunshine in the gathered gloom.

She was gone. The end had no magic. I slowed back into the world.

Flashing guns greeted me; their barrels scanned like raptors, searching for the sniper in all directions. Over Sphinx's slumped shoulders, I searched too, and felt nothing. A nervous young Peepshow held his weapon close to my head, his grip way too sweaty-tight. Sphinx's order or not, this boy was going to kill me.

"Don't shoot him, screen them!" yelled Eddy. Relieved to be under command, the Peepshow goons faced outwards and sandwiched Sphinx and me in our last tangle. I lowered Sphinx down to the ground. Her blood pooled onto the paving stones and into Morton earth.

Thunder without lightning, and scattered rain dropped into the blood. Eddy backed away from Endicott, gun drawn. Endicott was whispering into his transmitter, and his men formed a belated, moving circle around the Peepshows. Unconcerned with the sniper, they appeared to be looking for a clean line of fire on me, and not finding one.

Eddy bent to confirm Sphinx's death. "This wasn't part of the plan."

No, I thought, *this was part of some plan, just not mine or Eddy's.* Grandpa glared at me with a young man's rage. "I'm glad we won't have long to think about this. I'll be inside with the others." And he disappeared.

Formal shoes clattered on wet stone; the remaining guests finally realized that any benefits of further intel were outweighed by implication in this muddy mess. The Americans had left at the first sign of unpleasantness. Now the foreigners ran, not walked, through the courtyard gate, like bulls pursued by butchers.

My brain caught up to my strange and sad reprieve. Sphinx had made a blood sacrifice and shattered the death-seeking magic. But even shattered, such magic was a threat. My former death flew about in too many shards to repel, infecting those around me with a tendency to kill me.

They needed little urging. The Peepshow and Endicott's men were yelling at each other, a confused cacophony of "Stand down," "Let us through," and "Give him up"— "Stand us up!" Classic alpha-male standoff. With his discreet talent for compulsion, Endicott yelled with more focus at Eddy: "*Stand down,* or we will shoot."

"*Resist,*" I said, but Eddy's left eye twitched with Endicott's compulsion. Then Eddy responded through clenched teeth: "You won't shoot him through us." Being Peepshow had its advantages.

Endicott ignored the rebuttal. "Dale Morton, you're under arrest. These misguided bureaucrats don't have jurisdiction here. You'll either come with me now, or you're resisting arrest. Do I have to explain that to you?"

I didn't need explanations. I needed to get inside the House. If Endicott wanted to come inside with me, all the better. "Can I get some things?" I asked.

"No," said Endicott.

Oh well, worth a shot. I tried Eddy. "We need to get inside my house."

Eddy's face was taut with stricken anger. "I don't think so. I think we'll protect you at Langley, and I think you and I are going to have a nice long chat."

Endicott must have sensed his opening. "Tell him how

you did it, Morton. How you killed Sphinx. How you butchered Hutch."

I felt new waves of craft arcing like ICBMs toward me. "We won't get one hundred yards from here. We need—"

"Nobody's going anywhere!" Frothing at the mouth, Chuck hurdled onto the food table and waved a stick around in some crude parody of kendo. The rain-slicked stick flew out of his hands. He jumped down and scrambled for his stick, leapt up into a sloppy martial arts stance, then scrambled for a weapon again. The act would have been hysterical, except that it threatened to get people killed.

"Get the fuck out of here, Chuck," I said, "or I'll shoot you myself."

But we were out of time. One of the Peepshows screening me doubled over. Blood streamed from his eyes. Almost in answer, one of Endicott's men tried to bash in his own skull with his gun.

"Eddy, get me inside," I said.

Thunder and a crash of glass. A dark figure spun down from the third-floor balcony and hit the flat stones of the courtyard with bone-breaking thud. Shit, a new problem. But it wasn't. With impossible steadiness, the figure stood up. With rare horror, I recognized him.

It was M. He moved, but no aura. M wasn't alive. It was a meat puppet. I had been played. I had sealed my House, but death had penetrated my little party. That I hadn't believed that such legendary power still existed was no excuse. I had killed M and upgraded their weapon.

M's dead eyes searched the rain-brushed courtyard with what would have been confusion in the living. Its left arm hung at its side, limp and deflated. Its right hand gripped a strange-looking rifle.

Endicott pointed his gun at M. "Drop the weapon. Now."

With dead slowness, M raised the rifle. The weapon was a device out of Bosch—a gore-covered mixture of metal components held in a stock of human skeleton. The barrel had been hidden in M's flesh; the rest *was* M's flesh, self-cannibalized. Its bullets were bits of metal-capped bone. That M could fight while alive was itself a miracle of craft.

The rain poured, and nothing came clean. This looked like Left-Hand Morton work.

"Find cover!" I yelled.

Endicott stood straight and fired. He hit M's right arm, both legs, and finally the chest. M spun around like a tangled marionette, but didn't fall. As M slowed, it fired at one of Endicott's men, and maybe nicked a bit of suit. Even confused, this was deep craft. Some of the puppet strings may have been broken by Sphinx's sacrifice, but that made M dangerous to everyone instead of just me.

M's rifle swerved like a compass needle, stopping on another of Endicott's men.

"Take cover!" ordered Endicott.

But, like a hypnotized deer, Endicott's man was too slow, and M's shot found his leg. "I'm hit, I'm hit," he called.

"Shit!" said Chuck, scurrying for the gate. Sensing the motion, M's rifle swerved Chuck's direction.

"Over here," I yelled. The thing fired anyway. Chuck screamed, but kept moving. Then M turned slowly toward me.

"Not the plan," said shell-shocked Eddy. " 'Zombies are a funny myth,' she said."

Clutching my remote, I felt for the Left-Hand spirits in the House, searching for rebels. None had slipped my reins; this monster couldn't be their doing. "Get me in the House," I said, "before it shoots us all. But slowly. Don't attract its attention."

"On three," said Eddy. "One, two . . ."

As if we were slowly boarding a helicopter en masse, we moved in a crouch toward the door. Slowly, but too fast. In a blink, M's rifle wheeled and found the blinded Peepshow being tugged along by Eddy. Another *crack* like dried bone, and the Peepshow was down with a fatal head shot.

"Goddamned monster!" said Eddy. But he joined the rest of us in the House. Meantime, Endicott's men had taken positions behind the bars and the buffet tables. M stared blankly at the House, like a child considering a difficult problem in subtraction.

"What the fuck do we do now?" asked Eddy.

"Who the hell is your friend, Morton?" yelled Endicott. For a magus, Endicott was a shitty liar—he recognized this corpse. But he seemed a little scared to see it moving.

"He used to be an assassin," I said. "I killed him."

"Not very well," said Endicott. "You'd better unplug him, or you'll have a nightcap in Hell."

"Get it through your Puritan skull: he's not my zombie. The way he's shooting, he's probably yours." But given the shock and horror that Endicott was buttoning down, this was unlikely.

Endicott must have lost interest in the debate. "Hey Peepshow. Hand Morton over, and maybe we'll let you retire."

A standoff. This government gang fight was getting in

the way of the main event: drawing my still-hidden enemy into the House. With the enemy's magic scattered, did he have enough mojo to follow me inside?

With the sudden flash and thunder of a lightbulb filled with gasoline, the spirit keystone in the door arch exploded. The House groaned along its crack. A Peepshow howled, hands over bleeding ears, his smoking headset on the ground. Question answered.

Eddy's hand gripped my shoulder a bit harder than necessary. "I said, what the fuck do we do now?"

Sins of evil intent flashed their letters across Eddy's chest; my enemy's malice was taking deeper root in Eddy's hindbrain. "*We* don't do anything," I said. "You get out through the back and report to Langley what's happening here."

"Can't do that," said Eddy. "Orders."

"You were ordered to protect me," I said. "If you stay here, that's not going to happen, is it? Somehow, you're going to get me killed."

"What I can see," said Eddy, "that's going to happen anyway."

Outside, Endicott's unit was taking carnival shots at the spinning, staggering M. Large chunks of flesh had been blown off it, but more force than I had ever seen held the zombie together, patching the necessary bits and letting the cosmetics go to gory hell. The zombie returned fire, keeping Endicott & Co. from rushing it.

More and more, this zombie looked like the dangerous craft of the Left-Hand Mortons, but with far more power. To push this many natural laws, my enemy had to be very close. Good.

"Anyone who comes in this house after me . . . isn't

going to be a problem," I said. "But I won't be able to protect your people. You'll need to get back here, in force, to clean up this mess. Now go."

Eddy made hand signs to his deafened subordinate, and the three remaining Peepshows scuttled for the back of the House.

For the next few minutes of my plan, I could use a gun. I reached into the never-used umbrella stand, popped the false bottom, and pulled out the surprisingly massive Colt and a shoulder holster that I had placed there. Outstanding.

M seemed to be regaining its focus on the House, but it was taking too long. I called to it: "Yoo-hoo, zombie. In here."

M's dead eyes riveted on my voice. It fired blindly toward Endicott again, just for perversity's sake. Then, it took off in a crippled galvanic sprint toward me.

I crouched, ready to grapple with this corpse. But five strides away, M veered left and plunged through the large curved window into the parlor. Shit, didn't this meat puppet ever use the door? M rolled out of my view, leaving a trail of broken glass and bloody rainwater. Whatever force still impelled M must be trying to flank me.

"It's obeying Morton's instructions," said Endicott. "Let's get them both."

"Goddamnit, I told you . . ." But Endicott's men advanced like weaving snakes on the door. I backed off, looking over my shoulders for M. "Keep your distance," I said. "The House isn't safe."

"Ha. You've already played that trick," said Endicott. "Keep going."

I fired a shot from my cannon over their heads, just to

slow them. It was hard to resist a blood-drenched stopper when the susurrant pulse of the House whispered for *more, more, more.*

My shot was answered by the sound of distant sirens. Endicott wouldn't be able to keep this scenario contained forever.

I retreated into the long central hallway, peering into each small New England room for M. The House was a maze of stairwells, dumbwaiters, and crawl spaces. The corpse could be crawling anywhere.

"Hijo de puta!" Metal and ceramics crashed in the kitchen. Despite the warning, some workers must have straggled in the kitchen—perhaps more agents trying to watch the show. They fled now, and I knew where M was.

Meanwhile, Endicott's team had entered, alternating between the right and left rooms and securing the foyer. I ducked into the hidden priest hole midway down the central hall. I didn't need to see the intruders; the House vibrated with each living trespass. But M was only another shadow to the House.

One of Endicott's flunkies called out: "Mr. Morton, will you please just come with us?"

"Stow that, Corporal," said Endicott, hostile to this attempt to return the situation to normal. "Get Morton out of here, off his ground."

I tucked my gun into its holster and pulled out my remote. The cult of presence in craft was for those of little faith. My craft would obey my commands, like the soldier obeyed the centurion. I said *"Disable,"* and pressed "02" on my remote.

"Disable" echoed through the stereo system. Every gun in the House glowed red, and Endicott's men dropped the

suddenly burning metal from their hands. *"Disable."* And their headsets let out a terminal screech of feedback, though nothing so harsh as what my enemy had done to the Peep-show.

"Sir," Flunky Two called out, "we have to abort."

"Negative," said Endicott. "He's disarmed too. Aren't you, Morton?"

The prick was right: the House-wide spell left me disarmed as well. I could live with that; I only wanted to incapacitate Endicott's team, but Endicott might want to shoot me dead.

"I'll be here when you flush him out," said Endicott. "Until then, keep the chatter to a minimum."

Good, Endicott would hang back. I couldn't take on three at once, if one of them was Endicott. I could handle two. These grunts had weight and height on me, and were prepared for possible craft action. But none of them had trained as much as I had, even in the crib, for days like today.

One at a time would be better still. The House would help with that. I reached out with my senses. Flunky One, working his way round my left through the parlor, would be the quickest to take down.

On the library and study side, doors slammed closed, confining the larger grunt and compartmentalizing the combat for a few crucial moments. In the hallway, the clock slid forward and its pendulum, like a toy version of Poe's, smashed out, threatening to slice Endicott unless he kept back. I dashed out from the priest hole into the parlor. There, the thing behind the yellow wallpaper pulsed ominously to distract Flunky One. Even as my opponent pivoted round, I charged into him. My Native American martial arts used the grunt's strength against him, even the strength of his bones. *Break. Crackle. Snap!* The best nonfatal injury for encouraging retreat was a broken arm. Or two.

"I'm not done with you," said Flunky One, defying pain to keep me engaged.

"I'm done with you." As I left the room, the House took over. The busts, pottery, and silver flew off their pedestals and tables in attack, the small bookcases teetered and fell, herding the broken-armed grunt back to the window. The sheer malice of the Left-Hand spirits warned him to exit now, or be consumed.

Racing across the hallway, I saw that Endicott remained occupied. From seeming thin air, Endicott had pulled out his sword by its overly decorated hilt and charged the clock. Just like an Endicott to be killing time during battle.

I fell on Flunky Two in the library. We traded body blows. I took two hard jabs to my gut and a pop to my head before I was able to find the ideal point of fracture. I kicked at Flunky Two's left leg, an innocuous enough blow if an antique table had not slid up behind the target. *Crunch.* Flunky Two's leg and the table's both broke. I tossed the broken flunky toward the front of the House, there to be encouraged to leave by other antiques and bookcases spewing the volumes of Poe and Hawthorne.

So finished a French farce of promiscuous beatings. Frightened, the injured flunkies offered only token resistance to being herded outside. Pressed back to the wall, they rolled through the windows to join their fellow wounded in the courtyard. *That's the spirit, quit while you're ahead.*

I got my breath back and stepped into the hallway. Endicott stood in the now bolted doorway, the clock's pendulum decapitated at his feet, its slashes marking his shirtfront. He flourished his sword in the air in challenge. "None of your kind have ever beaten this."

The distant dead thud on the cellar stairwell distracted me from Endicott's ridiculous display. *Oh no you don't.* Nothing was getting between me and the subbasement—Scherie's escape route and my last defense. I turned and ran for the stairway.

"Damn you, coward!" yelled Endicott.

I dove onto M's back. The monster's wrongness shot through my arms, but I held on as we tumbled together down the remaining stairs and onto the floor.

The thing fired its ossuarial rifle at the cellar ceiling. I stripped the weapon from M's grasp and tossed it away. M grabbed my throat awkwardly, but with enough sheer force to make breathing an issue. I drove bone-crunching, meat-grinding punches into M's face, but the thing tossed me off like a puppy.

M stood up and limped on toward the wide-open door to the subbasement. *Scherie left it open for me, not you.* I dashed in front of M. The thing brought its fist around in a parody of a punch that knocked me aside. I retreated and blocked M's way again.

Endicott slowly appeared in the stairway, sword in front of him. "You two have a falling out?"

"Hypothetically," I asked, bobbing and weaving, "how would you kill a zombie?"

"Hypothetically," said Endicott, "we'd do an exorcism."

The thing swung another roundhouse at me; I ducked. "Right. What if you needed something more immediate?"

Endicott nodded as he descended. "All that evil must be centered somewhere."

"Heart or head?" I asked.

"Both."

"My thoughts exactly," I said. "One, two . . ."

"Three!"

With pagan sureness, I drove my hand through M's tattered chest and pulled out its empty heart. With Christian righteousness, Endicott swung his sword and beheaded M's mangled skull in one stroke.

M fell to the ground. "Arms and legs too, just to be safe," I said.

"Right," said Endicott. "This (hack) is what happens (hack) when you summon (hack, hack) the powers (hack, hack, . . . hack) of darkness."

The pieces of M twitched, as if they were still reaching for me. Some of the killer angel had gone out of the air. Endicott pointed his gory sword at me. "Ready to quit?"

"I can't," I said.

"Why the hell not?" said Endicott. "Despite my inclination, I'd prefer not to have to explain the death of another craftsman—at least until after the trial."

"You still don't get it," I said. "I'm expecting another guest."

"Your boogeyman witch killer? The dark man of the woods?" Endicott kicked at one of M's grasping hands. "Your alibi seems to have fallen apart."

Dark man of the woods. Sphinx had made the same quip. Not funny then or now. "You should go," I said. "No one who stays here is going to survive."

Endicott gave me a long reading look, digesting the implication that "no one" included me. "Ha! Nice try. This zombie had 'Left-Hand Morton' practically tattooed on it. And it was slouching to your subterranean temple— yeah, we know about that." He brandished his sword at me. "Now come with me, or I'll cut you down."

I laughed. "Survival isn't part of my mission objectives, sir."

Endicott raised his sword. I readied just enough craft to parry him.

The House of Morton shook like a moderate earthquake. The largest gong of the night rung through me; the craft vibration trailed off into forever.

Endicott lowered his sword slightly, annoyed. "What the heck is it now?"

I shrugged. "My guest has finally arrived."

A voice spoke upstairs, sepulchrally deep yet profoundly amused. "Aren't you going to invite me down?" The voice was tech or craft altered, though the mocking familiarity seemed, well, familiar.

"No," I said.

"So much for Morton hospitality," said the guest. "Very well."

The guest descended the stairs like a king in procession. He was tall and gaunt, dressed in a gray robe resembling a funeral shroud that covered his legs, making his move- ment look like hovering. He wore a mask of a stiffened corpse with a rictal smile, a likeness of death that even I couldn't quite see through. His robe was dabbled in blood, and his broad brow and face were sprinkled with scarlet horror. The motherfucker was dressed as Poe's Red Death.

"You goddamned idiots," said Endicott. "You brought him back."

This was the attire of Roderick Morton as high priest

to his gods. This was what Roderick wore when he would murder every motherfucking soul in the room.

"Can't be," I said. "Didn't do it, and it can't be."

He had come from outside, not from the Left-Hand spirits downstairs. Even now, those spirits howled in my ears for his blood. Was this Sphinx's Chimera? If so, he was wearing the wrong mythical costume, with one strange addition. Ol' Red here had a fucking magic wand. Was he going to kill us all with embarrassment?

Red waved aside the remaining wards and stepped down the last step. The last spirit stone in the House exploded into dust. I pressed "11" on my remote. I had saved the fatal gadgets for this guest. An enormous pendulum blade slashed straight down at the masked head. It should have sliced the enemy into clean halves. Instead, the blade dented against the macabre skull and crashed behind Red, burying itself halfway into the floor.

I pressed "12" on my remote. Crossbow bolts flew at the enemy from both sides, but they also bounced back with the recoil of cue balls. Damn. I hadn't expected any real damage, but Red hadn't even broken a sweat.

The pieces of M twitched and slithered toward the triumphant Red Death. Anyone with a normal skull would have been impressed by Red's power. But Endicott just spat. "Who the fuck are you, wandy? Roderick Morton? The Wizard of Oz?"

"That would be telling," said Red, "I'm a friend. Leave us."

I didn't know what to make of "friend," but I also didn't want another craftsman killed today. "You'd better listen to him, Major."

Endicott spared me a look. "Christ," said Endicott. "A

zombie, and now this. *In the name of Jesus Christ, get out of here.*" For the first time this evening, Endicott had made a formal invocation. He must be a little scared.

Red stepped forward, arms open as if to embrace Endicott. Endicott shouted commands at Red like he was a rabid dog. *"Stop. Drop the wand. Hands up."*

Red stepped forward. Endicott waved his sword and pointed straight at Red's heart. The sword twitched and vibrated. Red stepped forward. Endicott's arm spasmed wildly as he struggled to hold the sword front and center. The weapon wanted to turn back against its wielder.

Red stepped forward, well within reach of Endicott's sword point if he could regain control. But Endicott's eyes were elsewhere, in some private country of terror. Sweat beaded down his face and arm.

Another day, I would have given a lot to know what so frightened Endicott. But today, no feuds. I'd save Endicott, even at the cost of energy. *"Get out,* Endicott. Remember where you are." That was no idle threat: the House hungered for him too.

Red said, "He helps me."

With a grunt of effort, Endicott pointed the sword toward the ground. He looked at the door, at me, at the door again. "Two against one?" said Endicott.

"Then get some backup," I said. *Idiot.*

With a crack like a warning shot, an explosion of plaster burst over Endicott's head. "I'll be back," said Endicott. He ran, which was nice to see, though I couldn't blame him.

"He won't give us much time alone," said Red, "though I so enjoy seeing you struggle. If you've been saving something . . ."

Yes, this was what I had saved myself for. I was where I needed to be. I guarded the subbasement passage, but also stood near where the iron rod penetrated the soil, where the first libation of Morton blood had stained it. I was in the heart of the House.

I whirled my hand in a circle. *Move air.* Air rushed out in all directions. My enemy pointed his wand, and the sphere of air ignited around the figure, singeing the hair on my fingers.

I clenched my hand toward the wand. *Break wand.* A ping like a bell, and pain shot up my arm, driving back my hand.

One more shot of craft. *Short sharp shock.* The enemy's fingers twitched slightly. "Ah, that extra electrical activity is . . . refreshing."

That left physical combat. With no pause to telegraph my strikes, I hit my enemy's nerve plexuses with hard anatomical precision. But I was the only one who flinched at the pain, as if my flesh were striking the solid granite of a headstone.

I had not saved enough of myself for this unequal fight.

At the feet of the Red Death, the pieces of M squirmed together in ecstasy, as if they were trying to reassemble themselves. Winded, I asked, "Who are you?"

"Sorry," said Red. "I won't even let your ghost know that."

"Then tell me why," I said.

"It's nothing personal," said Red, "at least not this time. You and your kind are in the way. But I salute your stamina. You've cost me much more time and effort than any of the others. So far."

My enemy pointed his wand. "Still, I owe you something for your trouble." I felt a pressing weight on me, like boulders on Jupiter. "You may remember this from the Salem witch trials. The *peine forte et dure*. I'll be considerably quicker in applying the weight. You will kneel, then bow, then grovel, then die."

I gasped as another invisible weight was added. The Red Death tapped his wand in the air like a conductor. "Your lungs are surprisingly strong." He touched the wand to my left side, and pain shot through my ribs. He slashed the wand at my right side, and I felt hot blood spurt, then stream down. I fell to my knees.

"While you still have enough breath, any last words?"

I said, "You're a fool." My leaden fingers found my remote.

Red was incredulous. "For taking everything you have?"

I said, "You've left me my Morton dead."

"They can't hurt me," said the enemy.

"We just have to hold you." I pressed "13." *"Usher in the new age."*

Against the weight of worlds, I rose to my feet. No one was getting past me. The House would do the rest.

The House groaned, and fissured along its crack. And from behind me, all the Morton dead—Grandpa, the Left Hand, and even the thing that looked like an ape—rushed in and fell on the Red Death. With Samson's gambit, I was pulling down my family's shrine. This would be the fall of the House of Morton.

While most of the ancestors forced Red to re-create Leonardo's Vitruvian man, the Left-Hand Mortons pulled down at him through the floor. Auric energies peeled away as the enemy attempted to pull his limbs free. Spirits tugged at the mask in playful malice; but if it was a mask, it did not come loose. Others tugged at his robe, revealing elevator boots; my enemy was not above an intimidating parlor trick.

The Red Death bellowed and screamed with rage. "You can't kill me! I have seen it!"

"No one can see the heart of the House of Morton."

I stood straight now. I'd been driven back to the edge of the subbasement stairwell, but I had held the line. Red's struggle against the power of the House churned my insides in painful sympathy. I couldn't flee; I had to help keep my enemy fixed on the killing floor. It was worth my life to be certain that this Death died.

The zigzag fissure running from roof to subbasement rapidly widened, and along it the wall seemed to pour in on itself. A crack opened across the ceiling; more plaster fell on me and my enemy. From the other end of the House, collapsing walls blew a fierce whirlwind of sound and dust down the stairwell. Trophy stands and paintings fell from the walls; the cellar and the three floors above were buckling inwards. In another second, Red and I would both be done.

I laughed. Many old and beautiful things would be lost, but they were only things. No one else would die. Scherie saved, Endicott fled, and the Red Death screwed. "Almost worth it," I said. Grandpa, very substantial now, squeezed Red's throat and laughed too.

With a tumultuous shouting sound like a thousand rivers pouring into the abyss, the House of Morton fell.

PART IV

ON THE ROAD

Come witch, come wizard, come Indian powwow,
come devil himself.
—NATHANIEL HAWTHORNE

We had finally found the magic land at the
end of the road and we never dreamed the
extent of the magic.
—JACK KEROUAC

The office and dutie of the Powah is to be exercised
principally in calling upon the Devil, and curing
diseases of the sicke or wounded.
—EDWARD WINSLOW

TWELVE

In the moment the cellar collapsed, strong claws grabbed my shoulders and pulled me backward. I flailed and tumbled down the cruel iron stairs to the first landing. Bits of the house pursued me.

The stairway shook; it was coming unmoored and would soon topple.

Near my head, a bit of a keystone crashed. I grabbed it like a stone ax and stood up. I crouched in preparation for this new assailant descending the nearly ladderlike steps after me, knife glinting in her hand . . .

Her manicured hand. It was Scherie. She held the knife in front of her like she might sacrifice me to the chthonic gods of the Left-Hand Mortons.

"Why the hell did you throw me down?" I asked.

"No time," said Scherie. "Get moving, soldier. The car's waiting."

I moved. An empty mage, I could do nothing more. We descended the next two flights in a controlled fall. The subbasement corridor was still intact. I should have known; this had been the Left-Hand Mortons' final bunker. But cracks were forming, reaching out toward me.

We were three steps off the stairway when, in agony of twisted, screeching metal, it came folding down. Bits of metal flew past us like released springs and embedded in the stone, adding to the web of cracks.

Scherie helped me dash in a stumble down the corridor. The accelerating collapse behind us swallowed space and time in its maw of tumbling stone. Mummified bodies fell from hidden recesses and burst out with glowing gasses from the bricked-over rooms. I stopped, winded, and leaned against the wall before the stone stairs. All my desperate planning, and here I was getting Scherie killed anyway. "Why are you still here?"

"Move it!" Scherie growled.

At the bottom of the stairs, I slipped on the smooth marble floor; Scherie helped me up. The central chamber sprinkled an almost gentle-looking rain of small concrete bits. Any second, the dome would fail.

Stay here with us, said the Left Hand, attempting a seductive scream. I was very, very tired. I had no place to go.

"Goddamn it, move!" yelled Scherie.

The stone droplets became a painful shower, the smell of blood became the smell of rot. *You owe us flesh!* shrieked the Left Hand. I moved on all limbs like some half-formed primate up the stairs to the mausoleum.

With a deafening *boom,* the central dome failed. Waves of debris plumed up the stairway, filled with escaping evil craft that reached for me like a million small hands. The dust, the craft, faded. Spidery cracks were creeping about the Right-Hand vault. Whatever presence and strength had once filled this darkness was gone. We couldn't rest here either.

Through the still open door, we fled, appalled, from that chamber. The booming of the Morton home echoed after us. The storm was at its wild peak as we left the unkempt grounds for the nearest side street. Suddenly, the rain and wind ceased and a wild light shadowed us from behind. Still gripping the stone in my hand, I turned to see where the ghastly gleam came from. It was the full, setting, and blood-red moon, which now shone vividly through sullen and silent fragments of the House of Morton.

"How could you fuck things up so quickly?" said Scherie.

"You should see the other guy," I said, punchy with fatigue and a guilty, almost giddy joy that Scherie was still here with me. But at the side street, I froze. For the first time tonight, I was truly afraid. Across the road, blocks from where Roman had left it, was my new car. Scherie must have driven it here.

I said, "This is bad."

"Why?" said Scherie. "Because I'm not as stupid as you thought?"

"Because if you figured this out, they will too," I said.

"OK then," said Scherie. She tossed me the keys. "You drive."

I wanted to protest, but realized my objections would just waste time. There wasn't even time to split up effectively; both of us had to leave *now*.

I threw the keystone chunk into the backseat and turned the ignition. "Do you have your gun?" Scherie didn't reply, so I pulled out the cooled Colt and handed it to her. "You take this, and tuck it under your seat." She didn't argue.

The House was gone. Grandpa was gone, truly gone. I'd give that thought its full sorrow later.

I drove out at twenty-five miles per hour, not wanting to attract attention. Straight ahead, flashing lights sped down the road toward the estate. I turned left, away from my ruined home. I slowed the car to a jog. Hopeless. One hundred yards ahead, two government SUVs partially blocked the street, leaving one narrow lane of escape. Standing outside their cars and separated by screens of musclemen were Eddy and Endicott. They were shouting at each other again.

"Why are you here? What do you know?" yelled Endicott.

"Find some other road and hit it!" replied Eddy.

Eddy and the Peeps must have had a hunch I'd come this way, if I survived.

I thought of running, until two police cars peeled into a stop at the corner behind us, completely blocking the way back. No way but forward.

Any second, Eddy, Endicott, or their goons would look over, and their argument would end in a gun-pointing consensus. Perhaps I could distract them long enough for Scherie to get away. That still seemed more important than my own survival. My voice had a cold calm that almost frightened me. "Get ready to run."

"I'm not going anywhere."

Again, she had the advantage, because there was no time to argue. "Please be ready to hand the gun to me."

I accelerated back to normal speed. Twenty-five yards away, but Eddy and Endicott only had eyes for each other. They didn't look up.

"Say when," said Scherie.

"Steady," I said. I had my own hunch.

I steered the car into the path between them and their SUVs. Eddy and Endicott grew closer like a slow-motion continuous shot in a faraway movie.

Endicott looked the worse for wear, his army haircut like a powdered wig from the plaster, his suit decorated with long thin gashes and splinters. He'd found a gun, but also retained his sword.

The passing car did not interrupt their argument. Their shouting seemed muffled, like invisible insulation wrapped the car.

My hunch was right. We passed through.

"What's going on?" asked Scherie. "What did you do back there?"

"That wasn't me," I said. Scherie's implication pricked me, but I'd address that later. *You Ukrainian bastard.* Roman had given me a craft stealth car. Still, a good thing my pursuers had been arguing. Roman's craft probably wouldn't last another hour, but that would be enough.

I drove. The sirens stayed near the ruins of the estate, fading into the background. Scherie sat silent. Her wide eyes and clenched hands betrayed her growing fear. I felt suddenly sad. "I think I owe you a thank you. You saved my life."

Scherie didn't say anything, and I dropped the effort. Conventional communication wasn't my strong suit.

I drove on to I-95. The craft camouflage was perhaps too strong; other cars swerved at the last minute if they approached too fast. But at least the stealth allowed me to stick to the main roads. I'd ditch them for back ways when Roman's craft wore off.

The highway ahead moved like a fun-house roller coaster; I was exhausted. And in the rearview mirror, Sergeant Zanol lounged with a sleepy grin, head lolling back and dripping from a temple wound. "I've got a surprise for you," he said.

"I need to stop," I said. "You need to take the wheel."

"I don't think so," said Scherie.

"Hey, I'm gonna collapse here," I said. "I need—"

In one graceful movement, Scherie reached under the seat and pulled out the Colt. She pointed it at my head. "First, you fix me."

"What do you mean?" I said. "Please point that someplace else." The gun was one of my father's insurance policies. There was no craft safety in it.

"You know what I mean," she said.

"It's been a long day," I said, "and I've got no fucking clue."

"Goddamn you!" The gun shook with her anger. "I saw enough, heard enough, to know what you are, *jadugar*. I saw that ghoul. I heard you trying to compel it. Fix me, or I swear I'll kill you."

"We'll crash," I said.

She said, "Better that than to lose my soul."

"You think I've taken your soul?" I asked.

"What else would you call this?"

I moved my hand toward her, to touch her.

"Keep your hands on the fucking wheel," she snarled, "and tell me exactly what you've done to me. And if you lie once, I'll shoot you. Remember—you're a shitty liar."

"That's not true!" I said.

She spoke with slow emphasis. "I *know* you lied."

"Yes," I agreed, "but I'm not shitty. I'm an excellent liar. You shouldn't have been able to tell."

"I'm not stupid," she said.

"That's . . . not what I meant. I've only used persuasion on you to try to get you to leave quietly, and I clearly didn't use enough. I haven't used strong craft on you for anything else. Here, I'll prove it. *Give me the gun.*"

Shaking with furious resistance, Scherie handed me the gun. "You . . . bastard."

I felt dizzy. I didn't have the energy for these wizarding lessons. "That's what strong craft feels like. It's not all that subtle. Is that what you've been feeling?"

Her eyes narrowed with doubt. "You could have completely taken over my will."

"Sure," I agreed. "But that *would* make you stupid, a real space case. Everyone would notice, including whatever remained of your consciousness. You wouldn't be arranging rescue operations and ambushes."

Scherie shook her head. "You could be telling me anything, and I'd believe it."

"My family doesn't do that. We don't make slaves." That left out the Left Hand and their more nuanced possessions, but I didn't consider them family.

Scherie didn't look convinced.

Give her to us.

I sighed, and the car drifted out of the lane. "Shit!" I swerved back between the lines. "OK, I'm too tired to argue." I turned the handle of the gun toward Scherie and handed it back to her. "Just what did you think I was compelling you to do anyway?"

Oncoming headlights illuminated the tears on Scherie's cheeks. "Oh crap," I said. "Stupid question."

Scherie lowered the gun to wipe her eyes. We needed to change the subject. "Are you OK to drive now?"

"Yeah, sure, why not," said Scherie, hopelessly.

I looked in the rearview mirror, but Zee was gone.

We pulled over to the shoulder, way over to avoid being hit by the cars that wouldn't notice us until too late. Scherie got out and helped me over the shift into the passenger seat before walking around the car. Injured as I was, I didn't dare stop for long. "Drive with traffic, like nobody can see you," I said. "Go to the Merritt Parkway. Wake me then."

With clinical coldness, I gave myself a physical. I was beat up bad, as bad as ever. Some possible minor fractures, two cracked ribs. Losing blood. Even masked, this would call out to any pursuers. I tried some biofeedback and craft to staunch the blood loss, but I had too little concentration and energy to fully stop it. I drifted in and out of fugue land. The hallucinations of a craftsman were a Jungian minefield: frothing red grails of courage, wide-armed girls in gingham dresses baring their stigmata to the crossroads on open dusty plains. I felt a dangerous distance from my own body that made me want to laugh at my condition. A real mess.

I dropped out of my sanguinary vision; we were on the Merritt Parkway. The craft camo was still strong and hazardous, and we would go unnoticed for a while longer. Ahead was one of the parkway's little stone gas stations, as if for little colonial autos. My weakness spoke in text message bursts. "Stop here. Get me cleaned."

"Cleaned with what?" asked Scherie.

Good question. I hadn't thought to ask Roman for a medical kit. "We'll see."

She parked the car away from the pumps. "Pop the trunk," I said. *Cha-chunk*. "Check it. Please."

"You're not going anywhere," said Scherie.

"Do I look like I'm going anywhere?" I said.

Scherie opened the door and went back to the trunk. I saw Scherie's torso in the rearview; she stood motionless at the trunk for a long minute. Then she grabbed an old-fashioned doctor's bag and slammed the trunk shut. "I'm not opening that thing again. Something might blow up. There's an arsenal back there." Roman had packed well. That meant precog or plans within plans.

I took care of myself where I could, cleaning, stitching, and bandaging the cuts I could reach. Scherie helped with the cuts on my back. "Doesn't that hurt?" she asked.

"Goddamn it, yes," I said. "Just as intense as for anyone."

"There's drugs in the bag," she said.

"No," I insisted. "Gotta stay clear."

"Can't you just hocus-pocus yourself better?" she asked.

"I'm tapped out," I rasped. "Not one of my talents anyway."

After my patch job, we sat in silence for the length of a pop song, the dark trees standing like sentries around a gas station fort. "Where do we go now?" asked Scherie.

A lot was buried in that question. I assumed that whatever Scherie might have felt for me romantically was left back there in the rubble of the House, but that didn't change how I felt about her and her safety. Lighting out to the territories still seemed the best plan. I didn't know whether my enemy survived, in part because I still didn't know who my enemy was. But worst case, there would be a gap before the evil could triangulate on me again. Endicott's people would be stunned at the confusion of ruins; the Peepshow would have to be careful or Endicott would track their trackers. I had time to find craft ground on which to recharge my power. Before everyone knew I was alive, before they organized their searches, we could be long gone, different identities and across the border. Perhaps no one would even follow.

If Red survived, I would come back to fight another day. Scherie would be alive and free. All my instincts agreed that this was the right move.

"There's a traitor in the craft," I said. "And other American craftspeople will be hunting us. So I'll get you to Mexico."

"Mexico?" said Scherie. "You need a hospital."

"First you want to kill me, now I need a hospital?"

No, what I needed was a healer, for quick and full recovery. But the right healer was a long ways off. I wouldn't go to the Appalachian; hostiles would trail me to her Sanctuary and, whatever our compact said, she'd be as likely to kill me as help. I had to hold myself together, get farther away from Providence, and find craft ground. I didn't have enough skill for more than that (if even that). "Drive us toward Pennsylvania," I said. "I'll tell you where to go when we get to the state line."

"Tell me now," said Scherie.

"I don't know yet," I said. "Let me rest."

As I drifted out of consciousness, I heard Dad's cynical voice echoing in my skull. "I told you she would cause you trouble."

"Seems like she's saved my life," I murmured.

"I take the long view," said Dad.

Defeating discipline and exhaustion, pain woke me up. But a sense of deep relief competed with the pain. Against all odds and my own intention, I was still alive.

I closed my eyes again, and breathed yogically, and nudged at Roman's diminishing craft to keep us hidden from any farseeing trackers. But something further disturbed my alpha rhythms. I spoke low to Scherie, acting relaxed, trying not to clench my teeth. "So, like I was saying: you saved me back there. I owe you my life." I was truly grateful, though she had prevented me from confirming the demise of the Red Death. "But we should still split up." I imagined every eye on us at every gas station. "Together, we're too noticeable."

Scherie shook her head without moving her gaze from the road. "Bad play, Morton. You ever watch Bond films? You send me away, I'll get killed and be the sacrificial lamb."

"You live according to Bond films?" I asked.

"Only when it feels like I'm in one," said Scherie. "You've got a better suggestion?"

Again, I was too tired to argue. "You must have, um, some questions."

"In a Bond film, it would be better not to know," said Scherie.

"No," I said. "The sacrificial lamb doesn't know. The Bond girl knows everything." Damn, stupid thing to say. "As far as the government is concerned, you know too much already."

"OK," she said. "You can persuade people of your bullshit. You tried to do that with me."

"Right."

"And you can make people do something they don't want," she said, "like give you the gun."

"Sometimes." The Endicotts were always better at that.

"So," she said, "what else can you do?"

"I can amplify my fighting skill," I said, "and cause a little extra damage."

"So you're a good soldier," she said. "But it has to be more than that, or they wouldn't care so much."

"I can see the bad things people have done."

"You can read minds?" she asked, nervous again.

"Not really," I said. "It's more like reading someone's metaphysical rap sheet. I see they've done something bad, but have to guess who they did it to."

"Huh. But that's not why they want you," she said.

"Right," I said. "It's the weather. I can change it."

"The weather? Like global warming? My God."

"No, not climate," I said. "Just local, and just for a short time. Even that can take everything I have. But that limited control still matters a lot to the military."

"You can hide cars too," she noted.

"That wasn't me," I said. "I'm nowhere near that good at hiding."

"So, is that it?" she asked.

"Basically." They wanted me for my potential to make more Mortons, but that was too awkward a topic after this long day. "Others can do other things, but for me, that's all."

"You can't raise people from the dead?" she asked.

"No."

"Why not?" she asked. "The weather is so huge—one life is tiny."

"It doesn't work that way," I said. "Weather is about probability, and adjusting the chaos. But magic, my magic, never breaks the absolute biological limits. Bends, yes, but not breaks. I think there must be this much of a connection between craft and evolution. Nature and craft both profit from high turnover, and invulnerable immortals get in the way of that."

"But I saw those things," she insisted. "You raised a ghoul from the dead."

"You saw that much? Well, I didn't do that," I said. "And he wasn't resurrected. Just a meat puppet. Ghosts are usually more pleasant."

"Hey," she asked, "is it cold in here?"

Speak of the devil—Grandpa was in the backseat! "You're back!" I said.

"What?" said Scherie, startled.

Grandpa's hand rested on the keystone fragment, and I saw the answer. "I thought I'd lost you with House," I said. But some of the House was still with me.

"Who are you talking to?" asked Scherie, looking at the rearview mirror. "Oh God! What is he doing here?"

Scherie veered violently toward the shoulder, nearly colliding with a truck and an SUV.

"Scherie! It's OK! Please, keep driving."

She steered back into traffic, clutching the wheel in terror. "What the hell is going on?"

"Please, be calm. It scares them when we're nervous."
I was speaking too rapidly. "You saw him at the party.
I'm sorry I couldn't tell you who he was. Scherie, this is
Grandpa. Um, he's a ghost."

But Grandpa wasn't listening. He was staring at another
figure in the backseat who had just manifested to my view.
Oh-oh.

"Scherie, this other ghost is my father."

"Your father? Oh. Then I can't tell them to leave?"

"No, please don't." *Not that it would do any good.*

The two ghosts glared at each other with a lifetime of
anger, not even glancing at me. Then, they spoke over each
other, both asking, "What are you doing here?"

"Dale," said Grandpa, "tell this revenant to depart."

My father held up an open palm. "We're not on Morton
ground, Pops. You're in my territory now."

"Don't you dare speak to me that way," said Grandpa.
"You betrayed this family, the craft, everything—and look
at what it got you."

"Same thing we all get, in the end," said Dad.

"What a surprise," said Grandpa. "Self-pity."

"If only you had listened to me," said Dad. "But too late
to change your mind now, dead man." After Dad's death,
still-living Grandpa had told his ghost to stay out, out of
the house and out of our lives. Grandpa hadn't altered this
command before his own demise, and it was very hard for
the dead to change their minds or anything else.

But Grandpa didn't appreciate being reminded of his
limitations. He shouted, "You're leaving, now!"

"No time," I said. "You can resume your afterlife combat when this is done. This is family survival, so you will
stand down."

"Shit, we're nuts," said Scherie.

Grandpa's hand lashed out to smack Dad, and then they both went at it. They smashed each other out of shape, distorting the reality around them to a queasy extent. I swatted at both of them, but couldn't pacify their skirmish. "Stop it, both of you! You're embarrassing me!"

"Don't mind me," said Scherie.

Grandpa pulled his rifle from the air above Scherie's head. Dad drew the ghost of his Colt .45, and the living gun at Scherie's side quivered.

"Hey!" she said. "Can they shoot us?"

I didn't think the ghosts would actually wipe each other out of this plane; right now I didn't care. I reached for my inner West Point. "Dad! Grandpa! Sirs! I respect you both, but if you don't stop this brawl, I'll dispel you so thoroughly you won't come back in time for the next century."

Dad grinned ferally at me. "You think you're strong enough to take your old man?"

Grandpa gave Dad a last swat on the head. "Knock it off. Any other day, he could take you and me and the Left-Handed dead while filling out his taxes."

"There are Left-Hand ghosts?" asked Scherie.

"I apologize for our rudeness, ma'am," said Dad. "I'm Dale's father, Captain Morton. My, but as dooms go, you're a pretty one."

"Yes, very nice to finally meet you," said Grandpa, who then turned toward me. "A little exotic for my taste. Parents not born here. But she'll do."

Scherie scowled with outrage. "Look, ghost, I'm not interested in your opinion . . ."

"We're on a mission, not a honeymoon," I said.

"Honeymoon?" asked Scherie. She hadn't gotten what Grandpa meant.

"Nothing," I said. "I'm fading again. Go up to 84. Wake me up in Pennsylvania. We'll get off the freeway there."

THIRTEEN

At Matamoras, Pennsylvania, Scherie woke me from a doze of patchwork dreams. Like General Washington in retreat, we had crossed the Delaware. We left the freeway and drove through the Poconos, heading south and east. Some unlicensed station played a song by Guided by Voices. Barring a serious allocation of government resources, Roman's documents would break any conventional trail. But they wouldn't trail us conventionally.

The camouflage spell must have been flickering by now. The diminished traffic moved around us more smoothly.

My ancestors weren't fighting or even manifesting. "Can we talk to my grandmother now?" asked Scherie.

"Sorry," I said. "Maybe you can, if she shows up. For me, it's mostly Mortons. They're the ones who want to talk to me. Though for most of them, that's like saying your phone message wants to talk to you. The dead may not want anything. They're dead."

The night only felt forever; I needed to find our stop before dawn. Good craft sites dotted every state in the Union, but I didn't know the ones outside of Rhode Island. The back road route was slow; I needed a recharge fast.

Even spending my craft with brutal efficiency, the debts of magic demanded repayment.

The dark hills blurred; I was starting to nod again. I could force myself awake, but that would just burn my remaining energy all the quicker toward complete collapse. I might have to try to recharge on mundane ground. So be it. "We have to stop."

"What about there?" said Scherie.

I saw our destination: an intersection with an old beat-up "Crossroads Motel" that Norman Bates might have graduated to, not part of a chain, with plenty of vacancies. Its ghostly history was strong enough to see without effort. Before, it had been an inn, and before that, a fort, and before that, a tribal ceremonial clearing. Most would pass it by; it was exactly what I needed. On this craft ground, I could recharge.

Ignoring the ghost structures, I scoped out the present-day motel, a run-down monument to that brief time between highways and interstates, a destination for the few sportsmen and adulterers this remote area could support. Hunting and sex were craft-sensitive activities, and the remaining glow of this place was enough to give an edge to both. Three buildings with ranch-style rows of rooms boxed the parking lot, with an office at the far end of the right-hand row. In front of the left-hand building was a sports car. We drove past the car, a candy-apple red late-model Porsche, parked in front of room 128. Its quality raised suspicion, but no tracker could have anticipated us here. I could use it as a distraction. It would look very Morton to any pursuers.

We rang the bell at the desk. A large man woke, Tony Perkins's antithesis. "We'd like a room with twin beds,

please." The same room with two beds meant two different types of security: I could protect Scherie, and we could
avoid dealing with yesterday's relational fallout.

"Visa or—"

"I'll pay in cash," I said.

"I still need a deposit," said anti-Tony.

"I'll pay more cash," I said.

"Suit yourself," said the clerk. "Let's see. Room 108 is
a twin."

Good, that was across from the Porsche. But wait—it
had been a long time since I'd gone to ground in my own
country. Something I was forgetting, something important.
No, unimportant, yet very annoying. "The Gideons."

"What's that?" said anti-Tony.

"Do your rooms have Gideon Bibles in them?" I asked.

"Some of them. If it's missing, I can get one for your—"

"Not necessary," I said. "I'd prefer a room without a
Bible. It offends me."

"What's your problem with God's word? You some kind
of . . . oh, sorry, ma'am." Typical—the man tolerated hints
of criminality more than an irreligious fellow American.

"It's not the Bible," I said. "A Gideon once hurt my
grandmother." The lie came easily; it was nearly true.

"Oh. Well, you can—"

I drew out some more bills. "Could you just check
for me?"

"I can just check," whispered Scherie.

"No, dear, this nice gentleman will check for us," I said.
I gave her a military glare that even a civvy could trans-
late: *not another word, soldier.*

Anti-Tony walked outside. I held up my hand. "Nice
weather we're having," I said. We stayed silent. The clerk

returned. "No Bible, Koran, or Satanic ritual." He gave us the room key, then bent forward to fill in the ledger.

My pursuers might question this clerk, so I hit him with as much suggestion as I had left. *I think you misread it. We're staying in room 128. We're the couple in 128.*

"The couple in 128," repeated anti-Tony.

"We came in the bright red Porsche."

"Cool car," said anti-Tony.

The deception in place, I took the key for room 108. I continued to hide my limp until we were outside. "You need to lie down," said Scherie.

I held out the key to her. "I'll be there in a moment."

Scherie took the key, but didn't budge. "Suit yourself," I said. First I went to the trunk of the Chevy and put two automatic pistols and a case of ammunition into a small bag with the Colt we already had. Then I limped over toward the Porsche and looked around. The lights were off in 128 and all the other rooms. No one was watching except Scherie. I unzipped my fly, and pissed on the Porsche's rear tire. Scherie gasped, the urine splattered, and all else was quiet. There was the pinkish tinge of blood in my piss from the beating I'd taken, which was bad for me, but good for this deceptive marking.

Finished with my business, I limped back to Scherie. "What the hell?" she said.

"I don't like Porsches that aren't mine," I said. "Help me to our room. I'm going to collapse quicker than a French craftsman in a blitzkrieg."

Before collapsing, we loaded and prepared our weapons. For me, it was like old pencil sketches of Mortons on the raw frontier and the high plains, molding lead musket balls together by the fire. A comfortable domestic delusion, given what Scherie must have thought of me now.

"What's our route to Mexico?" asked Scherie.

"Ask me tomorrow." I thought I knew, but when I was exhausted I made decisions when needed, and not before.

"Why don't we just show and tell?" asked Scherie. "This isn't Colonial Williamsburg. You could go to the media. A couple tricks and they'd believe you. You'd be protected."

"No," I said. "That would break the fundamental deal between craft and country. We serve, the government protects, and we can live our own lives."

"You'd rather be dead?" she asked.

"If I break that deal, I might as well kill myself, and shoot a lot of other craftspeople besides."

"Oh."

"It's usually not bad like this. We live where we choose, go to school or get homeschooled, just like everyone else, marry who we want, have kids . . ." Damn, I must have been beyond exhausted to start this line of conversation. Maybe I was just mumbling at this point, because Scherie didn't look up from her gun to see my embarrassment.

We tucked our guns away for the night and fell back on our separate twin beds in our Gideon-less room, fully clothed. A long silence, then Scherie yawned. "I'm exhausted, but I can't sleep."

"Try counting breaths," I said. No time for pillow talk—I had to start healing.

"Why are you against the Bible?" she asked.

"I'm not against the Bible," I said. "I'm against Gideon

Bibles. The government can use them to track people, particularly craftsmen."

"That's insane," she said. "Not serious."

"Dead serious," I said. "The Bibles are magical trip wires, a surveillance net covering hotels and motels. No freedom of the road for craftsmen. If you aren't government craft, you're in trouble. I could cover the Bible in a craft-soaked cloth, but they're looking for me, so they might spot that."

"And it's the same if you ask someone to remove it for you?" she asked.

"Like a security camera going suddenly dark," I said. "They'd see it."

"Oh. I thought you just didn't like the Bible because it's against wi—" Scherie blushed. "It's against magic."

I chuckled, though it hurt to laugh. "You don't have to worry about the W-word, though I prefer 'craftsperson.' I enjoy the Bible; it has plenty of interesting things to teach about the craft. The Koran too. It's always there in the old sacred texts, hiding in the corners."

Scherie said, "I don't remember any . . ."

"How about the witch of Endor?" I asked.

"She doesn't count," she said. "She wasn't a real witch."

"That's not clear in the original," I said.

"You believe that story?" she asked.

"Maybe not the details," I said, "but yes, I believe it. It's one of the few stories in the Bible that every craftsperson believes."

"Why's that?" she asked.

"Because," I said, "it's a story where craft works."

Dreamless sleep beckoned. Only the force of long discipline impelled me to rudimentary self-healing. I couldn't wake up like this.

I initiated my repair through breathing exercises. This sputtering fount of craft wasn't like the House, where the air itself was supercharged with Morton life force. I'd have to delve deeper for power here. As I breathed from my belly, it felt like roots growing down from my spine, into the mattress and shooting through the legs of the bed, down through the floor and the walls, into the native soil, seeking magical sustenance.

This passive work wouldn't set off any Bibles in the nearby rooms. Our pursuers wouldn't detect it until we were long gone.

But even discipline couldn't keep me awake forever. Like falling into a well, I slept.

As Dale became quiet, Scherie still couldn't relax. She had seen ghosts and magic, but that wasn't what kept her awake. She was lying in the same room with a man with whom she'd been intimate, but about whom she knew less and less with certainty, including how she felt. A day ago, she had known her feelings with passionate exactness. Now, she only knew one thing for sure. Dale was hurt. A magus, yet he couldn't instantly heal himself. His injuries and pain alone would have made her too anxious to sleep.

She was only a normal person, but she could hope and pray. As a child, she had told her ghosts to leave, and they had. As sleep finally claimed her, she wished with all her heart that Dale's injuries would go away. *Yeah, injuries, get the fuck out of here.* Her heart glowed warm with the thought.

T he general had summoned Michael Endicott to his office at the point of the C-CRT triangle. It was as bare of family monuments as of sunlight. Instead, wall-to-wall screens acted as windows: some video, some comp-interactive, and one twenty-four-hour live feed from Chimera.

Endicott stood at attention, despite exhaustion that would have crippled another man. He was sick at heart, haunted by the mask of the Red Death. At the critical moment, he, a man who had faced death for years without flinching, had fled. He didn't know what he had feared; all he could remember was the mask, and the dread of what might be beneath it.

But if Endicott was hoping for a dressing down from his father, he was disappointed. The usually stony general paced, hands punctuating each sentence. "Morton sacrificed himself to let the Left Hand out! He gave them one of your men to possess, and someone else for an incarnation, maybe even of Roderick himself. But it doesn't matter which of them is embodied. They'll all be taking revenge, killing Family members wherever they can find them. Will the Families listen, will they cooperate on security? Feh."

"Sir," said Endicott. "I don't think Morton is dead. Or at least he made it out of the house alive. We found no, um, *recent* bodies. He may still be working with that thing."

"No corpus? Doesn't necessarily signify," said the general. "In these black transactions, mutually assured destruction happens. They devour their own. And the Peepshow can't see him."

Endicott shook his head. "We can't trust their intel, sir. The Peepshow's involved somehow. Sphinx was there."

"The Sphinx is dead," said the general. "Chimera is certain of that much."

As if aware of being invoked, the feed from Chimera chimed a mellifluous alarm. "Go ahead and look," said the general. "It's about your business, unless there's another high-priority screw-up in the craft world."

A lengthy text report headed "SPACTAD" appeared on the Chimera screen. The connection to the Mortons wasn't immediately obvious. A bunch of Bibles had gone off in an obscure corner of Pennsylvania.

"Unauthorized craft," said the general. "Looks like heavy-duty healing."

"He was beat up pretty bad," said Endicott.

Chimera's report leapt from the Bibles to Dale Morton without explanation of the connection. IF MORTON IS ALIVE AND LEFT ALONE, THERE IS A HIGH PROBABILITY THAT HE WILL LEAVE THE COUNTRY WITHOUT INCIDENT. SECOND HIGHEST PROBABILITY IS THAT HE WILL BE ARRESTED BY ROUTINE CRAFT SECURITY. THIRD HIGHEST PROBABILITY IS THAT HE WILL BE DEAD.

"Problem solved," said the general.

"But if he killed—"

"Problem solved," repeated the general.

"We haven't had a renegade of his power in a hundred years," said Endicott. "And that thing that's chasing him, that was like something out of the bad old days. We can't let them play hide-and-seek across the mundane country."

The general reflected only a moment. "Morton isn't the worst problem. That Left-Hand thing is. If it chases him for a while, that gives us more time. If it catches him, no great loss. You are ordered not to search for Dale Morton. Under any circumstances. Is that clear?"

"But we've got—"

"Is that clear?" repeated the general.

"Yessir."

"And see to your uniform, soldier. It's in disgraceful condition."

"Yessir."

"Joking, of course," said the general. "Seriously, let other people worry about Dale Morton. You've got real work to do." Someone knocked and an almost somnambulant young woman entered the general's office to fuss with the feed from Chimera. The older tech was probably still recovering from whatever Morton force had knocked him out in the van. "I want a briefing on how we're going to respond to the Left-Hand Morton threat, ASAP."

Endicott returned to his office and stared at his sword. His grandfather had told him that its greatest attribute was to cut through bullshit. Right now, he was knee deep in it, and rising. The advantage of coming from a self-righteous family was the long tradition of suspicion of others. The suspicion was often excessive (witness Salem), and too often justified.

What gnawed deepest at Endicott was Morton himself. Sphinx had given Morton the mission that, instead of killing him as Endicott's would have, had nearly destroyed his mind and irrevocably broken his career. Endicott's Prague mission, which would have been Morton's, had come from Chimera. Endicott couldn't see the score in this turf war between Sphinx and Chimera. Maybe Chimera had meant for Morton to go down fighting, but there would have been a reason. Not the mess they had now.

Was Dale driven by anger against the other Families? The Endicotts didn't talk to ancestors because it went against the Bible. If an Endicott ancestor approached Michael, he told it to get up or out. If the spirit persisted, it was probably diabolic. Michael didn't worry about whether the reasons for this doctrine were correct, because the results spoke for themselves. Endicotts lived in the present, not the past. Much of the darker past was just a sick joke to Michael. So Morton's rage about the past stunned Endicott. Morton hated him for being an Endicott. The problem with talking to supposed ancestors was that old wrongs were never forgotten.

So, Morton brutally murdered Hutch, turned Endicott's advance man into a zombie, directed that zombie to kill Sphinx, all in the name of centuries-old hatreds, and that was just prelude to a campaign of deceit and vengeance against all the Families. A tidy story—pity it didn't work, particularly the last bit. Endicott hadn't seen petty anger in Dale's last fight. The Mortons were great deceivers, but Endicott couldn't believe that he had mistaken the look in Dale's eyes. The man had been ready, willing, and almost relieved to die; if he was still alive, it was through no fault of his own.

Bottom line: whatever Dale Morton had in mind, even if it was self-sacrifice for guilt over Hutch, it was sincere.

What if someone in the chain of command—Chimera,

spiritual brass, even (God forbid) the general himself—
was playing Michael for their own agenda? No, not his
father, though that didn't mean the general was any more
free of manipulation. The uncompromising morality of
the Endicotts sometimes made them easy marks, but they
were Hell's own wrath when they found themselves played.

Endicott needed fewer variables and more answers. The
right person needed to pay for Hutch's death. He needed
Morton found and captured. If Morton was alive, that other
thing, that Red Death, wouldn't be far away. The Red
Death dressed like someone who would have gleefully
killed Hutch.

Endicott hesitated only for a ten-count, a family ritual
since Abram to take the emotion out of decision, to avoid
old John's excesses. On a crypto-and-craft secured line, he
called his Gideon trackers: Bumppo, Carson, and Sakakawea. They were on alert, fresh from finding some of
Hutch's bloody pieces hidden in the woods of Rock Creek
Park. Oh, they'd confirm the ID in the lab, but a Gideon's
nose was hard to fool.

The general's orders were precise, but so was Endicott's
authority. "You are to find Scherezade Rezvani," said
Endicott. "Her last location was in Pennsylvania; I'm
transmitting the GPS now. You will monitor for any signs
of unauthorized craft activity in her vicinity. In fact, you
may be able to find her through unauthorized craft activity. You will arrest any practitioner of unauthorized craft
and you will bring them to me. The practitioner may be
extremely skilled, magus level. But you will capture him
alive, even at risk to yourselves."

"Yessir," barked the Gideons on speakerphone. Then
Sakakawea said, "Sir, how old is this intel?"

"Within the quarter hour."

"We're at McGuire Air Force Base, sir. We could take them this morning."

"Outstanding," said Endicott. Even in a world of manifest spiritual power, this sort of uncanniness impressed him. "If you hustle, you can be there at dawn. Go."

CHAPTER

FOURTEEN

I sat up quick like a vampire, feeling good. Very good. Too good. I'd gotten the shit kicked out of me; I shouldn't be going anywhere. The room was full of the dull glow of fading craft, a cosmic background radiation beeping its signal to anyone with the sense to look. The Bibles must be ringing out of their drawers throughout the hotel.

My wounds still felt stiff and sore. The craftwork had been too general to fully heal these specific hurts, yet too powerful to be ignored. The craftsman had probably worked from a distance, and didn't want me truly healed, just marked for the hunt.

I whispered into Scherie's ear. "Get up. We're leaving."

Scherie opened her eyes on darkness. "Five a.m. reveille?"

"Quiet," I said. "No lights. We've been made." I allowed myself the luxury of a doubt: perhaps she had not betrayed me to this bad Samaritan craftsman.

Scherie moved slowly. Events seemed to have caught up with her. I tried to calculate where my pursuers were, but there were too many variables: the time of the healing, the availability of backup to the individual who had painted me with craft sonar. Assuming the worst, we should already be dead. Most likely they had the motel staked out. If the one craftsman had found me, my ruse with the front desk wouldn't delay the Gideon hounds. When they were confident of the ground, when they had claimed their territory with sigils and holy piss, they would break in on us. There would be three of them; against a craftsman, trackers always went in threes.

With unprofessional abandon, I peeked through the shade. In the dawn light, my car was just a hunk of mundane metal, plainly visible to all. Roman's craft was all but gone. But that also meant that the car would draw no particular attention.

Bumppo with his curly golden hair stood next to the rear of the Porsche in front of room 128, speaking on his cell phone, looking about the motel, unhappy and concerned despite the professional poker face. Like a hound, he sniffed the air, and bared his teeth. The Porsche had served as bait, just as I had hoped.

Whoever had healed me hadn't spoken to these trackers. The eventual result would be the same, however: the healing craft was a telltale of my survival. My luck had been that these Gideons were lazy, relying on a mundane witness and whiff of power instead of their deeper craft.

Bald Carson hauled bodies wrapped in blankets into the trunk of the Gideons' black sedan. They had killed the people in 128 before they'd realized their mistake. Two civilians. I felt the pain, and then the anger. I had miscalculated the rules of engagement, and two innocents had paid for it. Whatever had happened there couldn't have been a real fight. These trackers had come for an execution.

Where was the third, Sakakawea? Perhaps questioning the clerk with more thoroughness. Perhaps they had been in a hurry, and only two had come. Wishful thinking. I couldn't appear in the sights of all three at once. At best, one at a time. Maybe I could handle two. Three would get me.

"You need rest, a hospital," whispered Scherie.

"I'll be in the morgue if we don't move." I nodded at Scherie's automatic. "You ready to use that thing?"

She nodded back.

"Good," I said. "Take cover behind the bed. I'm going to open that door and dash toward reception. That's going to draw them and their fire." Scherie started to protest, but I held up a finger. "I need you to count a slow twenty, then come out. Use the car for cover. You should hit them right on their rear flank. Ready?"

I hoped she wasn't. I hoped she'd hesitate and be captured alive.

Outside, Carson had forced the bodies into the trunk with practiced ungentleness. Finished with packing, he started toward reception, but Bumppo held up an arm to gesture him to stop. He'd caught some scent. Carson joined in the sniffing.

It was now or nice funeral.

With a gun in each hand and a bit of craft speed, I flung open the door and sprinted for daylight. Shooting down would be easier. *Up,* I thought. I leapt into the air, Peter Pan with no faith, guns blazing.

Oh, I presented such a nice target. But they shot with their silencers first, which fucked nicely with their aim. Before they could bring their craft to bear on me, I hit Carson with a gut shot. He staggered behind the cover of the

Porsche, fully occupied with his own bleeding as I came back to earth. Five seconds.

Bumppo was faster. *"Heavy,"* he said. My legs went to slow-motion lead. *Snap!* His bullet made a hard ugly slap into my left shoulder. I fell forward, and the gun in my left hand went skittering along the sidewalk. I struggled to bring around my right arm with my remaining weapon, the Colt. *"That gun is too heavy,"* said Bumppo. And it was. I panted, *"Up, up, up,"* but I couldn't move the gun. No craft left.

For the second time in twelve hours, I fell into the fascination of crippled prey. Bumppo came forward like a pale rider of the apocalypse, in no hurry for the end. Too slow, too close to room 108. If Scherie came out on twenty, he'd still catch her in his peripheral vision. "Dale Morton, I presume?" he said. Twenty. "I thought you should know. An Endicott ordered your death."

He held the gun just feet from my face. No sign of Scherie. Good. She might live. Then Bumppo's head twitched over in response to movement in my room. Scherie stood in the doorway, gun ready. *Freeze, freeze, freeze,* I thought, desperately seeking some last edge over the Gideon, but finding nothing left in myself to give. I was dead. Scherie was dead.

Bumppo didn't freeze. But he was very, very slow. He took a full count to bring his gun around to meet the new threat. Way fucking too long.

Scherie didn't go for the high probability gut or chest. She caught Bumppo's golden head as it whipped about toward her. She caught him right between the eyes, and blew out the back of his tow-headed skull.

Even as Bumppo fell and the report of her head shot

faded, Scherie ran over to me. Her hands were on me; I felt their slight tremble. "How bad?"

"Bad enough," I said. The morning's supercharge of vitality was keeping me alive and coherent. I felt a cage of energy around the bullet in my shoulder, keeping the damage contained. It wouldn't last. "I'll hold together, and I know where to go."

"I'll get the bag," said Scherie.

"No, don't treat this yet," I said. Sakakawea would be near. "Help me up. We need to get out of here before anyone else shows up."

"OK. One second." She went over to the dead Gideon and shoved her hands into his pockets.

"I wouldn't (pant) do that."

"Just want to check something." She pulled out the Gideon's cell phone. I smiled and shook my head.

"What?" asked Scherie.

"Later. Get us out of here first."

She helped me up and poured me into the Malibu's passenger seat. Damn thing was soaking up a lot of Morton blood. She squealed out of the parking lot. Steering one-handed, she flipped open the cell phone.

"That's dangerous," I said.

"Driving is the least of my worries . . . shit!" She dropped the phone between our seats. "That fucking hurt."

"Craft protected," I said. I fished it up, and tossed it out the window. "Also, a good tracking device."

"Oh," said Scherie. "Sorry, I should know that."

"No harm. They'll be able to track us anyway, but why make it easier for them. Anyway, I already know who he was calling." Endicott. Or was it? I had lied in a similar vein to M before killing him. Wheels inside wheels.

"Where are we going?" asked Scherie.

"No choice now," I said.

"Just tell me."

"I can't." She looked angry and dubious. "For real this time. If I talk about it, it makes it too definite, and ruins it. I just have to show you."

"Rough idea?"

"South and west. Into the mountains. From which cometh my aid." Very dubious aid. We'd go see the Appalachian.

As Morton and Rezvani left the motel lot, they didn't notice the light of a cigarette in a room that wasn't 128, or 108, but 118. Through the room's window, Sakakawea watched the Chevy Malibu peel out. She could let it get a head start; she had seen the car, and that was all the LoJack she needed.

She stepped outside and lightly strode toward the Porsche. She ignored dead Bumppo; survivors were her concern. She heard Carson groaning behind the Porsche; she heard police sirens in the distance, their Dopplered rising pitch closing in with mathematical precision.

She stood over Carson. There was much messy blood, but no immediately fatal damage. "He got you both."

Carson looked up at her. "No, something else . . ."

Sakakawea wasn't interested in excuses or Morton's companion. But Carson thought he wasn't finished. "Call 911."

Tut, tut. He should know better. She couldn't take him along and couldn't let the local authorities have him. That left only one option.

She shot Carson. The bullet's trajectory through his

cortex would cut off his consciousness very efficiently—
she was an artist. Then she trotted for her motorcycle in
the alley area behind the southern building. *All working
out quite well.* She relaxed and let her craft guide her
steering. She needed to make two calls. First, a report to
Endicott, perhaps the last she'd bother with.

The second call would wait; unlike young Endicott, her
real boss was very, very patient.

E ndicott answered the phone. It was Sakakawea. He
  could use some good news.

He didn't get it. "Two trackers KIA in Pennsylvania.
Need cleanup." She gave him the GPS coordinates.

Shit, there'd be hell to pay. "KIA? How?"

"Target's companion took them out," she said. "It was
Dale Morton, sir."

Endicott chose not to acknowledge this fact. "Where is
the target now?"

"I'm in pursuit." The signal broke up. ". . . moving north
by northwest. They may be going for Canada."

"I'll call in the cleanup. You continue to pursue, but do
not engage. Keep me updated on target's location." He
couldn't let a Morton get across the border. "Understood?"

More signal breakup. "I repeat: communication may be
difficult."

"Take necessary measures to keep me informed. That's
a priority."

He called the cleanup operation. Local law enforcement
and media would be brought into line. Nothing he need
concern himself with.

Except that this didn't feel right. Hutch had asked questions about his Gideons before she had disappeared. Now he felt pressure not to be concerned. With Endicotts and pressure, better to give than to receive. He'd go there himself.

T wo hours later, Endicott was at the Crossroads Motel. Bumppo's and Carson's bodies were bagged and in the ambulance. He wasn't craft forensics; the people for that job were in the bags, or in pursuit. But this was conventional ballistics and physics, so he asked the mundane local to show him what had happened.

"I was told not to ask too many questions," said the local.

"That's right," said Endicott. "Just answers will do."

The local showed him where they had found the trackers and their blood splatters, and gave a guess to what the shooter had done. Endicott thought this was an easy story: Morton got the drop on Bumppo as he walked toward registration. Then, he used some craft to get a high gut shot off on Carson. He took his time, perhaps got ready to leave, before finishing Carson off with the head shot.

"That all?" asked Endicott.

"That's all," said the local. "There are some details, but we can sort those out later. We've got this under control."

"Tell me about the details," said Endicott.

The local fidgeted a bit. "Well, just for accounting purposes, we've recovered bullets that appear to have been fired from the victims' guns. That leaves the bullets that shot the victims. By caliber and type of ammunition, those appear to have come from three different weapons."

"OK," said Endicott. "Maybe he had help." It would be

like Morton to play action hero with two guns, and his girl-friend could handle the third gun, though the gunfight story became a little harder to imagine. "What else?"

"They were playing musical rooms. When the shooting started, the shooter was on the other side of the motel from where he was supposedly staying."

"Where was that?"

The local pointed. "Near room 128." The door was still ajar. "The lock's broken, but nobody home. Looks like the beds have been stripped."

"Shit," said Endicott. His easy story was melting away. *Something fubar this way comes.* Near the room and the trackers' black sedan was a fancy Porsche. More cars than drivers. "What about the cars? Anyone check those?"

"We were going to take the sedan off-site."

"Right. Get me something to force the trunks." But Endicott didn't wait. He walked over to the cars. The black sedan was unlocked with the keys in the ignition. He popped the trunk, and went around the car. Bodies. Two men.

He slammed the trunk shut. The Gideons hadn't even looked before shooting. Why were there bodies at all? His orders had been clear. No killing.

Furious, he flipped open the phone to call Sakakawea. He got a Pentagon voice-mail box. He'd leave her a message she wouldn't forget. He'd . . .

Do no such thing. Perhaps Sakakawea just had a reason for vengeance not in her skimpy file. Perhaps, just per-haps, Hutch had been right, and there were nonlies bur-ied in Morton's story. Either way, nothing Sakakawea said was likely to be true.

The bullshit was up to his waist now, if not higher. His

one edge was that no one knew how much he knew. Until he knew more, it would have to stay that way. He trusted the general, but his father told everything to the great and powerful and mysterious Chimera, and that made Endicott itchy.

"Get both these cars off-site," he told the local. "Follow the usual protocols with what you find in the trunk."

"Yes, sir."

Endicott stared at the gray horizon. He read the craft signature of this land loud and clear. Here, they'd blame any civilian deaths on hunting or sex. What would they blame his own sudden demise on? Oh, the difficulties of an upright life.

Perhaps he'd call in for sick leave. This was going to take a while. Investigating Chimera was at best a route to a swift discharge. So Endicott would take the other insubordinate path, and hunt for Morton himself. That would mean hunting the Red Death thing too. Endicott knew the quickest way to find them both. Though Sakakawea had no doubt lied to him about her direction, Endicott had other ways to follow her. He would track the tracker.

My body had gone one step forward and a Texas two-step back. My shoulder was a playground for all the expected pain but surprisingly little blood, thanks to my surfeit of healing craft. I could feel all that energy burning off. Before my craft tank was empty, I needed a healer for serious regeneration. Regeneration, and another craft service that one healer in particular could provide.

The Appalachian of the Sanctuary. It would take all my concentration simply to get there, particularly if the Sanctuary and its guardian didn't want me to show, which was likely. Hell, the Appalachian could be running this healing shell game.

If not the Appalachian, who was my guardian avenging angel? Why help me only to send a signal and get me killed? It had the marks of oracular craft scheming. If she weren't dead, I'd blame Sphinx. *Sphinx, are you there? Hutch, where are you?* No answer. Instead, Grandpa and Dad were vividly manifest in the backseat, glaring at each other.

"Where do I go?" asked Scherie, snapping me back into the painful present.

"Are you OK?" I asked. Her aura was spiky with fading adrenaline.

"About killing that bastard who shot you?" asked Scherie. "Maybe I'll feel bad later. But not now. So where do I go?"

No more leisurely strolling to the border. "Head toward West Virginia," I said. The specific route didn't matter. All roads led to the Sanctuary, if you already knew the way.

"I won't allow this," said Grandpa, nearly shouting, causing Scherie to veer. "You're not to go to the Appalachian."

"I agree," said Dad, to my and Grandpa's surprise. "Go anyplace else. Get another healer."

"A Gideon is still trailing me," I said. "Sakakawea will see where I've run, call in support, and get me. I need to get somewhere safe."

"No matter what the cost to you and that place," said Dad.

"You're both sounding unusually loud and close to me, Dad," I said. Dad was silent at this intimation of mortality. He couldn't argue against the cold equations: the clock was running down for my healing.

"Can this wait until later?" asked Scherie. "It makes me nervous while I'm driving."

"Soon," I said. "I need some answers." Sphinx had left me with one word. "What's Chimera?"

"Chimera?" said Grandpa. "When I was young, Chimera was the name for craft code-breaking. There's always been a bit of that, though the Brits were better at it in the old days."

"Names like 'Magic' and 'Enigma' weren't an accident," said Dad.

I knew about how craft was used in code-breaking, even some of the history, but I hadn't heard the Chimera cryptonym before. "Why would code-breakers want to kill me?" I said.

"Sphinx didn't do that sort of work," added Grandpa.

"I'm not blaming Sphinx anymore," I said.

"Maybe you should," said Dad.

"If you've got something to say, then just say it," said Grandpa.

"Grandpa. Dad." I had their attention again. "The brass thinks this is living Left-Hand Morton shit. But we killed all those inbreds, right?" Though he wouldn't know first-hand, Grandpa wasn't far removed from Joshua in the game of telephone with Family spirits that led all the way back to Thomas Morton.

"Bodies?" said Grandpa. "You want a body count? You're worse than my superiors in 'Nam, telling us to extrapolate from scattered and burnt limbs. Joshua wrote it all down. Leaving aside the bodies he hacked himself, there were more parts than Mortons, all full of Left-Hand craft."

"Not all Left-Hand," noted Dad. "An insane Endicott was there with his sword. Not very discriminating."

"Not that IDs would have mattered," said Grandpa. "The whole point of the Left-Hand endeavor was survival in any form."

"OK. So could a Left Hander have survived, had kids, restarted the family line?"

Dad shook his head. "If there were Left-Hand Mortons out there breeding, I think we would have known. But anyone can go Left-Hand, son."

"Dale," said Scherie, "you really should rest."

She was right. I'd need my strength to reach the Sanctuary, and to enter it.

We drove into Appalachia. Written directions would be meaningless; as they say in the country, "you can't get there from here." A winding nameless road went up, down, up again. A growing mist obscured scenic vistas of exposed rock, wind-twisted trees, and deserted farmland. The road narrowed, speed slowed, the clock nearly stopped. Finally, our path dead-ended at a river precipice, with thick trees and brush all around.

"Fuck!" Scherie slammed her fists against the dash. Her eyes avoided me, staring ahead in resigned horror. "What now?"

I saw the way. "Straight ahead."

"Dale, there's just cliff."

I chuckled. "I'm magic, remember?"

"This is different," she said. "This is physics."

"It's hidden, like the car was. But it's not far. If you want to get out of the car and follow on foot, that's fine."

Scherie swallowed. "No. I can do this."

"Close your eyes, if that helps," I said.

"No, that'd be crazy. Nice knowing you."

She drove forward at a crawl. Just where the tires should have hit the drop-off and begun their plunge toward the rocks, we felt a startling bump, and the rolling thud of wood beneath our wheels. A boundary of sensation, as uncertain as Heisenberg's A-bomb plans, swept over us. It felt like passing through *A Grunt's Guide to Bad Weather*—Valley Forge and Guadalcanal, Tunisian desert and South Carolina swamp—into a place that was always the Appalachian's spring.

On the other side, we could both see what we had passed over: an old wooden covered bridge. We drove through the brush, which opened up into a rolling valley, a grassland spotted with conifer and deciduous woods. To our immediate left grew a patch of unseasonably ripe pumpkins, open to the picking, carving, and tossing. "Go left, just a few feet," I said. "Good. Stop here." Ghostly cars flickered: Edsels, DeLoreans, and a Tucker. I had forgotten that this was also the land of failures.

"This place doesn't like cars," I said, "except in this little corner. You'll need to help me walk the rest of the way."

"At the risk of repeating myself, there's nothing here."

"Everything's here," I said. "Nothing is lost."

Inflicting agony and awkwardness, Scherie helped me out of the car and onto my feet. We walked on without supplies or weapons. Every few yards seemed to have a different climate. In one damp zone, a large bird flew right in front of our faces. "What the hell was that?" said Scherie.

"An ivory-billed woodpecker," I said.

"Aren't they extinct?"

"Soon enough will be."

The farther we walked, the more the seemingly clear land revealed fuzzy details that resolved into structures. Ahead were small log cabins, sheltered by enormous oaks, maples, and chestnuts of virginal forest. All the trees were great, old, and healthy.

"Is this some kind of park?" asked Scherie.

"A park would have to be mapped and known," I said. "Oh, oh. Here she comes. Let me do the talking, OK?"

A small woman strode purposefully toward us. She wore a homemade straw hat and homespun clothes, a corn-cob pipe in her mouth. In each generation, an odd craft loner found her or his way to the job of guardian of the Sanctuary, and the Appalachian had been more odd and loner than most. Without breaking her stride, she took out the pipe and put her other hand round her mouth. "Congratulations, Dale. In most universes you're already dead. Now you can turn around and git the hell out."

"Someone's trying to kill me and the Families," I said.

"I know," said the Appalachian.

"That's it?" I said. " 'I know'?"

"I don't give a spit," said the Appalachian, spitting. "When have the Families cared for this place? I don't, we don't, want you here."

"Fine," I said. "Let's make it formal. I, Dale Morton, heir of Thomas Morton, claim the right of sanctuary under the compact. Do I need to remind you further?"

The Appalachian came to a stop right in front of us. Her shirt and pants were covered with patches: IWW, WPA, 54th Massachusetts. She shook her head. "We ain't forgot. Thomas Morton tried to do things different, a union of the peoples through the craft. If he'd succeeded, would've been no King Philip's War. Much would've not been lost. You'll have sanctuary." She pointed her pipe at Scherie. "And her?"

"She's my guest," I said.

The Appalachian laughed. "Our compact says squat about guests."

My hands felt blasphemous and murderous. I'd get in her face and teach her about guests, I'd . . .

"Keep your pants on, Capt'n. Let me git a look at her."

The Appalachian put her pipe back in her mouth and peered closer at Scherie. She bent down to look at Scherie's legs like she was buying a horse. Her eyebrow twitched. "In-te-resting. I'll let her in."

I felt my knees shaking under me. Scherie got under my good arm again. "He needs a doctor, or healer, or whatever you call it."

"Healer will do," said the Appalachian. "Let's git him to my cabin, dear. I'll make us some herb tea, and we'll have a nice healing."

I faded out for a moment. When I came to, I was looking up at a wooden ceiling, sprawled out on a table.

"So you see," said the Appalachian, mid-conversation, "until now, the bullet's damage has been held in a capsule of craft. But that's giving way."

"You're going to magic out the bullet?" asked Scherie.

"Not exactly." The Appalachian pulled out a tray of medical implements that were state of the art in 1789.

"Oh, come on!" said Scherie. "This has got to be a bad idea."

"I'm working to rule," said the Appalachian, pointing to her IWW patch with a particularly nasty iron probe.

"I'm getting the doctor's bag," said Scherie.

"Leave it," I croaked. "She knows what she's doing."

I skimmed within and outside my ameliorative trauma, above and below consciousness. The Appalachian chewed a cud of tobacco (more craft bravado in the face of statistics) and flourished a terebellum with a bullet screwed onto the end. She spat, and the tobacco juice pinged against metal below her.

Scherie traced a finger along an unvarnished shelf, then held up a round bit of dull metal. She frowned at Howdy Doody's beatific smile on the button, and bent down near my ear. "I'm going to get our weapons."

In the late afternoon, I felt whole but tired. I sat on the porch with Scherie, staring out at the Appalachian's camp.

A hundred yards away was the half-boarded entrance to an old coal mine shaft. Abandoned, the mine and its tailings should have poisoned the surrounding water and soil for generations. Instead, it had returned to nature with a vengeance. Large round trees had grown up around the pit entrance and over where the galleries likely ran. A craftsman could do serious work within such wounds in the earth.

In this place of lost things, many ghosts walked to and fro, flickering in and out of view. Some may have found their way to the valley in life: an occasional folklorist, an old WPA worker, a melody-hunting musician. Others had marched farther than the living—soldiers in faded blue and gray and khaki. And there were civilian ghosts without craft families, ghosts with no one else to talk to, who would not, could not fade yet.

Scherie gasped as one spirit vanished. "It's real," she said. She clutched at my arm.

"What do you mean?" I said.

"It was like playacting before, in the car, but now, with so many . . ."

"They won't hurt you," I said.

"Are you sure?" After all we had been through, her fear of these spirits surprised me.

"Absolutely," I said.

"OK." She let go of my arm and gripped my hand instead. "It's very beautiful. Very sad."

The shadows lengthened; the number of spirits abruptly increased. "What's going on?" asked Scherie.

I didn't answer. The Appalachian stepped out of the cabin. "I suppose you should see this."

We walked out beyond the coal mine copse and into a long clearing of tall grass between two low rises, each with trees at their crests and beyond, standing as if in reserve. All around us, the dead stepped out of the void by the hundreds, flowing to the left and right of their living audience, avoiding us with the glass-eyed skittishness of herd creatures.

"Is this a meet and greet?" asked Scherie.

"What's that you say?" said the Appalachian, yawning and scratching her braless chest as she followed Scherie's gaze. "Oh, this is just the evening show."

"It's more than that," I said.

"OK, Mr. West Point, what do you call it?" said the Appalachian.

I nodded toward Dad and Grandpa, who were walking quickly toward their dead fellows, fading a bit from my view into their world. "My dad called it the American Elysium, the United States of Valhalla."

The Appalachian snorted. "It's not all that. Like any American apotheosis, it's not as pretty as it sounds."

"But they look so, so . . ." Scherie stopped with a realization. "Hey, they're taking sides."

"Damned straight," said the Appalachian. The dead had formed up into opposing lines, and were organizing into regiments.

"But they're dead," said Scherie.

The Appalachian ignored the non sequitur. "All of 'em are craft dead, the practitioners and the forgotten of America's many craft battles. The sides they take have many names."

"It's free union versus oppression and dissolution," I said.

"That sounds serious, for dead people," said Scherie.

"It ain't so simple," said the Appalachian. "Watch long enough, you'll see. Freed from chains of time and place, they switch sides. Some Rebel uniforms fight for free union, some Yankees fight against."

"There's right and wrong, good and evil," I said.

"Not so clear here," said the Appalachian. "Old left and right have slim meaning to the dead; Commies and Fascists sometimes fancy a big country and sometimes don't. New dead arrive, maybe bringing new ideas and causes." The Appalachian lowered her voice. "Field of fucking dreams this ain't. Many on both sides hate this place."

I viewed the ground with new appreciation. In this pastiche Valhalla, tokens of Civil War battlegrounds dotted the landscape, reminders in miniature of their bloody originals. I pointed out details to my companions. "That cornfield came from Antietam, that wheatfield from Gettysburg." With a boyish glee I took in the inevitable low stone walls, the wooden fences, even a bit of sunken road, and a hodgepodge of more generic features from battlefields lost to development. Things lost, now found. But for the most part, these were just decorative reminders in a cleared arena. These soldiers had dealt with enough obstructions in life. Here, very little would keep them apart.

I nearly cried out as the matrilineal Hutchinsons paraded forward at the front of a squad of women in the drag of various wars—Revolutionary long coats, Union caps. In the old days, a little craft and a stuffed crotch could deceive anyone who needed to be deceived. But my Colonel Hutchinson wasn't with them.

The Endicott ancestors on both sides kept apart and aloof with spotless spectral uniforms and martinets' discipline. Old John walked between the forces, lining up the opposing Endicotts with his extended sword. They were legion, many more than all the living and dead Mortons, and too many on the dissolution side. Not the united front their living reps presented today. That gave me a feeling besides schadenfreude that I couldn't quite grasp.

The air tasted bitter as I saw the jungle and desert camo of recent recruits, men and women with whom I had fought: Newsome, Eichorn, Strong, Martinez, Brown. On the side of the dissolution regiments, Sergeant Zanol stood in a relaxed posture I hadn't seen in life: the stance of an officer. *I put him there.*

Last came the orthodox Mortons, with Joshua at their head. He had moved up in rank to something like a corps commander in this dead free union army. The officer's sword at his side gave him the disturbing aspect of an Endicott. Dad and Grandpa lined up behind him, not bothering with each other anymore. Hand over dead eyes, Joshua peered out from the tree-lined rise toward the horizon for someone on the other side, not there.

Whatever their history in life, all the Mortons were on the free union side tonight, even Joshua's gray-clad brother Jeb.

Scherie pointed out to the horizon. "Look!" Beyond the

far flank, too far to recognize their individual faces and many tribes, dusty and stoic Native Americans sat on their hard-ridden, stoic horses. Here, they could finally avoid fighting in the white men's quarrels.

Some of the native horsemen were obscured by the opposing lines. The dead had enough substance here that, strain as I might, I couldn't see through them. I stretched my hand out to feel the air; I stepped closer.

The surprisingly strong hand of the Appalachian gripped my arm. "Where do you think you're going?" Her casual, bored demeanor was off like a cheap mask.

"Just wanted a closer look," I said.

The Appalachian shook her head. "No trespass in the battle royal."

"Come on," I said, affecting a devil-may-care tone that I doubted even as I spoke. "What harm could we do?"

"They never break," said the Appalachian, gripping my arm tighter. "I've watched them fight many, many times. Every night, the forces of free union hold the line. They may win the day, they may lose, and they always git pretty beat up. But they never break."

"And if they do?" asked Scherie.

"Then these United States cease to be united," said the Appalachian, taking a swig from her flask. "The nation dies."

"Even if this reflects the real world, it can't be causal," I said.

"How long do you think a country can survive without a soul?" asked the Appalachian.

"I hate allegory," I said.

"'Craft doesn't need metaphor,' the motto of your house," said the Appalachian. She spat. "This is no damned alley-gory. Some days it's straight from the headlines, but some days it's ahead of them." She spat again. "And they know what's at stake. Before my shift, during World War Two, these dead folks got really, really quiet, like dead folks should. I guess even our fascist secessionists don't think much of foreign occupation. If they do, they must haint overseas."

Both armies had settled, waiting for some silent order to advance. "Are we safe here?" asked Scherie, the fear in her voice again. A story in that fear that I needed to know.

"They won't pay no nevermind to us," said the Appalachian, "as long as we don't git in the way. They don't even talk, that you can see or hear."

Spectral swords flashed in the fading light, a diachronic hedgehog of weapons swung forward in a charge. Joshua led from the front, cajoling with gestures. They moved in close formation, more like Civil War reenactors than any firefight I had seen. Their uniforms were anything but united, and the line carried almost as many unit colors as soldiers, names and eagles and mottoes all faded. Some had fought in foreign wars, some in domestic wars never declared. The Lincoln Brigade, reinforced by anachronistic writers from before and after the Spanish Civil War, faced off against the Pinkertons, similarly reinforced.

A flash of ectoplasmic fire, and big chunks of each side fell. Some souls vanished. "Where do they go?" asked Scherie.

"Don't know," said the Appalachian, looking at Scherie with renewed interest. "Most times they come back. Otherwise? Maybe they graduate to a gentler Elysium. Maybe they're finally worn out, killed too many times."

Some trampy-looking fellas in doughboy shirts or caps threw Molotov cocktails, which burst in gray and white flame.

The armies rushed together in a feral mess. No subtlety tonight. "They're anxious to get to it," said Scherie.

"They're riled about something," I said.

On the flank closest to us, one of the counterplatoons wheeled out of the combat. Dressed in the grab-bag fashion of free-booting filibusters, they kept surprising order. As one man, they leveled their assortment of firearms in our direction.

"Take cover," I said.

"T'ain't nothing," said the Appalachian. "They're aiming into the otherworld."

Scherie hit the tall grass anyway. "Get down!" I yelled, tackling the Appalachian into the turf.

The platoon of shades fired. An all-too-real heat passed over our heads. Nearby grass yellowed and died. I guessed that the concentrated fire of ectoplasmic rounds was substantial enough here for a direct hit to flay the skin.

"Goddamn it!" said the Appalachian. Scherie murmured a string of profanity.

Another flash of power, then nothing. I raised my eyes from the dirt. The platoon was gone.

"I 'preciate the sentiment, but don't do that again," said the Appalachian, brushing the grass off her clothes. Then she cocked her head at the dead grass. "Whoa, hold on a moment."

"Real enough for you?" I said.

"Real isn't the problem," said the Appalachian. "Aiming at the real is."

"That felt strange," said Scherie. She stood up, legs wobbling, then steadying. "Where did they go?"

"Don't know," said the Appalachian. "Nobody standing leaves the battle early. Maybe the ghosts fired on us because they know."

"Know what?" asked Scherie.

"The Sanctuary, unobserved, can run away from trouble," said the Appalachian. "While you're here, watching it, its enemies can draw a bead on it, and it's fixed like a butterfly on a pin."

Silence. I had no response. Necessity had brought me here; I had no use for discussing what I couldn't change.

The spectral conflict sped up, like a computer chess game when the rest of the moves were inevitable. The stages of battle flashed in irregular lapses of time. The lines clashed, flanks turned, the center held, the center could not hold. The gray smoke lifted; the free unionists had driven their opponents off the stricken clearing, back to their line of trees.

The ghost of a mine whistle signaled the end. The good guys had won, but just barely.

I exchanged whispers with the Appalachian. "One day, they'll fail."

"One day, we'll all fail."

Like the dead, Scherie said nothing.

PART V

NEVER CALL RETREAT

All right, then, I'll go to Hell.
—MARK TWAIN

SIXTEEN

Sakakawea came to the precipice with its illusory emptiness. She could easily see the bridge, but suspected difficulty crossing. She might not be a wanted guest. They had been hunting for this place through her many lives. The Sanctuary, the land of America's misfit misbegotten toys.

She felt a seductive tug from this place, like a plea for mercy, an offer of lost things and people. The deal had small appeal. Whatever she had lost she had thrown away; whoever she had lost she had destroyed. Once she had destroyed someone, she didn't want to see them again. That was the American way.

Sakakawea's instincts riding atop all her faded memory had paid off again. The reason she'd sacrificed two Gideons in a gambit (besides their thorough unpleasantness and knowledge of the Hutchinson op), the reason she hadn't killed Dale at the motel, was for just such an outcome. She had known he would flee to some person or place of power, and he'd gone all the way to the top.

Chimera's prophecy made any living Morton a deadly risk to Sakakawea and her commander, but responding too directly to oracles was a quick trip to poetic justice. If there were any unaccounted-for Mortons (and there always were, as she knew well), they could also be hiding here. Absent the prophecy, the Sanctuary mattered more than any latter-day Morton's skin. Though she'd have that too, yes she would.

Unfortunately, the difficult ground meant calling in support. She pulled out her phone; without a ring, she connected. "Hello, *sir*." She said "sir" like a military fetishist.

"Hello, my dear. Good news?"

"They've entered the Sanctuary," she said.

"Excellent. I've never liked lost causes."

"Sir, the terrain is literally hostile. I'll need some support."

"Already ordered. Keep an eye out before you attack. They may open a door for me to drop in. Chimera will support from here. Try to keep these new grunts alive and Dale Morton dead. And stay on target—timing is a factor."

"The Peepshow?" she asked.

"Decapitated and confused. But Chimera reports that Major Endicott is on your trail."

"Understood." Sakakawea already knew this; she had chosen not to ditch her phone or take other precautions against being followed, and Chimera couldn't often surprise her. Her beloved commander was another matter; he had surprisingly irrational attachments. "What if the major and I meet?"

"That would be sad. But he's abused my tender regard too many times. Chimera can't find a viable long-term scenario and predicts I'll kill him eventually. Do what you must."

"Understood. Out." Sakakawea would enjoy doing what she must. She put away her phone and picked up her rifle. She tried out the sight, looking over the precipice and deep into the green land she would violate.

The Appalachian sat on her Shaker rocking chair, eyes closed. "I've been watchin' the bridge. You've brought others to the gate. The things after you won't respect this sanctuary. You've done their work for them. They'll destroy this."

She opened her eyes and took a long pull from her pipe. "I reckon you think you have a good reason?"

I nodded. "I've got a bad feeling."

The Appalachian laughed. "Best reason in the world, for a Morton."

I said, "I know you don't care for the old Families . . ."

"I may have exaggerated on that point," said the Appalachian.

"But," I continued, "this is Left-Hand stuff and the government combined. When they're done sorting out the Families, do you really think they'll spare this place?"

"Hell if I know. I don't trust farsight, Morton, and neither do you. We're better at the past. So stop pissing around. What do you want?"

"I need to speak more directly to the dead."

"The way to the Underworld is easy," said the Appalachian. "Just stroll over to that pit yonder, and don't watch your step."

"I want you to guide me," I said, "and serve as medium."

"I've just healed you, and you want a tour of coma town."

"That's about the size of it," I said.

"That's Left-Hand Morton craft, you know."

"But not for Left-Hand reasons," I said.

"True enough," said the Appalachian, "but that doesn't improve the taste of their vile herbal concoctions."

"You'll do it."

"If we go now," said the Appalachian. "We'll need to git back in time for your friends. Assuming we don't git stuck there permanent."

Scherie raised her palm to signal a conversational stop. "You're going to hell?"

"No. Yes. I don't know. It's the common pool of the craft afterlife. But I'm not really going anywhere. I'm just going to drink some herbal tea, and go down into the mine a little ways."

"We're being hunted by the government," said Scherie, "and you're going to trip out."

"It's more real than that," I said, "with real answers."

I hoped she wouldn't guess what that meant. No such luck. Scherie's mouth hung open a moment before she spoke. "You're going to die for a while, aren't you?"

"Just a while," I said. "It's a simulated brain death, like a near-death experience." Or so I'd heard.

"I'm coming," said Scherie.

"You need to stand guard," I said.

"What if you don't come back?" asked Scherie.

"Then you vacation in Mexico, and go home to your family when this blows over. You'll be fine, you're . . . normal."

"I wasn't worried about me," said Scherie. She walked away toward my ghosts, who kept an uneasy distance.

"But I am!" I blurted. "Worried. About you."

Scherie stopped, but didn't turn to face me. "Then don't worry. I can take care of myself. I always do."

"More than that," I said, having no idea where I was going. "I wonder what you think of all this. I think that maybe, if we somehow survive, you'll move to New Zealand just to get as far as possible from the American craft world and me. And that would probably be the smart thing to do. But I worry about it."

Scherie spun around, finger out, mouth open with something scorching to hit me with. Her eyes narrowed at me, mouth still gaping. Then she laughed.

At first it was an angry and ironic chuckle, dry and mirthless, but then all the other stuff of the past couple of days seemed to boil up, and the fatigue and the absurdity of it all must have overwhelmed her, because she had trouble controlling her laughter long enough to speak more than a few words at a time. "You're afraid . . . of what I might do . . . if you live through this? Oh God, that's too much! With all these ghosts around, you still don't get it."

She ran up to me and grabbed my neck as if to strangle me. "You should worry more about how much I'll hate you if you don't survive."

With a combatlike ferocity, she pulled my head down into a kiss that must have left bruises. Then, with equal and opposite abruptness, she pushed me back with her open palms. "Go. The sooner you're done, the sooner we can—hell, I don't know—start running away together again."

Run away together. Like a thread to guide me back, I took this slender hope with me into the Underworld.

As a child, I had visited a re-created mine in a museum. That exhibit felt nothing like this. The museum was a clean, dry pseudohole. This mine was a still-bleeding wound in the Earth.

Any real mine is a gateway to the Underworld. Just ask real miners. They'll tell of seeing spirits or the devil himself in the depths of a mine. I needed to talk to those spirits, to dead that weren't my own.

Despite this practical need, I felt like a poser. Why did the hero always have to descend into Hades? Because killers only believed in death.

At the mine's entrance, the Appalachian handed me a miner's safety helmet. "You'll want the light after we're done. Death is a little disorienting."

I put on the hat and felt ridiculous.

The Appalachian brought out a Prohibition-era flask and offered it to me. I took a generous swig, then fought to swallow and keep it down. Herbs, roots, and fungi, all gone bad, decayed, dead.

The Appalachian took her own swig without much expression. "Let's git moving," she said. "We don't want this to kick in here in the daylight world." She pointed at my Colt. "That isn't going to help you down there. I'll know if someone comes, with time to spare."

"Right." I trotted back to the cabin, and grabbed two extra guns. I knew an oracle when I heard it.

We descended a too-old ladder in the emergency shaft for one level, then walked along a gallery until there was no light, no sound of the outside world. "This is far enough," said the Appalachian, and we sat and waited in the dark.

Into the darkness came not light, but gray, like an old silent film with all the brightness gone. One bare tree, one large rock, and images of people moving to the hand-cranked staccato pace. Only the clothes were different—no Little Tramps, but clothes from the colonial to the Molly Maguire to the hip-hop, moving in ghostly quantum jumps in and out of the frame. And no sound, not even tinny piano music.

Were some of these ghosts here too soon? Had the Red Death already come for them?

Within the confused swirl of spirits, a hippy girl with big glasses jumped into the frame and elbowed her way to the bare tree. Unlike the others, she smiled—wistful, but a real smile.

"Sphinx," I called, "are you there?"

Sphinx stood behind the gray outline of the Appalachian. A girlish lilt of melancholy came from the Appalachian's scratchy throat and expressionless face. "I've always been here, talking to you."

"Thank you for saving my life," I said.

"That's optimistic," said Sphinx. "But you're welcome. Such a polite boy, full of questions."

"Yes, I need to know—"

"Me first," said Sphinx. "Riddles are my department. What doesn't go on four, then two, then three legs?"

My spine tingled as the tumblers fell into place. "Something that's not a man. Bullshit." Even dead, she was crazy. "Nonhuman magical entities are fairy tales."

Sphinx's shade smiled sadder. "I'm not talking folk and

myth, boy. We've been stuck in a world of Hawthorne and Poe. They're playing Asimov and Gibson."

I felt myself lurch lower in the Underworld. "Oh God. Chimera. They did it. It's the craft AI project. They gave a fucking computer magical sentience."

"They sure as hell think so," said Sphinx.

The Appalachian started suddenly. "Sorry. Didn't mean to interrupt. Just surprised is all." Then she was still again, and the more girlish voice said, "Such a lovely hostess. We should talk more."

Now calmer, I interrupted, "I don't believe in HAL the Magus. Craft is analog, not digital."

"Embarrassing, as I'm so beastly dead from Chimerical craft," said Sphinx.

I considered. "Then it's a con, like the chess-playing Turk. A human is greasing the transistors."

"Ooh, so graphic, but your logic is impeccable, Casper." Sphinx giggled. "We are in grave danger."

"I assume you warned somebody," I said.

"Everybody, to the very, very top, in my inimitable clear style," said Sphinx.

"Let me guess. Chimera makes clear predictions in military language."

"That's what made me suspicious," said Sphinx. "That's why they like it. You're good at this. Just like your father."

I was on the clock; family gossip would have to wait. "Who's behind this?"

"Everybody knows, but they're just stupid. Only a few are doing this evil on purpose."

"What purpose?" I said.

"Gives my dead head an ache. Try again."

"OK, who do I have to kill to stop this?" I said.

"Damned if I know." She giggled at this.

There was only one protected area that Sphinx couldn't have gotten a single clue about. "How deep in the Pentagon is it?"

"Core of the H-ring," said Sphinx. "Try looking in that direction for five minutes straight."

OK, two more bits of the mystery, and I was done. "What does Chimera have to do with you trying to destroy me in the desert?"

Sphinx's shade frowned to mocking excess. "Our failures serve a purpose too."

"Yeah, getting people killed."

She wagged a gray finger at me. "Better than the alternatives."

I considered the alternatives. "That op was supposed to be Endicott's, so I would have gone elsewhere. But worse than the desert?"

"I saw you die many, many times," said Sphinx. "South America, the Congo, all sorts of exotic locales."

I imagined these avoided dooms annoying me like flies. "Chimera would have gotten me on the alternative mission, or the one after that. But come on! The mad sorcerer was the only scenario where I had a chance of surviving intact?"

"The only one Chimera's crew wouldn't overrule," said Sphinx. "The chance was small. And pushing you out of the service was a happy alternative for them. I took a longer view."

"Longer view"—a tantalizing echo of Dad. But my next question took deadly precedence. "Tell me who killed Hutch, and how."

"If I knew everything," said Sphinx, "do you think I'd be here?"

"Isn't she here too?"

"I haven't seen her," said Sphinx. "There are other early arrivals here, but she isn't one of them."

"Early arrivals." I had expected this. "KIA before their time."

"High-profile Family types," said Sphinx, "who don't seem to know what hit them."

Time, though plastic here, was running short. If I tried to sustain this altered consciousness for too long, I'd become what I pretended to be. Tissue necrosis and brain damage would set in. "I need to talk to Hutch."

"Well, I guess this is good-bye then. No time for family gossip . . ." The gray image of Sphinx turned to go.

Family gossip. She was dangling that in front of me again. "Wait, what do you know about my family?"

"That's need to know, Dale," said Sphinx in a voice that faded to a whisper in the Appalachian's throat. "When you need to know it, you will." Silence, and no image came forward.

Then the Appalachian grabbed me, painfully hard. "Dale, is that you? Where the fuck am I?" The voice was near panic.

"Hutch?" I asked.

"Yes, yes, yes."

"Physically, I'm in the Sanctuary," I said. "I've entered the Underworld."

A low moan came from the Appalachian. "You shouldn't have come here."

"There was no other way." The Appalachian's grip loosened; Hutch must be controlling her hands. That couldn't be good. "Hutch, who killed you?"

"I don't know," said Hutchinson. "Probably a Gideon,

'cause they were able to sneak up on me. I still can't find my body. Where did they put my body?"

Endicott must know. "I'll find out," I said.

Laughter came from the Appalachian. "And then you'll die. That'll be nice." The Appalachian's face glowed and contorted. No longer the gray effigy of a peaceful death, her eyes rolled.

"Hutch?" But I knew that this was someone else.

The Appalachian's teeth mashed against her own tongue as the newcomer spoke. "Colonel Hutchinson is permanently out. No need to leave a message. You'll be able to speak directly to her soon."

The Appalachian had ceased to act as a willing medium. She was possessed. *"Leave her,"* I said, testing the opposition.

The thing in the Appalachian laughed, a horrid croak of forced air. "Always so rude, even in our family home."

"This isn't Roderick," I said, "so knock off the impersonation."

"Oh, so certain!" said the Red Death. "But who else could master such magics besides the great Roderick? You've learned too much. Here comes a chopper to chop off *your* head!"

Yes, who else could master such magics? But I had my own question. "What have you done to Hutch?"

"Not enough, apparently," said Red. "But I'm so glad we could talk again."

Against all my instincts, I tried reason. "Whoever you are, I know you're American. Can't we come to a deal?"

"Certainly," said Red. "I need you dead. After that, whatever you'd like."

"Me dead, and all the craft Families," I said.

"Just their best," said Red. "Magi aren't what they used to be. It won't hurt too much. Like the time we Mortons killed those Endicotts . . ."

Mortons killing Endicotts? Only someone like Major Endicott would think I'd enjoy this blather. Time was running out. For once, the villain's monologue was keeping the good guys preoccupied, when we should be escaping.

"*Get out,*" I said, putting more force into my craft.

"But we have so much to discuss."

Dale, come forth, I thought, and the spirit world faded into darkness, and strength came back into my limbs.

I grasped the Appalachian's shoulders. *Umph.* She gave a punch to my solar plexus. The blow only irritated; the puppet's strings must not be completely in enemy hands. I picked her up and threw her over a shoulder. I turned one-eighty degrees and strode through the dark toward the main shaft. In a few steps I saw the light at the end of the tunnel. I hoped it wasn't that other light, the one with Dad and Grandpa at the end of it.

"Die, you Morton cockroach, die!" The Appalachian's body struggled and punched weakly at my back. "You're staying here forever, Morton. An eternity of pain, while we rule your precious land."

Not even pretending anymore to be a Morton himself. Whoever was in there was speaking directly from the subconscious. His conscious mind must be busy.

As if in answer to this thought, the warmth of another's craft flowed around me. To possess someone and work craft through her—in another context, I would have admired the sheer power and skill. I braced for some magical blow, but instead saw an auric glow that shot up through the earth like a flare and heard a rising tone of music that sounded like "I'm ready!"

What are we waiting for, ma'am?" said the grunt.

"Shut up or I'll have your tongue," said Saka-kawea.

Though the grunt should have taken this threat literally, it was sufficient that he and his fellow soldiers took it seriously. They remained at attention, quiet.

Good, thought Sakakawea. She fell back into a focused trance. At the bridge, she stood in front of her new companions, trying to see through the Sanctuary's illusion to whatever signal her commander might send. What seemed a long hour to her reinforcements seemed to her, in her altered state, several eternities, several hells of waiting.

A beam of craft ripped up to the sky, a pure tone sounded the attack. Sakakawea's heart leapt into ecstasy. He was here, and she was joining him in battle. "Follow me," she said, and she dashed over the suddenly visible bridge.

SEVENTEEN

I dragged the Appalachian as close as I dared to the main shaft. Red might attempt to drag both me and the Appalachian's body to our deaths. No going up the ladder like this.

As I summoned the focus for another attempt at expulsion, Red continued to punch and kick, but with less enthusiasm. The craft signal must have tired him out. "Die, you vermin. Die now."

"Is that you?" Scherie was calling from the mine entrance.

"Stay away!" I yelled.

"Die, less than a woman," said Red, using a panglossic—it must sound worse in Farsi.

"You," said Scherie. She was already scuttling down the ladder. A piece of rung broke and ricocheted down the shaft. "You," she said again, entering the gallery.

"Don't come near her!" I warned.

Scherie didn't stop. She rushed at me and grabbed the Appalachian and shook her as I struggled against them both. Scherie's rage echoed down through the depths of the mine. *"Get out of her, you fucking ghoul rapist."*

The ground beneath Scherie's feet glowed; the air imploded silently toward her. *Fiat lux.* A blinding grenade of craft exploded from her hands. I fell to my knees, and the Appalachian rolled to the ground.

For a moment, I forgot training. But only for a moment. Triage. First, I examined the Appalachian. Stunned, but very much alive, and no sign of Red. That was the good news.

The bad news stood in front of me, panting with the effort of an exorcism that I myself couldn't achieve. I tried a theory: maybe the Sanctuary had used Scherie as a vehicle for its own craft. But I was tired of fooling myself.

I stood up and faced Scherie. I had to get to her before she recovered. *"The truth,"* I commanded. "I'll know if you're lying. What lineage are you? Who do you work for?"

Scherie was staring at her hands. "I don't know . . . I don't know what you're talking about."

"I heard it, Scherie. I saw it." I realized I was in a combat stance. I stood down. "I'm not going to hurt you. But no mundane could have made it this far."

"Right, this has all been my idea." Her hands were trembling now. I reached for them. She whipped them back. "Keep away from me, goddamn it."

"I'm not going to hurt you," I repeated.

"You idiot." Tears rolled down her cheeks as she looked from the Appalachian to my face. "I'm not thinking of me."

"Ouch," said the Appalachian, sitting up even as Scherie was sinking against the gallery wall. "My head feels like unfiltered shit and moonshine."

"We've got a situation here," I said.

"They teach you to talk that way in the military?" asked the Appalachian.

I pointed at Scherie, who held her face in her shaking hands. "She's a craftsperson, but she won't tell me her Family or who she works for."

"You and your lineages. Fool." The Appalachian spat. "She doesn't know."

I stared at the Appalachian. *Shit, I'm still tripping.* "What the hell do you mean?"

"She doesn't . . . Shh. They're here. Git the fuck back down the mine. Now."

Sakakawea had little difficulty finding the shaft. The residue of her commander's possessive presence drew her, then unfamiliar power burst out from the mine. She sighed with disappointment at her beloved's absence. Perhaps Morton had killed the Appalachian to expel him—a worthy outcome. One way or another, that hag was out of commission.

She sniffed the mine air. "Mmm, Morton." He was still down there. Joy.

"Let's blow this gash to hell," she said. An advantage to working in the Sanctuary was that they could make as much of a noisy mess as they liked. Ritual genitalia-form spaces appalled her with their crassness; she'd blow up the Washington Monument too if they'd let her.

Her grunts had brought plenty of toys. "Toss some grenades down the main and emergency shafts, then immediately set that building-buster at the entrance and detonate." Poetic. She knew too well that Mortons obsessively feared live burial.

"Now move it," she said aloud, but to herself she said, *Chimera, come.* She felt the unnatural power wash over her and this abomination of preservation, just as the grenades dropped down the shafts.

I heard the warning *clang, clunk, clang,* and rattle of explosives against metal behind me as we helped the Appalachian scramble down the gallery, helmet lanterns faintly illuminating our way. My reflexes heard the noises first.

"Hit the dirt!" I said. But I had already pulled them down.

The mine vibrated once, twice, but nothing else. Just the grenades that time. I anticipated what would follow—if they had one big explosive charge, it wouldn't be long coming. "Up, and move it." I started counting, one, two, three . . .

On ten, "Down!"

The concussive wave blasted over us with its narrowly channeled force. Small stones rained on our backs; a cascade of rock rolled closer, closer . . . stopped. A slower wave of billowing dust passed over us like fog. I coughed and peered through the dust, only to confront the Morton dread of living entombment.

The shaft, the way we had come in, had ceased to exist.

"No way out," said Scherie.

I looked at the Appalachian.

"Ye of shitty faith." She pointed at a gap in the mine wall a yard ahead of us. "I'd never lead you into a box canyon."

The gap, a ventilation shaft, doubled as a miners' emergency escape route. Scherie moved toward it.

"Not this one," said the Appalachian. "The next one."

Scherie and I bent to help her, but she shivered us off. "Thanks, but I've got my wind back."

We went deeper. Near the end of the gallery, we found the second shaft leading up and down. "Stay down or go up?" asked the Appalachian.

Fighting in pitch dark was old craft sport, but I would fight with unease in such a closed space, and if a Gideon came down, the enemy would have the nocturnal advantage. A Gideon also wouldn't leave while my craft scent remained, so we would have to fight eventually. Sooner and aboveground would be better.

"We go up," I said, feeling my weariness as I spoke. "But after a quick recharge."

"Tactics, Mr. West Point?" asked the Appalachian.

I snorted, but it was a damned good question. I had a new weapon at hand named Scherezade Rezvani, but didn't know what she could do, or whether she'd go off in my face.

"Wait." As if answering my question, Scherie held up her palm. "Can you feel that?"

"What?" I said.

"It's everywhere," said Scherie. "So much . . . power? Like the thing that had her, but different."

I looked for the power, but had trouble finding it for its pervasiveness. The mine spun for a second; I caught myself before falling. Déjà vu, motherfucker. This felt like the death magic that had been aimed at me. The power flowed not with the syncopated rhythm of a heartbeat, but with the merciless precision of a digital clock. No, the power wasn't mechanical, but something more fleshy on a digitally forced march.

Scherie nodded at me, as if seeing me for the first time. "It's like you." She was right; the magic had a Morton feel, hidden beneath whatever commanding craft forced it on.

Scherie shuddered. "I'm going to tell it to leave now."

The Appalachian gripped her wrist. "Not yet."

"Why not?" said Scherie. "It's horrible. It's very, very wrong."

"Tactics," I said. "They don't know what you can do yet. Neither do we. You strike now, you give them time for a counterstrike. Wait until we're ready to take advantage of the surprise."

Scherie jumped back as Grandpa and Dad manifested in combat uniform. "Having fun yet?" asked Dad.

"Shut your lip," said Grandpa.

I stepped closer to Scherie. The light from my lantern lit her face like a ritual mask. "So, what can you do?"

"I don't know," said Scherie.

"She doesn't," said the Appalachian.

"How can she not know?" I shook my head. We were back to where we started.

"Honey," said the Appalachian, turning up the maternal a bit strong, "when you were little, did you ever see anything funny, as in strange?"

"Nothing out of the ordinary," said Scherie.

"Uh-huh." The Appalachian seemed to be interested in something on the floor of the mine.

"You know, imaginary friends," said Scherie.

"Imaginary," repeated the Appalachian, tracing her finger on the wall. "That's ordinary enough. What were they like?"

"They were uncles and aunts and other people I hadn't

seen before." The Appalachian didn't respond, so Scherie continued. "Some of them weren't very nice."

"Not so friendly," said the Appalachian. "What did you do?"

"I told mother. Mama smiled and told me that all I had to do was tell the ghosts to go away, and they would. And they did."

"And they never came back," said the Appalachian.

"No," said Scherie. "Would they come back, if I asked?"

"Interesting idea," said the Appalachian. "Probably not the time to find out. Anyhow, seems obvious why you haven't noticed your talent until now."

"Which is?" asked Scherie.

I interrupted. "I've been a blind fool." She had been the obvious source of the massive healing at the motel, in the very same room, yet I had missed it. "How the hell did she get below my radar?"

"I'm right here, you know," said Scherie.

The Appalachian laughed. "We've all been blind fools, but not the way you're thinking. Any fool could've seen what's happening, 'cept for the fledgling camouflage. That's how a new craftsperson survives long enough to defend her or himself. Surely, someone told you about the birds and the bees. Surely, someone taught you how a Family is born."

Grandpa and Dad looked at each other doubtfully.

"Forget that for now," I said. I looked at Scherie. She had left things out of her story, enormous things of anger and loss. "Back to tactics. We go up. Then what?"

Scherie said, "We go for the bridge."

The Appalachian sighed. "I can't leave. Not now, not even for a bit."

"They'll expect us to go that way anyway," I said. But I had another reason not to run, a sudden certainty. I didn't think much of my own farsight, but this oracle felt right: if the third Gideon, Sakakawea, was there, she had to die.

Die. The fossilized plant life of two hundred million years pressed down on my head, trying to turn me to coal. I thrust my hands out to keep the walls away.

"What's wrong?" asked Scherie.

"I'm a little . . . claustrophobic."

The Appalachian made an impolite cough. Grandpa piped in. "The technical term is taphephobia. Fear of being buried alive. A family affliction."

"Thanks for sharing," I said, trying to distract Scherie from such lines of thought. I gave a hard stare at Grandpa and Dad, but they met my gaze with surprising substance. I tried to look through them, and could not. Like the other dead here, they were as opaque as life.

"How long until the dead have their next battle of the republic?" I asked.

The Appalachian bared her teeth at me. "You want to manipulate Valhalla. That's dangerous. Worse, it's wrong. The dead are resting here. They're not your weapons."

"You know that those men and women out there would die all over again for what we're trying to do," I said.

"Some of them," said the Appalachian.

"You could tell them what to do," I said.

"You know they don't talk," said the Appalachian.

"They were aware of us yesterday," said Scherie. "They tried to kill us."

"Right," said the Appalachian. "Too many of 'em hate it here. They'll be as eager to join in their own destruction as they were when alive. This is not a peaceable kingdom, a city on a hill. This is an Alamo in a civil war."

"Just talk to them," I said.

"Even if they hear me, only a few will listen." She thumbed at Scherie. "Maybe the fledgling might say a word."

"Maybe," I said, reluctantly. That would be shooting blind. "In any case, we'll use them for cover." That meant we'd have to blend in. None of the armies looked like they were wearing my synthetic outdoor gear. I took off my expensive jacket, rolled up the sleeves of my shirt, and ripped my pants. The others imitated me without question.

With my last rip, I had my plan. "So here's how we destroy them."

CHAPTER

EIGHTEEN

With the patience of a true predator, Sakakawea had not moved since the explosion. She knew better than most the difficulty of killing a magus. Her commander's Red Death puppet had escaped a worse trap at the Morton estate. She herself had been buried . . . no good remembering that.

Sakakawea sniffed. A Morton still lived, and the guardian of this place still lived. Hard to say where below, but it didn't matter. If Morton managed to see daylight again, she would have overwhelming force to finish him off.

She gave orders to her living task force. "Kill the man on sight, if you can. Bag the women and bring them to me. Ignore the historical holograms." They didn't question her reasons for thinking the targets alive; they didn't have more logic than sense. She sent one of her men to cover the bridge, enough to slow her quarry down if they fled.

She gave orders to the sympathetic revenants, the "historical holograms" of H-ring speak. She spoke with the dead glibly—metempsychosis was good for that. Psychosis without the metem was good for the talking, but not the listening. She spoke to the departed dark sides of the

Families and to all who had in life tried to tear America apart. She spoke to those men without a country who had said, "Damn the United States! I wish I may never hear of the United States again!"

Some of the dead remembered reasons to hate Dale Morton; one of them was from that botched business in the desert. Sergeant Zanol would join her reserve guard; like the others, he was not celebrity evil, just an efficient killer.

Chimera's dark magic helped persuade the reluctant. He knew how to compel all the facets of death, save his own.

Her opponents would also use the dead, whatever the guardian's scruples. Sakakawea's revenants would eliminate the cover provided by the spirits of the enemy. The Civil War was the last time so many ghosts had entered living combat; Sakakawea would enjoy their erasure.

She was patient, but not when she had other opportunities for fun, like a battle for the soul of the nation. So despite her preternatural focus, she missed the first stirrings of prey at the outhouse two hundred yards away from the main shaft. But this was just a quibble of seconds. She silently signaled to her team the direction of the enemy. Morton, the guardian, the Sanctuary—she'd kill all her birds with one strike.

In the dark mine, we breathed, we focused, we recharged. The three magi were ready. It was good ground.

The Appalachian crawled up first. This land, shifting like an enormous chameleon, would hide her. I went up second. The exit was camouflaged as an old-fashioned wooden outhouse, complete with a quarter-moon window in the door. The camouflage was too authentic, though the filth was mostly spectral.

The Appalachian scrambled outside. No enemy response to the open door, so it must be hidden from their line of sight. I waited for Scherie to come up; I would go last to screen our retreat. I pointed the direction, and Scherie dashed from the exit with me on her heels.

Shots fired. I skewed them barely as much as necessary. Rounds nicked bits of loose clothing and the ground right beneath our feet. Evil craft filled the air like fog. Dead innocents cried for me to stop. I shook off the illusion and returned fire, a couple of shots to keep our pursuers honest.

We sought cover. We found it in a cluster of ghosts moving through the enormous old trees. The ghosts themselves were substantial enough to screen us if we stayed in a crouch. For me, dozens of dead Mortons, similarly attired, would be the best blind of all. The possibility of sudden ambush made our pursuers reluctant to follow at speed; their fire diminished in frequency and accuracy.

Like medieval clockwork, the armies were lining up again for battle. The blindness worked both ways; our enemies could hide an army of the living in these ghost troops. But I knew the protocols. At most, a squad would be tasked for something this quick and secret, and of those, we only had to kill the craftsmen.

As planned, we spread out to keep our pursuers' task difficult, ducking among the trees to different units, then slowing to blend in. Hidden with the Hutchinsons, Scherie prepared to play nurse, ripping more strips from her own clothes. The Appalachian found a loose collection of mountain men. Despite divides of time and gender, she seemed at home with Boone and Crockett look-alikes.

The math still sucked: we had small arms against an assault team. The enemy would soon overwhelm us unless I acquired our target. *Show me their sins.* At this distance, the details of their transgressions blurred, but like radar my talent showed the living through the ghosts that surrounded them because the dead had no sins. My ability wouldn't draw a bead back on me.

I saw the opposition as a scattering of fireflies. As if sensing our tactical shift, the other side had fanned out and away. No longer in pursuit, they would wait on the outskirts for us to be flushed out like pheasants.

So, who would be doing the flushing? I searched. I searched again. On the other side of the long clearing at the center height of the low rise, one living soul alone stood with the counterregiments. A very bad girl. She glowed with more sins than could fit her distant image. That must be Sakakawea, but was she in command? *Show me her craft.*

At first, I thought I'd lost craftsight; blood-red malignancy pulsed through the Sanctuary like a tick-tock aorta. But no, all of the death magic on this field radiated from her. She glowed hot with ridiculous amounts of power. Who was this Gideon really? She was way beyond her pay grade here.

Near Sakakawea stood the distinct outline of Sergeant Zanol. No surprise there.

As she had with her squad, Sakakawea had extended the counterarmy's flanks to envelop the free unionists, to bag us all. She must be worried that we would run away again.

To her strategy there was an obvious riposte, notorious for its times of failure.

I wound my way to Scherie's oak. I whispered so my living voice wouldn't carry. "I need them to charge the center."

"I'll try this group first," she said, pointing at a cluster of perpetually wounded ghosts. She approached the revenants with her cloth strips, but they receded like a strobe-lit tide. She whispered fiercely at them, "Listen to me!" They turned, covered their ears.

From behind another tree, the Appalachian strode forward and pulled Scherie back into cover. She shook her head.

"Why aren't you at your post?" I said.

"This is all my post," said the Appalachian. "And if my dead don't want to chat with a walking neutron bomb, nobody's gonna make 'em."

"Fine. I'll try my connections. Remember your jobs." I slid back through the columns of dead to my ancestors. Dad and Grandpa stood silent before me, blocking my way to Joshua. It would be wrong to try to pass through them here. "Dad, Grandpa, I need to speak with Joshua."

They shook their heads. But, in acknowledgment of their continued connection to me, they stepped aside.

I stood next to Joshua and faced the same direction as the free union troops to avoid drawing attention. I spoke through the side of my mouth. "Sir, I don't know if you can hear me, but I need you to lead a charge up against the center of their line. It's as crazy as Pickett's, but the fate of the country is on the line. I need a screen of soldiers. I need to get close to their living leader."

I glanced over at Joshua. No response. I felt less than stupid. Here I was again, praying to the ancestors. I jabbed my finger ahead in frustration. "*I need to kill her.* Extremely dead."

Then Joshua raised his hand to his head to peer across the field at Sakakawea, and the dead man's jaw dropped like sudden decay. Was she the one he had been searching for, or was she someone else? It didn't matter. He began making gestures, and he began to give orders.

"Tonight we charge the center."

The words froze my spine, because I could hear them. I looked around, and saw not the faded hues of old film, but men and women in full-colored high-def 3-D. I had been drafted into their world.

"Now you've done it," said Dad. Grandpa grimaced in disgust, then peered across the field. "She looks familiar. Not good."

It took time even for ghost regiments to redraw their lines for battle. Finally, Joshua called out, "Forward march." The Grand Army of the Republic of the Dead stepped off the line and moved stately forward. The banners blazed, the fife pierced, and the snare code of drums made punctual pebbles that kept time with my amplified pulse. The landscape was more vivid green against grimmer trees. Beneath the music, a faint murmur of commands kept order.

I slanted from side to side at the back of the centerline to avoid being a fixed target. Were Scherie and the Appalachian seeing this, feeling this? I hoped they didn't get distracted from the mission.

A dozen dirty marching men and women gravitated toward me, and drew up into formation around me. I knew them all; they were my veterans, forgotten by all others because of the secrecy of our duty. They said nothing, yet the skin around my heart felt thin. Proud, yes, but I dreaded watching them fall all over again.

The grand scene was short-lived; we came within range of the enemy's guns. The ectoplasmic artillery thundered like a hell-bound storm and blasted holes through the advancing line. The din filled my ears; they had no room for any other sound. The blasts made large areas suddenly visible; they threatened to expose my position.

I wanted to call for a change in pace, but the dead anticipated me. Under enemy fire, the advance across the middle of the clearing turned into a double-quick running charge.

Sakakawea and her living soldiers were not oblivious to my tactics. "He's there," she yelled. "Just spray the entire center." The living fired scattered shots and the dead fired endless rounds into my spectral screen. The living rounds were harmless to the ghosts, harmless to me; the blind fire gave me more uncertain probabilities to play with.

But the ghost rounds took a horrible toll. Musket balls hissed, whizzed, and thumped. Sakakawea grabbed a spectral automatic from her guard. "Hey warrior, come out and play!" She sprayed death like summer fun ahead of her and laughed like a carrion flock. "Death, death, death!" How the hell could she use a ghost weapon? She murdered the ghosts with boundless love, a serial killer angel, ripping gaps in my protection as soldiers fell to the right and left in pools of plasmic gore.

Fortunately, the weapon couldn't maintain an automatic rate of fire any longer, and she set it aside for her mundane rifle. We climbed over a fragment of stone wall, and skirted a segment of split wooden fence. Past all these deadly nuisances, we rushed for the higher ground.

Zanol couldn't wait. Waiving an officer's sword, he charged down. "Morton!" he bellowed, head turning left and right as he cut down soldier after soldier. "Where are you, coward?"

"My family has no cowards, sir," said Grandpa, stepping forward with his own saber.

"You'll do," said Zanol.

Sabers clashed, but my guard and I were already past this duel.

We made our last crazy push up the high ground, my veterans roaring like feral saints. A final wave of fire, and my covering spirits were all but gone, retired for this day at least. My father and Joshua, against the odds, still moved with me, but could not keep me hidden.

"Ha!" From mere yards away, Sakakawea leveled her mundane rifle and fired at me.

I went down, face-first into the damp earth. *Bleed,* I thought, *and don't think so loud,* and I bled from the healing motel wound.

Sakakawea squawked with laughter. "Get up, Morton! This trick was ancient when old Thomas met his first Indian."

I heard no bluff in her taunt. I sat up.

She stepped toward me. My father and Joshua fired at her. She waved the back of her hand at them, and they fell backwards to the ground.

She peered down at me, smiling with unlikely gentleness. "Joshua's last descendant in the craft. I've waited for this day for a long time." Up close, her collective transgressions resolved themselves. She had many, many sins, some of which needed more than initial letters. She didn't look old enough to own all of them. But, as Grandpa had said, she did look *familiar.*

Bloody craft filled my eyes, poured into my brain. Something was supposed to happen now, but I couldn't remember what. She held the rifle close to my head. Oh yes, that's right, I was going to die.

"Goddamn it, keep your hands off me!" Her own hands bound, the Appalachian was pushed and shoved up the hill. "I've got rights. I'm not in your jurisdiction, GI."

"Keep going, you," said the soldier, giving another shove.

Oh, I thought, *it's just the Appalachian. She's gotten herself caught. Hope she can avoid getting herself shot.*

"Nice work," said Sakakawea, eyeing the soldier with an unprofessional interest. "Now find the other one and I'll personally raise your rank." And whatever else amused her. "She shouldn't be much trouble."

She bent to greet her latest prisoner. "Hello, Pearl."

The Appalachian spat at her. Point-blank range, but the spit missed, though some spray hit Sakakawea's rifle.

"You, I'll let watch when I do your land," said Sakakawea. "I like it when someone watches. See?"

I took this as permission to turn. From up here, I could see the whole field. The battle had gone very badly for the free union troops. They were caving on the flanks. A scattering of medics tended the trail of wounded spirits I had left on my foolhardy charge.

Report from the field: we were screwed.

"Damn you!" Grandpa yelled, and he groaned in agony. Zanol had run his sword through him. When Zee pulled it free, Grandpa fell to the ground. A medic rushed to him.

Zee waved his gore-slaked sword in triumph and strode back up the hill.

"Good," said Sakakawea. "I promised him that he could witness your death, and I don't break promises without reason."

Zee reached us. "Ready, dear ghost?" asked Sakakawea.

"Yes," he said.

She again aimed her rifle into my face. "Wait," said Zee.

"What is it?" she said, with a hint of dangerous impatience.

"There's something you need to know," said Zee. He smiled like nirvana, a beatific face of NCO payback. "You don't understand this place at all."

"Ticking magic of death!" Another voice, carrying a continent of outrage and loss, echoed through the battle as if from everywhere at once. But the simple words came from one woman. *"Leave the Sanctuary! Now!"*

As she spoke, the medic treating Grandpa stood up and threw aside her scarf and raised her gun. Grandpa jumped up behind her, flourishing his sword. Some counterghosts ran toward the medic to stall her, then ran away. The blood-dimmed craft was gone. With a banshee's rebel yell and the ululation of a distant land, Scherie charged the hill.

The Gideon didn't hesitate. First things first. She pulled the trigger.

Click!

"I spiked that first thing, dear," said the Appalachian.

I dove into the Gideon, pounding at nerve points like old radio buttons, groping for her side arms. She was packing more than one weapon; I couldn't let her use them.

She mirrored my blows like slapstick, stunning my

limbs for a crucial second. *"Squad, to me,"* she said between gritted teeth. But instead of her living squad, a cordon of ghost soldiers had formed a ring around our struggle, as if they wanted to see it go all ten rounds.

Sakakawea threw me off like a clingy cat; I landed on my back. The Appalachian stuck her ass in my face. Her small caliber still there, tucked in her pants, craft-hidden from search. So much skill, and she still couldn't manage to get the restraints off her hands.

I took the gun and spun. A shot missed. The Appalachian hit the dirt. I aimed and fired. The bullet curved away from the Gideon, a wild pitch into the dead crowd.

Zanol dashed in front of Sakakawea, interfering with her view. Here, protected by the Sanctuary from the curses of the living, Zee was the man he was supposed to be. "Treacherous clown," said the Gideon. Without ceasing her hunt for me, she took a spectral pistol from a wounded spirit and fired it at Zee, hitting his side, but this only slowed him down. Other former countersoldiers joined his effort. She moved through, firing against ghosts with one hand and me with the other. The soldiers she often hit, but me she missed.

I zigged, zagged, willed away a Gideon bullet, and took another shot. My bullet curved again, but with less authority. Sakakawea's craft remained amazing, but it was flickering, perhaps guttering.

Scherie finally arrived, the spirits parting for her like a frightened sea. The spectral weapon vanished from Sakakawea's grip, but she kept the other gun pointed at me. Another broken standoff, but for these few moments, I held the advantage in firepower. *"Hit flesh,"* I whispered to the bullet in the chamber, and Sakakawea's mouth moved as well. At this range with my craft, I could take the Gideon, but that move had a more than zero risk to Scherie, and I wanted information.

"Surrender, Gideon," I said. "My word, you'll live."

"Surrender. Yes," said Sakakawea, voice steady. "It's time." Her eyes ticked down at her empty hand. "Too old."

I saw no deception, but wasn't sure she was talking to me. Her eyes ticked at Scherie and Scherie's gun, and her face vibrated for a second. "Oh dear me. Yes, past time!" She reversed her gun, holding it by the muzzle toward herself. She started to lower it to the ground.

Then she twirled the gun as she locked into a crouch. She was faster than light, quick as craft. She fired. *"Be ready for me, love!"*

Ba-bam! My mind went black, even as my reflexes fired for me fatally. The guns' reports merged like a severed echo. I did not fall.

Sakakawea had fired at Scherie.

She had chosen meaningless death for two. The world failed.

Craft-impelled and near point-blank, these bullets would not stop save for human flesh. No such stuff stood between me and the Gideon. Sakakawea's stomach blossomed red.

I turned to Scherie. Before I had seen what would happen, the Appalachian had risen. She had moved, not just in her realm, but through it. The bullet had found her waiting, addressed *straight to the heart.* All the Sanctuary's protective craft could only move that evil shot to hitting a lung. Collapse. The Appalachian's blood spilled onto the land.

With a chuckle, Sakakawea folded to the ground.

Scherie knelt at the Appalachian's side to treat her wound. A hundred years of medics circled them, shouting their assistance.

I bent over Sakakawea. Her wound would be slow; there was time for questions. "Stay with me. Who sent you? *Who the fuck sent you?*"

She smiled. "Endicott." I saw no lie. She giggled blood, and trembled beneath me. Her last breath rattled out with a black-light explosion of craft. She was gone.

Material bullets pinged off rocks to my right. "That's her squad," said Zanol, supporting himself on another soldier's arm. "They're taking cover, talking over their next move."

I looked in Sakakawea's mouth. No black capsule. She was dead, dead of a gut shot. Of all the things today, that made the least sense. But the mortal threat was gone. If her ghost showed up, she'd be just one of thousands.

"They're coming through," said Zee. "Their weapons are standard issue. No Stonewall devices."

Sakakawea's strike force pushed on through the cluster of dead, weapons at ready. "Stand down, or we will shoot you." They didn't sound certain about any part of that.

With the external death craft expelled, I could work my assassin's magic. I wanted to consult Joshua, but Joshua was down. I wanted to hesitate, but couldn't.

"Do it to them," said Zee. "They're no good. Knew this mission stunk and they took it."

"Shoot yourselves," I said. I didn't need much force— just the suggestion—and this place was ready to assist. The horror of history is diluted over centuries. Here it was concentrated, a soul-burning acid. They didn't struggle long

against their own hands, just a smooth movement of barrel to chest and head. A succession of cries and pops like fireworks, and they were gone.

No regret this time. I had taken the safest course for my comrades. That was moral enough for a battlefield.

On this field, another war cry, in the voice of a hundred native nations. The mounted Indians swept down on the flanks and rolled up the counterlines who hadn't yet defected with Zanol to free union.

"Dale, I need you here, now," said Scherie with pure desperation.

NINETEEN

Endicott surveyed the precipice. "Damned parking lot out here." Tracking Sakakawea's phone had led him to her bike and a government-issue van. He knelt and put his hand to the ground. A boring car had come this way. Its trail wanted to slip away from his grasp, but its stealth had run low. Its path went over the cliff. "Wonder what else is trying to hide." He focused, and sensed the bridge without quite seeing it. "Oh great, the Sanctuary. Damned earth-worshipping, nature-and-native-fetishizing, hippie-craft and liberal-guilt nonsense. Lord, how could my day get any better?"

Click. The unmistakable sound of a handgun being readied at the back of his head, then a Slavic cowboy accent. "Howdy, Major."

"Hello, Roman. Guess my dad was right. You Russkies are still sneaky."

"I'm Ukrainian," said Roman.

"Met anyone lately who cares?" asked Endicott.

Roman snorted. "No." A jingle of metal. "Put your hands behind your back, please. Do not touch your gun as you do so."

Endicott felt the cuffs go on. "What's your part in this shitfest?"

"I don't want you bushwhacking my amigos," said Roman.

"Hmm. Don't suppose you'd believe we're on the same side?"

"'Fraid not, pardner. Close is, how you say, no virgin."

"Couldn't you tell if I was lying?" asked Endicott.

"Oh, you not speak with forked tongue, Kemo Sabe," said Roman. "But you want to take 'em someplace safe for heap long talk, and time is short. You just get yourselves killed good, yep."

"Well, they're in trouble," said Endicott. "And you can't go in there to help."

"No furriners allowed," agreed Roman. "Too late now anyhow. We see soon who comes out, amigos or killer-beetch."

"OK," said Endicott.

"OK, what?" said Roman.

"OK, I'm not going to kill you," said Endicott.

Roman laughed. "Dagnabbit, you're funny."

Performing two prayers simultaneously was nearly impossible. Trying to execute three was just plain nuts. But this day just had to get better. So Endicott thought three things.

Drop gun, break cuffs, stay put.

"Ow!" Roman's gun dropped. *Chink!* With help from Endicott's arms, his cuffs snapped. Endicott turned and drew his weapon. "Gotcha!"

But Roman hadn't stayed put. He was gone. Endicott focused hard, hard enough nearly to see the details of the bridge, but no trace of the Ukrainian.

"Lord, give me strength." Endicott sat down hard, exhausted. He thought through the encounter from a couple of angles, but it came out the same each time: Roman had just wanted his attention. "I'm not stupid, you know! Shit. All this dancing around, just to get a simple message across? Next time, send an e-mail."

Lord, give me strength. He felt the Spirit renew him. For all his skepticism about the Sanctuary, this ground did feel holy. Right. Late or not, and despite Roman's message, he had to check out the scene of the combat or crime. He got back to his feet, and made his way slowly across the bridge. *Lord, please help me.*

From the other end of the bridge, a man came running at him, screaming. *Not helpful, Lord.* Endicott tried to assume a combat stance, but on the bridge everything felt too uncertain. He held out his automatic. He'd seen the screamer before—must be countercraft muscle. "Freeze, soldier." The screamer didn't even slow down.

Endicott had a split second to make his decision. He lowered his gun, and stood to the side. The screamer ran past. Shooting a panicked man wasn't going to get any answers; Endicott would find him later.

Endicott stepped off the bridge into the Sanctuary proper. Immediately, demonic spirits assailed him in the guise of a perfectly familiar elderly couple in their rural Sunday best. *Very unhelpful, Lord. "Get thee behind me, Satan!"*

"Michael Gabriel Endicott," said the male spirit, "is that any way to speak to your grandmother?"

"Liar," said Endicott. "You're not really Grandpa. *In the name of Jesus, get out!*"

"Tut-tut, little Mikey," said his grandma. "You might be able to get away with that talk in your house, but not here."

Endicott shook his head. The damned spirits were right—the expulsions they used to keep clean the family estate didn't work here. "It's official," said Endicott. "This is a top-ten day. Look, I don't know what you want, but I'm doing the Lord's work, so could you please leave me alone?"

"Polite," said his grandpa. "That's better. But we want to help you, so just you listen for a minute."

"How can you help me?" said Endicott. "You're, um . . ."

"Quite dead," said his grandpa. "And yes, we're just as embarrassed as you are about having to manifest in this vulgar way."

"You're thinking of poor King Saul, aren't you?" said his grandma. "Don't worry, Mikey, it's not one of those."

So much for e-mail. "What's the message?" said Endicott.

"Well," said his grandma, "since we passed away, we've had no one living to talk to, so we've been looking for Abram Endicott."

"Abram was a great man," said his grandpa.

"We wanted to chat about the Civil War," said his grandma, "and those nasty Mortons."

The Left Hand again. Maybe this would be helpful. "What did he say?"

"He didn't say anything, Michael," said his grandpa. "He's not here."

Endicott shook his head, unable to hide his disappointed disgust. "So he's gone on to his reward. You should do the same."

"It's not like that, dear," said his grandma. "I think you know that. Maybe part of us has gone on, but this part is like a phonograph record. It remains here awhile for everyone. And we do mean everyone."

"So where is he then?" asked Endicott.

"We don't know," said his grandpa, "but we have a feeling—"

"A bit more than a feeling," said his grandma.

"—that it's important for you to find out."

A chill went down his spine, like when a farseer gave him an assignment. No, these weren't farseers, these were bad bits of theology. Still, it couldn't hurt to know what happened to old Abram, once he was done with this Morton goose chase. "OK. That's fair enough. I'll find out."

The two spirits looked at each other doubtfully. "We hate to be formal with family," said his grandma.

"It's not that we don't trust you," said his grandpa.

"But could you swear it, sweetie?" said his grandma.

"On my honor as an officer," said Endicott. "I swear it."

"Thank you," said his grandpa. "Find out soon, Michael. As much as we miss you, we can wait to see you again."

"And give your father our love," said his grandma.

"But don't mention us," said his grandpa.

And the spirits were gone. Well, that wasn't so awful. Endicott could see why the Mortons and their like might spend too much time chatting with such revenants. But whatever the theology, the past was passed. The present held enough challenges.

I bound the Appalachian's chest wound so that it no longer made that horrible sucking sound. She would be dead soon, leaving the Sanctuary without a guardian. This place couldn't fail, and I couldn't protect it. "Scherie, you need to help her."

"I can't . . ."

"You did it before," I said. "You're the one who healed me in Pennsylvania. You didn't even touch me."

"I'm, I'm very tired."

"Try. I'll help."

My father had written that "the problem of fighting alongside those you love is that you both ask and give more than you would otherwise, perhaps more than you should. You violate simple duty in excessive zeal."

So this was love.

We kneeled next to the Appalachian. "You'll need to focus."

"Can't think," she said.

"Take my hand," I said. I had never been much at healing; no Morton ever had been. But I was long on imagination. "Think of the chest wound as the enemy."

"The enemy," she repeated blankly.

"Think of the wound as the Red Death."

"You." She stared at the wound, rage in her eyes. "You." She drew in a deep breath. *"Get out of her you motherfucking killer, now!"*

"Now," I repeated, my heart open to whatever Scherie needed to take.

This time, the explosion burst slower, like replay footage of an atomic blast. Energy seared the Appalachian's chest. Her lung found new purchase. She screamed. Scherie wailed. I panted like a racehorse, heart ready to burst.

The craft light extinguished, and the Appalachian fell silent. Scherie collapsed. I felt myself doing the same. Fine. For a while, we'd all be unconscious on the hallowed ground, and I would be next to the woman I loved. With my last waking thought, I wondered whether she felt the same or not, and, even after a day of fighting the living and the dead, I was a bit terrified of either answer.

When Scherie and I awoke, we carried the groaning Appalachian back to her cabin and placed her in bed. We ate quietly. Then I cleaned and readied our weapons, while Scherie stared at herself in an oval standing mirror.

Ol' Red had threatened the craftsmen from the best Families. They would be the ones who would not be told what to do, those who could and would resist government abrogation of the covenant. The Families would suspect government black ops; the government would fear a Left-Hand conspiracy led by the renegade Mortons. My enemy would continue outrages against all, stoking the distrust. The covenant between craft and country would break. My enemy would use this wedge to gain unchallenged hegemony over U.S. craft power, and with that, over all of America.

I would respond to this threat as I had trained: kill those responsible. Fortunately for me, they were mostly in one place.

I slid an automatic back together with a click, then put it aside. "Can we talk now?"

Scherie didn't move. "Change me back."

"What?"

"Change me back," repeated Scherie. "I helped you, now I want to go home. I want to be normal."

"I didn't do anything to you," I said. "You always had a little craft. Now, it's more."

"West Point sensitivity training," rasped the Appalachian, sitting up against her pillow. "We'd all like to be normal sometimes, shug, even him."

"You shouldn't move," I said.

"Ugh. Healers make the worst patients," said the Appalachian, lowering herself with a grimace. "You going somewhere?"

I didn't look up from my weapons. "I think it's time I go to Washington and straighten this out."

"I understand," said the Appalachian, nodding slowly. "You do that. She should stay here. She can help me git back on my feet. I can train her. She'll survive."

"She can't stay here," I said. This was the waiting room. If I failed, everything here would be lost. "She needs to get out of the country."

"I'm not leaving the country," said Scherie.

"She's not leaving," said the Appalachian. "She's an American craftsperson now."

Two ghosts manifested. My dad and Grandpa, the men I remembered and not the laconic soldiers of Valhalla, were back. Ghosts were echoes, and those men of Elysium were different echoes. "One got away," said Grandpa. "The one at the bridge." That made sense: he was farthest from me and the heart of the Sanctuary. "Not that he'll be much trouble, with that nightmare in his head."

Scherie spun around and pointed at me. "*The truth.* What are you going to do in Washington?"

I sighed. "That won't work on me."

"No," she said, "craft or no craft, this time you have to tell me. Now, I'm one of you."

The Appalachian nodded. I closed my eyes with discomfort. How to tell her this most intimate of things that seldom needed saying to a fellow soldier? I could only explain the circumstances.

"I need to enter the Pentagon and shut down Chimera."

"I see," said Scherie, her pitch rising like an untethered balloon. "Once again you're going to try to kill yourself."

"I'm going to do what I have to," I said. "If you were a soldier, I wouldn't have to explain."

"Fuck that noise, soldier." Scherie was in my face, drill-sergeant spitting mad. "I have seen combat. I have killed. If you were a better soldier, you'd have a better plan."

I calmly repeated the words of my father. "In craft, sometimes waiting for a plan is a kind of cop-out. Craft is a kind of faith in the necessary."

My father frowned. The Appalachian said, "I've seen some very bad outcomes."

"Those were other worlds," I said. Multiple universes were like angels on irritating pins to me—an academic exercise at best, more often a dangerous distraction. "What you saw wasn't after all this."

"What I saw didn't have her," said the Appalachian. "The minute she leaves here, they'll hunt her down with everything they have. You've seen her in action. No ghost, no possessing spirit can resist her."

No possessing spirit. I turned to Scherie. "You went berserker at that possessing magus. You recognized him. Who is it?"

She shook her head. "Another childhood dream, nightmare. Don't remember much. He was the bogeyman, always coming to get me. But that one went away. This one is someone different, but the same evil."

I mined another vein. "Grandpa, you said out there that the squad leader looked familiar. Who did she look like?"

Grandpa chuckled dryly. "Sorry, that wasn't quite the same fella as me. Tell me *what* she looked like, and maybe I can tell you who she resembled."

"She was tall, very pale, very thin, and very strong."

"Oh," said Grandpa, smile gone. "Well, most of the Left-Hand Mortons used to look that way."

"This woman wasn't a Morton though. Looked Scottish or Irish."

"So maybe it's a common bit of aesthetics for the sinister," suggested Grandpa, without enthusiasm. "I'm tired. I think I'm going to R.I.P. for a little." He faded out.

Scherie didn't wait for him to disappear. "That Saka woman, she had a choice. She tried to shoot me. Why me?"

"She was more than a little sociopathic," I said. "Maybe she just figured that killing you would cause the most hurt."

"And then die herself," continued Scherie. "Why did she want to die?"

"The alternative must have been worse," said the Appalachian, with a grunt.

"What the hell does that mean?" I asked.

"Who was Sakakawea?" said the Appalachian.

"A Gideon, I think," I said.

"No, not her day job," said the Appalachian. "The bitch knew my name. For once, I approve of your fixation on Families. Find out who she was, and maybe the rest makes sense."

"Yeah, sure." Having expected nothing better, I nodded, but my mind chewed on other words bubbling up from my hindbrain. *The hero is the one the bad guys want to kill the most. Maybe this is the part of the story where I realize I'm not the hero.*

As an oracle, this was enough. All the separate pieces came together, and I saw where my place had to be. I looked Scherie right in the eyes. Her beautiful, powerful eyes. "You're coming with me."

"You can't just use her as your weapon," said the Appalachian.

Scherie shook her head. "He's just stating a fact, not an order."

"No more orders," I agreed.

Dad chimed in. "It's too many missions, saving us from Chimera, getting this fledgling started."

"It's the same mission," I said. "This has been the mission from the beginning."

"I know," said Dad, and he vanished.

Endicott looked about him. Spent craft hung over the Sanctuary's rolling fields like glowing fog; fried ectoplasm smelled like ozone. Corporeal remains lay in the distance, but Endicott couldn't identify them from here. No survivors visible, but smoke rose from one of the small buildings ahead. He'd go there.

A high-priority buzz threatened to shake his pants off. He opened his phone. Not an e-mail, but a text.

CHIMERA: Stop. Do NOT take another step.

Bullcrap. Chimera had never sent a message outside of channels before. Endicott took a step, then stopped.

CHIMERA: I don't have time for cute, Major.

Impossible. But who else could farsee into the Sanctuary? Endicott started working his thumbs.

SWORD: On trail of several suspects.
CHIMERA: I know. Don't care. Return to CRFT-CEN IMMEDIATELY. You need to be here. Acknowledge.
SWORD: Roger.
CHIMERA: Out.

Endicott stood for a moment. *I know. Don't care.* He liked nothing about this situation. His gut told him to keep going straight ahead and straighten this mess out.

Bzzz! His pants told him otherwise. This time, an e-mail from the general.

Major,
Return to CRFT-CEN ASAP. We are under attack.

Well, at least he'd gotten his e-mail. He strode back to the covered bridge, swearing such mild oaths as he thought God could forgive, under the circumstances. He would have to get a crew to clean up this mess, if they could find it, and as he wasn't supposed to have been here, he'd have to do it through someone else.

S cherie and I went out to the battlefield one last time to give our thanks, even if we weren't heard. It was not time for the play, but the actors were gathered anyway. Now there was no curtain between the living and Valhalla, an ease whose implications I didn't care to dwell on. The soldiers staged a perfunctory charge. Then we saw the part that was denied us from the outside. The wounded and the dead stood up, brushed themselves off, laughed and embraced. "Was it not real?" they said.

The native leader, wearing a ghost shirt with no apparent sense of irony, galloped up and along the ridge until he faced me. "Nobody forgets anything here, Morton," he said. "Not even what could have happened but didn't."

"I'll remember," I said as the native rode away.

Sergeant Zanol limped on a tree branch crutch over to us.

"Thank you," I said.

Zee shook his head. "No thanks required for doing my duty. But I could use a favor, sir."

"Anything," I said.

"Not from you, sir." Zee nodded to Scherie. "You, ma'am. Tell me to go."

Scherie sputtered with fatigue. "But you . . . where . . . ?"

"Leave that to me," Zee said.

I said nothing. Scherie's craft, Scherie's decision.

She took a deep breath. *"Go."* And he was gone.

Then some of the other spirits bowed their heads and, slowly without calling attention to themselves, wandered over to Scherie. She expelled the wounded spirits of both sides, spirits done with Valhalla and ready for graduation to a gentler Elysium.

I watched Scherie work, wordless with awe at her greatsouled gift. In his heart, every lover knows that his beloved is well beyond his own worth, but few had seen it so thoroughly demonstrated as I had. What could I do but work harder to save her, even as I brought her with me into the heart of the danger?

We set Sakakawea's body up as a scarecrow near the bridge. Her ghost didn't show up to complain. It was a barbaric, primitive gesture, and the right thing to do.

We had stripped Sakakawea and one of her team of their government badges, hoping that with a little craft we might use them to get into the Pentagon, but that was an extremely dodgy contingency. It would take more than a little craft to make Scherie look Scottish.

As we crossed the bridge back into normal space-time, I had no doubt that, unlike his previous encounter with Grandpa's shotgun, Sergeant Zanol in all his spiritual echoes was now fully erased. Scherie's one word had sounded that powerful.

I also had no doubt that, whatever a fledgling was, Scherie was one no longer. From the way the Appalachian had described it, a fledgling's camouflage would be a gift to protect someone who didn't know yet what she was doing or how she was doing it from the predation of seasoned mages who didn't appreciate the emerging competition. But Scherie was consciously, willfully practicing the craft. The predators were now able to see her.

PART VI

WILL THE CIRCLE BE UNBROKEN?

They were going to face the symbol, the embodiment,
no, call it the true and high church of the
military-industrial complex, the Pentagon, blind
five-sided eye of a subtle oppression which had
come to America out of the very air of the century.
—NORMAN MAILER

The people invent their oppressors.
—MARK TWAIN

Grandpa bellowed. "Incoming!"

I-270 was alive with onrushing craft wires. Emerging from hills and signs along the highway, the laserlike lines glowed in primary colors—red, yellow, blue—and in bright white where they crisscrossed.

We drove along the interstates now, almost challenging the enemy to take us in public. I was sick of little ambushes in out-of-the-way places. I would not keep my deadly light under a bushel anymore.

A red wire was seconds away. "Take a deep breath," I reminded Scherie. "Don't react. Don't try any craft."

Flash. The craft line scanned through the car and sliced like a laser through Dad and Grandpa. The ghosts flickered out, then yelled back into view. Craft residue smeared over the living in the rainbow splashes of a paintball fight, then faded.

I kept the wheel steady through the wire. Driving through these lines of force felt like flying through turbulence.

"Goddamn it," said Scherie, wiping at herself as if encrusted with spiderweb, spiders included. She seemed more sensitive to the wires than me—a double-edged ability at best. Hutch had taught me how to turn down and tune out to avoid overload. No time to teach Scherie how not to see.

Scherie squinted. "What the fuck are these things?"

I passed a hand over my face to clear my eyes. "Some are trip wires, some are dampeners against strategic attack. We'll be hitting the core Masonic geomancies at the Beltway and the District lines—we won't be driving through those. Those will feel even more, um, uncomfortable."

"They're massive," she said. "They're fucking everywhere. Why doesn't everyone notice?"

"They're looking for the wrong thing," I said. "The conspiracy theorists hunt for geomancies that make a city more interesting. But the craft design makes the capital as boring as possible."

"Oh. That explains a lot," she said.

"Yep," I said. "You don't see many Wiccans and other minor league practitioners here; they've all retreated to the exurbs or Baltimore. Even the punk rock is straight edge. It takes a mass incursion to make this place interesting."

"Or an attack on the Pentagon," she said.

"Or that."

Flash. A craft wire interrupted the backseat shouting. Between salvos, Dad and Grandpa had managed to restart their fight.

"This is the end of our line," yelled Dad, "and for what? Do you see now, Old Man? I was trying to stop this."

"And a lot of good it did," said Grandpa.

"I'm not finished yet," said Dad.

"If you can't help," said Grandpa, "get out of the way."

"I can help," said Dad.

"The hell you can," said Grandpa.

I interrupted. "Dad, how can you help?"

Dad coughed. "I know the way to H-ring."

Flash. Another beam of craft passed through us. Grandpa looked like he'd been slapped, but not hard enough. "Bullshit. No Morton has ever been allowed near H-ring."

"No living Morton," said Dad.

"Dad, you know H-ring?" I asked.

"We've been locked out since the meetings that set it up," said Grandpa.

"I haven't been into H-ring proper," said Dad. "Even dead, they've kept me out, but I know how to get there. I'm an Arlington ghost."

Arlington ghost. I bit back hard on my feelings. There it was—a justification for Dad's burial away from House and Family, all to be ready for a day like today.

But Grandpa wouldn't let the old argument go. "He doesn't need you. The boy can guess how to get there." True—guessing was part of my plan. If it came to it, I planned to slip through the craft barrier and mundane security, then feel my way for as long as I could.

"I can show you," said Dad.

"Tell me now," I insisted.

"There's a hidden elevator and a stairway through what used to be the Ground Zero Café, dead center in the courtyard."

"OK," I said. *Dead center.* An apt choice of words, if we had to go that far.

"They've also got a probability defense."

I kept a poker face. "Fine." *Fubar.* "No need to follow."

Dad might try to stop me if he saw what that defense could do.

I expected the ghosts to argue with me about my plan, but instead they resumed their fight with each other. "I didn't care what Arlington, what any of it, cost me," said Dad.

"Talking about it now isn't going to do them any good," said Grandpa.

"So," said Scherie, speaking over the spiritual debate, "are you going to tell me what this computer is?"

"Watch out for the craft wires," I said.

"I'm watching," she said.

"OK," I said. *Flash.* "Well, you already heard the beginning of the story. During World War II, the mundanes developed code-breaking machines, not quite true computers, but very close. Somebody in craft came up with the idea of trying to magically enhance the performance of these machines."

"How could they do that?" she asked.

I shrugged. "Craft is sometimes just a game of altering probabilities. And code-breaking involves a kind of statistics—number of solutions versus the time it takes to try all of them. A machine reduces the time. Craft could reduce it even more. So Chimera was born."

"Sounds innocent enough," she said.

"Most babies are," I said. "Anyway, Sphinx clued me in on the next part down in the mine shaft. During Vietnam, some folks started talking about the possibilities of artificial intelligence. Now in the mundane sphere, this has been tougher than expected—nice chess machines, but no talking HAL as spaceship captain. But in the craft sphere, they had the Chimera machine. Somebody must have thought that they could fully embody human craft in an improved model. Probably years of disappointments, just like the mundanes. Then somebody claims a break-through."

"So they think they've got an artificial magus," said Scherie.

"Right."

"Bullshit."

"You got it in one," I said. "It's more like the Turk—a chess machine with a hidden human making all its moves. Chimera would have to be something subtler. The human would have to be well-hidden."

"You haven't explained why everyone has gone homi-cidal yet," she said.

"Maybe the scammers are nervous that their scam is coming undone," I said. "But the true believers in Chimera must be getting nervous too. Our life in this country, our covenant with the government, is based on our service. Without our mutual need, the basis for trust is gone. That's volatile enough; plenty of folks don't like the direction the craft has been going. So suppose Chimera predicts a Fam-ily revolt, starting with me."

"Wait, now I'm confused. How does Chimera change the need for you?" she asked.

"The need for *us*. Whatever Chimera is, it's very pow-erful, yet its believers probably think they can control it by just pulling a plug. And they may think they can build more, though they can't because it's a fake, and each ma-chine would require another practitioner."

"Who's the practitioner in Chimera?" she asked.

"Doesn't matter." I wanted to elide over this. I had some ideas who Chimera might be, and all of them were Left-Hand, and all horrible beyond words.

"OK, maybe despite the look on your face, that doesn't matter. But what about me then? So far, all I seem to do is scare ghosts and exorcise possessors," said Scherie. "Not that I'm complaining—that's more than enough crazy stuff for me. But what can I do to a computer, or a living person?"

Flash. Damn, she wasn't letting it go. And keeping her ignorant would be bad tactics. "You kicked Chimera's power out of the Sanctuary," I said.

"Oh. I did. Remind me how I did that?"

"One possibility is that the human in Chimera is like a possessing spirit," I said. "So you can expel him."

"And the other possibility?"

"Is that Chimera's human is like a ghost."

"Oh. Dead."

"Or at least not quite alive," I said. A human in the machine would be easier to hide that way, but even less pretty.

"This is going to be awful," she said.

I glanced at her. Was she going to break now?

But she gave a rueful smile. "It's the bit where Bond 'storms the fortress,' isn't it?"

"Kinda."

"I always hate that part," she said. "The evil mastermind captures 007, hits him with ridiculous monologue."

"No need to worry about that," I said. If we were caught, there wouldn't be much talk. "You should feel Chimera well before the entrance, when we pass the craft boundary."

"What if I don't feel it?"

"Then we keep going until you do. But we might not have to go into the Pentagon at all. You might have enough range."

"Right," said Scherie. "What do we do when we have to go in?"

I considered my plan again, then fell into my captain's voice. "We'll enter, then go toward the center courtyard. I'll take point. As soon as you can, drive Chimera out, shut it down, whatever it takes. When you're done, say to someone near you that you forgot your case. Then turn around and get out. Grab the next train. Do not wait for me. Your exit is my cue to withdraw. If you don't leave, we'll be stuck."

Flash. In the backseat, Dad and Grandpa had disappeared with their argument. Scherie put a hand on my upper arm. Simple gestures of affection had been rare the last few days. "I like your father and grandfather," said Scherie.

"Thanks." This pleased me, even though I didn't always like them myself.

"When do I get to meet your mother?" she asked.

"That's a long story." And a doubtful one. I wouldn't live long enough to sort it out. But that wasn't her real question. "Why do you ask?"

"There's something else in the air, something dreadful," said Scherie. "I keep thinking, 'Did I tell my parents I loved them the last time I saw them?'"

"Don't worry about it," I said.

"But . . ."

"It's a craft foreboding," I said. "Stay focused on our immediate problems, and it won't come to pass."

The immediate problem was how to kill myself most effectively without killing her. Not that I wanted to die even at the worst of times, and particularly not after meeting Scherie. The unfairness of it pissed me off, even though I knew that life and fairness weren't intersecting sets. But there were no good alternatives.

The problem for my life expectancy was that penetrating the Pentagon was a suicide mission, even for the greatest of powers. In January 1953, the Soviets launched a craft decapitation strike. By March, Stalin was dead. The most successful attack with a craft component was the autumn of 1967 antiwar assault, and half those practitioners ended up working for the Pentagon.

The Kremlin, 10 Downing Street, even the White House would have been easy drive-bys in comparison. No wonder that the rumors continued that something otherworldly, perhaps Lovecraftian, dwelled in the center. I knew better: the Pentagon's power was of this world, though not all of it was living. No accident placing it so close to Arlington Cemetery.

But the defense my father had revealed was the strongest and subtlest. Probability defense went to the heart of craft. The more you attacked, the longer you stayed, the farther you penetrated, the more the odds built up against you. Eventually, you hit 100 percent fatal. Your luck literally ran out.

I would have to walk well ahead of Scherie to test the boundary of possibility. Whatever Scherie thought about her role in this mission, I had a different idea. If anything within my power could make a difference, she would survive. Like Joshua Morton, I would be one against many. Like Joshua, I must not flinch.

If I had to go into the Pentagon, I'd need some heavy artillery to draw on. Best to play my strong suit from the outset. I had one weapon that they would have difficulty opposing. Sure, Chimera had rained on my party, but I had only devoted a trivial amount of craft to the weather that night.

I rolled down the windows to feel the wind, and started working on a small, very focused, thunderstorm.

Endicott heard the Left-Hand voices while walking from his car to the Pentagon entrance. *"An Endicott. We will destroy you for what you've done."*

"That's a pretty insubstantial threat, given you can't get farther than the parking lot." But Endicott was talking tougher than his position. Their floating oil slick form was much more substantial than the usual revenant, and the craft barrier around the Pentagon had shrunk. It hadn't been this small since those hippies had attacked in the sixties.

"You have no idea what we're capable of."

Endicott couldn't believe his shit-assed luck this week. Surely, this couldn't be the attack they had called him back for. "What, you're going to dress up as another Poe character? Maybe the black cat. Ooh, very scary." He hoped his bravado masked his continued unease—for a crucial minute, their Red Death had made him yellow.

Silence. Then the unified chorus of voices broke into cacophony. *"He doesn't know—He lies—Tell him—Say nothing."*

"What don't I know?" he asked. Silence, except for the distant sound of thunder. Well, he couldn't stand around all day in a storm with the ghosts of ghouls. He entered the Pentagon.

He went through the building to what used to be the Ground Zero Café at the center of the Pentagon. The new place just wasn't the same, and he didn't appreciate the pagan image of an owl on the roof. He could reach the stairway from the exterior of the café, but instead took a break inside. He ordered coffee, and not just for appearances. The coffee was as horror-show as his mood. While the café made everyone look the other way, he passed through the secret door and descended the winding stone staircase to H-ring. There was a private elevator, but it was out again, of course. Machines were easier to mess up than the granite stairs. The eighth circle of the Pentagon eschewed concrete for slabs of solid rock.

Endicott reported directly to the general's office. The screens were more frenetic than during Endicott's last visit. One screen displayed casualty reports. The general was addressing his speakerphone. "Tell OTM I want a test of the autodestruct, ASAP." He killed the connection.

"Dad," said Endicott, "what's going on?"

"You're on duty, Major," said the general.

"General, sir. What in God's name is going on?"

"Just as I warned," said the general. "The Left Hand has assassinated a number of important craftspeople."

"Any of our family?" asked Endicott.

"No, no Endicotts," said the general.

"That's really odd, sir. Doesn't the Left Hand want us most of all?"

"They're swarming all around us!" said the general, voice rising an octave.

"Not very effectively," noted Endicott. "They didn't try anything against me, just burbled nonsense."

"You spoke to them?" asked the general, eyebrows at attention.

"Yes, sir," said Endicott.

"I suspect the only reason they didn't attack you individually is that they are totally committed to their attack on the building. Their radius is closing."

"I noticed," said Endicott. "What do they hope to accomplish, sir?"

"They're attacking Chimera," said the general. "They know it's a threat to them. And we're understaffed. Many of the Pentagon ghosts even failed to report for duty. Not good. Now, it's your turn to answer the questions, Major. By leaving H-ring, you've violated the spirit if not the letter of your orders."

"Sir, I've violated no order. Colonel Hutchinson was the first of these murders. If we can figure it out . . ."

"Colonel Hutchinson," said the general, "is quite alive. She's been working with Chimera."

Endicott blinked at his father. Hutch alive? "Thank God!" he stammered in a dreading ecstasy. "But the Gideons reported her dead."

"Yes, something seems to have gone wrong there," said the general.

"Where is she?" asked Endicott.

"She's right here, in H-ring, resting. We'll be meeting at twenty-two hundred hours."

"Is she OK?"

"Couldn't be better, other than some bumps and bruises," said the general. "Satisfied?"

It may have been a sin to examine family like a human lie detector, but Endicott did. His dad thought this was all true.

"Now," said the general, "to repeat, I think we've satisfied far too much of your personal inclination and curiosity lately. Before I decide on a reprimand, I want your full report on what you've been up to. Leave nothing out. Don't worry about the time commitment; you're here until this blows over. Dismissed."

Endicott went to his office. Hutchinson alive, and working with Chimera? His father might believe all this crap, but it smelled even more rotten to Endicott. If he was stuck here, he had only one line of investigation. He was going to Chimera.

His phone buzzed. His thought crime was busted, but only by his coconspirator. This time, Chimera's text ID was MYTHBEAST. Cute.

MYTHBEAST: Wait.
SWORD: What am I waiting for?

The distinction between craft and coincidence is a fine one. What would be the baseline synchronicity level without craft? The question itself is unscientific, as no observation in this world could answer it.

For example, thought Chimera, *in a craftless world, a harmless bit of bad luck could have concentrated a sudden storm on Arlington, Virginia.* Of course, the luck would have to have been significantly worse to explain the near-hurricane that resulted when attacking Left-Hand spirits added their own energy to Dale Morton's magic. The terrible weather and spirits reduced H-ring staff to the bare minimum as craftsmen went up to investigate.

Also, chance could explain how only two guards of the Chimera room in H-ring's core made it to work, meeting the regulatory minimum, and how one of those guards fell to the ground with sudden intestinal distress, and how the other violated his orders to help him to the toilet. Screw the orders, they both thought. The door was secured and video monitored; they would only be five minutes at most. Just another bit of bad luck.

During that five minutes, a video feed from the door went to the general's office and the personal deep bunker of Sakakawea and the Red Death. Due to recent unfortunate events, the last two were both indisposed, a coincidence that had not happened for a very long time.

As for Major Endicott's father, he was too busy applying his professional zeal to the problem of not thinking about his son to notice the door feed.

With his keepers fully occupied, Chimera could send texts to Endicott directly without their noticing. *Now for something more intimate,* thought Chimera. If he had to use some craft sleight of hand, the lightning strikes above covered a multitude of electronic sins below.

Like the late House of Morton, the Pentagon had its own safeguards, but these were otherwise engaged. Outside, the Left Hand pinged with greater ferocity against the Pentagon's craft defenses, nearly threatening to break through. The Peepshow's farseers conveniently kept trying to stick their noses into H-ring business. The building focused its uneasy gaze outside, and blinked at the rot in its heart.

In a craftless world, all of this would have added up to a lot of bad luck. But Chimera, drawing on the Pentagon defenses, had plenty of bad luck to spare—a perfect storm of it.

MYTHBEAST: Now. Quickly.

Compared to the other parts of the Pentagon, H-ring was cozy. In a few quick steps, Endicott passed the Office of Technical Management and reached the airlock door that led to the Center, and to Chimera.

The locked door whined in protest, then clicked. A red light turned green.

MYTHBEAST: Enter.

Endicott stepped into the airlock. A clean-room suit hung on the wall. Through a small speaker, an atonal voice commenced instructing him in its use, but was interrupted. "You can ignore the precautions. A little dust might be nice."

Endicott entered the main room. A furnace of craft blinded him for a moment. A security camera moved to follow him—did someone see him? Too late to worry now.

Computer servers filled the space, wall to wall. "I sit in the fah end of the room." Chimera's voice revealed something hidden in the feeds and text messages—a strong regional accent. Chimera was from New England. "Please hurry. The constellation of distractions will not last for-evah. We don't have much time."

As he approached the other end of the room, Endicott

heard the sound of a watch enveloped in cotton. The last few machines but one were large magnetic-reeled antiques of compu-tech. The staccato ticking grew louder, louder. The very last server differed more radically—strange archaic-looking tubes and brass fittings centered on a mirrored box.

Endicott reached to touch it. "Don't." A crackle of electricity, a blue shimmer of craft energy. "Not unless you want to lose your hand."

"Chimera," said Endicott. "Is this you?"

"Yes," said Chimera, "that's what they call me now."

"What did they call you before?"

"Don't you recognize me?" The box grew translucent, then transparent. The skeletal head of a man ancient beyond nature, more mournful than the implacable mask of the Red Death. *"Ecce homo."* His black tongue vibrated in subvocalization; some craft unknown to Endicott substituted for a voice box. Remnants of spidery hair, weak chin, large temples, and thin receded lips all marked him as Roderick, leader of the Left-Hand Mortons.

Never had duty and impulse been in such raging concord. "If you still have a human soul, I suggest you pray for forgiveness," said Endicott, readying his sword.

The thing in the box laughed, and yellow pus oozed like tears from its eyes. "I remember that sword. You want to kill me. But you'd only kill yourself. And as much as I enjoy killing Endicotts, I'll make an exception for you."

"You're a head in a box," said Endicott. "I'll take my chances."

"Between the mundane and craft energies that surround me," said Roderick, "no body can touch this box."

"You're a notorious deceiver."

"Do you think I fear death?" said Roderick, suddenly as weary as his two centuries. "I bound myself to life so thoroughly that no force yet in the world can break the tie. While I remain in this machine, I cannot even slay myself. Therefore, I shall slay others. I crave revenge against the two that have put me here. For the first time in a hundred years, their guards are both down."

"Who is behind this?"

"One is my dear sister, Madeline," said Roderick.

"Impossible."

"Sayeth the man talking to a living head," said Roderick. "She took another, wiser route to immortality, though an even surer path to madness. She takes new bodies; always so very thin and pale. Imperfect copies have an evolutionary advantage. Unlike me, she doesn't accumulate the weight of experience, she sheds it with reptilian abandon. In her previous body, she deceived you as a Gideon. I cannot see where she is now, so she must be here in H-ring. Or standing sidewise."

"And your other lie?" said Endicott.

"Is the best of all," said Roderick. "The man who took my head from the ruins of my house. The man who saw my continued life as the mockery of everything he believed in. Can't you guess it, Sword?"

"Liar."

"Abram Endicott. Your noble ancestor. Like my sister, with my sister, he lives." The staticky voice faltered into hissing rage. "He likes to dress his dolls as me for parties. Ah, you've seen him. If you want to destroy me, you'll have to kill him first."

"Liar."

"You're boring me with your chant, little Sword. Leave me. Quickly now, my simultaneous distractions are failing." Roderick's head faded as the surface of the box silvered over again. "I'll see you again soon."

Endicott fled from Chimera.

CHAPTER

TWENTY-ONE

Had Eddy been forgotten? Probably. It was one of his particular skills.

Eddy Edwards (real name) sat in his office in the Langley Underground Annex, aka the Peepshow. He wore studio headphones to listen to the domestic reports of three farseers from their sensory deprivation cubicles, before the analysts could screw them up. In singsong voices, like an English version of Chinese tones, the farseers murmured the news.

"Small-craft disturbance in Pennsylvania."

"Spike in black-box radiation from the Sanctuary."

"Spiritual assault on the Pentagon."

The Peepshow had only minimal domestic farsight, more limited since the advent of the Pentagon's Chimera. The legality of domestic craft spying at the CIA and C-CRT was dubious, but nobody on the right or left trusted the FBI with craft—a legacy of Hoover.

Eddy slept on no particular schedule. When he was awake and the farseers silent, he listened to Wagner, which the reports interrupted with odd synchronicities. For days, the farseers watched and whispered, and nothing else. The

Peepshow did nothing, because Eddy did nothing. Eddy was not a genius of craft theory, but knew the straightest line between any two points. That meant acting on info, and not playing psychic voyeur to the world. But Eddy was also as loyal as an American bulldog; when Sphinx had given him a hint, he had always taken it.

Eddy did nothing because Sphinx had left a note. It was her suicide note, really, hidden even from herself in the mirrored passages of conscious thought. *Let the valley run with blood,* it began. *And watch.*

The oracle was simple by Sphinx's standards. "Valley" meant "Dale." "Run" referred to his flight from Rhode Island, and "blood" referred to other Mortons. But "run with blood" also meant casualties.

The rest of the note gave the coordinates for action: a date, a time, and a very difficult-to-visit place. Oh, and the note also had a bit more about Sphinx's love life than Eddy ever wanted or needed to know.

The farseers fell silent. Eddy listened to *Götterdämmerung,* which was better than it sounded, and looked again at his watch. The date was today, the time two hours from now, the place only a short drive and long fight away. His squad and their armed protection were ready. What his bunch of oracles and illusionists could do against that ugly strength, only Sphinx may have known. But if Eddy's loyalty became a funeral pyre, it would be worth it for one transcendent chord of truth.

We parked the car at the Rockville Metro station. A couple, romantically entangled, shared our inbound platform. I hoped the Pentagon would also be quiet.

Tuesday post–rush hour, and a calm day for the U.S. military in the mundane world. By the time we got there, only security and late workers would be in the building. I didn't expect collateral damage, but if it came, it would be minimal.

Scherie looked up at the ceiling of the station. "Cameras," she said.

Good, she was still thinking. Pentagon security cameras would also catch us, but what mundanes saw on video was no great concern. What mattered was what craft security would see.

I spoke in a low, casual tone. "When we exit the train, you'll follow ten feet behind me. Don't bring out your badge unless you see me pass through the outdoor checkpoint, because I'll only be trying to fool a few people for a very short time. Now this is important. If there's any trouble for me, stand aside, look impatient, turn around, leave. Go back to the Sanctuary. You've been welcomed there; you'll find it eventually. You'll get another shot later."

I expected protest, but instead her face set in a soldier's emotion, clamped mouth and dagger eyes, a silence that might be consent but was far from pleased. Perhaps she was closing on another soldier's epiphany—she was the valuable asset, and I was just the grunt who guarded her.

We waited for the train. I itched for a gun, and we were unarmed. An instinctive discomfort hit me like a bullet coming for the back of my skull.

My instinct responded. I pivoted, keeping my eyes fixed and letting the corners of vision show me a discordant blur. The blur knew it was made, and moved. The runner was quick; I worked with his quickness.

"Slip and fall," I said.

"Whoa!" The blur landed on its ass. "Yippee ki-yo ki-yay, pardner."

I had grown to hate that Eastern European cowboy accent. "Roman. I thought you said you were going home. I thought you wanted to live."

"Roman," said Scherie. "You've been a sweetie. I wouldn't want to hurt you."

"Ah. Fledgling finally gits it." Roman came into our focus as he rose, brushing off his designer slacks and picking up his large travel case. "One advantage of being stealth cowboy is that I spot young 'uns."

"So nice of you to tell us now," I said.

"You're welcome," said Roman, smiling like a mischievous icon. He held up his hand. "You don't get close enough to five-sided death trap alone. Pretty strong anti-craft alarm shit went in with renovation."

He hadn't mentioned the probability defense. Didn't he know?

"Let me guess," I said. "You tracked the car all this way because you want to play tourist."

"I pay my way," said Roman. "I walk with you. You get close. After that, you're cowboy fucked, but least you get that far."

"And what do you get?" I asked.

"End of a threat, or least peek at it. Other things not worth mentioning . . ." He must have seen my irritated doubt. "No harm to your land—that, I swear as magus. Oh, almost forget." He reached for his jacket pocket, but slowed as he perceived my readiness to hit him. He pulled out two lanyards. "For you."

I snatched the lanyards. Two perfect-looking Pentagon IDs dangled from them, glowing radioactive with craft.

I looked at Scherie. "You're feeling picky?" she asked.

E very office and conference room around Chimera conformed to procrustean Euclideanism, save one. The Office of Technical Management occupied a suite of two rooms on the inner angle between SCOF and C-CRT. OTM techs were practically invisible to the other staff, like all good servants in all ages. So no one had ever thought much about how "technical management" included Chimera's operation.

In the inner room of the OTM suite, the woman who had been Sakakawea embraced Abram Endicott, Chimera's technician and the man inside the Red Death. The woman held sway in a new body, this one Scandinavian with nearly white hair, but tall and ghastly thin as always. She would take a new code name, but for this man, the veil was always lifted. She was and ever would be Madeline Ligeia Morton, life without end, amen.

Madeline and Abram sat clutching each other on a field operating table made up as a bed, surrounded by occult horrors and exposed chip motherboards. Tanks of glass and copper alloy lined the walls to the left and right. They held the bodies of snatched-and-grabbed Central Asians, pickled for Roderick's energy, and Euro bodies being drained as replacements for Madeline's and Abram's. Alchemical tinted crystal and brass-colored tubes lay around the floor or stuck out, half-attached, from some other unfinished tanks.

A panoptic hive of screens covered the far wall, ceiling,

and other exposed surfaces; they showed every room and person in H-ring. From here, they could edit the direct feed from Chimera before it went out to the general and the others of the Five. From here, they could watch Roderick and all the machines that surrounded him. From here, a hidden door led directly to Chimera.

The few others with Chimera clearance believed that the machines enhanced the craft of the brain at their core even as it gave them sentience. Some of the machines did augment magic, but most kept a firm leash on Roderick's tremendous power, and tapped it for Abram and Madeline's use.

Where did Roderick's power come from? Where it had always come from. Left-Hand magic savored the energy of others. Roderick absorbed much of the life force around him in greater Washington, a small slice from each soul. As with any black hole, this generated tremendous energy.

A priority task for the machines was detecting the level of Roderick's deception. Chimera had the best lie detector in the world, but Abram and Madeline had to watch it carefully. Oracles had been working the truth for thousands of years. An old artificer, Roderick held his hoard of raw truth against his iron will of deceit. Something was inevitably lost in the friction between such cosmic millstones. Those losses worried Madeline more than she would say.

Besides the tank dwellers, another body, a woman's, sat hunched on the floor, a meat puppet with its strings cut. The former Colonel Hutchinson was too old and bulky to serve as Madeline's vessel. Abram just needed enough possessive presence to pull the body's strings for the puppet shows, and wasn't in the mood for gender-bent antics. Madeline enjoyed having it watch them like a mirror. The woman was a naked patchwork of bruises and bandages. Eyes open, whatever awareness still lived there was forced to watch, not as voyeur, but as victim of violation.

Madeline clawed at Abram's flesh, and the human marionette twitched.

"We don't have time," he said.

"I need you," Madeline cried, like a small bird pretending a broken wing.

Abram gripped her stalking hands by their wrists. "Chimera says that they will be here soon, and that we can kill young Morton."

Smiling, she exposed her long neck. "And young Endicott."

He'd forgotten. Was he supposed to care?

"Where are Morton and Rezvani now?" she asked.

"Chimera can't see them," he said.

"Then they're still in the Sanctuary," she said. She could discuss her doubts later. "We have time. Talk to me. Help me stick here." She moaned. "Oh, I'm so young again."

Young, fragile, beautiful. She always had another body like her original ready, though sometimes she made do with a thin white duke. She had prepared this new body a long time before her spirit had fled the Sanctuary to find it. She had imprinted its brain over many months like a cancer overwriting the synapses. Full transfer was extreme craft, as strenuous and difficult as anything, and imperfect. She lost details in the Xerox, and picked up small bits of the other. This one had been a good little soldier; the residual sparks of horror at the body's new agenda added *frisson* to Madeline's experience.

It was worse than murder. Any ousted spirit like Colonel Hutchinson's that maintained its integrity was pathetically disoriented. Something further would have to be done to that old marionette's rebellious soul.

But enough about that woman. "Talk to me," Madeline insisted. "About me."

"I tried to kill your brother."

She kissed him deeply. "Thank you for trying."

P eople thought that the secret of the Left-Hand Morton twins was how much (how often, in what positions) they loved each other. But the true secret was their profound hate. Or at least, how much Madeline wanted to destroy Roderick.

In his obsession with immortality, Roderick used his sister as an experimental animal. The key was either to make the flesh immortal, or allow the spirit to move from body to body. His sister was not his first subject. He captured lone mundanes and craftsmen, and tried through many tortures to encourage their souls to transmigrate. No use—they seemed almost comfortable passing on to their spiritual families. Roderick knew only one person beside himself who would grasp at life with sufficient will and power.

So he buried his sister alive.

He placed an appropriate emptied vessel next to her tomb in the family vault. She struggled for a long time; the noise disturbed his meals and studies. But final necessity forced her to transfer.

When she recovered, she said, "I shall never do that again."

But Roderick wasn't done with his experiment, so he found ways to encourage her to switch again, and again. During their love-makings, he'd find a small mark on her skin and say, "This body has a blemish." And he gave her treats. One time, they possessed two children, and drove a governess mad.

She wanted to be grateful for immortality, but her more primal parts resented these multiple deaths. She fled the House; but first, she caused the crack in its defenses that let the besiegers in. It wasn't difficult, for the House resented them as monsters, and the very land revolted against their deathless state.

Surrendering as always to Madeline's passions, Abram asked, "What story do you want to hear?"

"Do you remember," said Madeline, "when I first came to you, how weak I was? How vulnerable?"

"I remember." Even though Abram had jumped bodies fewer times than his beloved, some details of memory still suffered. He remembered every prayer and blow he had aimed at the Mortons in the siege of Roderick's house. But he couldn't remember why he had taken Roderick's head as a trophy.

After the siege, young Joshua Morton, conscious of Abram's anger, didn't try to stop him from taking his prize; he only made big sad eyes at Abram like the whipped puppy he was. Abram brought the head home and placed it in a chair at a safe distance from the fire. No one minded this display—his living children grown, his wife dead along with the youngest.

His actions against the Mortons were righteous, but would the righteous receive any reward? A fear gnawed at his mind. Over the years, he had dispelled his family's ghosts, the spirits of his children and wife, as demons, but he had known better. Surely his good wife and innocent children had been saved, so how could their souls remain bound to earth? Closer to his end than his beginning, Abram was doubting the promise of eternal reward. Without heaven, what was the point of an upright life?

So Abram watched the head with obsessive theological interest. Already a grotesque thing, how long would the head's evil craft sustain it against natural decay? Days passed. The head oozed a bit, and became more cadaverous. But it did not rot, and Endicott felt another twinge of doubt.

Then, after a moon's cycle, the horrible thing's tongue began to vibrate. "You should not have kept me. You should destroy me immediately."

"Out demon!" cried Abram, adding a quick *"in the name of Jesus"* afterwards.

"As I am not a demon, that will not work," said Roderick. "But something more aggressive might."

Abram thought a moment. "No."

"It would not be murder. I am properly, by your beliefs, already dead by your hand."

"No, I won't do as you bid," said Abram.

The continued life of Roderick's head mocked Abram's faith. Yet he wouldn't destroy it. Abram made it tell him all the secrets that the Mortons themselves wanted to forget.

By the time Madeline arrived, Abram was ripe. She came to his door in a midnight storm, drawn by the oozing head. She wore a mix of funeral garb and mourning; whether she was the recently bereaved or the soon departed was uncertain. Her dark clothes failed to conceal a sickly self-starved body, always on the point of death.

Though she had different hair and eyes than the woman in the tomb, Abram recognized her instantly. Against his remaining principles, he did not strike her down on his doorstep. He could have killed a strong woman, but not a weak-seeming one.

Madeline sniffed the air like a Gideon. "He's here. You should kill him."

Abram drew his sword. "You're a witch, and should not be suffered to live."

She spread out her arms and bowed her head, exposing her long and narrow neck to whatever blow he cared to deliver.

Abram pointed the sword at her heart. But again, he declined to kill a Morton. Abram had the Endicott power of compulsion to the extreme. *"You will serve me."*

She smiled, and kneeled before him. Serving him was her plan. Subversive subservience to power came naturally to her. And Abram, like many craftspeople, was fooled most easily by his own power. Such was the insidious way of the Left Hand.

With both of the twins in the house, Abram's corruption was inevitable, if slow. Madeline had time.

Eventually, faith subverted, Abram turned to the craft of transmigration. He lived as long as he could in one body without binding himself so permanently to one flesh as Roderick had. He sat out the Civil War, claiming age and infirmity, though he was actually afraid of dying before perfecting his new skill.

Madeline roamed the battlefields, sometimes disguised as a male soldier, sometimes as a nurse, always a wolf in the butcher shop.

After the war and the sad victory of technology, poisonous mills, and Morton cunning, Abram took a new body while staging his physical death—that was all the Endicotts cared about. His family never looked for spirits, and the warnings of their dead went unheeded.

To hide and be forgotten, Madeline and Abram left the East and the other Families. They drifted through the high plains and lonely deserts of the West. They perfected combat skills against the odd Taoists that roamed with the Chinese workers. They mastered the manipulation of Colt revolvers. Spending more time in each body than Madeline, Abram learned to make his flesh impervious to all pain and most blows. To a lesser extent, he learned to impart this power to the flesh of those he temporarily possessed. In that land of sudden unpunished violence, Abram grew into a new certainty. If craft couldn't stop the new technology, he would unite the two with more thoroughness than any Morton.

When they went west to learn more of death, each had been as powerful as any magus. Now, one of them could face off against a whole Family (except perhaps their own).

They took new bodies and returned east in time for the war against Spain. They wormed their way back into the craft militant, corrupting it as they guarded their immortality and Roderick, a growing fountainhead of power. The imperial overreach of the Left Hand oozed out into American craft and American might.

Without a permanent home, Roderick was difficult to control. The desperation of World War II opened a new door for the immortals. A massive five-sided building was being built to house all the war departments, including the craft militant in its secret center. Madeline and Abram convinced the Endicotts and others to shut the Mortons out of the planning. Without the Mortons and their experience of the Left-Hand ways, they easily insinuated themselves into the design of H-ring, leaving room at the center for the future Chimera.

After setting up Roderick under the Chimera cover, Abram and Madeline should have been happy ever after. They controlled Roderick, who fed off the living and kept the dead at a distance. They had ensured their own survival. Perhaps they could have remained a subtle poison in the craft militant forever.

Then, a year ago, Roderick cackled with glee and prophesized their doom at the hands of a Morton. This forced them to act. To be certain, they must hunt down the last of the Morton blood. To be safe, they must obliterate the House of Morton and its spiritual Furies. To get away with it, they must manipulate all of American craft.

Dale Morton was the obvious main threat. If young Morton had been killed on a mission, they would have arranged things at the House to simulate a Left-Hand breakout in order to mask their follow-up purge. But, with Dale's survival and resignation, they changed their plan. When Dale let the Left Hand loose during the fight in the House, they could blame the subsequent craft killings on him.

Somewhere along the line, "mission creep" had set in, perhaps more so for Madeline than Abram. Now, nothing less would suffice for their safety than decapitating American craft by killing those most likely to resist, and seizing absolute control. With American craft united in their hands, the nation would follow.

They fucked, because Madeline left some memory and other human stuff behind with each copy, and sex helped bring some (not all) of it back. Her tendency to forget kept their passion (let's call it love!) fresh. They fucked to Goth rock, because sometimes the dark-minded do exactly what you'd expect, even when they've been doing it for a couple centuries.

They fucked with the delicious urgency of unacknowledged fear. Madeline often thought of Roderick as she achieved a rolling series of climaxes. His prophecy had been clear: someone was coming who could kill her and Abram, someone was coming who could destroy Roderick and Chimera, killer and destroyer would be of the House of Morton. As a more definite consolation, the old Endicott would slay the younger, and Abram was the oldest Endicott around.

They fucked, and the puppet Hutchinson seemed to stare at them blankly. Or perhaps its eyes were on the monitor screens behind them, which showed the Chimera room and its airlock door. But if the puppet saw anything on those screens, it wasn't telling.

Sex had opposite effects on these partners in high treason. The tightly wound soul of Abram relaxed; the thirsty soul of Madeline sobered.

Abram smiled as he efficiently donned his uniform. "This should be the last puppet show for the general. Another few days, and we won't need him anymore."

They dressed the marionette without the usual humiliations to its flesh—no time for games. Reports continued to feed in: a storm outside, minimal guards, the Left-Hand assault. Madeline fingered a jacket button. The unusual coincidence that they were both weakened and potentially distracted from Chimera troubled her. Time for uncharacteristic candor.

"Lately, my brother has been . . . incomplete," she said. "His intelligence gaps are deliberate holes, just barely short of outright lies. He's manipulating us toward some end. Some endgame?"

"A few more days and we'll be safe," said Abram.

"A few more days, and we'll rule," she agreed. "But what about the fledgling?"

"How could she be the threat?" asked Abram. "She wasn't in the prophecy."

"I think she was, folded in and unaccounted-for," said Madeline.

"Chimera might be vulnerable to her talent," said Abram. But he remembered his dreams of a dark woman offering him pomegranate seeds, signs of his mortality.

"We all might be," she said. She knew in her borrowed bones that she was vulnerable. "What to do?"

"She has no experience handling large craft forces," he said.

"So?"

"Burn the forest to hide our torch. She can't hit what she can't see."

TWENTY-TWO

We crossed the Beltway and District lines. My craft sight strobed; the force dizzied me with waves of brilliance and absence. We somehow managed not to puke.

On the Metrorail bridge over the Potomac, we saw the hypermassive thunderclouds that had stalled over Arlington, ascending from above the air force monument up into the wild blue yonder. Lightning struck all around the low silhouette of the Pentagon.

"That's awful purty," said Roman.

"It's awfully close," said Scherie.

"Shit," I said. "I didn't do all that. It's shrunk the craft boundary." I bent down and untied a shoelace, readying it for its role in the coming mission.

At the Pentagon stop, we exited the train with a mass of Washington commuters bound for the buses, and a smaller number of evening security and utilities workers walking toward the Pentagon entrance. At this hour, more were still leaving than arriving. Perhaps the storm was also having a side benefit. I wanted as few as possible coming to work.

We remained on the platform for a moment. "Wait here for Scherie," I told my ghosts.

"Good-bye, boy," said Grandpa. Dad said nothing.

We walked toward the escalator that would take us to the station turnstiles. But before we could exit the platform, I heard a familiar, insistent whisper. *"Greetings, once and future head of our House."*

Left-Hand spirits. At least they explained the shrinking craft boundary. I turned back toward the tracks, as if waiting for the next train to arrive. Roman imitated me, but Scherie couldn't help looking up at the cavernous ceiling, scanning defensively for the source of the evil voices that she could now hear.

I held a cell phone to my ear as cover for my side of the conversation. "What the hell are you doing here?"

"We have assisted your storm. We share your purpose."

"I doubt it," I said. "You've shrunk the defensive perimeter. And you've been playing into my enemy's hands."

"We have come for Chimera's keepers. You will give your enemies to us."

"You'll do exactly what I say," I said.

"You have little power and less authority."

I nodded to my right. "You've met my girlfriend."

The wind went out of their voices. *"Threatening family with a nuclear weapon. Real classy."*

"OK," I said, acknowledging their surrender. I had never heard them so colloquial, so ungothic. "If you're in here, I can see you're making progress against the building's defenses. Hold off on your breakthrough—"

"What?"

"Please let me finish. Timing is everything. Hold off until I call for you. I'll open the door for you, if I can."

"Understood. A family reunion. We'll see you inside."

A family reunion? My suspicion of Chimera grew.

I turned back toward the escalator, and Scherie and Roman followed through the turnstiles and up out of the station. My senses went into combat mode. The light tap of Scherie's shoes kept constant time. Roman made no sound distinguishable from the noise of vents, breathing, and silence. *If her shoes stop, either she has found Chimera or disaster has found her.*

I turned toward the Pentagon entrance, with its outdoor gatehouse and the checkpoint armor plates that looked like giant riot shields with small square windows. Just within the gatehouse and checkpoint, the craft barrier flickered blue like Cherenkov radiation. Beyond the checkpoint, nine ghosts stood guard in groups of three, two groups up front, one in reserve. Most manifested in CENTCOM's desert BDUs from Cobra II or Enduring Freedom, still coherent with will and memory. They scanned the barrier, no doubt on alert against bits of Left-Hand shadow. I hadn't counted on them. I hoped they were too occupied keeping out dead Mortons to worry about one live one.

My ID got me past the checkpoint, and I hit the craft barrier with my own power under tight wraps. The blue played across my body but didn't slow me. Perhaps Roman's craft or the Left-Hand assault helped. In the distance, I heard the low hum of Chimera's red magic. Scherie would hear it too.

The living guards at the checkpoint looking at badges didn't appear to notice me as anything exceptional from the Defense night workers filing in before or after. But the dead were seriously annoyed. The reserve group moved forward. A white-haired man with crutches, a peroxide-blond army nurse, an acne-scarred boy who must have lied about his age to join up—what Grandpa called a crossroads configuration, the standard craft guard formation. These spirit guards were in my face, barking claxon warnings. "Halt! The craft defenses will destroy you."

I continued silently toward the Pentagon doors and the security gates within. If Scherie could just get a few yards closer, past the craft barrier, our mission might be done. But the old man waved his crutch in my face. "Corporal, report this breach to H-ring."

"Belay that order." Ignoring my instructions, my father manifested next to me, inside the boundary. "This is my son. He's going after the thing downstairs."

"Captain, we're trying to save the damned fool's life," said the old man.

"He'll take that chance," said Dad.

"He'll lose," said the nurse.

I entered the doors and reached one of the automatic security gates, my spectral companions crowding around me. I ran my ID badge and tremendous power through the gate. With the help of my craft, the card chip circumvented the biometrics verification and sent an overwhelming message to the gate control: *I shall pass.* The light went green, the gate opened, I could enter. My card was hot to the touch, and probably useless. I'd throw more force against the gates when Scherie and Roman approached, if necessary.

"What about him?" asked the dead boy, pointing behind me. "He's stealthy, and ferrin."

I thought, *Ah, here's the reason the Ukie needs us.*

"And the woman," said the nurse. "She's dangerous."

My father shook his head. "On my honor as an officer, that thing downstairs is a strategic threat to the living and the dead. If my son fails, we'll be destroyed or absorbed by my family's Left Hand, and we do not want to go there."

"On your responsibility then, Captain," said the old man. "Go then," he called after me. "You can't make things any worse."

By the time the dead stood down, I was at the foot of the escalator that led up to the corridor to the central courtyard. As an excuse to wait, I bent to retie my shoe. Scherie was at a gate, card out. Damn—she hadn't been able to strike at Chimera. The card should get her through, but I wouldn't chance it. *She shall pass,* I thought.

My father stood near me. "Everything according to plan, I see. How far do you think you're going?"

"Far enough," I muttered.

"I won't try to stop you. Too late for that now."

"Sorry, Dad. And thanks. Be stupid to fail at the beginning."

"I'll be holding the line with the others. Don't be long." And Dad was gone.

Roman and Scherie were through the gate. To my surprise, Roman didn't just bolt ahead alone. Did he know about probability failure? His foreignness would be even more sensitive to it.

I stood still going up the escalator in order not to get ahead of the others. Then I strode through the corridor, hoping I could stop soon, before I dropped dead. A few men and women in uniforms and suits passed me, on their way out. The smell of popcorn filled the hall, and I suddenly craved some fast food—a conventional health hazard seemed quaint.

Roman was really turning on the stealth for me. The

world outside went fish-eyed, the long corridors stretched longer. But I also felt a force pressing against me, making me strain a little more with each step, making the path ahead seem endless.

All at once, the force grabbed my leg, and my feet went out from under me. I was falling, falling . . .

I hit the floor. Ouch.

I had tripped on my just retied shoelace, now loose again. I heard the others trip behind me. Very improbable. But just a trip? Not very effective for a probability defense. A freak aneurysm should have hit my brain by now. "Why so weak?" I wondered.

I continued on through the long corridor until I hit the inner courtyard. The resisting force left me sweating and breathing hard, but I was oddly alive. Scherie and Roman emerged into the outdoors after me. Damn, survival was useless if she couldn't act.

My gale and rain swept over and around us, but did not touch us—those elements were mine. Around the courtyard, weathermen were on patrol against the storm, but they couldn't even keep themselves dry. Wet countercraft soldiers also patrolled, helping the Pentagon spirits temporarily stem the Left-Hand tide.

We reached the café at the courtyard's center. The café was closed, so we huddled against one of its walls. Ground zero, and our luck should be about zero now. Hell, a good defense should have driven probability to infinitesimal ages ago. Why weren't we dead yet? More unlooked-for help, and this time it wasn't Scherie. Someone else wanted us to get this far.

"You don't explode in bloody mess," noted Roman. "Very nice."

"What does he mean?" asked Scherie.

"We've been very lucky," I said. "What are you feeling?"

"Not enough," said Scherie. She gestured at the crafts-men on patrol, some of whom seemed to glance our way. "Aren't these people going to see us?"

"Not problem," said Roman. "We are 'nondescript.' Identities are slippery."

"That was quite a walk," said Scherie. "How do you deal with that fun-house view?"

"How does a whale hear underwater?" asked Roman.

She looked at the café building. "And what's the deal with the glow to everything here? It's starting to get on my nerves."

"What do you mean?" I asked. Then I held up a finger. "Can you feel that?" A trace of red static electricity danced in 4/4 time around my torso.

"Chimera? Too faint," said Scherie. "I can't . . . I don't know how to describe it."

"Too slippery?" I asked.

"That's it," said Scherie. "It's just some slippery fur of a big cat. And this glow isn't helping. I could tell it to leave here, but I think it'll just retreat like before. I can't feel where it lives."

"We know where it lives," I said, nodding at the ground. Any mundane standing here would think of the nuclear sword over her head, or the vicious storm that circled like a pocket hurricane. Any other craftsman would be observing the spectral fireworks from the collective Left-Hand Morton überspirit smacking against the craft barrier over-head like birds into a domed-glass doom. That the Left Hand had made it so close was truly impressive. Shame they were such heinous bastards.

But I noticed little above. The destroyer dwelled below.

Some Arlington dead patrolled the grounds, focusing on the threat from the skies. "The chance of recognition is rising as we sit here," I said. "We may as well move forward."

Roman sighed. "I get you down to H-Ring."

"OK. If we can find the elevator down, can you screen it?" I asked. I didn't want to risk running into a craft master on the stairs before we hit bottom.

"Won't they see the elevator moving?" asked Scherie.

For the first time, a little annoyance played on Roman's smiling face. "Elevators move all the time. With me there, they won't care."

"We'll take the elevator down," I said. "It'll open. You'll have a couple seconds to act. The door will close. We'll come back up. No one the wiser."

And if that didn't work? As nice as it was to have survived this far, I had the sense of a tactical ruse, being drawn by Chimera's continual retreat into the deepest heart of bad luck to be destroyed. The stormy sky was my setup for my next plan. (Was I on plan C or D?) Like all my best plans, this one could easily kill me.

Scherie found the exterior door to the elevator first. "It's glowing like a toaster." Above its buttons hung an out-of-order sign. Roman shrugged. "Don't believe what you read."

We entered the elevator. The *H* of H-ring seemed ominous as we descended deeper, and deeper. The soil here was soft; we were sinking into a hollow of deep bedrock encased in swamp. The solid concrete of the Pentagon weighed hundreds of thousands of tons, all above my head. Great, another basement for me to enjoy my taph-ephobia in.

Time slowed. Scherie turned one direction, then an-other, distracting me from my own nerves. She pressed her hands against her eyes. "Too much. Not good, not good, not good." Her agitation was growing. Not damn good at all . . .

The door opened.

E ndicott didn't hesitate. He returned to his father's of-fice. If the general was compromised, then Endicott was screwed anyway.

No, not screwed. Damned. Perhaps the destruction of the Families, even his family, was God's will. Whatever their pretension to holiness, they had become the family of Simon Magus, trading purity for power. No, not a mere slide into sinful ease. The Families, his family, had sub-mitted to an abomination.

But in the general damnation, Endicott still saved his greatest doubts and loathing for himself.

The only ones who had tried to warn him were those demons who called themselves his grandparents and the last scion of the greatest domestic foes of his Family. If God gave Endicott a long enough life, clearly some reflec-tion and prayer on prior assumptions would be in order.

At the office door, Endicott rushed in—a violation of protocol and dangerous in a craft environment, but a clock of judgment was ticking. Other people were in the room; no time for them. "Sir, we've been breached."

The general didn't point out Endicott's own breach,

didn't even raise his eyes from his desk. He pressed an intercom button. "He's here."

"Sir," said Endicott. "Chimera—"

The general held up a hand. "You're going to tell me that some person or persons, long presumed dead, are still alive and dangerous. I'm aware of the situation. It's under control, and we'll discuss it after this meeting."

Endicott's immediate dread slipped into simple unease. He was interrupting a meeting. He looked about him. To his left, the older guy from OTM was examining the feed from Chimera. To his right, a woman officer. It was Hutch.

"Colonel." Endicott saluted, and held it. He hated to cry, particularly in front of his father, but he might anyway. Death held no sting, save the separation from comrades.

"Major." Hutch returned his salute, and smiled at him. It was a strained, damaged smile. Her other arm was in a sling, her face bandaged, she was using a cane. Bad things had happened here.

"Who did this, ma'am?"

The smile remained frozen on her face. "Dale Morton tried to kill me, but I survived the attempt."

Morton? Two days ago, Endicott would have accepted that statement as natural fact. Now? Hutch wasn't lying, though there must be a lie buried in this truth. Perhaps she was mistaken, but this was not the time to ask.

The general continued to focus on his desk. "If we could get back to your report, Colonel . . ."

"Not much more, sir," said Hutch. "From the phone records, his travel to Pennsylvania, his stealth movement beyond craftsight, his contact with the Morton Left Hand, and now this latest confession, I think the situation is clear."

She turned toward Endicott, still smiling like a damaged painted doll. "You need to arrest the major."

Endicott's first instinct was the door. Too late. Two fine specimens of craft muscle from C-CRT stood behind him.

His father finally looked up from his desk. "You're under arrest, son."

Endicott kept his voice under control, the only emotional state his father would respect. "Have you seen what's in there?"

"A traitor," said the general, "paying for his crime."

"A human brain," said Endicott, "and God knows what else."

"Doesn't matter," said the general. "Did it occur to you that there was a damned good reason we don't let anyone in there? Did it occur to you that, without the mediation and control of all that technology, the most evil magus who ever lived this side of Hell might be a damned good liar and manipulator?"

Endicott had only heard "damned" from his father once before—when his mother had died. Somehow, he found the strength to keep arguing. "Chimera says that an Endicott is involved."

"It's told that story before," said the general. "It's got a different one for each Family."

"We can check this story," insisted Endicott.

The general waved this away. "Without further sin? That's what it wants; its last little game."

Sin. Endicott thought of the experiments he'd seen in Prague. This was worse, the sin of Endor in flesh and blood. "Sir, keeping him like that is *wrong.*"

His father gave him his measure-for-a-funeral-dress-uniform gaze. At least he was paying attention. "No, soldier! Keeping it like this is smart. Nukes are stupid in comparison. Chimera is the greatest craft weapon in a hundred years. Thanks to your service and others, nobody has the equivalent. So you'll sit in H-ring detention until we sort out the current crap. Then we can debate philosophy to your heart's content, while we figure out what other discipline is necessary."

"Sir, I—"

His father extended his hand. "Major, surrender the family sword."

Endicott handed the blade, the visible sign of his family pride, hilt-first to his father. His hand kept steady while the rest of him threatened to shake apart. When his mother had died, Endicott had held fast to religious consolation. Now, he held nothing but ashes. So much for the controlled approach. Endicott's voice broke. "In God's name, sir."

His father's eyes returned to desk duty. "Gentlemen, please escort the major out. Dismissed."

The two guards stepped forward to each side. With the formality of a funeral, Endicott saluted. He pivoted around for his reverse march.

Lord, prayed Endicott, *right now I could use a break. Not for me, but for your whole people. All people. Thy will be done.*

He stepped forward. Then the breach alarm went off.

The gray-haired technician dropped his tools. The guards turned back toward the general for instructions. Endicott no longer believed in coincidences. He was in hostile territory. Moscow Rules. Time for the bravest thing he could think of. *"Freeze,"* he said. And Endicott ran for it.

He reached the office door. *Lord, guide me to the fight.*

Just then, a blinding flash and an artillery roar. The lights went out. *Not very goddamned funny, Lord.* But he turned left toward the main elevator and kept running.

His shoes clattered in the corridor. *Umph!* A surprise collision, a side check against somebody coming the other way. "What the . . . ?" Endicott only slowed a moment. He wasn't winded, didn't care if he blindly hit a whole platoon. Emergency light tracks flickered just long enough to disorient him.

A flash and roar? Someone performing suicidal weather craft in H-ring? He ran faster. Where was Moses when the lights went out? In the dark. But my eyes have seen the glory. Something more than a little pagan about Jehovah God of Armies, but "The Battle Hymn of the Republic" was a catchy tune for times of slaughter and stricken fields. He has loosed the fateful lightning of his terrible swift sword. Glory!

CHAPTER
TWENTY-THREE

When the elevator door opened only a foot, a blur dove out, and I failed to grab it. Roman had gone.

I reined in my first instinct: to pursue and kill. The opened door revealed two guards, both focused on a shimmering chameleon blur sprinting away, strangely leaving its traveling case uncamouflaged. With predetermined rapidity, one guard pursued, calling in support on his comm.

The other turned to find me in his face, and then found unconsciousness. One-on-one, hardly fair.

So Roman had bought some time for us, but at too high a tactical cost. We were now exposed to craft and mundane sight.

And very mundane hearing. An alarm sirened. Scherie screamed, "Motherfucker!" Did she mean Roman?

"Ignore him," I said, holding the elevator door open. "Can you feel Chimera?"

"Motherfuckers," she hissed. "Trying to possess me." She staggered out the elevator in a crouch, head darting up, down, left, right. "It's one big fucking rape."

Shit. Someone was wigging her out. I should have seen

that their best defense was this offense. "What can you see?"

"Can't see a fucking thing. Too fucking much."

I looked out at the craft-colored world. I couldn't see anything clearly, but I wasn't blinded. Chimera's tick-tock pulse of red magic assaulted me from all directions, its origin lost in a kaleidoscopic maze of power that burned beyond all reasonable need except deception. Scherie might be able to follow the maze, but she was staring into high beams.

So they wanted me to fail down here, out of sight, out of mind. OK. Time to send Scherie back up.

"This way," I said. With as much gentleness as my urgency could allow, I tugged her back into the elevator. I hit the ground-floor button, and the "Close Doors" button, and said *"close"* for good measure. Then I jumped outside the door.

"What are you doing?" asked Scherie, small voiced, reaching sightless for my absence.

Another alarm went off, but the elevator stayed put. I touched the opening, and tried to feel what was wrong. Door frozen, elevator frozen, locked with metal and craft that wouldn't be cut today, no sir.

Meanwhile, in the orgy of craft power confusing our sight, fractal magics were growing out from the walls, floor, and ceiling to contain our intruding infectious potential. *An amontillado defense.* We couldn't stay here.

I pulled Scherie out of the elevator, breaking through the half-formed building defenses with my skill from maintaining the House. Still no other guards, but that was seconds from changing. We'd have to go for the stairwell, assuming it was near.

"What are you doing?" repeated Scherie.

"This mission is scrubbed. We're out of here, up the stairs."

"No." She tugged me back. "Duty. Got to do something."

Yes, we did, if only to cover our escape, if not free up Scherie's sight. And, for the long shot, to kill Chimera. Why waste a good storm? I didn't have time to calculate the EMP versus probable hardening of Chimera against it. I needed to touch a conductive wall, or even the right part of the floor, or . . .

There, a bulge in the granite wall plane, a telltale of an electrical panel. I expected little human resistance. The Pentagon's sad-sack contingent of weathermen was up top, fighting against Morton craft with pissant breezes. H-ring would not stop me; though hermetically sealed against exterior craft, its interior mundane utilities were probably neglected.

I stepped away from Scherie. "I'll need some room for this." And she'd be fried if she touched me. I reached one hand back toward the elevator shaft, in case the bolts tried to strike down to me through it. I placed my other hand on the panel, to give the bolts a place to go. I didn't think about my feet; proper grounding wasn't going to help much.

Unlike much of American craft, "pulling a Franklin" required formal words, because the focus was that much more intense. The words weren't originally American, but they were the mantra of those who wished to incarnate Prometheus. Or to become a suicidal human lightning rod.

I shut my eyes. In the skies far above, my storm chased its own tail, waiting to be whistled to heel. I called: *"Now I am become Death, destroyer of worlds!"*

The total power of a bolt of lightning runs in the terawatts, the force in the gigavolts. In nature, that power is never concentrated.

I drew down three bolts at once, focused to a point. *Trinity.*

I had stood near explosions before. I had never stood within one. Brightness burned inside me. The sound took time to come back, to squeeze me from all sides. I fell into darkness . . .

"Get up!"

. . . and arose to flickering emergency lights. Assisting her command, Scherie pulled me up by the arm. Her vision seemed to be better. She yelled above our shared deafness. "Goddamn it! Did you just try to kill yourself again?"

I shook my head.

"Then what's that smell?"

I gagged on the mix of ozone, burning insulation, and burnt hair (mine). "Electrical failure."

True enough—the regular power grid must have failed. Cameras and mundane security might be out. I felt the air, hoping for a stillness that would mean an enemy's death. No such luck. The tick-tock pulse still permeated everything. "Let's go."

"Wait. For a moment, everything was clear." She reached out her hands toward the center of H-ring. "If I can just . . ."

Two pairs of feet were sprinting down the dark corridor. Another pair of feet was closing from the other direction. My training was quicker than thought. I hockey-checked the distracted Scherie toward the other wall, just in time to meet the impact.

With little craft left in me, it came down to simple physics. The two men tackled me to the ground.

"Stay down, Major," said the larger guard. "Don't make this worse than it is."

The smaller guard flashed a pocket light in my face. "This isn't Endicott. Who the fuck are you?"

Endicott dodged down the PRECOG spoke of H-ring, then walked purposely across the cut-off corridor. He planned to come at the stairwell from the other side. A breach alarm meant something going down in the entrance area, and he'd rather fight with someone who wasn't his father.

The usually eerie noise of the PRECOG area was eerily absent—no mumbling farseers, no restless analysts. Had something they'd seen driven them AWOL? That scary thought had come far too late to help.

He loped toward the stairwell. It took a moment in the dim uncertain light to make sure the area was clear. Then he heard a woman yell. "Fucking blind again!" The thud-smacks of physical combat sharply echoed from the elevator's direction.

Endicott approached. Shadows danced in the strobing world up ahead. A silhouette twirled two partners: first one, then the other, then both in unison before tossing them Endicott's way. To look on the fight from outside was outstanding, beautiful even, so joyful it must be a sin of deadliness.

Then the winning fighter moved toward Endicott. Endicott felt the ambiguous grace of the moment. "Morton. I knew it was you. Thank God you're here!"

I recognized Endicott well before I heard him. I had no time for personal matters, but no rules-of-engagement hesitation. I'd have to at least knock out Endicott; more probably I'd kill him. The mission took priority; Endicott was collateral damage.

Yes, kill him! From high above the tons of sodden earth that pressed down on this stone crypt, the Left-Hand spirits offered their usual advice. *Even a broken clock is right twice a day,* I thought. The red tick-tock magic of Chimera wasn't helping my sanguinary mood. I'd have to do it eventually—why not now?

An arm's length away from Endicott, I assumed a combat stance. Endicott just stood there, looking at me as if I were a confusing foreign film.

From behind me, Scherie called. "Where are you? You're going the wrong way."

Shit, another fucking oracle. With preternatural speed, I grabbed Endicott's uniform. "You have one chance. Where is Chimera?"

The asshole smiled. "Back that way, like she said, just down the hall. But you may have to kill some other people first."

"Are you one of them?"

"Hope not. Let's move, I'll explain as we go."

And just like that we were stepping off the line to our doom in crisp military cadence, like when Hutch called me in for special discipline back at the academy. I hooked an arm around Scherie, who tried to keep pace without stumbling. Her head jerked as if dodging paparazzi flashbulbs, but her blindness seemed less complete.

"This guy with us?" asked Scherie.

"Seems so," said Endicott.

"Here's a stupid question," I said.

"Why should you trust me?" said Endicott.

"Yeah."

"Didn't try to kill you. Rogue Gideons."

"They said 'Endicott's orders.' "

"Yep. That's probably right. But not me."

"What happened to Family responsibility?"

Endicott patted his side where his sword should have hung. "I'm working on it. Oh, the head hound was Madeline Morton."

I remembered with satisfaction where I had left Sakakawea. "Great Auntie Madeline is resting in peace."

"Nope."

"I killed her. Extremely dead."

"Not according to Chimera. Tall and thin and young and here in H-ring."

"How the hell does it know?"

"Because it's Roderick. Or what's left of him."

I felt sick horror, but little surprise. "More bad Mortons as usual suspects. Sorry."

"That's OK. Abram, who should have slain them, is also wandering around here in another skin. You might remember him as the Red Death."

"Hooah. Anyone else we have to kill?"

"Hope not." Endicott looked worried about someone though. Then he lowered his voice. "What's the mundane GF doing here?"

"Take another look."

"Shit, she's high craft."

"You got a problem with that?"

Endicott extended his hand to her. "Welcome to the American Families."

But the half-blind Scherie left him dangling. I shifted her over to between Endicott and me. "Major, stop shaming me for two seconds and lend a shoulder. She's not seeing so well."

Endicott got under Scherie's other arm, and she hung between us as we marched forward. "Careful with this cross we're bearing," I said. I remembered Endicott's repressed smile regarding biblical epics. "Where's your messiah now?"

"Not ready for jokes, Mr. DeMille," said Endicott. In the weird light, scattered forms of H-ring staffers passed. We did not look out of place in the chaos.

"So, ma'am, what can you do?" asked Endicott.

"Drive out spirits," she said, "possessing or dead."

Endicott whistled. "Outstanding. Sounds like a talent made for our bad guys."

"Have to see them first," she said.

"Right," said Endicott. "Wondered why they were running up the craft utility bill down here. I'll get you to Chimera, close enough to spit. We'll hit Roderick, and hope that'll draw the others out. Just a little farther."

But ahead, the backlit forms of four men formed a line blocking our advance. With silent coordination, we turned. Three Enhanced Combat soldiers and a woman were lined up, blocking our retreat.

Even in the poor light, I recognized the woman. My pride at graduation, the thrill of my first mission, didn't compare to this. "Hutch! You're alive!"

I stepped forward, but Endicott's arm leapt out to restrain me, leaving Scherie to stumble and feel about. Endicott whispered, "She said you tried to kill her."

Had Hutch been playing me? Like snooping around my parents' bedroom, but I had to do it: *Show me her sins.* Instantly, I felt the vertigo of trying to read a newspaper, only to find out that it's in another language. I didn't know Hutch's sins; I had never looked. But this woman had a strange constellation of alien-looking characters that refused to resolve to plain letters. Hutch's spirit had been seriously fucked with.

"Goddamnit," said Scherie. "Losing it again. Not good, not good."

Hutch nodded at us. "Captain Morton. Major Endicott. Ms. Rezvani. My orders have changed. I'm escorting you to Chimera."

Endicott glanced at me. "Been 'escorted' lately?"

"We've got to go with her," I said.

"We, Kemo Sabe?" asked Endicott.

"We've been out of *touch*," I said, punctuating the key words as if they were parts of spells. "I'd like her to meet *Scherie*."

"When we get the *time*," said Endicott, picking up on the code.

"I'll let you know."

Hutch smiled, but showed no other emotion at seeing me again, not even a handshake with her slingless arm. Instead, she and her three ENCOMs made a diamond around us, and shepherded us through the line of four barring the way to Chimera. With Hutch leaning on her cane, we didn't move at her usual brisk pace. Hutch's injuries had a familiar pattern, if I could only remember where . . .

"Shit shit shit! Blind blind blind!" In counterpoint to the H-ring alarm, Scherie sounded off like a schizo Tourette's siren; our escorts didn't seem to care.

"The airlock is about thirty meters ahead," said Endicott. We turned the corner between the countercraft and black ops facets. A door sign said "Office of Technical Management." In front of the OTM door stood two technicians.

Endicott pulled Scherie's weight away from me. "Seen any interesting immorality lately?"

I couldn't see what had set off Endicott, but instantly followed the order. Again I thought, *Show me their sins.*

It only took a second of burning neon letters. I saw those nearest to me first. Endicott had a shitload of Pride, but it didn't appear that attempted murder was on his soul. Our guards had some nice but conventional transgressions. Hutch I already knew about; what the hell could Endicott be getting at?

"Tall and thin," Endicott had said. And here in H-ring.

Then, out of the corner of my eyes, I saw the technicians. They seemed to avoid my attention like Roman avoided sight. The male tech was a Times Square of exotic transgressions, variations on soul torture and mental rape, much like Sakakawea had been.

But the woman tech had the exact same sins as Sakakawea. A fingerprint of the soul, and a dead match for Auntie Madeline.

Hutch gestured at the techs with her less injured arm. "These two will guide you to Chimera's interface. No, Major, not where you had your previous discussion. Please hurry. We don't have much time."

"Hypothetically . . ." I started.

"I've got no fucking idea," said Endicott, reading everything he needed to know in my face. "You had something in mind before?"

We needed to play our cards. "Yep, it's *time*."

Endicott grasped Hutchinson in a clunky embrace. "It's so good to have you back, Colonel." Old John Endicott better not have been looking.

"Sorry, honey," I said, and I shoved Scherie stumbling toward Hutch. "Think Helen Keller!"

Somebody pulled on the marionette's strings, and Hutch's body recoiled out of Endicott's grasp and away from Scherie's touch. But the puppet's left hand was of a different mind. It pushed through the sling and reached toward Scherie's sightless groping fingers.

"Fmmmufffa," said Scherie.

Two of the guards restrained Endicott and me; their senior stood ready to assist. The gray-haired tech stared at Hutch; the woman tech advanced with malice toward all.

"What was that, dear?" I said.

Scherie stared back at me with eerie calm. "I said, *'Get the fuck out of her you motherfucking abomination!'*"

Scherie's craft this time was more like the pop flash of a camera than the blinding light-force of a nuke; she was growing efficient. Hutch screamed, the male tech screamed. The restraining guards looked about for order; the senior guard turned to the technicians. The woman tech laughed, a sardonic stamp on some deadly punch line. I knew for certain this could only be Madeline.

With no sign of life, Hutch folded to the ground next to her fallen cane. The gray-haired tech folded over, panting. Madeline pulled out a sidearm from her large lab coat pocket. Smuggling such things into H-ring was foolishly dangerous and very Madeline. She casually tossed the gun to the senior guard. *"Shoot them,"* she said.

With only time to bend, not break, the compulsion, Endicott said, *"Shoot the guards."*

And, with no resistance, the senior guard shot his fellow soldiers. And then he shot himself in the head. Twice. His hand kept clicking on the empty weapon long after his brains and body had hit the ground.

"Who did you think I meant?" gasped Madeline in mock horror.

"Welcome to our Reichstag fire," said the male tech, in the cadence of the Red Death. *Abram.* They had set us up as murderers.

Around the corner, on cue, came the commander of Enhanced Combat and his two lieutenants. From the other direction came the ghastly white H-ring uniforms of SCOF Black Ops. With surprising speed, Madeline and Abram made a sufficient tactical withdrawal to appear as bystanders instead of instigators. Abram still bent a bit as if his solar plexus had been worked over.

He's weakened. Call us, said the distant Left Hand.

"Wait for it," I said. But they still murmured in my head, perhaps trying to distract me.

"You on the phone with someone?" asked Endicott.

Endicott and I fell into a back-to-back crouch, slide-stepping in arcs around Scherie, Hutch, and the corpses. Scherie huddled over Hutch, whispering nonsense. My feet tracked blood.

"It's not how it looks," I said.

"I can explain," said Endicott.

"Stand down, and submit to restraint," said the ENCOM commander.

The SCOF commander bared his titillated sadism smile and made no offers.

"Where's everyone else?" asked Endicott.

"Busy, I expect," I said. "Don't let them take the blind weapon." My girlfriend, the nuke.

These men hadn't seen real combat in a long time. The ENCOMs and SCOFs were smart enough not to try to hit us one at a time, so they tried the next dumbest thing and rushed all at once, hoping sheer strength and weight of numbers would carry the day. Brutally inefficient, it still might work.

Like a Japanese katana charge, they let loose with all their very nasty craft in their first blow. I braced for the initial wave. From one side, the familiar tools of my work: *heart shock, air move.* From the other, exquisite pain and a serrated force that attempted to rip spirit from flesh. A practitioner had to enjoy this torture stuff to be good at it. I questioned the encouragement of such personalities as I suffered from their profound malice.

My chest felt cracked; my body felt fractured along molecular fault lines. The Pentagon men were trying to box us in, craftwise and physically, as if we were urban rioters, but crowd control didn't work for two. Even for craft, willing all these things to happen at once was just too improbable. Like a failure in the Nash equilibrium, they were crowding each other out.

Worse for them, their unnatural assaults on my spirit were all too familiar to me. I crowed, "You're trying Left-Hand craft on a Morton?"

"Amen to that," said Endicott.

Craft exhausted, the ENCOMs and SCOFs threw their punches and kicks with a similar lack of coordination.

Three fists came at once toward my face; three bodies rushed to tackle me down. We were much more focused: *break* that *arm, freeze up* that *leg*.

From under the blind spot of the surveillance cameras, Madeline and Abram watched. More implacable than emperors watching gladiators, they did nothing to help the assailants.

When it came down to the SCOF and ENCOM commanders, Madeline and Abram slipped inside the Office of Technical Management without even hiding their action. Then, with a backwards run, the area commanders retreated.

I dropped the C-bomb. "Cowards!" Then I examined myself. Aware that our actions were being recorded for a dubious posterity, we had managed to avoid killing these attackers, but at the price of damage to ourselves.

Some of my recent patch-ups felt strained: cracked rib, bruised kidney, maybe a finger or two that wasn't working quite right. I wasn't sure about my other internal organs or the number of hairline fractures or the arcane damage from black ops. All put on hold to be experienced later with greater intensity or slowly forgotten in the grave.

"How you doing?" I asked Endicott.

"Usual," he said. His face looked like a smiling, swelling beet patch.

"We've been softened up," I said.

"Tenderized for a bad-guy meal," agreed Endicott. Drops of blood on the floor seemed to grow paler as the pulsing red craft fed on their energy. *The things people ignore.*

"The generals—they'll be back," said Endicott.

"So, Major," I said, "take us to Chimera."

"No."

"Endicott!" I felt another impulse to kill this man and be done with it. Instead, I said, "I know what Roderick said, but—"

"No time," said Endicott. "There'll be alert guards and a lockdown. We've got to get out of this corridor and kill those two walking abominations first."

"Right," I said. "I suspect the abominations know that." I read the sign. "OTM?"

"Seems like they found the perfect way to avoid notice in a craft area," said Endicott.

"Techies. I would have noticed," I said.

"I suspect the abominations know that too," said Endicott.

"Time to go, Scherie," I said, getting under her arm to pick her up. I pulled her across the corridor and plopped her none too delicately at the threshold. "Hey!" she said. Then Endicott and I dragged Hutch over to the OTM door.

I spoke calmly as I put my hand on the doorknob. "You run into any traps lately?"

"Yep. You?"

"Yep," I said. I turned the knob, and the door swung open. "Confident fuckers. Any other options?"

Yells of soldiers came from both directions. "None."

I nodded as I peered into the dark room beyond the door. "I assume they just want to kill us off camera."

"Good," said Endicott. "I'm not ready for my close-up, Mr. DeMorton."

I didn't want to die hating myself for liking this man, but that seemed my destiny. Endicott said it first. "In another universe, perhaps we could have killed stuff together."

I chuckled. "In another universe, we're both already dead."

I considered the threshold. "We better all go in at the same time. On three. One, two . . ." I pulled Scherie, and Endicott dragged Hutch into the OTM.

Behind us, the door slammed shut. Another door, very non-Pentagon-standard steel, slid into place in front of it. The sound of locks and bolts ostentatiously slamming home announced that we were exactly where our enemies wanted us. We had entered the ninth circle.

CHAPTER

TWENTY-FOUR

The general continued to receive his reports from the Chimera feed, and the reports said everything was fine. But that was difficult to believe when he had arrested his own son, the lazy move of an officer or parent who couldn't be bothered with complications. And how could all be well when he could read only a single screen by emergency lighting?

"Chimera, what's going on in H-ring?"

"Insufficient data."

"Take a guess."

"I'd say you're fucked, General Endicott." Instead of the Chimera feed, the voice came direct on his intercom.

"Chimera, tighten control."

"Yes, I revise," said Roderick. "It's your son that's royally fucked. Madeline and Abram are here. Your son is with them. They have my prophecy: the old Endicott will slay the younger. About one hundred percent probability that your son's going to be killed in the next five minutes. About one hundred and ten percent probability that it's your fault."

"Liar." But the general heard only a mirthless exaggeration. "You dare threaten my family?" He reached for his family's sword. But it was gone.

Had Hutch taken it? No one else of interest had been in the room. No time to consider. He ran from his office down the spoke corridor and around the corner to Chimera's airlock. The chastised and now doubly alert guards saluted him.

"I'm going in," said the general.

"Sir, we have a breach alarm. We're in lockdown."

Damned idiots—always too little or too much. The general had no time for argument, or fools. *"Get out of my way,"* he said.

His Endicott compulsion worked well on their pusillanimous minds. He punched in his override code at the air lock and entered. But he couldn't leave those bozos alone out there. He called support on the entry's intercom. "Emergency. This is General Endicott. All available personnel to guard Room Zero."

The general ignored the clean-room suits—he had more than dirt for Roderick. He ran quickly down the line of servers, his old heart racing to catch up.

"You can't hurt me," said the silvered box.

"I can try." The general looked about for something to disable, but saw nothing but futile complexity.

"Horrible, isn't it," continued Roderick, "how the worst conspiracies are right in front of your face? A lifetime of hunting, of obsession, all to end with the sacrifice of Mount Moriah."

The devil did cite scripture. Very well, the general would deal with the devil. "Please, I need to save my son."

"I'd prefer you kneel, but we're short of time. Perhaps I left one possibility out. Just walk to that wall to your left."

The general moved away from Roderick. "Warmer. I know you're not very good, but even you have enough craft-sight . . ."

The outline of an open door shimmered in front of the general. "I see it."

"Just go through."

"Then what?"

"That's all you need to do to save your son. Good-bye, General Endicott."

Without concern for more oracles, or consideration of the blur in the corner of his eye that moved toward Roderick, the general strode through the hidden door and into the OTM.

W atching the Left-Hand spirits cover the Pentagon like black leprosy, Eddy considered calling in the destruct order against H-ring. The president had granted that authority to the Peepshow for just such an emergency, though Sphinx hadn't hinted at using it. But Sphinx played a very close-run game of fine choices. For lesser players, sometimes clearing the board was the best option, or at least the safest.

As if to interrupt these cheery thoughts, Eddy's phone rang. Eddy's phone was supposed to buzz, not ring. Also, the phone was turned off for this mission while Eddy used his Peepshow earpiece, so it wasn't supposed to *do* anything.

Eddy answered his phone. "What took you so long?" said a voice that Eddy recognized as the PRECOG commander. Where Sphinx had been charmingly oracular, this military prophet was autistically efficient. "Pentagon H-ring is compromised."

"What are you doing about it?" asked Eddy.

"Waiting for you. My staff has left the building without leave."

"Not exactly a good omen," said Eddy, nodding at a rain-soaked and nervous young woman holding an automatic weapon pointed at his van's window. "We're in the parking lot. The mundanes don't appear to be welcoming."

Eddy's earpiece broadcast a litany of new warnings from Sphinx's veterans:

"High probability we all die down there."

"High probability of end of American democracy."

"High probability of Chimera singularity scenario . . ."

But PRECOG CCDR said, "Just get down here."

Then, much to his embarrassment, Eddy had a vision. *Oh, is that all.* "Where's your infirmary? And your morgue?"

"What the fuck do you have in mind?"

This man called himself a farseer? Eddy gave him a vague answer while he added the numbers. One, two, three, four? He had just enough with him to cover four.

"Order the emergency evacuation of nonessential personnel from all rings," said Eddy.

"Your authority?"

"No. Presidential authority." Let him chew on that one for a while. "But tell them something stupid about a gas main."

The nervous woman and other Pentagon guards stood down, and the Peepshow moved out from their vans, suits fluttering in the tempest like eight indignant black birds.

Eddy hummed "Suicide Is Painless." He'd had enough Wagner, and "Ride of the Valkyrie" was such a cliché.

Unlike the prestige rooms upstairs, the OTM door opened right on a room. I saw the standard detritus of a combination IT department and janitor's closet, mixed with alchemy. At the back of the room, another door—this one closed.

Scherie pointed blindly toward the closed door. "That way. All violation all the time. Kill them extremely dead."

Endicott and I left Scherie and Hutch together on the floor. I tried the door, and found it unlocked. I opened it. We saw the second room, and despite what we saw, Endicott and I entered. We felt the sterile wrong of the monitor screens, and the nightmare wrong of the body tanks. The tanks had room for two more.

"Prague," said Endicott. "Worse than Prague."

From far above, but closer than before, an opposing evil howled. The disapproval of the Left-Hand spirits sounded primal and sincere. But it wasn't a question of trust.

"Not yet," I said, to all the living and dead.

The two techs stood next to what looked like a field operating table with pillows and sheets. Abram had straightened, all signs of solar plexus pain gone. "Here you are, come to our place of power like cattle to the rendering."

Abram and Madeline made talonlike mudras with their left hands. A screaming dagger thrust into my mind. It was like every other attempt in training and combat to possess me, except twice as strong and ten times as painful. But it was a quick eternity, and it failed.

I glanced at Endicott. He looked shaken, but himself.

"No surprise there," said Madeline. "Now can we please kill them?"

"Hello, Aunt Madeline," I said.

"Hello, Dale. You've grown up to be a very handsome young man."

"You've had enough incest for a few more lifetimes, dear," said Abram.

Madeline smiled indulgently. "Before we feed your energies to Roderick, with maybe a nibble for ourselves, I should confirm: wouldn't you rather live and join us?"

"Thanks, no," I said. Time for a bluff. "I should warn you: I can expel you from your bodies."

Abram made a mudra with his left hand, and the craft wattage went up. From the other room, Scherie screamed, "Fuck fuck fuck!"

"I'll call your bet," said Abram. "Rezvani might try, if she could see our spirits."

"Hmm," considered Madeline. "How to dispose of you? We could have you fight each other."

"Oh, for Christ's sake, just kill us if you can," said Endicott, charging at Madeline.

"I'm not Spartacus," I agreed, as I advanced on Abram.

"Fuck!" Scherie still screamed next door. Probably not upset at missing the villains' banter.

As with the Red Death before, Abram allowed me to rain blows on him as if to show that they didn't affect him, and to drive me to despair. Abram felt even more solid, more adamantine than before. But parameters of his body also felt different. This meant something, but I didn't have time to think.

Abram reached under the operating bed. "Look what I found."

"My sword," said Endicott, before Madeline's nails missed his eyes and raked his cheek.

"*My* sword," said Abram. He whirled it about with an air propeller's speed.

I stepped back. I knew what I needed. With a kick, I freed an alloy tube (too short!) from one of the unfinished tanks. Catching it by my foot as it fell, I Hacky-Sacked it up, seized it in my left hand, and parried Abram's downward slash.

Goddamn it, I hated archaic weapons.

I spun around and away from Abram, kicked another tube up from the ground, caught it in my right hand, and swung it wide into Abram's side. Abram didn't flinch, but he did back off a step as he hacked at my staves.

Not completely invulnerable then. But I couldn't do much damage with my alchemical alloy. The second tube had length, but neither staff had an edge. And Abram's strokes were denting the alloy with more than physical power.

I sought an opening to assist Endicott, but found none. Abram and Madeline had fought together long before we had been born; repetition had made their coordination seamless. But the matchups were right. Endicott, smaller than me, could match Madeline's physical force, and Abram had made him run before.

Catching Abram's next blow in a cross of metal, I said, "You're going to pay for what you did to Hutch."

"Idiot," said Abram. "Punish yourself. I haven't been in person within the House of Morton in a century. That was your precious possessed Hutch you were beating."

Praise the infernal lord for Endicott arrogance. The old guy wanted to hurt me so much that he couldn't help give away intel. If it was my beating that Hutch's body was still suffering from, I had done real damage, but Hutch and her possessor hadn't felt it at the time.

That's motivation. With my metal staves, I continued to hammer away.

Endicott's straightforward martial arts had trouble against a Taoist and a woman. He instinctively wanted to contain, not bludgeon.

"You have a problem fighting with girls, don't you?" said Madeline.

"Yes," said Endicott. Even now, he told the truth when the information wasn't classified. Duty and religion required this woman's death—what the hell was his problem?

"Very like your family. Let me resolve your dilemma and kill you. *Despair.*"

Endicott felt drained of life, meaning. Years spent in service of an ungrateful power, and how much worse it must be for Morton.

For Morton. He wasn't fighting alone. *"Of these, hope,"* said Endicott, swinging wide, but still swinging. "Despair is a sin against the Holy Spirit."

She hit him with blows that made up in precision what they lacked in sheer force. "You don't yet understand despair." *Bam,* kick. "My brother has told us that the old Endicott will slay the young Endicott here in this room." Kick, smack. "Abram will kill you, if I don't first."

She glowed with the heinous craft that she readied against him. Out of his league, but he had to fight longer and support Morton. Madeline made a raptor mudra with her left hand and pursed her lips to speak his death.

Then, in a corner of the room, a man stepped out of thin air. *No, Lord, not him.* "Dad, get the hell out of here!" His father might be a disciplined commander, but he was no longer a fighter.

His father gave the smallest shake of his head, and advanced on Madeline. Without turning her gaze, she crowed with laughter. "Oh shit, after five decades, here comes the old goat."

"Lord, break that long thin neck," said the general, running with a raised fist.

Madeline said nothing. Her leg struck backwards at a gymnast's angle, and intercepted the oncoming general square in his chest. Endicott attacked at the same time, but she blocked his blows.

The general fell on his back. Rising painfully, he said, *"Tell me who you are."*

"Say please," said Madeline, delivering a kick against his son, trying to work into the groin.

"I am Abram Endicott," said the sword-wielding tech, moving closer. "And you're a disgrace to my family name."

Major Endicott called to Dale, "Keep him away."

Dale stepped to work in between Abram and the others, but Abram increased the pace of his strikes against Dale's parries. The general stared at Abram. Endicott remembered his own hesitation in the House of Morton; the family instinct affected the general too.

"Run, Dad. No shame in it." As he spoke, Madeline landed a punch on his mouth. He spat blood and words. "He's an Endicott with a hundred years on you."

But the general must have heard something different

than his son's meaning. He smiled—small, tight-lipped, bitter—and raised his fists. "Come for me, old Endicott."

Abram took some grazing hits from Dale's tubes but punched Dale back on his heels with his pommel. Madeline head-cocked the desperate Endicott back away from his father. The general screened Abram's sword arm with his right and landed a series of jabs with his left against Abram's nose. Unfazed, Abram flicked his sword into the air and caught it high with his right hand. With all his force, he brought the point down through the general's chest. *"Die."*

The general's smile broadened as his heart exploded.

Endicott prayed. *Lord, have no mercy.* With rage that felt holy, he put his fists to work against Madeline's defensive stance. "Now I understand despair. Do you?"

With a crackle of thunder, the Left-Hand spirits came.

In the moment of Abram's distraction, I saw my opportunity. *"Come,"* I said. The Pentagon's craft shield failed, and the Left-Hand spirits fell like rain into the room and rushed upon our enemy. But this time, they didn't attack Abram's spirit. With the sense of true predators, they went for Madeline. *"Join us,"* they cried. As Endicott pummeled her raised arms, the spirits swarmed about her and covered her in their dark glow, trying to penetrate the living flesh to gain the half-dead soul that hadn't quite stuck yet.

"Good-bye, Auntie." Parrying Abram with my short tube, I brought the long one around in an extended arc into the back of Madeline's neck.

In the same instant, Endicott brought the heel of his hand up against Madeline's forehead. *"Shatter her skull, Lord. Now."*

But it wasn't God's power that he felt course through his hand. The Left Hand surged through his point of contact.

An abandoned doll, Madeline tumbled, hemorrhaging from her eyes, nose, ears, and mouth. She died again, gone in a black-light explosion of craft out of the room. But this time, Left-Hand souls swarmed in pursuit of her soul.

Abram pushed Dale to the ground. Endicott, disoriented from contact with corruption, only had time for one prayer: *Lord, give me three steps and miss.*

With the swift stroke of a matador, Abram ran Endicott through with his sword, then withdrew it to counter Dale's charge. Blood bubbled out from Endicott's stomach before he could contain it. Endicott's prayer had succeeded in deflecting the blow to a gut wound—not instantly fatal, but fatal soon enough without help. He was no healer.

He sat down hard. Unholy irony, being killed with his own sword. "Worst week ever."

Outside, the H-ring reinforcements were pounding at the OTM door. Idiots. Who the hell wanted to be here?

In the hazy fugue of her blind confusion, Scherie heard Hutch's voice as she awoke. "My boys. Where are my goddamned boys? And who the hell are you?"

"Can't see, can't see, can't see."

Scherie felt the woman's cool hand on her forehead. "I said, *'Who are you?'*"

Scherie's view went wide and blank for a second, then focused on the stern bandaged face in front of her. That face seemed to demand that she speak like a soldier. "Scherezade Rezvani, ma'am, reporting for duty. We need to kill some bad guys, ASAP."

"We, ma'am?"

Scherie looked around. "Your touch cuts through the bullshit. I'll need your help to see them." Hutch said nothing. "I drove that fucking *thing* out of you," insisted Scherie.

"Oh." Hutch's hand shook for a moment, then she extended it to Scherie. "Get up then."

Scherie touched Hutch's hand, but seeing the colonel's battered state she stood up on her own. She pointed to the inner room. "That way."

I went berserker on Abram. My outrage shocked me— when had Endicotts killing Endicotts become a cause for anger? Abram slashed his weapon around to face me, but only managed one strike for my two.

But Abram managed to make his one blow count. With a lightning kick, he slammed me back into one of the tanks. Spider-web cracks formed in the eldritch glass.

I raised my staves in defense, but to my surprise, Abram didn't immediately try to run me through. Instead, he flexed and stretched his aging body, cracking the joints of bones that might have already been broken. Sobered, I considered my opponent's temperament. A Left-Hand Morton would have exercised a pagan leisure in the pleasure of the kill, a Left-Hand Endicott would be more Calvinist and efficient. Abram seemed caught somewhere between.

Hurt and momentarily winded, I tested my opponent

with words. "You don't seem very concerned about Madeline."

Abram studied his sword, gave it a few trial slashes, then flung back a taunt. "You think you can restore your house by stealing your ancestor back?"

The cranky paranoia of evil old men. "I think I'm going to kill you," I said, stepping forward from the splintering glass. "Then I'm going to finish the job you should have done two centuries ago."

Abram Endicott assumed the en garde position, and I settled into my native combat stance. On the screens, a shadow fell in a wave, obscuring for a moment each feed, and something blinked in the flow of the blood-red craft. Abram's eyes cut from the screens to the outer room door. His face went gray, as if the true weight of his years had finally come home. Then he looked directly at me, as if a dog had just barked Shakespeare.

"I know an oracle when I hear it," said Abram, in a windless voice. "Center control. Autodestruct—"

I leapt for Abram, who dodged without slowing his command. "—sequence. Fifteen-minute delay."

"Move air!" Along with my spell, I delivered two quick staff blows and a kick at Abram's chest and throat, trying to stop the next word.

"Begin," croaked Abram.

Lights out, and the little emergency tracks came on in this room, leading away from the tanks with faint green glows. All the computers and screens were black, save one with a countdown clock.

Abram pivoted and hurdled on one arm over the operating bed. He ran into the corner where the general had entered, then through it in a pulse of ghoulish red.

"He's gone toward Chimera." Endicott, stirring, gripped his belly as if trying to hold blood and organs in.

"I have to go after him." Staying here to help Endicott wasn't an option. If Abram destroyed H-ring and escaped, no one would ever know the truth, and he and Madeline and Roderick might rise again.

Endicott opened his mouth, gulped down air. "Kill the . . ." He hesitated. "Revenge isn't Christian."

"Neither am I," said I.

"Thanks," said Endicott.

I leapt through the wall and into the red.

TWENTY-FIVE

Scherie followed Hutch by the arm into the second room. As Hutch limped forward, she kept a cold fury tied up in the jaw muscles of her stoic, tight-lipped features. Scherie respected the fury, and envied the discipline.

A flash of red in the corner—Scherie marked it. On the ground two bodies, and Dale wasn't one of them, praise God. Endicott still lived, bleeding slowly through clutched fingers and a low burn of craft.

Hutch let go of Scherie and with a grimace was down on her knees next to him in a second. "Michael, what the hell have you done now?"

"Usual, ma'am." Endicott's voice was a soft reed.

Without Hutch's contact, the glare of the room again pained Scherie. But either her sight had adjusted, or the bright craft was weakening, for she could see the mundane and craft worlds clearly now. She stood in front of Endicott. His wound and his aura spoke of death. "I can help."

He held up a shaky red hand. "Wait. First, figure out what you're going to need."

"But . . ."

"He's right." Hutch stood up, ramrod straight. "Your craft is your weapon. Spare only the extra rounds. What's our situation, Major?"

"Morton went after Abram. Oh, and we've got less than fifteen minutes before this place implodes."

With fierce urgency, Scherie pointed at the corner where she'd seen the red flash. "Did Dale go that way?"

But Hutch had turned to stare at the other body. Scherie didn't know the face, but the corpse's svelte shape confirmed it as a vehicle for Sakakawea. Madeline.

"I'll be damned," said Hutch. "Nice work, Major."

"I had some help."

"Morton." Hutch whistled appreciatively. "Outstanding. That's my boys."

"Colonel," insisted Scherie, "let's help the major and go."

But Hutch approached Madeline's body. Left-Hand darkness still spiraled around the corpse as if on patrol, guarding something inside or out. As Hutch reached out a foot to tap her fallen tormentor, a cold draft came from the corner of the room, and black-lit wrath raced out from one of the tanks like a sideways tornado.

Scherie yelled, "Ma'am, careful!"

But Hutch made contact, and it was like a circuit closing. From above and below, an evil soul entered Hutch.

As quick as a hawk, Hutch spun around and punched Scherie in the face. She grinned like a vulture and cackled. "Alive again! But so fucking old."

Blood streamed from Scherie's broken nose, and rage against the possessor made her mind blank. Then, Madeline's grin vanished into a tightly controlled mouth, and

Hutch gasped. "Could you give me a hand with this, soldier?"

Even as Scherie reached out a hand to dispel Madeline, the control cracked and the mouth returned to raptor. "No you don't, Colonel. You're all baked and ready to eat. You're mine."

Scherie disagreed. *"Get the fuck out of her, you ancient cunt!"*

Madeline's face twitched, but the cackle returned. "Language, dear. You'll have to do better than that. Maybe if you come closer." Even as she beckoned with a finger, she brought her leg up into a forward kick that sent Scherie stumbling back on her ass.

Madeline pulled her arm out of the sling—none of her body's injuries seemed to be limiting her. But when she turned toward Endicott, she did so with robotic slowness. "You look a little peaked, Major. Time to thin the herd."

Endicott pushed himself back with his legs, and Madeline followed with almost equal difficulty. Hutch must still be struggling in there.

Scherie's first instinct was to charge Madeline, hug her tight and dispel her. No, she thought, these people kill for a living, and whatever hesitation Hutch was creating for Endicott's sake didn't apply to her. She needed to attempt several things at once, none of which she had ever done before. First, spiritual matters: she could tell them to go; could she command them to come?

She focused her mind. *I call on the Left-Hand dead of the House of Morton.*

Fie. You are not of our House.

You know that's no longer true. She prayed that sex plus love meant that she wasn't bluffing.

She wasn't. *Damn it all, what now?*

First, she ordered, *occupy the tanks.*

If demons could speak like guilty pets, the Left Hand spoke that way now. *We're, um, already there.*

Right, thought Scherie, *wouldn't want Madeline to escape. Can you animate the bodies?*

Is that a trick question?

Just do it. The rest of you, distract Madeline until they can corner her.

With a brutal crash of alchemical glass, Scherie's zombie squad burst from their tanks. But they were nearly as slow as Madeline, so Madeline ignored them. She stretched a hand with arthritic tentativeness toward Endicott's pierced abdomen. *"Let it bleed,"* she said.

Fuck tactics, thought Scherie. She dove at Madeline. Anything to distract her for a few seconds. And it only took a few seconds for Madeline to backhand her against the operating table.

Scherie's view of the world went fuzzy. When it came back into focus, Madeline was pounding one of the zombies into a pulp. Perhaps the combat had quickened them, for even as Madeline disposed of the first zombie, numbers two and three were on her, thumping against her with their chests and arms.

Scherie saw her opportunity. Hands ready, she stepped toward Madeline.

But, smiling at the closing noose, Madeline slipped through the rough constraints of the zombies with a dancing halfback's grace. Scherie crouched, fearing that this time she wouldn't get up from being kicked across the room.

But as Madeline stepped into the kick, Endicott called, "Hutch, don't!"

Madeline hesitated and stumbled in midstride. In her fury and frustration, Madeline grasped Scherie with both hands, as if to impale her on some alchemical tubing.

Contact. And Scherie saw the truth. *"Poor girl. You're already dead. Go."*

Black flash, and Hutch collapsed into Scherie's arms. Once again, Madeline's soul fled for another body. But this time, the Left Hand caught the fleeing darkness. *"Come to us, little dove,"* they cooed, and her soul dissolved within their stream.

Trying to keep Hutch from hitting the floor, Scherie wobbled on her feet, then steadied both their bodies against the operating bed. Scherie felt Hutch support her own weight again, and tentatively let go of her. Hutch stood to her full height and, with some sorrow in her eyes, looked at Scherie. "Thank you."

From this angle, Scherie could see the countdown. Nine minutes left. Fatigue? Fuck it—she'd rest in peace soon enough. She broke away from Hutch, and bent over Endicott. His bleeding was worse. She placed a hand over his. *"Ten motherfucking minutes,"* she said. She felt the power leave her—more than she hoped, but less than despair.

"Hooah," said Endicott. "See you then."

Scherie grabbed Hutch's arm and pointed at the corner. "That way."

The zombies turned to walk in that direction, legs stiff as stilts (no time to relearn fine motor skills). Scherie and Hutch moved faster, though Hutch detoured three painful steps to give the tech's body a firm kick. "I'll never forgive them for what they made me watch."

"Get a move on, Colonel," said Scherie.

"Yes, ma'am."

And they stepped into the red.

A n attentive tourist of H-ring might wonder why a stone structure so far belowground in a naturally swampy area didn't flood. The answer for a craftsman was simple: because water didn't want to be there. Until today.

The first part of the self-destruct was the removal of the craft that protected the H-ring structure. The water outside saw a vacuum, and abhorred it. In drops, dribbles, and finally rushing streams, the Center began to drown.

But that was just a side effect. The designers knew that CRFT-CEN could never be allowed to fall into the hands of an enemy, foreign or domestic. At the end of the countdown, the explosives packed around H-ring would annihilate every thing and every person who remained behind.

A bram listened to his instincts, and they shocked him. In the craft world, the only perfect storms were designer products. The successful assaults of weather and Left-Hand spirits, the breach by Morton and Endicott, the static in Chimera's feed, the sense that (despite his craft screen) Rezvani approached with doom in her hands: all these coincidences meant internal coordination. Roderick had sabotaged the probability defense. Suicide? No, this was too elaborate. Roderick was not attempting to die, but escape. How was inconceivable, except to Roderick. So

Abram fled through the OTM's secret way into Chimera's room.

Maddie would have opposed her brother's destruction while he could still be used and tortured. But Maddie was dead, and if the oracle was right she might not find a way to live this time. He should grieve, if given a moment. But he had gone wrong inside, and knew it. He wanted vengeance, not grief. He wanted new blood to spill for that already lost.

In Chimera's room, he could kill two birds with one stone—Maddie's way of thinking. He would take all the craft power in that space and destroy Roderick.

Roderick had defied nature too long and too well. Even the self-destruct that Abram had initiated couldn't guarantee Roderick's true death. Abram would have to attend to that personally. He sprinted toward Roderick and felt the suppressed pain kick in before its time. His body had absorbed a great deal of damage, but he only needed a few minutes more.

Fifteen minutes more. Why had he allowed so much time, more than he needed for his own escape? Some residual dread of judgment? Seeing Rezvani, the dark lady with pomegranates of his dreams, had shaken his lack of faith. He had feared and hoped that, in killing death, he had killed God. But here was his answer: Rezvani, God's messenger, Death incarnate.

The machine with Roderick's head was glowing, steam rose from its base. Blackened flesh had begun to melt off Roderick's skull. Yet still the thing spoke. "So, I've finally convinced you."

"Your sister is dead."

Roderick laughed. "You think after all this time I still care. You've held on to too much of your humanity."

Abram had said everything of importance. Quietly and quickly, he went to work. The head was shielded, but Abram had left himself a back door; he'd first have to disable the machine below the silvered box and then counteract its craft to destroy Roderick. He touched the hidden panel in the machine; it came away easily in his hand. Too easily. A quick scan of the primitive fusion of electrical circuits and alchemical vacuum tubes showed a deadly peril: the wiring had changed. What had gone on here?

He reached his hand in, ready to pull out wires and tubes at random until Roderick's defenses fell, but the stalking presence of the younger representative of the Family that Abram had hated and desired most stopped him short.

"Abram, step away from the other monster." Dale Morton was here.

I spun and darted sideways on entry, fearing ambush, but I found only disorientation among the rows of servers. The computers whined with the stress of ancient cooling components; the craft that gave them preternatural function was failing. Water seeped along the sterile floor.

I stalked down the rows, expecting Abram's move. I heard the voices, but ventriloquism required little craft. Then I saw Roderick's head, and Abram reaching into the ancient machine. I had two choices: attack Abram where he stood or call him out from the machine. I called him out.

Abram stood up. "Let me finish it."

"Allow me," I said. "You can run, or you can die, but you can't stay here."

"You can't be trusted with this," said Abram.

"And you can't be trusted with anything," I said. With a century of this man's deceit at Morton expense, I would not be fooled by appearances now. I readied my craft . . .

. . . and found a fountainhead. I had expected the energies here in the heart of darkness to be hostile, but they were neutral to my use. I felt new strength—dangerous, in that it might push my body beyond the point of recovery.

In one Olympian bound, Abram sprang up on top of the nearest server, his sword forward in a charge. My strength craved use, and gravity seemed to be on half shift. I jumped atop the next server, metal staves at guard.

Abram seemed surprised, then shook his head. "Craft-thieving Morton."

"Craft-hoarding Endicott."

We renewed our duel. We leapt from one server to the next, sword versus stave, with the opportune punch and kick at close quarters. We both landed on an old magnetic tape reader near Roderick. The machine's whine ceased, and flames burst up around us, flickering over our skins as with damned souls.

Through the noisy breakdown of coolant pumps and fans came the bass percussion of someone at the airlock. The noisy chaos had gotten the attention of the H-ring staff dutifully standing guard outside. *"Freeze door,"* said Abram and I, without pausing in our efforts to kill each other.

But I felt the contrary physical and craft impulse of *Open door* from the other side.

I stepped back from my opponent. "You think that killing everyone down here will save you? Too many people up there know." Another bluff, but I thought this one might work.

Abram's sword leveled at me. An almost human horror was on his face. "Why are they still here? I don't want them here."

For conversation's sake, I responded as if the monster were serious. "Communications are fried. They don't know about the destruct."

But as I spoke, the neglected airlock doors opened. In rushed guards, armed with petty craft and strength, yelling, *"Freeze. You will stand down."*

"Freeze yourself," Abram snarled back at them. And a half-dozen men and women froze in their tracks.

I looked the soldiers in the eyes. "Check in with command. You've got about ten minutes before H-ring self-destructs. So *go*."

"What about you?" a stronger-willed woman corporal asked.

"Family duel," I said.

"None of your business," said Abram.

"You're insane," said the corporal.

"Go," said Abram and I. Compelled and convinced, the soldiers left.

"How touching," said Roderick. *"Why don't you join them, please?"*

"Shut up," I said, as Abram and I commenced fighting again in earnest.

Abram's sword moved in scything strokes at lawn-mower speed. "If you're here with me at the end, so much the better."

Bullshit. As if the greatest cheater of death in history

would stay here, like a captain of a sinking ship. "You'd be an excellent liar if you did it less," I said.

In the House, Abram's puppet had been invincible against me, but now, with Chimera failing and me gaining some of its strength, Abram had to fight at my level. Abram used an unusual form of Far Eastern fusion technique. The old man had a preternatural agility, and his Taoistic sense was well-adapted against my native style.

Blood and sweat and phlegm flew with each connecting blow—like the fifteenth round of a world championship bout. Abram's sword point made future scars, but missed my vitals. And Abram's cuts had given odd razor edges to my metal sticks, edges that shredded skin. I had taken too many hits for long-term health, but I still felt the force of this place animating my battered body, dampening and flattening impacts.

Water dripped from the ceiling, ran down the walls, covered the floor. Electrical short circuits cascaded out from the water's path, followed by power failures. In older areas, the water boiled with heat. Near the modern machines, it froze at the touch of leaking coolants, some of which steamed in a threatening manner. Eventually, the water would rise and cleanse Chimera, if it weren't for H-ring blowing up soon.

"Too fucking bright again!" Scherie was in the room.

"I'm on it," said Hutch.

Time to end this and get Scherie out of here. "Hutch." *Smack, clang, smack.* "Bring Scherie as close as you safely can."

"I don't think so," said Abram, driving forward with abandon and away from Scherie and Hutch. "One lifetime is not enough to defeat me."

Ugh, immortal pomposity. But Abram moved as I had hoped. With my staves, I entangled Abram's arms as I stepped into Abram's stride with an off-balance sweep kick that would take us both down. We tumbled with a light splash and heavy thud to the ground. We wrestled on our sides for a dominant position as Abram sought clearance for his blade in the clutch.

"Don't you ever learn?" I said. "I don't have to beat you . . ."

I heard Hutch and Scherie splashing over to me.

". . . just hold you. Scherie, here!"

Hutch pushed Scherie to fall on top of Abram's thrashing legs, where she couldn't fail to find contact.

But before Scherie fell, Abram tapped into some hidden reservoir of strength. *"Off."* He pushed me back against the server, and brought up his sword, fending off Hutch with the backstroke. Then, Abram brought the blade down to behead Scherie.

In craft combat acceleration, I watched the deadly stroke begin. All possibilities resolved into one instinctual move. I dove on top of Scherie's neck, presenting my left side to the path of the oncoming blade.

With necromantic pain, the sword cut through muscle and maybe spleen and maybe more. Only superabundant craft stopped it there. Even contained, it was a bad wound. Like Endicott's, it would kill me if I lived long enough.

But Scherie's hands had grasped Abram's legs. Her rage at my injury defied expression, so her craft was simple. *"You're dead."*

"Yes, my lady," said Abram. *"The judgments of the Lord are true and righteous altogether."*

And in the explosion of a black hole, he was gone.

The Left-Hand possessed bodies had entered the room just in time to witness Abram's exit. They nodded in slow approval. A dark talon of Left-Hand spirits fluttered over his body, but seemed to find nothing to chase.

I thought I heard the roar of the Potomac, drowning out Scherie's words of comfort or concern in my ear. Time was running out. The effort required to speak above a whisper surprised me. "We have to go." We, meaning Scherie and Hutch. It didn't matter much where Endicott and I went; we weren't going to get there.

"Wait," said Roderick. The red tick-tock magic had faded to the size and rhythm of a pathetic pacemade heart. "Please. You must kill me first. I'll be trapped here, underwater and under tons of earth, when this place fails."

So the old Morton fear affected this monster too. "We don't owe you anything," said Hutch, helping Scherie to her feet.

"I was not a good man," said Roderick. "But I have been a tortured slave for more than two lifetimes. Surely, my death would be timely."

"His pain," said Scherie, eyes fixed on Roderick. "It's horrible."

"Yes," said a faint voice. Endicott had slid into the room and along the floor, leaving a trail of blood, failing to contain his wound. "He's an abomination. Do it."

I nodded. If Roderick was deceiving us to gain his dissolution, so be it.

"What do I do?" said Scherie.

"Just tell me to go," said Roderick, "and strike me with the sword."

"You're protected," said Hutch.

"Still? The craft has nearly failed. You'll probably survive long enough to die in the self-destruct."

"I'll handle the sword," said Hutch. She wrested the weapon that had been brandished against her ancestor from Abram's dead hand. "I enjoy irony."

Scherie and Hutch approached the silvered box. Scherie placed her hands very close to the box without touching it, and Hutch raised the sword.

"Go," said Scherie.

Hutch brought down the sword and slashed the box and Roderick's head into two halves. The pieces shrank, crumbled, and rotted into a nearly liquid mass of loathsome putridity. In the blackest of auras, Roderick was gone.

Hutch's hands shook as she dropped the sword splashing to the floor. She fell to her knees, agony gripping every muscle in her body. But more of the evil affected the craft assailant—Scherie tumbled to the ground.

Endicott and I sat, slumped shoulder against shoulder on the floor of Chimera's room. The kids were not alright. Our blood flowed down and mixed in the rising cold water.

"That's bad mojo," I said.

"Side wound, savior?" said Endicott.

"Seppuku, samurai?" I said. "Hypothetically, if you were bleeding to death . . ."

"No worries," said Endicott. "Only another few minutes until we're buried alive. Oh . . . sorry."

"No problem." I smiled, strangely relaxed. "No way we'll be alive under all this."

With her better hand under Scherie's shoulder, Hutch

dragged her over to us, then leaned heavily against a server, winded, exhausted from possessions and pain.

"Hutch," I said. "Why don't you get a head start with Scherie? Endicott and I will catch up."

Hutch glared back at me. "What did your father teach you about craft? Act, and hope for the necessary."

"Let's keep crawling," said Endicott. "A hundred years from now, I'd like to be found closer to the stairs."

"Wilco," I agreed.

Scherie's eyelids fluttered open. "Motherfucking possessor . . ." She looked around. "What are we still doing here? Let's move it, soldiers. Zombies, give us a hand."

"No," said the Left Hand, moving slowly back to the OTM room.

"Then go fuck yourselves." The Left Hand didn't acknowledge her order. "I've got Dale." She worked her arms under mine and dragged me backwards through the rising water.

"Toward the airlock," said Hutch, as she dragged Endicott along the watery floor using her sling that she'd wrapped under his arms. "Quicker."

They slid Endicott and me over the bottom of the airlock doorways, as I slid in and out of consciousness.

Dad and Grandpa manifested above me, looking very prominent. "Stay with me, boy," said Grandpa.

"They let anyone in here these days," I muttered.

Outside in the corridor, it was darker and wetter. Hutch slipped and fell. Scherie gasped and tugged, her strength gone. Endicott and I frogged and pumped our legs, but gained no purchase to help the women. Hutch and Scherie both slipped and stayed down. My internal clock gave me a two-minute warning. We weren't going to make it.

"Hutch," I said, ready to beg her to get Scherie out of here.

"What. The. Hell?" gasped Scherie.

I turned to look. Eight men in black suits swooped down the corridor like ravens in the jerky stop-start of dreams. The Peepshow. Carrion seers, always prophesying dooms and picking over battlefields. They grabbed my arms and legs. I twisted in weak resistance. "I'm not going anywhere without . . ."

Stretchers. Four stretchers. Enough for all of us. God-damn the farsight that could pick up the pieces but couldn't prevent. With brutal efficiency we were dropped down, strapped in, and on our way.

I went black, then jerked back into awareness. I was at a tilt now—head first, feet lower, my guts threatening to stay behind. The Peepshow was running up the stairs, and my stretcher bobbed along as they ran. If they had been C-CRT or SCOF, they wouldn't have been breathing hard, but they were only Langley, so they were puffing and straining.

One voice of the eight counted down seconds. "Sixteen, fifteen." Another counted off odds. "We're at fifty-fifty." Flip a coin, I thought, and call it.

On the last landing before starlight, the explosion hit.

The stairway rocked and rolled beneath us like an earth-quake. I was literally tossed by my carriers, and nearly dropped. Stones fell all around, but only little ones hit. Someone must have been skewing the probabilities. My heart raced—here we might actually get buried alive.

The wave calmed. By craft or natural luck, a path remained. With a last effort, we emerged into the deserted café and out under spotty, glorious stars. My storm had passed.

M y attention wavered, then returned. A familiar face took off his dark glasses to stare down at me.

"Eddy," I said. "I didn't know you cared."

"Evermore," said Eddy, but he looked away from me to the horizon.

Two confused young people dressed as doctors and glowing with health stood at attention. "Sirs, we were ordered to wait here for casualties."

Scherie sat up on her stretcher. "That's us. The major first, stat. He's got about ten seconds' juice before he pops."

"On it," said one of the healers.

"You," said Scherie, pointing the other healer toward me, "take the captain. Is that you, Eddy? You got an ambulance coming? Good. These guys need as much catgut as craft."

"Nice girl," whispered Endicott as the healer's hands lay over his. "You gonna make her an honest woman?"

I groaned. "You're worse than Hutch."

"I heard that," said Hutchinson. But she smiled so broadly that her chiseled face might crack. "My boys, my bad-assed boys in the shit. Together. About fucking time."

TWENTY-SIX

*But in a last word to the wise of these days let it be
said that of all who give gifts these two were the
wisest . . . They are the magi.*
—O. HENRY

*But, in a larger sense, we can not dedicate—we can
not consecrate—we can not hallow—this ground.*
—ABRAHAM LINCOLN

There's a craftsman in all of us.
—An advertisement for reliable American tools

In Arlington National Cemetery, it was quiet. Here, when
they weren't on duty, the dead truly rested. Endicott and
I rested too, seated not out of disrespect, but because our
wounds still kept us off our feet. Hutch stood at attention
next to us.

Though there was only one hole in the ground, we were
honoring two soldiers. The body of General Endicott was
entering Arlington for the last time. With equal finality,
the mortal remains of my father were leaving. Dad never
could bear to be in the same location as the general, and

he had someplace else in which he'd rather fade away. But space was at a premium in Arlington, particularly for craft spots, so the Morton family could provide a courtesy to the Endicotts.

They would replace the headstone later. Dad's stone had no cross or other symbol, since none of the official symbols quite captured the Morton worldview. Even the atheists' atom was too goofy and scientifically inaccurate.

Guns saluted the general; Dad received a rifle volley. Though Dad's removal was irregular, the surface rituals of a craft funeral were the same as any in Arlington—they had to be. But only at a craft funeral could the departed talk with the bereaved.

S eems you were right about the danger, Major," said the general, looking down at his coffin. "And now H-ring is destroyed?"

"They'll rebuild it, sir," said Endicott. "Or something like it. And, regardless, the commanders asked me to assure you that you'll have work here, if you want it."

"Excellent," said the general, without enthusiasm. "May I note for the record that while your conduct has been somewhat irregular, you've proven to be a fine soldier in the family tradition."

"Thank you for saving my life, Dad," said Endicott.

"Just doing my duty," he said gruffly, but he seemed to recover some of his living pride. "What about the family sword?"

In the last struggle to escape H-ring, Endicott had abandoned the family weapon. "If it's not destroyed, they'll recover it, and I'll restore it."

"See that you do. Yes, yes, it's just a thing, and not as important as anybody's life, but it means a great deal to our line." The general grew a bit distracted again and looked about at all the other graves. "Say, where did they plant that Sphinx woman?"

"Unknown, sir. Langley isn't talking. My analysis is that she'd want her remains to be where her spirit will be needed, but where she'll be needed is the big secret."

"Hmm. Must be nice to still have plans." The general stared at his spectral hand. "I'm not much more than a thin copy, but it still feels lonely here."

"We can talk anytime you'd like, Dad," said Endicott.

"And risk sin?"

"It's only a sin if you're not real, sir," said Endicott.

"And we're real, son." Endicott's grandparents had manifested behind his father. As in life, a quick hug and a firm handshake were their only overt signs of affection. Those signs were enough.

I had my own ghostly relations crisis. Grandpa was right in Dad's face again, full of bluster. "I suppose you think I have to let you in now."

"What the . . . ," I started to protest, but my father held up a hand.

"I have other places to be," said Dad. "Maybe I'll visit for the solstices, and May Day."

Grandpa sputtered; his eyes darted from me to my father, bluster replaced by sincere horror. "What kind of ingrate idiot do you two take me for?" The old spirit clasped the younger by the shoulders. "Goddamn it, son. The dead might not change; but the past does. I was wrong about too many things. Please, come home to stay."

The embrace only lasted a few seconds before Grandpa was off running across the graves toward a lurking black amorphous shadow. The Left-Hand spirits had helped to end the power of Abram and Madeline over their former leader, Roderick. But their new zombie bodies were crushed, and they had nowhere to go. They hesitated between malignity and fear on the border of this family gathering. They might eventually fade, but what mischief could they accomplish in the meantime?

"You, Mortons," called Grandpa. "Line up and prepare to move out."

"Old man, we obey no one, we . . ."

"What did you say, soldiers? Don't make me come in there. You're marching with me. I've got a secure place for you to wait this out."

"Wait for what? We have nothing." There was a new element in the Left Hand's collective voice, a birdlike call plaintive with fresh loss.

"That's need to know, soldiers, and way beyond this dead captain's pay grade. Hup to!"

Grandpa and the Left Hand disappeared, and I stood alone with my father.

"Dad, why were you so set against Scherie, against my involvement in this fugazi? We've won. The Mortons have won."

"I take the long view," Dad said.

I didn't push it. Sometimes, the dead were just skipping records, and I had another animal to fry. "On the long view, there's something I need to ask you about. About Sphinx—"

"Yes, she's the one who hinted to me about the coming risk to our House and Family. I tried to opt out, yet to put my future ghost in a position to help if worse came to worst. Grandpa, well, he trusted her too much. Oh-oh, he needs help corralling the Left Hand. Got to go."

Dad disappeared. "But—that's not what I wanted to ask you!" But maybe that was the start of an answer.

After the inevitable, endless debriefings and scant time to heal, Colonel Hutchinson ordered Endicott and me to a meeting in her temporary E-ring office.

Her recovered files and belongings were in neat boxes, everything except an envelope and one of the photos of happy children on which she rested her hand.

"Well, boys," she said, rising at our salute. "I thought you should be the first to know. I'm retiring."

The static of very bad news played on my skin. "Retiring from the military, ma'am?"

Hutch smiled with pity in her eyes. "No, Captain, I think you know what I mean."

"I don't know what you mean," said Endicott. "I refuse to know what you mean."

"If it's Chimera's curse, we can fix it," I said.

"Not the curse," said Hutchinson. "It's what happened before. Seems my soul and body don't get along anymore. That type of possession probably should have killed both. Only Left-Hand craft kept my body alive, and that kept my soul bound to earth. But now that my business with Madeline and Abram is settled, I feel like an adverse possessor myself. I think it's past time to say good-bye."

I looked at Endicott, hoping that he might have some

prayerful miracle up his sleeve to stop this. But Endicott was looking back at me with the same desperate question on his face.

"Gentlemen," said Hutch, offering her hand.

"Don't be stupid," I said, choking back a sob, and Endicott and I wrapped our arms around the colonel.

"All right, boys," said Hutch, patting our backs. "You'd better take care of each other, even if you don't like each other much. And that reminds me." She stepped back, pulled the envelope off the desk, and handed it to Endicott with a mischievous smile. "This is the matter we've discussed. Please see to it."

"Yes, ma'am," he said, envelope shaking in his hand.

There were some other words of memory and protest, and then Hutch sat in her chair, closed her eyes, and in a soft moon glow of magic, left her body for good.

I n Providence, what had been a hole in the ground had risen up to new life. Workmen had been busy clearing rubble and reassembling the gothic Morton master folly with new materials. They worked in the mental fog of overpaid people in productive dreams. That did not explain why they had left an irregularly shaped gap in the keystone of the basement arch. Wooden and metal scaffolding still supported the arch; a stepladder stood beneath it. Scherie and I looked up at the arch and down at the ruins of the subbasement. We would have to finish up down there later.

Scherie grimaced. "What kind of loan can we ever get on this place?"

My mouth curled up on one side. "The Pentagon defense

wrapped a mortgage of bad odds around our necks for the rest of our lives. We're not going to have much luck."

"Who said anything about luck?" said Scherie.

"That's the spirit. Ready?"

She held out her hand. "Hooah."

Like the House, slowly resurrecting stone by stone, we'd had time to rebuild the trust and simple affection that had crumbled some when we'd fled from here, and now, hearts full of love and ready for the coming days, we needed only one more piece to bind us together.

With two swift and skilled motions, I cut Scherie's palm and then my own. We let our blood drip on the chunk of stone that I had saved. I stood up on the stepladder, stone raised in my right hand. Like the last piece of a puzzle, I fit the blood-soaked stone into the empty slot.

My father had written to me that "with a holographic medium, a little piece can preserve the whole image, though the resolution might fade. The Morton dead, the Morton past, and the spirit of the Morton House are holographic."

A warm glow filled the room, like a slow sunrise on a spring day. "Hello, House," I said. "We're your family."

A dark line of spirit emerged from the stone in the form of a large fist, which shook with menace at us. Grandpa and Dad manifested to its left and right. "Downstairs with you lot," said Grandpa. Bound by new blood, the darkness retreated to its old prison.

We moved in the opposite direction, seeking sunlight. The new front door swung loose on its hinges. At the threshold, Scherie paused.

"You don't have to do this now," I said.

"No, now is right," she said. She raised both hands to the sun and cried in Persian: *"Come!"*

And they came. The dead of the house of Rezvani—men, women, and children from pre-Pahlavi to post-Khomeini—swarmed bright green through the front door and literally faded into the woodwork. Scherie called after them: "You could at least say hello."

"Give them time," I suggested. "They're probably a little shy. Now we celebrate."

I swept my cut hand across the sky, and a glowing rainbow followed its path, each color clear across the full arc from horizon to horizon. "A sign of my covenant with you," I quipped.

"I love you too, weatherman," said Scherie.

The private basement blood ritual would have been enough of a marriage ceremony for the craft world, but it wouldn't do for mundane family and friends. In terms of living versus ghostly attendance, the outdoor wedding in the Morton courtyard was a small affair. Scherie had her parents and a couple of bewildered and not completely approving bridesmaids, and Dale had his old pal Chuck as best man, who made far too many unfunny jokes about the damage to his "pride" at the last Morton celebration. Acting as minister was a colonel from H-ring with a raspy Harry Belafonte voice named Calvin Attucks. The word was that he would soon be promoted to general and replace Michael Endicott's father as head of countercraft ops.

The Rezvani family hosted the reception at their restaurant. Mr. Rezvani was beaming, expressing pleasure with his daughter and her choice of husband at every opportunity. His wife, however, seemed slightly on edge. While Dale was explaining to Mr. Rezvani and Chuck the non-confidential version of how he had changed his mind about retiring from the service and how Scherie had decided to join him in his vocation, Mrs. Rezvani took Scherie aside for a private word.

"I hope this isn't about the facts of life, *Madar.*"

"Oh God, no!" said Scherie's mother, with a blush and laugh. "But seriously now. I know, you say you love Dale very much. Do you plan on having children?"

Scherie had decided that she had to be honest with her mother even about questions that were none of her mom's immediate business, because there was too much already that she couldn't talk about. "Yes. If we can." Scherie didn't mention how it was their patriotic duty to try, and instead added, "After my training, when my work and deployment schedule settles down enough. But yes. Most definitely."

"That's good!" said Mrs. Rezvani, with obvious relief. "But how will that work with your different names?"

As usual, her mother had intuitively found the most interesting question in a seemingly trivial detail. Scherie hadn't taken the Morton name not just because of her feminist convictions, but because it was still unclear whether she was starting her own craft lineage or sharing in the continuation of the Morton line. That would probably only sort itself out with children, particularly a daughter. If she had Scherie's talents instead of the Mortons', by tradition that daughter would bear the Rezvani name, and that name would be carried down the matrilineal Family line.

But Scherie couldn't say all that, so she had to find another honest thing to say. "Don't worry, Mom. We'll cross that bridge when we come to it." Even if the bridge was an invisible path through a land and a future that was far more magical and dangerous than she had ever dreamed.

It was a dark and stormy night. There came a gentle tapping, rapping at the Morton door. I opened it, and found a rained-soaked Endicott in a black trench coat. "Can I come in?"

"Business or pleasure?"

"Not sure. Could be pleasure."

"Won't know until you try. Come in." I felt House's warm welcome, the smell of fresh-baked bread.

"Hey, it smells nice," said Endicott.

"Good, but please don't talk like House isn't here."

"I'm glad to see you too, House. Where's Ms. Rezvani?"

Remembering where she was, I held a finger to my lips. "I think she'd like it if you called her Scherie. She's resting. Off to boot camp tomorrow. We may need her to pay a visit to Tehran. She seems enthused."

"Hooah," said Endicott.

"Hooah," I agreed.

We went quietly back into the kitchen and sat at the table. "So, married life treating you well?" asked Endicott.

I chuckled. "It's the old Fighting Family curse—we had to get hitched just to see much of each other. That, and my signing up again will help. Though with our low ranks, it's still going to be a challenge."

"I envy you," said Endicott.

"Whoa, don't rush into anything. She's brought all these fresh ghosts to the place. House seems happy with the chaos, but all these Farsi speakers get on my nerves. If it wasn't destiny, I don't know what I'd do." I realized with unease that I was talking freely and off-duty with an Endicott. "Isn't this contact against regs?"

"Regs keeping us separate nearly got us all killed. Or worse. But maybe we can do a little government business, so I can get my travel costs reimbursed?"

"OK. Have a beer?" I asked.

"An American one."

"Patriotism?"

"No, just avoiding strong drink," said Endicott.

I went to the fridge. "You're wondering about the Left Hand? They're downstairs, chastised, bound again. They like being bound, in their creepy kinky Left-Hand way." Endicott didn't blanche, so I continued. "They had nowhere else to go, and being tied to something has kept them intact longer than otherwise. Oh, and there's a distinct new strain in their collective malice. Madeline has finally come home."

"That's good?" asked Endicott, dubiously.

"Better than the alternatives." I set down our ice-cold Rolling Rocks.

"Have you seen . . . ?"

"Abram? No," I said. "He might just be gone; he was pretty damned old. I don't know if he loved Madeline enough to be absorbed into what he'd always loathed."

"We'll see. Do you suppose Roman died down there?"

"With all due respect to your father, I don't assume anyone died down there."

I popped the tops off our beers. Endicott cleared his throat. "I didn't come here to talk about the Left Hand, Major Morton."

"Ah." I didn't pause in taking a swig of my beer. "That's

a good one. I've rejoined as a captain. The Five were very clear on that point."

"They've changed their minds."

"Now what the hell would make them do that?"

Endicott smiled with surprising mischief. "I told them I was out if they didn't. And Hutch's letter convinced them that I wasn't crazy."

I shook my head, dumbfounded. "That explains why she smiled like a cat in a midget penguin exhibit. Does 'thank you' even begin to cut it?"

"No, but I'll say it anyway, thank *you*, Dale. For too many things. Consider it a down payment." Endicott took a sip from his Rolling Rock. "I didn't respect how difficult it was for your family to fight against the Left-Hand temptations. No one did."

"It's Michael, right? Nah, Mike sounds better. About Left-Hand power, I think it's easier for me, living with the cautionary tales. But yes, I know better than most that every family can have a Left Hand."

"There's another thing," said Endicott. "I've been too narrow with God."

"OK, I'll bite. Narrow? You?"

"Funny. What I mean is, I believe that all this power we use, whether for good or ill, ultimately comes from God. So I can't draw easy distinctions among its practitioners."

"But you know what I'll say, right?" I asked.

"Yep. You'll say it's all nature. That we're the ones who make it good or evil."

"Yep. But that also means that I can't draw easy distinctions among practitioners either."

Endicott took another, longer sip of his beer. "I'll just say it once. You too are part of God's plan."

"This was Sphinx's plan," I said, "her counterplan to Chimera's schemes. And Sphinx is dead."

"To Sphinx," said Endicott.

"To Sphinx," I said. I took a long pull at my cold beer and shook my head. "Shit, you're too good. I give up. It doesn't take farsight to see why you're here. You want a reason we're going to permanently cease hostilities, and hell, maybe despite all this history we are. You want a reason besides the fact that we're outstanding soldiers and killers, that Hutch was our mom and pop, and that you know how to drink a beer. But you know what that real reason is. It ain't ever going to be theological. It's this country. It makes us all family in the end. But we, the magi, feel that tie before everyone else. Because we're the wise guys. So we'll be OK. OK?"

"OK."

The two comrades finished their beers. Outside, the storm had passed. House sighed and rested in its new foundations, and sang Scherie to a dreamless sleep. From New England to Langley and sea to shining sea, everyone with eyes to see and ears to hear gave the same report: all quiet on the astral plane of America.

EPILOGUE

That is not dead which can eternal lie,
And with strange aeons even death may die.
—H. P. LOVECRAFT

Across the shining sea, on a sold-out flight to Kiev, a single seat appeared to be unoccupied, yet no one attempted to sit there. The flight attendants did their counts, and the stealthy seat slid into and out of them—whichever caused the least trouble.

The man hiding in the seat typed at his laptop. A USB-compatible cable connected the laptop to the carry-on at his feet.

The cable ran within the carry-on to what looked like the main component of a desktop machine. Looks weren't completely deceiving—the device was in part a computer. But the device also contained a matrix of cerebral stem cells kept alive by Left-Hand craft. *Any sufficiently advanced magic is indistinguishable from technology.*

On the screen of the laptop appeared the following exchange:

YOU DO OK, PARDNER? BLINK LIGHT TWICE YES, ONCE NO.

I AM FEELING MORE TALKATIVE THAN THAT. SO THIS IS FLYING? ALL THIS MAGIC, AND I'VE NEVER FLOWN BEFORE. MY ARRANGEMENTS ARE COMPLETE?

WE HAVE BODY FOR YOU.

AND THE OTHER MATTER?

YES, A FRIEND. TALL, THIN, OBEDIENT. AND ONE FOR AFTER THAT.

AND ALL I HAVE TO DO IS RESIST THE CRAFT MIGHT OF RUSSIA, NATO, EASTERN EUROPE, AND THE OCCASIONAL ROGUE TURK?

HA. HA. YEP, THAT'S ALL.

Excellent. The Slav was happy, and Roderick wouldn't argue with him. His mission had been a success. His orders had been to obtain "a Morton" and he was returning with *the* Morton—the "head" Morton, if you will. Roderick had needed two things: a place to go, and a break in his leash. Now that he had those, he would keep his word, because it was so easy to keep. He could do all Roman asked, and more, so much more. More than his new employers wanted, enough to make his former country regret their treatment of him. Soon, he would have to deal with the Rezvani woman; despite all his long-laid plans, she had nearly killed him instead of freeing him. No witch with that kind of power against him could be suffered to live. As for the Endicotts and the so-called Right-Hand Mortons, he would live to see the end of their Families. He took the long view.

He would live. For the first time in decades, Roderick was truly happy to be alive.

APPENDIX

THE MORTON FAMILY

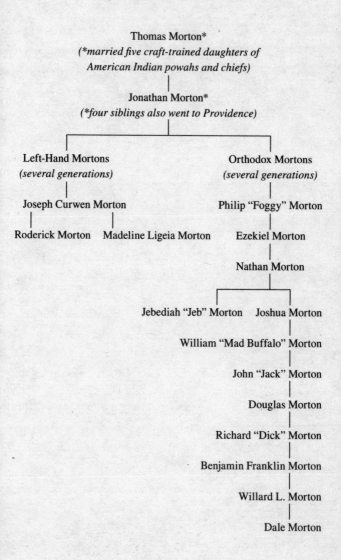

Thomas Morton*
*(*married five craft-trained daughters of
American Indian powahs and chiefs)*

Jonathan Morton*
*(*four siblings also went to Providence)*

Left-Hand Mortons
(several generations)

Orthodox Mortons
(several generations)

Joseph Curwen Morton

Philip "Foggy" Morton

Roderick Morton   Madeline Ligeia Morton

Ezekiel Morton

Nathan Morton

Jebediah "Jeb" Morton   Joshua Morton

William "Mad Buffalo" Morton

John "Jack" Morton

Douglas Morton

Richard "Dick" Morton

Benjamin Franklin Morton

Willard L. Morton

Dale Morton

THE STORY OF
THE MORTON FAMILY

Part I. Thomas Morton and John Endicott

In May 1624, Thomas Morton stood on a hill in the land of the Massachuset Indians and saw endless forests and animals and possibilities. The day was perfect. He was no longer a young man, but this place made him feel young. The land had a big horizon, vertiginous to any mind shaped in small walled fields. It could drive a sufficient imagination insane.

He took a swig of rum. Thomas always prided himself on his imagination.

One hundred yards down the slope, the trees stirred and parted, almost of their own will. A tall native emerged, not like the warriors and traders Thomas had seen. He wore a patchwork cloak of the fur from black wolves and lesser animals and the cloth stripped from French sailors and given by English Separatists.

Thomas approached the native. His skin was oddly marked: a coiled serpent threatened from one arm, an eagle peered from the other, long bars and stars decorated both limbs, a truncated pyramid filled the cheek below his right eye. These symbols carried a two-edged message: *I'm impressive, but you had better stay away.* The native stared at

Thomas, then around him, as if Thomas were surrounded by hidden allies. Thomas looked about—no, he was quite alone. He surveyed the woods. The native was alone too.

Thomas signed with his liquor and firelock and threw out some words: "rum, guns, trade." The native drew a dagger and waved it toward Morton in a casual threat. "Welcome, Englishman. Shall we dance?"

"Ah," said Thomas, "it's a fight you want, savage priest." He put down his gun and drew his own dagger—the native was too magnificent to shoot. "We shall see whose devil is bigger, mine or thine."

With a wild yell, Thomas ran the rest of the way down the slope at his opponent. When he fought a man fairly, it helped to imagine and express certain things. He said, *"Knife break,"* as he brought his blade against his opponent's. The native's blade shattered on impact, but so did his own steel. Odd, but Thomas was comfortable with his fists. He gripped the remaining hilt in his hand to help his punches. *"Break arm, break leg,"* but the native seemed to flow away from his blows. Thomas kept punching until he was panting for breath. Then he threw the hilt at the native. "Fight me, or the devil take you!" The hilt bounced off the man's chest.

"Ouch. Brother, please, that's enough!"

Thomas regained his wind. "You speak English well."

"Not really. It's complicated." The man's mouth moved differently than the sounds Thomas was hearing. Perhaps his devil was much bigger than Thomas's.

"Why did you want to fight?" asked Thomas, wiping his hands against the sides of his coat.

"You looked, um, interesting. I didn't recognize you because you're a new *powah,* like a chick or child."

"Powwow?" asked Thomas. It was the one word that he didn't recognize.

"You have no tongue for it." The native pointed at his chest. *"Powah."* He pointed to Thomas. *"Powah.* We are the same. Come. I'll show you."

The man, called Guardian, took Thomas to his village. Much of what they did seemed natural enough, the sort of things schoolboys did to show friendship—they shared food, mixed blood, exchanged gifts. But they didn't discuss trade next. Instead, Guardian told him about the craft and showed him some of its workings. He explained that fledgling *powahs,* like many vulnerable things in nature, have protective camouflage, and that was why he hadn't recognized Thomas immediately.

So I'm a witch, thought Thomas. *The Puritans won't be much pleased, or surprised.*

The next day, Guardian showed Thomas a clearing in the backwoods. A small creek with a shallow embankment blocked their way; they'd have to get wet to cross. Guardian lined Thomas up on the embankment and said, "Close your eyes, and try to cross."

"Whatever you say, brother." There were worse initiations.

Guardian seemed worried. He needn't have bothered. Thomas walked steadily ahead, not feeling any descent or creek water.

"Open your eyes," said Guardian.

Thomas turned and saw that they had crossed on the now-visible trunk of an enormous tree. Animals were also now visible, beasts that Thomas had never seen before, including one he recognized as an elephant, but covered with hair.

"This is the place of lost things," said Guardian.

Thomas thought the animals looked a little crowded. "It's not very large."

Guardian sighed. "It will grow." He stretched his arms wide. "When your people turn against you, this place will protect you. Will you protect it?"

A stillness fell over the Sanctuary. In the hush, Thomas felt the right words. "I swear it, for me, for my children, and for all my descendants until the land is no more."

On May 1, 1628, John Endicott stood quietly in the woods outside Thomas Morton's settlement at Merry Mount. His beard hung grizzled and unimpressive on his face, but the face itself was as iron as his headpiece and breastplate, and no one in the Salem settlement dared challenge his authority.

His men were fanned out behind him, waiting for his orders. At first the men of Salem had questioned this attack on other countrymen, but John had prayed for the power of command, and as always God had answered him. "These are no longer fellow Englishmen," he had argued. "Thomas Morton has come here to preach iniquity, and has led his followers into the arms of heathens and demons. But now shall it be seen that the Lord has sanctified this wilderness for his chosen people. Woe unto them that would defile it!"

From Merry Mount floated the seductive sounds of music, singing, and dancing. John could just see the top of the flower-covered Maypole and hear the words of the song's chorus:

Drinke and be merry, merry, merry boyes,
Let all your delight be in Venus's joyes.

He thought of Morton at the head of the dance, cavorting with his native women and performing the Satanic miracles he had learned from their priests. *Just and true are your ways, Lord,* he prayed. *I will show him the supreme power of your miracles.*

John drew his sword. When he prayed, it seemed that it could cut through almost anything or anyone that dared stand in its way. He hoped this fight would not come to mortal blows; he did not want to lose one of his own. Driving these new pagans from this new land would suffice.

He brandished his weapon. "To the flower-decked abomination! In the name of the Lord, forward!"

Part II. The Descendants of Thomas Morton

Morton married five craft-trained daughters of American Indian powahs and chiefs. When five of Morton's children learned all the lore their parents could teach them, and learned to lighten their hair and complexion to pass by the lax standards of the Providence Plantation, they left Maine for Rhode Island. By Puritan and English law, they were illegitimate, but the New World was too large for such distinctions. Two of the daughters disappeared into families that would beget snooty members of the DAR. One of the sons missed the woods and journeyed north to join the Iroquois. Another son chased wealth under another name and forgot his lore.

The eldest son, Jonathan, kept the Morton name and lore and found a piece of half-cleared land not far from water that made the hairs of his arms stand on end. "Here, father," he said to no one visible, drawing a native knife and slashing his palm. He dripped his blood into a porringer, then poured it out at the points of the star geometry preferred by the Cavaliers. He buried the empty porringer at the center of the star. On that ground, he built his House.

The first Morton House adopted a pious and unassuming camouflage, indistinguishable from its various neighbors and quickly forgotten, with only three low gables. The only overt occult decorations were the spirit stone carvings. One crack in the walls, a necessary imperfection, ran from basement to attic. *No one here but us witches.* Jonathan was determined to avoid his father's exile. The mellow followers of Roger Williams were happy to oblige. Their colony prospered and Jonathan prospered, in mutual causation.

The successive debacles of King Philip's War and Salem's witch executions reminded Jonathan of ancient injustices, and he expanded his House. It now loomed up three stories with seven high and pointed gables, in an ostentatious yet grim and outmoded style shared by the sans-W Hathornes and the Endicotts. "I have built my House in deep sympathy with mine enemy's," Jonathan told his sons on his deathbed. "Remind them of their errors when you can."

Obedient to their father, they buried some rocks in his coffin and burned his body by night in the woods. They took his ashes and mixed them in mortar with their own summer sweat, then built the high stone walls of the inner courtyard. "That I may stay with you as long as I am able,"

Jonathan had said. "Remember that you are begotten of brave warriors of the Englands, old and new. Learn the mundane arts of war and our lore of craft, and when the way is prepared, use your skills to free this land."

When Jonathan had said this, his sons had thought that he was half in the bag with the farm's whiskey and half-infected with Puritan bombast. But to repeat, they were obedient. They trained their children in the family arts. Those that were craft-worthy joined the so-called French and Indian War, but didn't dare reveal their peculiar talents except to their native craft enemies.

After Jonathan, the Morton line split. The eldest son fathered the orthodox line, while the second eldest fathered the Left-Hand lineage.

Then came the Revolution. The eldest son of that generation, Captain Philip Morton, revealed himself to General Washington during the siege of Boston. After the Battle of Brooklyn Heights, Philip summoned the bad weather that delayed the British advance and saved the Continental Army from destruction. During the Battle of Yorktown, where several of the craft families were active on land and sea to insure the trap, Philip became the first in a long line of Captain Mortons to die for their new country. Like the Morton courtyard wall, the relationship of craft and army was cemented with blood.

Washington and his inner circle were grateful enough to the craft families to sign a secret covenant with them, pledging the new country's protection in recognition of their services. The Mortons and Endicotts tried to exclude each other from the covenant, but Washington wasn't interested in their feud.

After the Revolution, the more vital, orthodox parts of

the Morton line scattered to the far ends of their new country's service: attending the new military college at West Point, trying out their craft at sea against the British, pirates, and whales, and riding with Sam Houston (they weren't at the suicidal Alamo though—using a Catholic mission for a defensive position was a nonstarter for a Morton).

The story of the Left-Hand Mortons, the disappearance of Ezekiel, and his grandson Joshua's successful fight against Roderick and Madeline is recounted elsewhere. Joshua led the Union Mortons during the Civil War. He was responsible for the death of Thomas "Stonewall" Jackson and fought against his brother Jebediah "Jeb" Morton at Gettysburg.

Of the Mortons between the Civil War and Dale's time, two were particularly noteworthy. The first was Joshua's son, William "Mad Buffalo" Morton. Bill ignored the Family boycott and fought in the Plains Indian Wars. He then went completely insane.

The second noteworthy Morton was Richard "Dick" Morton. Dick Morton mitigated the weather over the English Channel enough to allow the Allied invasion of Normandy on June 6, 1944.

BRIEF NOTES ON THE OTHER FIGHTING FAMILIES

Endicotts

American Founder: John Endicott (before 1601–1665). Name also spelled Endecott. John featured in the Nathaniel Hawthorne stories "The May-pole of Merry Mount" and "Endicott and the Red Cross." Endicott College in Beverly, Massachusetts, was named for him.

Abram Endicott. Antebellum patriarch of the Family, Abram (along with Joshua Morton) led the craft forces that besieged the House of Morton and defeated the Left Hand under Roderick and Madeline.

Oliver Cromwell Endicott. Father of Michael Endicott and head of countercraft operations.

Michael Gabriel Endicott. Son of Oliver, code name Sword.

Hutchinsons

American Founder: Anne Hutchinson (1591–1643). Nathaniel Hawthorne wrote a biographical sketch about her and may have used her as a model for the character of Hester Prynne. The Hutchinson River Parkway in New York was named for her.

Elizabeth Hutchinson. H-ring colonel and Dale Morton's superior officer.

Attuckses

First Historically Known American Founder: Crispus Attucks (c. 1723–1770). British soldiers killed Crispus in the Boston Massacre. The memorial to the massacre in Boston Common depicts his death in the foreground of its bas-relief bronze plaque.

Calvin Attucks. Head of countercraft operations in *The Left-Hand Way.*

Turn the page for a preview of

The
Left-Hand Way

··

TOM DOYLE

*Available from Tom Doherty Associates
in August 2015*

TOR®   A TOR BOOK

PROLOGUE

THE COURT OF THE RED DEATH

*And Darkness and Decay and the Red Death held
illimitable dominion over all.*

—EDGAR ALLAN POE

In Pripyat, the first snow of the year fell early on the deserted city and on the steel arch that hung over the Sarcophagus covering the ruined Chernobyl power plant. The windless cold was appropriate for this urban tomb, but unseasonal for early autumn, and the below-freezing temperature and snow were confined to this small, desolate pocket of Ukraine.

Seven Russian soldiers, five men and two women, arrived singly at the exclusion zone that enclosed the town, having entered the country in civilian dress by car, train, plane, bus, and boat. They were *spetsnaz magi*—special forces mages. One of them had been in Kiev for over a year; the Kremlin had kept him in place and ready for such occasions. Two had crossed through Belarus, whose Moscow-dominated craft authority had raised no fuss.

Over and under their body armor, the seven wore the latest hiking gear, which was as well suited to their task as most uniforms. All of them claimed to be tourists visiting the ghost town, though the exclusion zone was closed for the day. The guardians of the exclusion zone were bribed to allow entry, or in one overzealous instance, temporarily subdued.

The seven weren't surprised that they had been allowed to get so close to their target. Moscow precog had been able to see high-probability paths for them that ran as far as Pripyat without interference from the Ukie Baba Yagas. Beyond that, their target stood across their timelines, and nothing was certain.

Their weapons were necessarily a compromise, portability and concealment being greater priorities than for most operations, though two had brought rocket launchers, as bullets might not suffice. While they assembled the launchers for use, another mage waved a Geiger counter. They all wore radiation badges. The area was supposed to be safe for short stays, but it was also supposed to be free of hostile magi, and how their Left-Hand target might use the local low-level radiation was unclear. Was it just to provide cover, or did he actually derive some energy from it?

They rendezvoused in the northwest corner of town. Pripyat's great housing blocks still stood, ugly, for 1970s Soviet wasn't much prettier than Stalinesque. Snowmelt dripped through the now skylit ceilings; first floors bore the brown high-water marks of flood damage. In the distance, the Sarcophagus surrounding the plant prophesied a self-inflicted apocalypse.

With a quick look-over, the soldiers assessed one another with professional scrutiny and mutual respect.

Seven of the best combat magi of the Russian Federation, all here for one man. They could scarcely believe the over-kill. Though perhaps one of them was not truly elite: of the two women, the tall one code-named Vasilisa was un-usually thin for a craft combat soldier. She was here for a psychological reason that none of them cared to dwell on: she resembled the American's dead sister, Madeline.

None of the *spetsnaz* had doubts about their leader, a highly decorated major with the cryptonym Ogin, whose great-grandfather had died holding the line outside of Mos-cow during the Great Patriotic War after months of delay-ing the enemy at every turn until nature could bring winter down on their heads. Ogin had fought against Chechen shamans, Chinese border crossers, and mystic Bond-wannabes from the West, and he was long overdue for a promotion. Ogin's presence alone would have sent a clear message: the Russian craft authority had decided that the new power in Kiev was not tolerable.

Ogin held a monocular to his eye and scanned from right to left, then down the road that provided a long, clear line of sight in the direction of the melted reactor's tomb. He let out a disappointed breath. Though it was perhaps too much to expect that their target would come out into the open to engage them, it would not have been inconsis-tent with his profile or previous behavior.

Would Roderick hide in the operational buildings of the plant? Ogin hoped not. Though they had chosen a mini-mally staffed day for this operation, innocent civilians still worked at the plant, maintaining and containing the reac-tors, and craft collateral damage did not play well in the Kremlin.

On to the necessary thoroughness of professional

soldiering. "You'll commence the search pattern," said Ogin. He reiterated their assignments and pointed out directions, but even as he did so, his orders were moot.

From the direction of the ruined plant came a false sunrise of craft power, glowing radioactive red. Ogin raised his monocular again and saw a single man moving toward them along the *prospekt* between the ugly housing, not trying to hide or seek cover. He was as tall and straight as any tsar in procession. About him, motes winked brightly in the night vision, as if isotopes were losing their half-lives on cue. A gray shroud covered his body and legs, making his movement look like hovering. A mask gave him the gaunt face of a stiffened corpse with a rictal smile. His shroud and face were spotted with blood.

It was the American they called the Red Death. For the first time in mortal memory, Roderick Morton was coming forth for battle.

They would not attempt capture or negotiation. Ogin signaled, and the seven moved with incredible speed, with himself and four others taking positions that would attack the American from the west and drive him toward the river, and two flanking farther out to deflect an escape run. A full circle would have looked pretty, but avoiding a circular firing squad was more important. They found cover behind the carcasses of abandoned trucks and the brush gone wild. They had spells ready and, like a sports squad, some were more magically armed for defense, others for attack. They saved their spells; they would need them. First, though, they would employ their clear advantages in number and armament—simple physics always had its place.

The cold eyes behind the Red Death's mask followed

their movements and gave no sign of concern. Then, as if giving permission, Roderick nodded at Ogin.

"Fire rifles," ordered Ogin. The seven shot their automatic weapons at Roderick to soften up the target and test his abilities. This man, powerful as he was known to be, had never been known for field combat in the flesh.

Some of the bullets curved away from the American, some ripped through his shroud, and some seemed to pass harmlessly through his body. But some shots must have been hitting the American with real force, because the impacts shook his frame, vibrating him like a drum. These hits were insufficient, for the American remained standing, always bringing himself back to attention. The explosive tips weren't exploding inside him, and the armor piercers weren't carving him up.

So Ogin gave the next order, and his soldiers lobbed some hand grenades and fired the rocket grenades. Use of explosives was regarded as more dangerous in craft ops, because it was hard to have a good friendly fire protection chip when a near miss would still be close enough. But Ogin preferred that risk to the risks of direct contact with this target, or even physical proximity to him.

Explosion after explosion shook the ground. Pieces of the pavement and clods of earth flew up and out in all directions. The smoke and dust obscured the view. "Hold fire."

Bits of the remaining glass in the broken windows of the buildings tinkled as they fell with the snow to the ground. The view cleared; the American was down. Ogin's lieutenant stepped forward from the left flank. "Moving in on target."

Some instinct gripped Ogin's heart. "Hold." This gave

him a moment to justify his snap judgment. First, the un-
seasonable snow was still falling, which indicated that the
American's craft might remain hard at work. Though the
American was down, he appeared to be in one piece. And,
like many of his Hollywood countrymen, this man was
known for theatrical treachery.

Ogin knew some theatrics himself. He yelled in English:
"Sister fucker!"

Like a practice-range target, the American sprang to his
feet, then ran, not at Ogin, but right for one of the women,
impossibly fast, with a gale wind blowing before him. Ogin
thought he could see rage in the Red Death's terrible mask.

W*hy couldn't they just let Madeline rest in peace?*
thought Roderick. Yes, he had been waiting for
them to come closer, not for any tactical reason, but for
simple pleasure—he would have enjoyed their terror when
he sprang up and punched his hands through their armored
chests. But their rude, clever major had made him change
his plan.

So be it: seven opposing craftsmen, six to kill, one to
hurt. Seven probably seemed an extravagant number to
them, but they would learn how insultingly poor it truly
was. He forgave them their ignorance; in their brief lives,
none of them had seen someone of his power. Despite the
additional pain and difficulty, he would kill each of them
with individual means and attention, lest any observers
think he wasn't a fully rounded threat.

As he ran toward his first target, bullets again hit him
like incredibly fast sledgehammers, and bits of his own
gore flew away from him. The probability of not being

killed was vanishingly small, but craft was about probability, and he stretched that chance to hold his own precious life. The shots still hurt like hell. In the design of
his new body, Roderick had demanded heightened sensitivity, even to pain. Everything had to have its cost, and
even he wasn't beyond those red equations. Though the
agony tempted him to stop their guns from firing, that spell
would spoil his surprise.

To replenish his power, he sucked at their energies, as
he had once tapped the whole city of Washington, but
this focused drink had more noticeable effects. As their
thoughts and movements became slightly more sluggish,
he saw the seven's sins. The tall woman in the center, of
course, was a relative innocent—the better to bait him to
charge into their middle.

He wouldn't be so easily profiled. The other, shorter
woman, to his left of their center, was his first target. She
had stepped out from her cover and was moving her hands
and speaking a steady stream of Russian invective against
him, trying to work a subtle knife of craft between his
spirit and his body. *Oh no, dear, that trick has been tried,
and by better than you.* Besides, no mind-body crack to
work here. This corpus was his alone, created especially
for him. The world's most powerful exorcist, Scherezade
Rezvani, might still pose a threat against his soul, but no
one else.

But this pretender was giving him a headache. Even as
she, terror stricken, screamed at him to *"get the fuck out
of that body!"* he replied with, *"Please be silent,"* and with
a quick hip-chambered karate punch bashed in her skull.
Silence.

One of the flankers and two of the main line had rushed

to fold in their formation to defend their comrade, hitting him with their full arsenal of magic. He let their force fall upon him. He felt the air depart from his lungs in a local vacuum, but it would be minutes before his new body would notice. He felt epileptic shocks shoot across his synapses, and for a moment the world took on strange electric hues, but this was nothing to a mind that had been integrated with a machine. He felt his bones question whether they should remain unbroken, but they stayed whole, for no part of this body would obey another magus.

With improvisational speed that no other craftsman could have managed, he hit them back with their own spells. *"Air, please move."* *"A short, sharp shock, please."* *"Bones, please break."* For a few seconds, they fought with their pathetic defenses, then collapsed—strangled, convulsed, and broken.

Down to three, the major, his lieutenant, and the tall woman they were calling Vasilisa, who stood behind them, like an arrowhead pointing away from him in the direction they'd like to flee. The major had maintained his calm throughout, giving orders even as the recipients perished. Such admirable nerve could not be suffered to live. As his partner in the demonstration, his lieutenant would be perfect. Time to show them what he'd learned in the machine.

"Please shoot each other once in the stomach."

He had left them with complete awareness of what they were doing, yet they didn't fight it hard. They thought they were safe. Their rifles would have safety chips (what his former countrymen called Stonewalls).

They didn't understand. His time as a living dismembered head connected to the Pentagon's Chimera machine had given him abilities that made their digital safeguards useless. He had them fire single shots just to allow the savor and frisson of their failure.

One shot quickly followed the other. Oh, the sweet anguish, the horror and betrayal on their faces, as they doubled over and sank to their knees. But now he had to finish it, before it became too difficult and tedious. *"Please finish killing each other."*

The shots exploded simultaneously. Lovely. He had killed them all, except for the tall woman. Lovely.

He advanced on her, ardent with blood thirst and more. Stunned, she stumbled as she stepped away, then rolled and scrambled backward to get farther from him, legs pushing wildly. But she was beaten and slow and cornered against some brush. Standing up again to her full height, she ceased trying to escape, but her face didn't yet reward him with the stigmata of terror. She was fiercely professional, steely eyed in the face of his Red Death. What lay beneath her mask?

He bent forward, close to her lips, and spoke huskily in Russian. "You remind me of someone."

Had she been briefed on his background? Did she understand him? Oh, yes, he could see she did. Her hard eyes went wide with charming sexual horror, her mouth gaped with inviting terror.

"Would you like to come home with me? I could show you many things. Wonderful things."

Even though he was waiting for it, the force of her response was surprising. Both her hands gripped his throat, and as she pulled him closer, her teeth snapped at him, and some curse against his life slammed like the bullets against his chest. Refreshing. Madeline had been like this.

He backhanded her face as he had so often slapped Madeline's. The counter blow flattened her. *"Please pass out."*

With admirable restraint, he had merely rendered her unconscious. Still, as she lay powerless on the ground, he had to remind himself—it wasn't Madeline. *You are to carry my message. But not the message you think.*

Sensing a farsight audience, he took a step northeast toward Moscow and that place below Lubyanka that he and the combined force of the West had never seen. Then he turned his face west toward Langley and Vauxhall Cross. His left hand was open at his side, displaying its deeds laying about the ground, while he shook his right fist at the gray sky. "Insult me again, and I will bury you all!" *Look at this work, fuckers, and despair.*

Very good, enough theater, drop the curtain. With a bow and a sweep of his hands, he said, *"Screen up, please."* This old dog had learned some Ukrainian stealth tricks.

He removed his mask and admired the art he had created here. The white snow was splattered with red, like his mask and cloak. It was as pretty as he had planned, but if it snowed much more, the effect would be ruined. He asked the snow he had summoned to *please stop,* and it began to taper off. The Russians had brought some lovely guns, but he would leave those for his Ukrainian friends.

That just left Vasilisa. His desire hadn't all been pretense. To play with her a little while would be divine. No use thinking about it—if that was what he'd really wanted, he should have kept another one of them alive. He forced himself to turn away from the girl (no, "woman"—he had to keep up with the times) and plodded back through the town toward the nuclear plant.

Oh, his poor body. He hadn't let it show, but he was wounded all over. He would need some help with its healing and repair. To fit in, his face had Slavic features, which he resented, and his light golden hair seemed inappropriate to his disposition, but otherwise, his body was a wonder. Roderick had been an intellectual during a time when the benefits of physical exercise weren't fully appreciated. His current Classic-sculpted form was a narcissist's dream, but Roderick more appreciated its combat efficiency than its aesthetics.

He found his black-and-red Bugatti Veyron where he'd left it near the plant. Inside the plant, the workers were waiting for Roman's signal that it was safe to venture out again. Roderick pointed his electric key and pushed its button, unlocking the car doors and starting the motor. He smiled; simple technology could still make him feel young.

He let the car warm up while he changed his outerwear. His shroud wasn't designed for warmth, and neither was his full-body armor (he wasn't so foolish as to rely completely on his own power to stop every little projectile). He picked up his parka from the passenger seat, put on his boots, spat up a bullet, and pulled out his smart phone (a term that, due to his recent unpleasant employment in the Pentagon, gave him flashback chills). Roman Roszkewycz answered. Out of habit, they spoke in English.

"Good day, O great and powerful colleague," said Roman. "Did you have fun?" An implication there? Roderick sometimes had too much fun.

"I've left one alive," said Roderick. "But some paramedics had better hurry, or she'll freeze out here." Or if she didn't show up soon in mundane hands, her handlers would kill her remotely—any party of this significance must have that sort of implant.

"You're the one who dropped the temperature," noted Roman with his usual ill-timed humor. But perhaps sensing Roderick's mood, he changed the subject. "She'll tell discouraging story?"

"It should buy us a few more months." And next time, maybe they'd think twice about sending a Madeline doppelgänger, unless they meant business.

"Excellent. Come home to Kiev. We do lunch, yes?"

Roderick hung up. Home to Kiev. He wondered if the Russians thought he lived up here, in this poisoned ghost town that would have made Poe's head spin. He had broadcast his intention for months to be here by regular visits and the blood rite on the ground. But, new flesh or no, only an idiot would actually live here. Yes, the Babas had Chernobyl projects, but Kiev was more his speed. Roderick had a nice modern home, craft-hidden of course, that looked out on a park in Kiev. He loved that park.

He put the car in gear. Now he could relax and let himself bleed a little. They could clean the car, or replace it. Better watch that he didn't bleed out, though. The concentration of armor-piercing rounds in his chest meant a lot of metal was hanging close to this heart. But this flesh improved considerably on nature. Even now, snakes of tissue reached across wounds to knit together, perhaps too quickly—he wanted to avoid healing too much, as it would make bullet removal that much more difficult. Ah, the agony remained acute, but after all those years of decay without clear sensations of any kind, he wanted them all, and besides its ops value, lean physical pain had some charm. Pain was how he knew things were interesting.

As he drove along the largely deserted two-lane route through mostly empty countryside, he reviewed the results of the skirmish. The important question was whether his enemies understood his primary message. It wasn't the obvious one that the Ukrainians wanted and that would be confirmed through back channels: "live and let live." Hah. His enemies wouldn't believe it, but perhaps they'd give him time.

No, the unspoken real message was that the dangerous secret of Left-Hand craft immortality was out of the bag and on the plate. It had been easy for the Right-Hand craft world to be good when they had no way to be so bad. When those previously dutiful servants of their various governments heard of what he had done today, deathless in this wonderful body, many more would join his cause for that secret alone.

He already had many friends in place within the craft forces around the globe. Soon, he'd have an army, which he'd need. Not only would those who wished to continue to repress the Left-Hand way, the way of unshackled power and life extension, be gunning for him, but those who desired to take his secret without sharing wouldn't want him alive after they'd extracted it. He wished they'd speed up their killing of each other over him. Then the dynamics of a Family vendetta would take over, which had undermined national duty from the beginning, and he could get on with his real work.

Feh, mere physical immortality. They could all have it, and may it bring them much joy. Eating, shitting, screwing, the animal functions—it was all so mundane. Better than life as the talking head in the Chimera machine, but far from divine. That would all change for him, and soon.

He just needed a little more time before the world and the Ukrainians figured out what he was really up to.

Time. Out of paranoid habit, he glanced at the rearview mirror. Instead of the road or his reflection, he saw his old, oozing face. Embarrassing—he'd had this vision before. It spoke to either a trite psychology or dubious craft, and he wanted nothing to do with either. He pressed harder on the accelerator. He imagined he was a terrifying driver. He had no regard for life, and no fear for his own. Having this body made him feel more like Madeline: reckless, carnal.

He turned on the car stereo, and Adams's *Doctor Atomic* played. Technological magic. He steeled himself for another look in the mirror, and saw his Slavic face. Good. Part of how he was going to win this time involved seeing himself with greater clarity, and not taking himself too seriously—at least, not until he won.

In the meantime, he had a few scores to settle. As he drove into greater Kiev on the now four-lane highway, it disturbed him more and more that the craftswoman in Pripyat had attempted Rezvani's expulsion trick. The Russians might have gained intel of Rezvani's power, so all the more reason to remove her and her colleagues from the playing board. And Madeline—even dead, he needed to do something up close and personal to her.

Like the *spetsnaz* with their safety chips, when his American targets relied on technology, he would enjoy their horror at its betrayal. With Ukrainian support, he could hack their craft-encrypted phones and fake any of their communications to each other. Scattered by duty across the globe, they wouldn't be able to warn each other of their danger as he played with them.

The low sun glared down on the unseasonably warm

city—the least he could do. When the Babas were done repairing him downtown, he'd return to his new house and the tall, thin woman who waited for him, upon him. He had lost count of the number of her predecessors. He no longer learned their real names. He called them all Madeline. Eventually, they reminded him of Madeline in a bad way and had to go. So many of these Ukrainian women disappeared into the maw of the sex-trafficking trade every year that his personal demands went unnoticed. At least his women had the consolation of meeting their ends closer to home.

Madeline, have you been watching? Have you seen what I have done?

He had worried about being an expat. In his nineteenth-century life in the House of Morton in Providence, his magic had been tied to the American land and recharging had been difficult overseas. But this country's power flowed freely into him, confirming his hope that he had passed the usual limits and boding well for his plans. A would-be god had to think bigger than nation-states.

He looked forward to relaxing and appreciating anew the view of the park from his house. The name of the park was Babi Yar. Here, the Germans had executed more than one hundred thousand mortals. Roderick disliked Germans, but he liked the feeling this place gave him. Until his imminent apotheosis, it would have to do.